T0058669

FORGED
IN SMOKE

Also by Trish McCallan

Red-Hot SEALs Novels

Forged in Fire
Forged in Ash

Red-Hot SEALs Novellas

Bound by Seduction
Bound by Temptation

Other Novellas

Spirit Woods

FORGED IN SMOKE

A Red-Hot SEALs Novel

Trish McCallan

Montlake
Romance

This is a work of fiction. Names, characters, organizations, places, events, and incidents are either products of the author's imagination or are used fictitiously.

Text copyright © 2016 Trish McCallan
All rights reserved.

No part of this book may be reproduced, or stored in a retrieval system, or transmitted in any form or by any means, electronic, mechanical, photocopying, recording, or otherwise, without express written permission of the publisher.

Published by Montlake Romance, Seattle

www.apub.com

Amazon, the Amazon logo, and Montlake Romance are trademarks of Amazon.com, Inc., or its affiliates.

ISBN-13: 9781503945494
ISBN-10: 1503945499

Cover design by Eileen Carey

Printed in the United States of America

Sitrep

Lieutenant Commander Zane Winters and his fellow SEALs thwart the hijacking of flight 2077. During the resulting investigation, they are approached by FBI agent John Chastain, who enlists their aid in finding and rescuing his kidnapped family. The hijackers demand that Chastain turn over seven passengers from the flight, or else they'll kill his wife and children. But upon returning from the successful rescue, the SEALs find Chastain dead and the list of passengers missing.

Through Amy Chastain (John's widow), they learn a top-secret lab was recently bombed. Seven of the scientists affiliated with the lab had been booked on flight 2077. Convinced there is a connection to the aborted hijacking, the SEALs raid the lab and find Faith Ansell, one of the purportedly dead scientists, on the premises. Before they can question Faith, they are attacked. They capture one of the mercenaries, who goes by Pachico, and haul him to a safe house with Ansell. Ansell tells them that before the bombing her lab had been working on a new energy paradigm that would have replaced every form of energy known to man—and that her coworkers had been kidnapped, and their deaths faked, in order to duplicate the research. When the cabin is attacked, everyone flees into the woods. During the ensuing battle, Lieutenant Seth Rawlings is near fatally injured . . .

Cast of Characters

Commander Jace (Mac) Mackenzie—commander of SEAL Team 7

Lieutenant Commander Zane Winters—SEAL Team 7

Lieutenant Marcus (Cosky) Simcosky—SEAL Team 7

Lieutenant Seth (Rawls) Rawlings—SEAL Team 7's corpsman

Beth Brown—Zane's fiancée

Kait Winchester—metaphysical healer, Cosky's fiancée

Faith Ansell—scientist working on the new energy paradigm

Wolf—Arapaho special forces warrior, unknown team, Kait's half brother

John Chastain—FBI agent, murdered in *Forged in Fire*

Amy Chastain—the widow of John Chastain, kidnapped in *Forged in Fire*

Benji Chastain—John and Amy's youngest son, kidnapped in *Forged in Fire*

Brendan Chastain—John and Amy's oldest son, kidnapped in *Forged in Fire*

Russ Branson (aka Russell Remburg)—facilitated the attempted hijacking and kidnapping of Agent Chastain's family in *Forged in Fire*, killed by Zane

Jillian Michaels—sister to Russell Remburg, kidnapped in *Forged in Fire*, antagonist in *Forged in Ash*

Detective Pachico (aka Robert Biesel)—hired mercenary who was instrumental in the attempted hijacking of flight 2077 and the kidnapping of Faith's coworkers

Eric Manheim—one of the men funding the attempted hijacking and the kidnapping of Faith's coworkers

Marion Simcosky—Cosky's mother

Clay Purcell—FBI agent, Amy Chastain's stepbrother

Aiden Winchester—SEAL Team 7, Kait's brother, hero of *Bound by Seduction* (a Red-Hot SEALs novella)

Prologue

Sweet Jesus, Joseph, and Mary . . .

ENEATH SPLINTERED SHARDS OF MOONLIGHT PIERCING THE THICK
canopy of blue-black ponderosa pine, Lieutenant Seth Rawlings
watched Marcus Simcosky—better known as Cosky—roll a limp
body onto its back. Rawls had seen plenty of dead bodies during his
fourteen years as a corpsman—or medic—for SEAL Team 7 . . . but
none like this.

Gunfire lit the clearing, pinging between tree trunks. He tore his
eyes from the body on the ground in favor of scanning the trees surrounding him. He and his team had neutralized most of the assholes
who'd blown up their safe house, but a couple had escaped and were
holed up in the forest creating havoc. Who the hell were these assholes?

More importantly, who was funding them? Their anony-
mous enemy had deep pockets and military connections—a deadly
combination.

Another burst of gunfire erupted. Rawls flinched, hunkering down,
watching Cosky squat to loop the body's limp arm around his neck,
so he could drag it over his shoulder. In a half crouch, his teammate
raced for the closest tree. For a second, instinct kicked in and Rawls
tensed, ready to dive for cover. But the impulse quickly fled. From the

evidence dangling over Cosky's arms, taking cover wouldn't make a lick of difference.

He followed Cosky behind the thick protection of bark and watched his teammate roll the body off his shoulder and onto the ground, where it lay stretched out on its back across a thin pad of pine needles.

Disbelief swelled, vibrated against Rawls's chest.

Hold up. It's just a dream.

His gaze skated to the right, taking in the body's blood-soaked shirt and jeans. He recognized the cotton polo, the pants too, with their thinning patches of denim across the knees. He'd dressed in both less than forty-eight hours earlier, before the race to Seattle to investigate the incinerated lab and the detour to this supposedly safe haven in the Sierra Nevadas.

Rocking back on his heels, he stared down at the bloody cloth clinging to his chest. His shirt bore identical stains to the one covering the corpse on the ground. *The corpse . . .* yeah . . . he'd seen enough death to recognize its stamp.

Just like he recognized the high cheekbones, blue eyes, and gleaming cap of wheat-gold hair belonging to the man on the ground. Damnation, it was the same face he stared at every morning in the mirror.

If that don't beat all . . . that's you, hoss . . . you . . . dead on the ground.

He must be dreaming, although try as he might, he couldn't remember closing his eyes.

He swayed, his body lighter than air, and looked down. *What the devil . . . ?* Several inches of air buffered his boots from the pine needles matting the forest floor.

Another slew of gunfire hammered the clearing. The familiar sound centered him, and his feet dropped back to the pitchy earth.

Time to wake up. Wake up!

"Clear!" a deep baritone yelled a hundred yards away.

Next to him, Cosky ripped his night vision device off and dropped to his knees. Leaning forward, he pressed his fingers against the side of the flaccid neck.

"Son of a bitch." The words emerged on a low hiss and Cosky pulled back hard.

"Is he alive?" Zane Winters, his lieutenant commander, skidded to a stop next to Cosky and dropped to his knees. He didn't wait for a response, just dragged the strap from his rifle over his head, yanked off his NVD, and stripped off his shirt.

Rawls shook his head. "A little late, bro."

His voice emerged hollow—disembodied—and neither Cosky nor Zane reacted in the slightest.

'Course this is just a dream . . .

He pinched his forearm, or tried to, except he didn't feel a thing, and his fingers disappeared into his arm all the way up to his knuckles. *Holy hell . . .* He could clearly see the murky image of rocks and pine needles through his transparent flesh. But he couldn't feel anything—not the earth beneath his boots nor the wounds beneath his clothes.

As Cosky dragged his shirt off his head, folding it into a compression pad, déjà vu hit Rawls hard. A memory flashed through his mind. A blood-soaked body stretched across green grass. Tense faces and folded shirts.

Only Cosky had been camped out on the ground, and he'd been the one working frantically overhead trying to keep his buddy alive.

He and Cos had traded places. With one big-ass difference. Cosky hadn't died.

"Welcome to hell," a sour, yet oddly familiar voice said from behind him.

Rawls spun, and his body went light and floaty again. This shit just got weirder and weirder.

Wake up, hoss. Wake the hell up.

A couple of beats of his nonexistent heart later, and his boots settled back down. With a tight breath, he focused on the man behind him, relieved to find an actual person standing there. Until he realized the figure was translucent too. The hazy image of a tree trunk penetrated the guy's thin chest.

A second later recognition hit . . . a bald head, crowned by a bloody bandage . . . brown eyes . . . a big black knife protruding from a narrow chest . . .

Pachico . . .

Pachico, who'd died in their safe haven less than fifteen minutes earlier. Pachico, whose corpse had been unceremoniously cremated when their hidey-hole had been blown to Venus and back.

Sweet Jesus . . .

Disbelief swarmed, flooding him like helium, and his feet said *adios* to the ground again. The man—or *thing*—laughed, and the knife bobbed up and down.

Wake up. Damn it, time to wake up.

Kait, Cosky's brand-new girlfriend, flew past Rawls, her braid flopping against her back and gleaming like wet gold beneath the opalescent shimmer of the moonlight. She dropped to her knees and spread her hands. "Which is the worst wound?"

"Chest," Zane said, backing up to give her room.

"What the hell do they think they're gonna do?" the man Rawls had known as Detective Pachico asked. "Bring you back from the dead?" He snorted out a laugh.

Cosky's breath whistled out in a rush. "I got a pulse."

Pachico laughed again. "Wishful thinking on your buddy's part. If you had a pulse, you wouldn't be all floaty beside me."

A thick, static pressure swelled in Rawls's head. He recognized the symptoms of shock—the mental fog, the dizzy floating sensation, the white haze shrouding his vision.

Except, if Pachico was right . . . if he really had died . . . he didn't have eyes now, did he? Or a body? Or a life?

Wake up. He pinched his wrist again, grimacing when his fingers sank into his transparent arm. Stepping forward, he grabbed Zane's shoulder, and his hand vanished. Zane didn't even flinch. No reaction at all.

"You're not sleeping, dumbass. You're dead. As a doornail. Your buddies can't see you, or hear you, or feel you. I should know. I've been trying to catch someone's attention since you let me die in that damn kitchen." Pachico paused and then his voice rose. "What the fuck are they doing?" He stepped closer to the drama unfolding before them.

Rawls turned back to the nightmare playing out at his feet. Kait knelt on one side of his prone form, her palms pressed against the center of his chest. Cosky faced her, his hands covering hers. Frozen, they crouched there, staring down . . . waiting.

"Tryin' to heal me." Rawls twitched, startled by his hollow, disembodied voice.

"No fuck." Pachico laughed. "Good luck with that."

There was precedent for such a healing. Kait had fixed Cosky's knee after all, but then again—Cosky hadn't been dead.

How did one go about healing the deceased?

He turned in a slow circle, surveying the silvery trees and shrubs surrounding him. The clearing stood pretty much the same—other than the moonlight, which might be a tad more ethereal since his death.

If he wasn't dreaming, if he really *had* kicked the bucket, this didn't resemble any of the near-death experiences his patients had recounted during his surgical residency. No bright light lurked in the distance. Peace and love were void from the air. Gram and Gramps, Ma and Pops, Uncle Andy and Aunt Ruth . . . Sarah . . . Hell—not one of them had come to fetch him into the afterlife.

Apparently they still hadn't forgiven him for what had happened . . . which was fair. He hadn't forgiven himself.

He frowned, his gaze falling on a crumpled figure in the distance. He hadn't been the only one to die in this meadow. Where were the rest of the corporeally disenfranchised?

"Why didn't your buddy over there"—he nodded at the motionless form—"go all Casper on us too?"

"How the hell should I know?" Pachico scowled at him before turning back to the drama taking place beneath the mammoth pine tree. "I wasn't given a manual any more than you were." He watched for a moment before leaning forward, his eyes widening. "What the fuck! Do you see that? They're glowing!"

Rawls simply nodded, too startled to speak. Kait and Cosky had lit up like a pair of bright white sparklers. A dense bubble of silver cocooned the pair, flowed out of their hands, and plunged into his chest, where it advanced in a glowing puddle until it infused every inch of his inert form. With each second, the light intensified, blurring the outline of his frame into a pulsing rectangle of platinum.

Within the radiance something took shape—a thick, wavering snakelike tentacle. It unfurled from the luminous pool like a cobra poised to strike, and hung in the air, shedding silver sparks.

What the freaky, unbelievable, hell?

Rawls leapt back when it suddenly flew at him, but he didn't have time to evade the blow. As the appendage penetrated his chest, it delivered an electrical shock of such intensity it knocked him off his feet. Before he could scramble up, another static jolt hit him and then another, launching his incorporeal body into helpless, twitching spasms. A sharp prickle swept his body. As the current pooled in his head, a static buzz filled his ears.

And then suddenly he was moving. He dug his heels and hands into the earth, or tried to, but *zap,* another bolt of electricity lit him from within, and some immense, unseen force dragged him forward.

Zane loomed directly in front, and he braced for impact, except he cut through his LC's legs like Casper through a wall. He was still adjusting to *that* when his boots pierced his lifeless torso, and he sank into his limp body like a stone into a well.

His head spun. A dense, crackling hum flooded his brain. Black pinpricks blinded him. A sharp sense of confinement struck, as though he'd stuffed himself into a suit several sizes too small. And then the pinpricks swelled, encircled him, drug him into a vortex of unforgiving black.

Rawls returned to consciousness in increments of scattered impressions and sluggish memories. The heavy thud of his heart deafened his ears . . . something hard and sharp, bordering on painful, dug into his spine . . . the thick sense of claustrophobia faded . . . the static charge consuming his chest shifted to a distinct burn.

Breath by breath the discomfort edged into pain, and from there it shot straight to agony. A groan broke from him, which spawned an explosion of voices.

Light-headed, he struggled to open eyelids that weighed a thousand pounds apiece. One blink, followed by several more, and two worried faces swam into focus—Cosky and Kait, their faces tomato soup–red and streaming with sweat.

"Welcome back," Zane said, his voice rough with relief.

Rawls rolled his head, tracking his LC's voice, only to freeze as dizziness hurled his stomach into his throat. He gagged, desperately forcing the bile back.

"Easy," Zane said, his voice quiet and calm. "You took a couple rounds to the chest."

An explanation Rawls had arrived at himself thanks to the straitjacket of misery cinched around his ribs, along with that weird dream they'd yanked him from. He eased back on the breathing, taking shallow breaths that wouldn't expand his rib cage. Kait and Cosky must have healed him enough to keep him alive, although judging from the pain consuming his upper body, considerable damage remained.

He gingerly turned his head to the right, keeping his torso as still as possible, and searched out Kait's sweaty, tired face.

"Thank you," he mouthed.

The effort, small as it was, exhausted him. Relaxing, he allowed his eyes to drift shut and concentrated on his breathing. Slowly, the buzzing in his head subsided and the dizziness waned. The agonizing burn in his chest shuffled aside, lurking in the background. A steady drone of voices overhead lulled him into a stupor. He'd just rest here a moment. Recoup his strength. But it didn't take long for that strange dream to play through his mind.

If Freud's theory was correct, and dreams were nothing more than the subconscious mind's expression of wish fulfillment, what the devil did that say about his desires? Uncomfortable with that line of questioning, he searched for something else to occupy his mind.

Opening his eyes, he took stock of his surroundings.

He was lying on the ground, which explained the chilly dampness spreading up his spine. Shifting his shoulders to escape a sharp object jabbing into his shoulder, he winced as agony instantly swooped down, clawing at his chest.

Still, he'd take the pain over that disturbing nightmare. Pain meant he was awake. Hell, it meant he was alive.

Time to get moving, though—the devil only knew when those bastards would regroup and descend on them again. They couldn't afford to be caught in the open like this. With that in mind, he concentrated on his hand, willing it to move. It took far too long for the order to travel from his brain to his hand, and when it finally did register, the movement barely qualified as a flutter. At this rate, he'd celebrate his next birthday in this damn place.

"Give it time," Zane said, as though he'd read Rawls's mind.

Did they have the time?

"Sitrep?" The single question was all he had the energy or air for.

"Secure. We neutralized the last of the bastards." Zane straightened and arched his back with a grunt of relief. "Wolf and Mac mopped up the chopper guards and are sitting on the bird." He paused to shake his head, a grim shadow darkening his eyes.

Sitting on the bird . . .

The words echoed in Rawls's head. When had his CO and Wolf left? They'd been standing there moments ago. He frowned in frustration, realizing he was mixing reality with events from the dream.

"For a moment there, it didn't look like you'd be bugging out with us."

"That close?" Rawls asked, the strange dream still churning through his mind. He'd died in that silvery netherworld.

"Closer than Cos got." The grimness echoed in Zane's voice.

As Zane stepped back, the bulk of another man drew close. Although the new arrival was partially obscured by Zane's silhouette, a streak of moonlight clearly illuminated a bald head.

Rawls caught his breath and froze—tension hitting hard and fast. Their party didn't include a Vin Diesel wannabe. At least not now. Not for the last thirty minutes, not since Jillian had driven a knife into Pachico's chest in retribution for the children he'd stolen from her.

The shiny chrome dome atop the man's head flashed silver as he turned in Rawls's direction. A face came into focus—long cheekbones, a narrow chin, small mean eyes . . . *familiar* eyes. A bloody white bandage wrapped around a pale forehead.

The ground at Rawls's back heaved. Ice crystals hardened in his gut, chilling him from the inside out.

Not possible . . . not possible . . .

His muscles rigid, he reluctantly dropped his gaze to the figure's opaque chest, with its big, black protrusion of a knife.

The mud-brown eyes watching him widened, which was impossible since the bastard was dead.

Sweet Jesus, he'd watched him die, watched his body incinerate during an explosion that had sent flames twenty feet into the air. There was no way—absolutely no way—the man could be standing in front of him.

No. Damn it. No. This isn't happening . . .

Rawls stared at the translucent body identical to the one in his nightmare, and his head started throbbing like a smashed finger.

Wake up, damn it. Wake up.

Pachico chuckled—an ugly sound completely devoid of humor. "Well, fuck me. Looks like you're not gonna escape me after all."

Chapter One

ABOARD THE *ESME*, ANCHORED DEEP IN THE CRYSTAL-BLUE WATERS of Roquebrune bay, the final haunting note of a Celtic ballad lingered, echoing in the ocean-kissed air.

Eric Manheim's cell phone vibrated twice against his hip as the note finally faded. The aborted call meant the last of his associates were on board and secreted away below. Perfect. As scheduled, the evening's performance had concluded as the council settled in. Time to move the festivities along, off-load the guests, and get down to the real business of the night.

Claire Rendell, the reclusive Celtic singer his wife adored, offered him a small nod and placed her microphone on the piano. Inclining his head in silent appreciation, he tightened his arm around Esme's shoulder.

"Happy anniversary, darling." He bent to brush her satin-soft cheek with his mouth.

She tilted her face to his, her short platinum hair caressing the perfect shell of her ears, her eyes a dreamy blue and swimming with moisture. Rendell's music always touched his wife deeply.

As the singer stepped down from the stage, applause broke out, at first just a smattering, but it quickly turned thunderous, pounding the ballroom until the sandalwood dance floor and quadruple-paned marine windows vibrated.

Esme pressed her cheek against his. "Such extravagance, darling. A private performance, plus my very own song?"

As his wife's breath tickled his ear, Eric's heart rate increased. The clean, fresh scent that was uniquely Esme swamped him. Instantly his breathing quickened and his body hardened. It still surprised him that the woman he'd married to cement the power, money, and holdings of their two lineages, would turn out to be the other half of his soul.

He hated usurping their anniversary celebration. But necessity overruled privacy, and Claire Rendell's riveting and rare performance had kept ears and eyes tuned to the stage instead of the helipad at the back of the yacht, or the mysterious late arrivals.

Waving a waiter over, he snagged two crystal flutes of champagne. He handed one to Esme and then steered her into the sea of expensive jewelry, evening gowns, and tuxedos. For the next two hours they drifted through a glittering, fragrant mob of exquisitely dressed well-wishers. As they accepted countless congratulations on their first fifteen years together, or the occasional well-bred ribaldry, Eric locked down his impatience.

The men below deck weren't going anywhere, and this camouflage above deck was key to hiding the pending session. Until recently, secrecy hadn't been a priority. Immense wealth and power brokered a fair amount of privacy anyway, at least enough to mask the quarterly meetings. But when rumors surfaced about the alliance's directive, and conspiracy theorists had zeroed in for closer looks, concealment had become imperative.

He'd been lucky that his turn to host the quarterly updates had fallen so close to his anniversary. What better cover for a top-secret meeting between the most powerful people on earth than a celebration with many of the most powerful people in the world in attendance?

The press cameras pointed toward the *Esme* wouldn't have a clue what they were filming. And once aboard the yacht, privacy was assured. He'd spared no expense to make certain of that. From the anti-paparazzi shield, which used lasers to disrupt the recording of images, to the electronic jammers that filled curious ears with a flood of static noise, his floating mansion was preeminently secure and perfect for their agenda. Nobody would question the helicopters constantly ferrying people between the yacht and shore, not when every press rag between New York and Paris had heralded Eric and Esme's fifteenth-anniversary spectacular as *the* social event of the year.

Still, by the time the final helicopter merged with the sky, ferrying the last of their staff to the glittering Monte Carlo mainland for the remainder of the evening, Eric was ready to cast off the trappings of the camouflage and get down to business. Turning from the window facing the helipad, he lifted Esme's slender wrist to his lips.

"It's unfortunate our anniversary got caught in these"—he glanced around the empty stateroom to make sure the two remaining staff members—the captain and cook—had left them to their privacy as instructed—"business dealings."

"Ah well, it couldn't be helped, darling." She offered a tired smile. "Try not to let them keep you too long."

Eric drew back in surprise. "You won't be joining us?"

"Not this time." She lifted her foot and gingerly eased off a glittering red sandal. "All those rubies and diamonds might sparkle like a Christmas tree on the dance floor, but they're hell on the feet." She set her bare foot down and lifted the opposite foot, slipping that shoe off as well. "Go to your meeting. I'm going to take a nice long soak in the tub."

With one last fatigued smile she walked away, idly swinging her glittering, bejeweled shoes.

Once she'd disappeared from view, he stepped behind the ebony bar and pressed a button next to the enclosed liquor case. A narrow panel housing a button and a lever opened. The button activated a sixty-inch retractable television hidden within the bar.

He pulled the lever instead, twisting it to the right. A distinct metallic snick sounded. With a mechanical purr, the shelf slid to the right, exposing a narrow doorway and a carpeted ramp descending downward. The door closed behind him as he stepped inside. At the bottom of the ramp stood a well-lit room. There were no windows, instead three crystal chandeliers cast bright white light from corner to corner and bathed the sandalwood walls with a wet sheen.

Seven men, their attire ranging from designer jeans to designer suits, lounged in leather executive chairs around a huge, ornately carved ebony table. While their clothing, age, and physical appearance ran the gamut, each had one characteristic in common. They wielded an aura of authority with the same casualness they wore their clothes. A round of hails broke out as he stepped into the room, and the door at the bottom of the ramp slid shut and locked behind him.

"Manheim."

"About damn time."

"Bloody hell, Manheim, it's been hours."

"Manheim."

Eric nodded or shrugged in response as he skirted the breadth of the imposing table. The piece's legs were carved to resemble a Siberian tiger's limbs—complete with paws for feet. The dark sheen of the ebony wood shimmered with satin gloss against the Persian Vase rug below it and served as a physical reminder of the critical role he and his associates played in earth's future.

Ebony trees, and Siberian tigers . . . two of the most endangered species in the world, both protected, yet constantly available on the black market.

"I trust there were no issues boarding the *Esme*?" Eric asked as he slipped behind a compact bar tucked into the corner.

The staff had been occupied in the ballroom, at the opposite end of the vessel, when the helicopter had landed, and the chopper pilot had returned to Monte Carlo once his passengers disembarked. There'd been nobody to witness James Link access the secret passage from the main stateroom and lead the council belowdecks.

A chorus of negative replies circled the table before the men returned to their previous conversations. Listening to the discussion of thoroughbred racing, or the current crop of award-winning roses, one would never guess that the collective assets of the eight men in the room rivaled the combined resources of the United States, Great Britain, and most of Europe—or that the council controlled virtually every financial institution in existence, along with the bulk of the energy, pharmaceutical, and agricultural corporations.

He removed a bucket of ice from the minifreezer and grabbed a pair of tongs.

"Gentlemen, the bar is open."

He mixed the requested drinks, passed them out, then dropped a couple of ice cubes into a crystal tumbler, filled it with water, and carried it to the head of the table.

He was a big believer in a clear head, untouched by alcohol, when conducting business. However, it never hurt to mellow one's competition.

While the men chatting around his table weren't exactly adversaries, they weren't exactly friends either. They were simply men—dangerous ones—who shared a particular agenda, bought and sold lives with regularity, and wielded the kind of power that could gut the most prosperous countries and wrench them to their knees.

He couldn't afford to trust any of them.

"You've gone soft, Manheim," David Coulson announced in his habitually harsh tone that turned even a joke into a clipped accusation. He held his Waterford tumbler up to the light and glared at the amethyst ring circling the top half of the glass as though it personally affronted him. "You've turned sissy on us."

Eric smiled benignly, not bothering to dig deeper into the comment for a hidden indictment. Knowing Coulson, there was bound to be one. "A gift from Esme. She appreciates a more contemporary touch."

"Esme isn't joining us?" Samuel Proctor asked. At the shake of Eric's head, he reached beneath his jacket and liberated a thick cylinder of tightly rolled tobacco.

While the council was sensitive to Esme's distaste for cigars, the instant she failed to show for a meeting, the stogies came out. Eric accepted the Gurkha Black that Proctor handed him and lifted it to his nose, breathing in the musty fermented aroma with pure appreciation. Gurkhas were one of the rarest and most expensive cigars available, and worth every pound paid for them. There were few things he missed since marrying Esme, but Gurkhas were one of them. Reluctantly he passed the cigar to James Link, on his right.

"Right on then, Manheim. What of those SEAL chaps and Dr. Ansell? Where do we stand there?" Giovanni asked, his English as clipped and perfect as the royal family, even though his native language was Italian.

It spoke to their concern that the first topic to hit the table revolved around the mess Mackenzie and his men had stirred up.

"No sign of them, but their faces are on every television and newspaper in the country. Someone is bound to recognize them and turn them in for the reward," Eric said. He took a sip of ice water and shrugged. "We wait and move when we're sure the intel is solid."

From the frowns circling the table, his associates were no happier with that plan of action than he was. But then, he had no intention of waiting for random recognition to pin those bastards down.

"Mackenzie and his boys obviously have help," Link said, staring into the amber depths of his crystal tumbler as his long fingers slowly rotated the glass. "What of the property in the Nevadas? Did you track down an owner?"

"The owner died in 1972," Eric said. "No next of kin. No other property listed under his name."

A moment of tense silence touched the table as the council digested that news.

"An alias?" Proctor asked, fishing a platinum cigar guillotine out of his breast pocket and clipping the tip off the Gurkha. "Mackenzie, or one of his boys? Maybe the Winchester gal?"

"Maybe," Eric said after a lengthy pause. But his gut was telling him no. There was a third party involved. A well-heeled third party. "The best chance we have of locating our adversaries is through Amy Chastain—John Chastain's widow. All evidence points to close ties between Amy and her family. At some point she'll seek out her children. When she does, she'll lead us back to Mackenzie."

"You're assuming she's with those chaps." Proctor lifted a gold cigarette lighter and let the flame sear the end of the stogie. After a few seconds he lifted the tapered end to his mouth and drew deeply.

"She was on the lab footage," Eric said, dragging the thick, musty scent of perfectly cured tobacco into his lungs. "She hasn't been accounted for since. She's with them."

"You've tagged her boys?" Coulson's harsh voice sounded more like an accusation than a question.

"Her kids have been injected, and the data stream is live," Eric said after a quick glance at James Link for confirmation. The tracking technology was Link's baby. "Thanks to Agent Clay Purcell, the woman's brother." Or stepbrother, as Purcell insisted.

Eric wasn't sure what was driving the fed's betrayal. The pair had been raised as brother and sister since prep school, yet the man had been instrumental in his sister's kidnapping and rape as well as his brother-in-law's murder. There was obviously some dark motivation behind

Purcell's actions, but whatever the man's incentive, he'd made tagging the boys relatively easy.

With luck, the technology would work as well on Amy Chastain's children as it had on Robert Biesel, their late, unlamented team leader. Mackenzie had no clue that by capturing and dragging Robert back with them, they'd exposed their safe house. The tracking device embedded in Biesel's cells had given Eric an exact location. Too bad nobody had been in the damn house when the antitank missile had landed.

"We can't assume that Chastain's widow will retrieve her kids. Or if she does, that she'll return to where Mackenzie and his boys are holed up," Coulson said curtly, a heavy shadow brooding on his face. "We need a course of action that isn't so nebulous."

Of all of them, David Coulson was the most dangerous. Possessing a vicious temper and matching ruthlessness, he generally advocated the quickest and most bloody course of action, regardless of the circumstances.

Eric took a long, slow sip of ice water, forcing his face into stillness. "Amy Chastain adores those boys. It's been three days. She won't leave them alone or unprotected much longer. She'll want them with her, in a place they'll be safe. She obviously trusts Mackenzie and his men. She'll take her boys to them."

Coulson slammed down his whiskey glass so hard the ice cubes cracked like pistol reports. "Another assumption. You're full of them. Mackenzie, hell, the whole lot of them, are targets. She was a fed before her marriage, for Christ's sake. She'll know that returning to their camp would put her children in danger. There is no logical reason for her to collect her children and take them there. Not when her brother and father are feds and perfectly capable of protecting the kids themselves. Which means tagging them is useless."

Eric tensed at the derision in Coulson's acidic voice, then forced his muscles to relax. While Amy Chastain's brother was actively working against her, the woman didn't know that, so Coulson's words held weight.

"True." He held Coulson's cold gaze. "However, at the moment, we're out of options. The SEALs have gone off grid. Which makes it rather difficult to neutralize them." He paused, offering a derisive smile himself. "Amy will go after her children." Of that at least he was sure. "Even if she doesn't return to Mackenzie afterward, the tracking devices will give us access to her; through her, we'll find them." He paused, to lift an eyebrow. "I'm all for a proactive approach, if we had an approach to follow."

Coulson flexed his shoulders restively. "We force the bastards into the open. Mackenzie has an ex-wife; Simcosky, a mother; Winters, parents and brothers. We use them to bring those bastards to heel."

"And prove to the world that Mackenzie wasn't mouthing excuses when he screamed conspiracy?" Eric steepled his fingers and held Coulson's flat gaze. "Going after their families will bring notice. We can't afford notice, not yet. They're discredited, wanted by the police. We can afford patience."

"Manheim's right," James Link said, a note of finality in his quiet voice. "If we were further along, we could chance questions and deeper looks. But we haven't reached that point yet. It behooves us to exercise caution."

Eric relaxed slightly—time to shift the focus. "What of your newest acquisitions? Are they settling in?"

A slow smile, shadowed by cruelty, kicked up the edges of Coulson's thick lips. "It took some initial persuading, but things are moving along nicely now."

No doubt the convincing had been brutal and bloody—just as Coulson preferred it. Their American associate had the soul of a sociopathic thug. Eric found it unlikely that the man had joined their cause out of concern for the planet, or the survival of the human race. It was more likely he'd accepted the council's mandates in order to shoehorn his own agenda.

But then, it didn't matter why Coulson had joined them, because his methods were exceptionally effective when it came to getting the job done.

"If we'd moved on the lab earlier, right after the plane fuckup, we'd be a hell of a lot further along," Coulson pointed out.

"We agreed it would be a mistake to take the lab while Mackenzie and his crew were being hailed as heroes." Link responded in his habitually quiet voice. "They knew the hijacking was a ruse to grab the seven scientists from first class. If we'd targeted Benton's lab while Mackenzie's cries of conspiracy were the lead story across the States, we'd have bolstered his credibility and collusion allegations."

"*You* agreed to wait," Coulson snapped back. "I called bullshit."

Eric shrugged. "It's done. No sense in reopening that discussion. How long before Benton can produce another new energy generator?"

"A couple of weeks," Coulson offered readily enough, although from his scowl it was obvious he didn't appreciate the change in subject.

"That soon?" Eric dipped his head in surprise. Maybe they wouldn't have to adjust their time line after all. "It will be ready—tested and refined—by phase two?"

"Absolutely." Coulson smiled, cold detachment in his gaze. "Benton has impetus to produce rapidly and well."

"Is the design as easy to weaponize as reported?" Link asked.

Which was the trillion-dollar question. For phase two to succeed, they needed the device fully operational and capable of specific energy discharges.

"Indeed." Coulson offered an honest-to-god sincere smile. "With a bit of rewiring and a component swap"—he spread his hands—"boom. Through the sonic distribution we'll be able to clear millions of acres with negligible effect to soil, water, and vegetation."

Silence ringed the table.

An equally stunned silence had struck the room the previous year when Link had filled them in on Leonard Embray's pet project, along with the potential alternative use for the device.

Benton and Embray's original intention for the prototype would have proved catastrophic for the entire world. With cheap renewable energy available to everyone—*absolutely everyone*—the human population would explode. Famine and disease would vanish, at least at first. Wars over oil or other natural resources would disappear. There would be far more people being born into the world than leaving it.

Benton and Embray, the ideological fools, hadn't looked past the initial benefits. They hadn't questioned the eventual ramifications. The earth couldn't support its current load of parasites. Natural resources were vanishing at an alarming rate. The giant oxygen-producing rainforests of the Amazon were being cut down and plowed under at a rate of twenty-thousand square miles per year, and predicted to be completely gone by 2050—with disastrous consequences to earth's climate. With the water table shrinking by the month, and the ice packs melting, and dozens of species forced into extinction thanks to mankind's unabated appetites, someone needed to step up and make the hard decisions.

Eventually, when the aquifers went dry, and previously lush landscapes descended into arid deserts, and irrigation was no longer available, disease and starvation would step in again, and the human race would face a massive die-off. Only, by then it would be too late. The planet would be in its final death throes.

None of these imminent threats could be fixed by energy for all. Indeed, the new energy paradigm would accelerate planet earth's decay.

People were simply too selfish and blind and disinclined to change their behavior. They were incapable of making hard choices and standing by them during difficult times. And governments were no better. Not when they had to answer to the lowest common denominator within their populations.

Something had to be done on behalf of the planet, someone had to make the tough choices and cull the human population—but nobody was interested in stepping up and shouldering the thankless task.

The New Ruling Order had been born of that realization. Born to make sure that earth survived and the human race prospered, albeit at massively reduced numbers and beneath benevolent guidance so the current crisis never happened again.

The council would have moved on the new energy paradigm anyway, as soon as reports of it hit their table—just as the parents and grandparents of various council members had moved on similar projects during the past seventy years. Only this time, stifling the new technology wasn't about conserving their share of the energy pie. It was about saving the planet.

But then James Link had joined them and opened their eyes to an entirely new application for Embray's pet project. One that offered a complete reboot of the planet, with minimal loss to vegetation, soil, or water. Embray, the idealistic fool, hadn't seen the possibilities they'd offered him. The chance to mold the planet into a sustainable ecosystem.

"What of Embray?" Coulson asked, as though he'd read Eric's mind. "Has his condition deteriorated?" He frowned and ran the Gurkha Black that Link had passed to him beneath his beak of a nose. "It's a shame we can't accelerate his condition. It's dangerous to have such a threat looming over our heads."

Link was quiet for a moment before offering a shrug. "He's stable, at the moment, but the damage to his brain was extensive and permanent. He exists in a vegetative state, with no possibility of recovery."

Which served their purposes well.

If Embray had survived the stroke with his mental faculties intact, Dynamic Solutions would have been beyond the council's reach, and Embray would have taken the assembly's proposal public. However, if he died, with no heirs or next of kin, the company would pass into the public's keeping in accordance with the dictates of his will. Embray's death would have severely limited James Link's role in the company's stewardship. Link would have been one of many executives with limited power. His usefulness would have been critically handicapped.

The trick had been destroying the man's mental faculties without killing him outright. It had been the only way to keep the company beneath their umbrella. If the CEO of Dynamic Solutions were incapacitated for any reason, the vice president of operations, in this case James Link, would step into the chief executive officer's position until such time as the incapacitated officer recovered or died. So far the strategy they'd employed to ease Dynamic Solutions under the council's control had proceeded without a hitch. Which was a blessing. The corporation had been a technological windfall.

"Nobody has questioned his condition?" Eric asked.

"Not once they've visited him," Link said quietly, his eyes on the table.

Eric nodded in satisfaction. It had been Link's request to give Embray the option of joining them, rather than simply removing him from the playing field. Still, they'd gone into the meeting prepared to act, and they'd done so immediately upon Embray's appalled reaction to their invitation. The cocktail they'd injected into the roof of his mouth had been specifically designed to cause a massive stroke. He'd been comatose before his personal assistant had been summoned or the first medical professional had entered the room.

The fact that Embray had chronically high blood pressure, and was under a doctor's care, had lent weight to the diagnosis of a stroke. So had the fact that there was no other explanation available. The chemical compound they'd used wouldn't show up in a blood panel.

So far, nobody suspected a thing. And James Link had taken control of Dynamic Solutions with little fanfare.

Eric studied the tight face and empty eyes of his newest associate and sympathized. There was no question that Link's betrayal of his childhood friend and teenage bandmate had come at tremendous personal cost. There was also no question he'd do it again, in a heartbeat, if necessary. While Link and Embray had been united in their environmental concerns, Link hadn't shared Embray's idealistic belief that the various factions of the human race would eventually pull together in the common interest of protecting Mother Earth.

Rather, Link believed, as did the council, that the human race would continue to squander the world's resources until the planet hit the tipping point and spiraled down so fast it couldn't recover. To prevent the annihilation of the planet, someone needed to act, and they needed to do so *now*—while there was still time to reverse the ill effects weighing down their cosmic home. When he couldn't convince his best friend and boss of that, Link had successfully facilitated the removal of Embray from power and stepped in to guide the company himself.

Chapter Two

FIVE DAYS AFTER HE'D DIED AND BEEN DRAGGED—WILLY-NILLY—back to life, an icy chill still held Rawls captive. So did a translucent, obnoxious, troll of a ghost. Gritting his teeth, he stared furiously at the rocky bank that plunged down a foot or two ahead, and the boisterous creek babbling along below.

Wolf—their badass Arapaho associate—certainly liked his trees and privacy. The new sanctuary their host had ferried them to was tucked into the Cascade mountain range and completely obscured by trees. At the back of the property, a stream wound through thick clusters of ponderosa pine and Douglas fir, providing the privacy and cover to accommodate Rawls's teeth grinding and frustrated silence.

"Five hundred and twenty-nine bottles of beer on the wall, five hundred and twenty-nine bottles of beer . . ." Pachico belted the verse out at the top of his lungs.

If the bastard had lungs . . .

The creek bed at this spot cut through rough terrain, so the path was narrower and studded by clusters of thick, heavy boulders. The force of the water rushing through the rocks was louder as well. Almost loud enough to drown out the annoying asshole haunting him.

". . . take one down, pass it around, five hundred and twenty-eight bottles of beer on the wall. Five hundred and twenty-eight bottles of beer on the wall, five hundred and twenty-eight bottles of beer."

Pachico raised his voice even louder, as though his life depended on it, which was damn ironic considering ghosts didn't have lives. Neither did Rawls. At least not since the bastard stalking him had usurped his life.

As the apparition's voice rose again, drowning out the soothing babble of the water below, Rawls bent to pick up a rock. Too bad he couldn't knock the transparent miscreant on his ass, but the stone would just sail through his clear form.

Things could be worse, he supposed, a whole lot worse. Currently only one of the newly departed had taken to stalking him. Hell, one was bad enough, but a whole passel of the damn things would have proved even more aggravating.

"You ready to make that call yet?" Pachico interrupted his rendition of the most annoying song ever to ask the question he'd been asking every hour, on the hour.

Gritting his teeth harder, Rawls drew back his arm and sent the rock skipping down the stream. He tried like hell to ignore the jaunty tune as it started up again. Still, it quickly bore into his brain, drawing fresh blood.

If he could believe Pachico, the call would be harmless. A quick recounting of the man's death to bring closure to his family, followed by instructions so his parents could retrieve the sizable fortune he'd stashed away.

Except the demand held two big complications. One—he sure couldn't trust the man . . . or ghost . . . or whatever the hell he was. What if the number was tapped and ringing-in exposed their current location? And two—hell . . . what if Pachico didn't actually exist? It was the most likely scenario and the one directly responsible for the constant burn in Rawls's gut.

The only working phone in the compound was an Iridium Extreme satellite model located in the command center. Accessing it meant wading through his teammates and the civilians accompanying them. If Pachico wasn't real, and the number didn't exist, the imaginary asshole's ultimatum would expose the ugly truth to the entire camp—when Kait's magical hands had healed those two chest wounds five days ago, there'd been a price. A big price. His sanity.

Although, considering how Zane and Cos had walked in on him while he'd been ranting at the corner of the cabin for no apparent reason, there'd probably been plenty of conversations concerning his sanity already.

Pachico had been immensely amused by the incident and determined to engineer a repeat performance. Conversely, abject humiliation was something Rawls had no intention of participating in twice, so he'd locked down his reactions and took to fiercely pretending that the asshole tormenting him didn't exist.

If the bastard would just shut the fuck up and let him get a couple hours of shut-eye . . .

Suddenly the singing stopped. Surprised, Rawls straightened and turned to face his see-through nemesis. Had his frustrated mental demand affected the ghost? Could dealing with Pachico really be that easy?

A wolf whistle pierced the clearing, followed by the exaggerated lip-smacking sounds of kissing. "Look who's headed our way. Normally big tits crank my cock, but under the circumstances, that package of skin and bone will have to do."

What . . . ?

Rawls turned, following Pachico's stare, and heat instantly unfurled in his stomach and wound through his chest. The hot, itchy prickle marched straight up his neck and into his face as well. It was a familiar, and annoying, reaction. One that struck anytime Faith Ansell, the dark-haired, blue-eyed walking freckle they'd rescued during the lab recon, was in his general proximity.

The woman had some insanely strong mojo. Not that he'd noticed this mojo all those months ago when he'd first spotted her at the airport terminal while waiting for his flight to Hawaii to board. No, this damnable reaction hadn't infected him until he'd touched her back at her lab. Somehow the simple act of putting his hands on her had supercharged his physical awareness.

Of course she'd coldcocked him at the time with a piece of pipe. The incident still made him grin. Even though it had hurt like hell, he admired that kind of spunk.

As he'd been doing for days now, he ignored his body's awkward reaction. She was close enough he should have heard her approach. Would have heard her if a repetitive, annoying ditty hadn't decimated his eardrums.

"Tell you what, Doc. You do her here, and I'll give you the night off. How's that for a compromise?"

The hope that he'd stumbled on a means of dealing with the bastard fizzled. Obviously mental demands failed to flip the switch on the ghost's voice box.

"Lieutenant Rawlings?" The lilt in Faith's voice turned his name into a question and drove that scratchy, uncomfortable prickle straight down his spine, where it played hell with his heartbeat. She slowed as she approached, watching him with furrowed brows and tentative eyes. "Do you have a moment?"

"A gal like that, all buttoned-up and proper. I bet she's got a kinky streak. I bet she's into bondage or some shit. I bet you could get her on her knees with your cock in her mouth after a compliment or two."

Rawls's jaw tightened. He tried like hell to ignore the troll's words, but they lodged in his brain, a burning, vivid image—*that dark sleek hair of hers rippling like a waterfall below him, her soft mouth moving up and down . . .*

Sweet Jesus—

Grimly, he shook the image away. "What can I do you for, Dr. Ansell?"

Pachico's belly laugh rolled across the creek bank. Rawls prayed she hadn't guessed his train of thought as easily as his ghostly stalker had. But the fact that she backed up a good two feet, as her uncertainty devolved into outright nervousness, was a clear indication she'd picked up on *something.*

"Two dumb-ass doctors sitting in a tree—k-i-s-s-i-n-g." Pachico's voice hit a singsong rhythm.

Rawls winced. Devil take it. No doubt a new and equally annoying song was poised to drive him crazy.

"Dr. Ansell?" he prompted, trying to ignore how enthusiastically his body was appreciating her nearness.

The sooner he found out what she wanted, the quicker he could send her on her way. He tried a smile out on her and she backed up even farther. Frustrated, he dropped the friendly act.

"You need somethin', darlin'?" he asked, only the question came out much curter than he'd intended.

She tensed, and for a moment it looked like he'd unintentionally managed to drive her away. But then she squared her shoulders and lifted her chin, holding his gaze. His lips twitched; there was that spirit again.

"Rumor has it you went to medical school."

He'd bet his med kit that rumor had focused on his loss of sanity even more than his aborted medical career, not that he had any interest in digging up either subject. Besides, he doubted she'd gone to the effort to track him down to drill him about his schooling.

"And?" He scanned her inflexible figure and the heat in his belly spiked.

She looked fine. Okay, not exactly *fine*—she was too thin to fit that description.

He'd noticed how skinny she was four and a half months earlier at gate C-18 in Sea-Tac Airport. He still wasn't sure why she'd caught his attention back then—she sure as hell hadn't looked like a terrorist. But something about her had snared his gaze over and over again.

Her thinness had been readily apparent when they'd broken into her incinerated lab six days earlier and stumbled upon her shimmying her way beneath the particle accelerator. The woman seriously needed to eat, although if she hadn't been thirty pounds underweight, she'd never have fit beneath the machine. Hell, she'd been light as a kitten, and as combustible as C4, when he'd dragged her out from beneath the machine and half carried her from the building.

She'd also been covered in scratches. Scratches she'd refused to let him tend . . . He swore beneath his breath and ran a palm over his head. "I knew I should have ignored your objections and insisted on dressin' those gashes—"

"The cuts are healing appropriately," she interrupted.

His gaze was drawn to the thick band of freckles marching across her upper cheeks and the bridge of her nose. Her coloring was . . . unusual. Freckles were more visible on people with fair coloring. Yet her skin tone had a distinct olive tint to it, and her hair shone with blue-black luster.

And her eyes—deep, dark blue . . . He jerked his gaze away, struggling to remember where he'd been going with his train of thought.

"Oh, for Christ's sake, you moron, kiss her already. Get her out of that shirt. Let's see some tits."

Pachico's loud voice knocked him out of his stupor. He stepped back, scanning her face—relieved to find her expression unchanging. At least she hadn't noticed his momentary lapse.

"I'll bite, sweetheart," Rawls said, working overtime on his drawl. "If you don't need me to tend them cuts, what do you need me for?"

Her eyes widened for a moment and then narrowed again. The tight skin of her forehead furrowed as she pressed her lips together.

Just maybe that question had come off more sexual than he'd intended.

"Never mind," she said, and pivoted with such precision, she would have done the naval ceremonial guard proud.

"Now, darlin'." He stepped forward, fixing to chase after her. "Don't—"

"Rawlings." A deep baritone barked from behind him.

Rawls spun to face the new threat and found himself face-to-face with the bulky, broad-shouldered frame of Kait's Arapaho friend. Hell, the man moved as silently as an operator—of course, according to Kait, he headed some super-secret Special Forces team, which elevated him to an operator of sorts.

He shot Faith's departing back a frustrated glance and forced an easy smile as he turned back to Wolf. "Thought you knew better than surprisin' a person like that, hoss. Surefire way to get yourself gutted."

Then again, it was a good thing Wolf didn't have a hankering to use that wicked knife strapped to his belt, 'cause Rawls would have been the one filleted.

He was in pretty sorry shape, damn it. First Faith had managed to surprise him, and now Wolf. Inexcusable. He needed to screw his damn head back on. If the bastards hunting them pinpointed their new camp and stumbled onto him lollygagging off in oblivion . . . hell, his mental meltdown was going to get him dead. Get his whole team dead. Time to man up and start acting like an operator.

"A word." Wolf let go of Rawls's arm and crossed thick arms across a wide chest.

Rawls shrugged, forcing himself to hold his host's hard, black gaze. "Have at it."

Wolf glanced from side to side, his black brows drawing together. "Is it here?"

Tilting his head, Rawls studied Wolf's face. His new friend's tone had been raspier than normal, with an undercurrent of unease. "What?"

"The *biitei*." The normally velvety baritone roughened.

With a roll of his shoulders, Rawls sucked back a tired breath. Christ, he needed a few solid hours of sleep. "You're gonna have to speak English, hoss."

Wolf's lips tightened, and the disquiet lurking in his voice shadowed his face. "The *biitei*. He who walked the other side. He who followed you across the threshold."

The other side?

That strange, ethereal dream rose in Rawls's mind. "What's a *biitei*?"

Wolf actually hesitated before offering a shrug. "Ghost."

Pure shock rocked Rawls back on his heels. "You believe in ghosts?"

An asinine question since the big guy had just suggested Rawls had brought one back from *the other side* . . . which happened to be a pretty apt description of that eerie, silvery world in his dream.

"What makes you think I picked up a ghost?" Rawls asked.

"I know you crossed over. I know you walked the other side. I know you brought a *biitei* through the veil on return." With each clipped sentence, Wolf's voice hardened.

A denial teetered on Rawls's tongue, but he couldn't force it out. Damn it—he was tired of pretending. He was tired of not knowing. He wanted answers. "I died?"

"You deny this?" Wolf asked, anger flashing across his square face. He planted his thick black boots and glared.

"I ain't denyin' anything. Zane and Cos—they said I had a pulse."

Wolf didn't respond, but the anger faded.

"Hold up now," Rawls said, studying Wolf's inscrutable face intensely. "How'd you know there's a ghost?"

Which was as close to a confirmation as he intended to get. While his teammates clearly knew something was wrong, they hadn't identified the problem yet.

Thank you, Jesus.

Wolf's black stare flattened. "Who was the *biitei*?"

"I reckon I ain't sayin' there *is* a ghost"—Rawls tried to lighten his drawl—"but if there was a transparent troll hangin' around, it'd most likely be Pachico, our old friend from the lab."

Which reminded him. It wasn't like the asshole to stand on the sidelines when the conversation was so wickedly ironic. He glanced to the left, then the right, finally turning in a slow circle.

What the devil?

Pachico had vanished.

An icy chill washed down his back. For the second time in less than a week, the ground heaved beneath his feet. Pachico was gone? Rawls winced, massaging his temples, as a hell of a pounding shook his head.

What the hell? Had the asshole even existed?

Maybe he *had* been a hallucination.

But then Wolf's words flashed through his mind. The big guy clearly knew there was a ghost. Hell, he appeared to know more about Rawls's current situation than Rawls did himself.

Wolf dropped his arms, his body tensing. "The *heebii3soo* Jillian killed?"

"That's the one," Rawls confirmed absently, scanning the grassy field and scraggly brush surrounding him.

"Your shirt. The one you crossed over in. Where is it?"

"I tossed it." The question, odd as it was, barely pierced his obsession with the whereabouts of Pachico.

Where had the ghost gone? How had he gone? For the past five days he'd been leashed to Rawls, unable to stray more than a dozen feet, expressing his frustration in the most annoying ways possible. And now he suddenly up and vanished? Why? What had changed? Rawls froze as the answer hit.

Wolf.

Wolf had appeared, and Pachico had disappeared. That couldn't be a coincidence. Faith's arrival hadn't driven the ghost off.

He swung around to confront his host in time to witness the Arapaho warrior dive into the tree line, apparently heading back to camp at warp speed.

Rawls started after him, heading for the west edge of camp and the back of Wolf's cabin. With luck, he could avoid the rest of his camp mates. But just as he dived into the forest at the camp's perimeter, the distinct *whop-whop-whop* of chopper blades beat the air. The devil take it—there was no doubt in his mind that Wolf was on that bird. Rawls changed directions, heading for the north edge of camp and the helipad. He broke through the trees just in time to see the bird bank and climb into the sky, Wolf clearly visible in the passenger seat.

"Sure as hell they have eyes on your boys. You realize that, right? A rendezvous *will* spring a trap," Commander Mackenzie growled, bracing his fists against the table.

Faith Ansell glanced at the drama taking place across the kitchen counter. The three SEALs might outweigh the petite redhead by a collective five hundred pounds, but Amy Chastain certainly held her ground. Did the woman's self-confidence come from her years as a special agent with the FBI prior to her marriage and subsequent widowing? After all, climbing the ranks of the bureau's good old boys' club was certain to instill a belief in one's own abilities.

Mackenzie's voice rose at Amy's lack of response. "You go in half-cocked and you'll get yourself and those boys killed. I guarantee it."

Faith flinched as Mackenzie's voice scaled the walls of the combined kitchen, dining room, and strategy center. The commander, she'd discovered, employed two volumes—normal and nuclear. Too bad he didn't come with a kill switch, like Big Ben, the particle accelerator in her lab. If Benny threw off his calibration and started thundering, she just flipped the switch and shut his bellowing down.

"I'm not asking you"—Amy's cool hazel gaze touched Mackenzie's face, and then Zane's, and finally Cosky's—"any of you, to come with me."

In contrast to the commander's voice, Amy's was calm, the very definition of moderation. Yet it hit the edgy air like an electrostatic generator, shedding high-voltage sparks.

"The hell you aren't. You know damn well we can't let you go alone," Mackenzie thundered, even louder than before.

Faith winced and rubbed her temples. Lord, the man gave her a headache.

"This isn't open to debate. I'm going." Amy set her jaw, pulled back her shoulders, and squared her feet, settling into a boxer's stance, but with weapons composed of words rather than fists. "They aren't safe with my parents. And Mom and Dad aren't safe with the boys there. I'm taking them. Period."

Faith sighed with admiration before turning back to the oven. If she had a pictogram of Amy's confidence and self-possession maybe she wouldn't be entrenched in her current dilemma.

She opened the range door, backing off slightly to let the heat escape. Once the worst of it had dissipated, she leaned down, sticking a butter knife into a loaf of golden-brown zucchini bread. The utensil emerged with a smear of grainy, yellow-brown liquid.

As she straightened, the cuts on her shoulders and collarbone stung. It had been six days since Rawls had pulled her out from under the particle accelerator. While the cuts she'd inflicted on herself while shimmying beneath Big Ben hadn't turned septic, as Rawls had so obviously feared, they weren't healing quite as fast as normal. It had been the height of foolishness to refuse his ministrations during the van ride to Wolf's Sierra Nevada home. She couldn't afford to let the injuries become infected.

Her health was already compromised thanks to her twice-daily palmful of pills. It was the immunosuppressants' job to prevent her body from rejecting her heart, which left her wide-open to infections.

She knew better than to ignore a possible threat to her well-being. She should never have ignored Rawls's offer to dress her wounds.

So what if the man's mere presence brought on butterflies and goose bumps? So what if he plunged her limbic system into hyperdrive. She was a normal woman in the prime reproductive stage, with a fully functioning amygdala. Of course her hands would get all sweaty and her stomach tingly. The guy was gorgeous, after all. There was absolutely no reason to feel embarrassed about her reaction to him, or fear his awareness to said reaction.

"And you think they'll be safer here?" Mackenzie snapped. "For Christ's sake, use your head. We're in a Goddamn war zone. At any moment—"

"I'm not bringing them here," Amy interrupted with the same cool collection as before.

Faith shot a quick glance at her camp mates. The main lodge, which housed the kitchen and dining room as well as the command center, was an open-air design. One huge rectangular area separated into individual rooms by waist-high counters and the arrangement of furniture.

"Where are you taking them?" Zane cocked his head, his brilliant green eyes sharpening as he focused on Amy's face.

There were pros and cons to the layout of the room. On the plus side, she had a front-row seat to every strategy session or informational briefing and would know the instant they located her kidnapped coworkers.

If they located her fellow scientists . . .

A wave of regret and horror seared her chest at the thought of her friends.

An image pushed into her mind, a memory—*a short, wide hall, the smell of fireworks stinging the air . . . a limp body stretched across the gray-and-red linoleum . . . a rumpled, bloodstained peach skirt pushed high on plump thighs . . .*

Faith shuddered, hurriedly shoving the memory aside. There was nothing she could do to help her friends. And wallowing in horrific memories served no purpose. It certainly didn't benefit her coworkers. Or herself.

She had enough problems of her own. She needed to focus and concentrate on what she could do. What she needed to do. And right now she needed to slow her galloping heart rate and find a way to relax.

In the past, baking had provided the serenity her condition required, but being in such close proximity to the men with their loud, often argumentative voices . . . well, that wasn't particularly calming at all. And she *needed* that blissful tranquility, *needed* the relaxation of baking.

Her donor heart had been damaged during harvest, leaving her with a bad case of ventricular tachycardia. Double-blind testing indicated that arrhythmia was often a result of stress. Baking relieved stress—at least for her. Ergo, her baking might hold the tachycardia at bay. For a while, at least. Until she could get her prescriptions filled.

"I haven't decided where we're going yet." Amy turned toward Zane. "I'll pay cash so I don't leave a trail."

Faith's lips twisted. Well, at least she'd done something right after escaping the lab. She'd known better than to go home. And since the men after her could track her by her credit and debit purchases, she'd headed to the closest ATM and withdrawn her five-hundred-dollar daily limit on her debit card before bolting from the vicinity. Another ATM and a different debit card for another five hundred. She'd hit a third ATM for a cash advance on her credit card, and then another ATM for another cash advance. By the time her cards stopped working, she'd collected twenty-five hundred dollars. Enough to last her several weeks—if she remained frugal.

It was too bad all that money was sitting in the motel room, along with her medications. Assuming the desk clerk or one of the maids hadn't absconded with her belongings. If she had a dram of Amy's fortitude, she would have insisted that Commander Mackenzie swing by her motel and collect her meager possessions before hauling her off to the Sierra Nevadas.

Of course, back then she hadn't been sure she could trust them—she still wasn't sure she could trust them . . . at least not with everything. Besides, even if she had insisted they swing over to her motel to collect her belongings, those possessions would be ashes along with Wolf's Sierra Nevada home now anyway.

Zane frowned and ran a palm over his short-cropped hair. "You could head to where my dad took my mom. It's a secure location, manned by a team of ex-special forces turned survivalists—doomsday preppers. They're hard-core fringe riders and conspiracy nuts, but you and the boys will be safe there."

With a curt shake of her head, Amy dropped her arms. "Fringe groups like that don't take in strangers."

"They'll take you if Dad asks them to," Zane countered. "These guys are good, they know what they're doing. Hands down, it's the safest place you'll find." He paused, shot Cosky a quick glance. "Mac's right. This place—hell, any place we settle is a hot spot. I'm sending Beth down there. Cosky's sending Kait."

Amy studied Zane's face, then switched to Cosky. After a moment she raised ember-red eyebrows. "I take it you haven't told them yet?"

The men's silence spoke volumes.

Faith smiled wryly. She didn't know Kait and Beth that well, but she'd spent enough time in the kitchen watching the interaction between the SEALs and their women to know they wouldn't be happy about this plan. Indeed, the room was about to get extremely loud—assuming they informed the women of their imminent abandonment in the command center and didn't finagle them off somewhere private and sweet-talk them into the news.

Of course, the SEALs were probably planning on shipping her off to this survivalist group too. Faith frowned. From what little she knew about doomsday preppers, they kept to themselves, avoided civilization, and set up their camps in the wilderness. Rather like this place, but without the benefit of helicopter service. Still frowning thoughtfully, she turned back to the stove and yanked open the oven to recheck the zucchini bread.

It would be even harder to fill her meds from such a camp. As she slipped the butter knife back into the bread, she released a frustrated breath. She'd been so close earlier . . . if she hadn't lost her nerve on catching sight of Wolf, she might have a line on her meds by now. In retrospect, she should have stayed put and explained the situation. Wolf would need to know about her need for medication at some point anyway.

"What do you suggest?" Amy asked, her voice more polite than curious.

"That you don't contact your parents or brother until we're on scene and we give you the all clear."

Faith almost didn't recognize Mackenzie's voice, it was so startlingly cordial. And she must have missed a critical exchange in the conversation, because it sounded like they were going to help Amy after all.

"I'm not asking you to come," Amy repeated after a tense silence.

"I'm fucking aware of that." Mac's voice tightened and hardened, but at least it didn't rise. "We're offering."

Faith wondered if Amy got the same impression, that the men intended to accompany her whether she accepted their offer of aid or not.

"Her parents live in Bellingham," the commander said, turning to Lieutenant Simcosky. "We'll need to find a canyon about half an hour out. Single-access entry point, with enough elevation to give us a three-sixty on the eyes."

Both Zane and Cosky nodded in agreement.

"Wolf's bird would come in handy." Zane turned to Cosky and lifted his eyebrows. "Think you can sweet-talk your new BFF into loaning us his toy when he returns?" He paused to tilt his head. "And by sweet-talking, I mean without your fists."

Cosky grimaced, absently stroking a finger across his eyebrow. "I'll have Kait ask him."

A moment of silence fell.

"What about Rawls?" Zane asked, his tone careful. "We may need his med kit."

More tense silence. Along with furrowed brows.

As quietly as possible, so she wouldn't interrupt their conversation, Faith removed two loaves of bread from the oven and set them on the counter to cool.

"Have either of you seen him today?" Mac asked, scrubbing a hand down his tight face. At the shake of Zane's and Cosky's heads, he grunted. "He talk to either of you about what's going on?"

More head-shaking.

Faith frowned. There had been something strange about that situation involving Seth Rawlings in the woods after Wolf's house had exploded. Something odd, and it continued to itch at her. The man had been lying there, still as death, drenched in blood. She'd been horrified, mournful, certain he'd been dead. Only suddenly, he'd opened his eyes. And then there had been no wounds when Amy had wiped him down with the wet cloth.

Cosky and Zane claimed blood transfer was to blame for his saturated clothes—that the body he'd collapsed onto had been riddled with bullets and had bled out. But if that were the case, if Seth Rawlings hadn't been wounded, what had triggered his collapse and unconsciousness in the first place? What was causing his current erratic behavior? And even more troublesome, what accounted for . . . the glowing? Cosky and Kait, even Rawls . . . all three of them had been wrapped in a luminous silver sheen.

With a shake of her head, she shrugged the memory aside. Likely it had been a trick of her eyes, the play of moonlight against the darkness.

But still—something about that night prickled at her, and her instincts whispered that whatever had happened out there that dark, dangerous night played directly into Rawlings's erratic behavior of today.

"I know he's your medic, but if he snaps and starts shouting at an inopportune time . . ." Amy's voice trailed off.

From the grim expressions stamped across the three SEALs' faces, they shared her concerns.

"He's sitting this one out." Mackenzie turned to Zane. "Talk to him. He's a liability in his current condition. And for Christ's sake, find out what the hell's going on." His scowl disintegrated into a grimace, and then a sigh. "I'll talk to Wolf, see if he's got anyone with medical experience we can borrow."

From eavesdropping on the random conversations that took place across the kitchen counter, it sounded like Lieutenant Rawlings had more than mere medical experience. Indeed, he was as close to a doctor as one could get without completing their internship. Cosky had told Kait that Rawls had graduated from medical school and passed his medical exams, he'd even completed his first two rotations of internship. Why in the world he'd thrown all of that away to join the navy and eventually the SEALs, well, that just wasn't her business, was it?

What was her business was whether he was mentally stable enough to approach with her problem and whether he could write prescriptions. Or if he couldn't write her a prescription, whether he knew someone who could—someone who'd fill her prescriptions with no questions asked and no medical history required.

The medical history was bound to get sticky, considering she'd been listed as dead by the King County coroner earlier in the week.

She'd been off the immune suppressors for six days now. In most cases, donor rejection was chronic, rather than acute, so the damage to her heart would accumulate over a period of time. As long as the cyclosporine and mycophenolate were reinstated at a higher dose soon, the immune-system suppression should occur soon enough to prevent damage to her heart.

The ventricular tachycardia, however, was a different obstacle completely. She needed that prescription of Cordarone. Every day without it put her life at risk. She had four doses left in the bottle; after that she'd be courting a heart attack with every beat of her heart.

She was down to the wire now. She'd tried to find Rawlings time after time, but the man was a master at avoiding unwanted company. And while he wore a walkie-talkie, along with the rest of the men in camp, she didn't particularly relish the thought of her medical history floating over the airwaves and around camp. Unfortunately, she'd officially run out of time. She was going to have to approach Zane or Cosky and ask one of them to contact Rawlings for her. And no doubt they'd want to know why.

She shook her head in disgust and scowled down at the kitchen counter. She should have just stuck it out earlier, regardless of Wolf's interference, and asked the pair for help then.

"We'll discuss scheduling when Wolf returns," Mac said, his gaze hard on Amy's face, as though he expected her to protest.

"I want to pick up Mom while we have the chopper. She'd be safer with Zane's father and his crazy-ass friends than where she's currently holed up," Simcosky announced, his square face uncompromising. He held Mac's gaze steadily.

The commander shrugged. "That's Wolf's call."

Faith swallowed a comment. The whole operation would be Wolf's call since he owned the helicopter. But she didn't bring that salient fact to the commander's attention. Her standard operating procedure during the SEALs' strategy sessions was to pretend she was invisible. Sometimes it felt like she actually was invisible, the men ignored her so completely.

Not that she was complaining—there was a reason invisibility was considered a superpower.

Maybe by the time Mackenzie's contacts located Dr. Benton and the rest of her crew, she'd have eavesdropped on enough conversations to know whether she could trust them with the real reason her friends had been targeted and taken—assuming, of course, that they weren't planning on packing her off to God knew where with Kait and Beth and the rest of the women.

Chapter Three

TEN MINUTES AFTER WOLF TOOK TO THE SKIES, RAWLS DRAGGED ONE of the kitchen chairs into his bedroom and shoved it against the wall next to the window, angling it until he had a clear view of the helipad. He'd know the minute Wolf returned to the compound.

He scanned the room for Pachico's translucent form, but his ghost was still missing. The sudden silence after days of endless chatter, and obnoxious top-of-the-lungs singing, weighed on him, filled him with ominous portent. The calm gave him way too much time and peace to think, which led to questioning . . .

How much of the past five days had been real versus hallucinations? Had Pachico even existed? Or—more specifically—had the transparent version of Pachico been a product of a damaged mind?

Before settling into the chair to watch for Wolf's return, he backtracked to the kitchen, pulled open the cupboard above the stainless-steel sink, and dragged down the bottle of Jack Daniel's Tennessee Honey. Bottle in one hand and an eight-ounce juice glass in the other, he backtracked to his bedroom and settled into the wood chair.

He set the bottle on the windowsill and stared at it. The golden liquid inside glowed with molten intensity beneath the sun's rays.

Since that incident when Zane and Cos had walked in on him yelling at Pachico to "shut the Goddamn fuck up" he'd spent from dawn to dusk outside, avoiding his camp mates as much as possible. When he did return to the cabin, it was to sleep. Or try to anyway. Pachico had turned sleeping into an exercise of frustration and futility.

It didn't matter how much toilet paper he jammed into his ears, or how hard he pressed the pillow over his head, Pachico's voice never dulled. In retrospect, the fact that he hadn't been able to mute the bastard's singing lent credence to the possibility the ghost was a byproduct of blood loss and his oxygen-deprived, damaged mind. If Pachico had been a hallucination, external methods to muffle his yammering would prove ineffectual.

No matter how he broke it down, he couldn't escape one hard fact. There was absolutely no evidence proving that Pachico had actually existed in that incorporeal state. Nothing to verify that Rawls hadn't lost his damn mind and dreamed the whole damn thing up. Hell, even the conversation with Wolf earlier could have been a product of his overactive imagination.

It was hell not trusting your own mind.

With a tense hand Rawls reached for the bottle of Tennessee Honey, rotating it on the windowsill. He'd found the bottle three days ago. It had been full back then. It was still full. A miracle considering that every chorus of that endless song had pushed him closer to twisting the cap and breaking the seal. Thus breaking a promise he'd made thirteen years ago.

A promise to himself . . . and to his sister, even though Sarah had been dead by then—past caring what he did or didn't do with his life. Past blaming him for the trajectory her short life had taken because of him.

Past blaming him, something his mother and father—hell, even he himself—hadn't been able to get past.

He slowly turned the bottle again, watching the amber liquid inside the glass burn, as though the sun were boiling the booze trapped inside.

Tennessee Honey was the kind of smooth, sweet liquor Sarah would have appreciated back in the day.

He'd gone for the harder stuff, booze with a bite, although he'd never crossed the line between partier and alcoholic. He'd been too committed to medicine to make that mistake. Driven to join his father and grandfather in the family tradition of surgical medicine—in wielding the power of life and death. So while he'd partied hard over semester and summer breaks, it hadn't affected his studies, his residency, or his life . . . until Miami. Until his alcohol-induced recklessness had stolen Sarah's life and sent his into a 360-degree tailspin.

From his third year of surgical residency to Navy SEAL in six months. What a curve his life had taken. And once again he was reeling from a 360-degree wipeout. Only this time, he had no clue what his life would look like once the world stopped spinning.

"Jesus Christ, Doc. At the rate you're moving, you'll never get that damn shirt off her. How about—" Pachico's voice cut off. He rocked back on his heels and took a long, slow look around. "What the fuck . . . when—" His mouth snapped shut and an unsettled expression crossed his face.

Rawls staggered up from the kitchen chair, stunned by the hot rush of relief that hit him. Sure, the asshole's reappearance didn't prove Rawls's sanity. Pachico could still be a delusion, but when he was walking and talking, or more apt—singing—he didn't feel like a hallucination.

"What the hell happened to you?" Rawls asked.

Something had kicked his transparent stalker out of existence—at least this existence, this world. It hadn't been for long, maybe fifteen minutes, but if he could figure out how and why, he'd have control over the bastard, and the ability to boot him at will.

"What the fuck are you yakking about?" Pachico asked, but the uneasy expression in his eyes belied his truculent question.

Pachico knew he'd blinked out for a bit. The look of shocked surprise on his face to find himself in the bedroom instead of the woods
had been a dead giveaway.

"You disappeared," Rawls shot back. "You were gone fifteen minutes. Why? Where did you go?"

He suspected the questions were a waste of breath. If the ghost had
remembered going somewhere, he wouldn't have shown such astonish-
ment when he'd found himself back in the cabin. For the moment at
least, Rawls bet he had more answers than his ghost did. Or at least one
answer. The big one.

Wolf.

But he'd be keeping that name under his hat until he had a chance
to question the man.

"I don't know what the fuck you're talking about," Pachico growled,
a stony expression dropping over his face.

Sure he didn't. "We were out at the creek, then you up and
vamoosed. What's the last thing you remember?"

The real question was whether he remembered Wolf's approach.
Since the bastard had been totally focused on Faith, Rawls was pretty
certain the answer to the Wolf question was no.

"That it's none of your fucking business, that's what I remember,"
Pachico snapped. "And I think you've lost focus here, Doc. You ready
to make that call?"

"No," Rawls countered with a dry smile. "I reckon you were at five
hundred and one."

Through the bedroom doorway came the sound of a fist at the
cabin's front entry, followed by the squeak of the door opening and the
muted bang as it fell shut again. Rawls tensed, turning to face the hallway. Only his teammates would enter on a knock, without introducing
themselves first. The women in the compound were more polite; they
waited for acknowledgment.

He listened to the sound of boots hitting the plank floor. Zane from the sound of them. Cos had a quicker pace, and Mac was faster still—clipped and impatient rather than brisk.

"Five hundred bottles of beer on the wall, five hundred bottles of beer—"

Rawls groaned beneath his breath. Yeah, this conversation was bound to be fun. He'd be lucky to hear a tenth of what his LC had to say.

After another fist against the bedroom doorjamb, which Rawls saw but couldn't hear, Zane stepped into the room. He stopped halfway between the door and Rawls. And thank you, Jesus, Pachico shut the fuck up. Had Zane's arrival kicked him out of existence? It hadn't the last time Zane had visited. Rawls shot his ghost a quick look. It hadn't this time either. Based on Pachico's expression, he was simply more interested in what Zane had to say than torturing his ride-along.

"Who were you talking to?" Zane asked with a long, slow look around the bedroom.

Ah hell, apparently the cabin walls hadn't muffled his voice. Of course the living room windows were open . . . Rawls groaned beneath his breath in disgust. This was exactly why he'd taken to hiding out in the woods.

"Nobody." At Zane's raised brow, Rawls shrugged. "Talkin' to myself. Ain't no crime in that."

A tense silence settled over the room.

Zane was the one to break it. "You know we've got your back. No matter what. You can tell us what the hell's going on."

Yeah? How was he supposed to tell his best friend that he was quite possibly certifiably crazy—as in *actually* certifiably crazy? What was the protocol for that conversation? A case of Coors, a jumbo bag of chips, a ball game on the telly, and during the intermission just throw the admission out there like a mortar shell?

"Goddamn it"—frustration tightened Zane's voice—"you forget what being a member of ST7 means?"

Rawls stared at the ground so hard his eyes burned. He knew exactly what being on the team meant. Unqualified, absolute support from your teammates. But hell, there were certain qualifications an operator had to possess to secure that spot in the Zodiac. One of those qualifications was mental health, and the very definition of mental health was the absence of delusions involving ghosts.

How many of his teammates would jump into the beach boat beside him if they knew he was stuck in his own production of *The Sixth Sense*?

"Fine." Zane released a sharp breath and tightened his shoulders. Rawls knew him well enough to catch the displeasure and frustration lurking beneath his flat expression. "As soon as the chopper returns, we're headed out to grab Amy's kids and Cosky's mom." When Rawls's head came up, Zane shook his. "You're sitting this one out, holding down camp."

Rawls simply nodded, unsurprised. His LC's caution was well placed—they both knew it. He couldn't be trusted during the risky mobilization of a team insertion when lack of focus could result in casualties.

Zane cocked his head and studied Rawls's face for a moment, as though expecting a protest, before continuing. "Keep an eye on Beth for me. This morning sickness is giving her hell, but she needs to eat. She likes French toast. Maybe ask Faith to make some?" At Rawls's nod, Zane hesitated and shrugged. "Wolf's leaving one of his guys to help out in case of trouble."

Rawls's lips twisted. Wasn't that sweet? They were leaving a babysitter for the babysitter. He forced the self-disgust aside and concentrated on the subtext of the conversation. Someone must have talked to Wolf over the sat phone. What else had Wolf told them?

"Did Wolf say when he's returnin' to camp?" Rawls asked, working like hell to keep his expression neutral and his eyes away from the corner where Pachico was silently following the conversation.

Something told him Wolf was the key to dealing with his ghost.

Zane's brows crinkled. "He didn't say. He flew off with Jillian. He's not coming back for the op, but he's sending his pilot and his second."

Rawls nodded and swallowed the rest of his questions. If Wolf had told them about Rawls's ghost, Pachico's name would have been the first thing out of his LC's mouth.

"We're sending the women and the kids to my dad's doomsday friends. I know you're not close to your father, but you should contact him, convince him to join—"

"He's dead," Rawls interrupted.

Surprise swept Zane's face and then it closed down like storm shutters during a hurricane. "When?"

Rawls held his lieutenant commander's icy green gaze. He'd known from the get-go that withholding the news of his father's death and flying out alone for the funeral would eventually rouse confusion and ire with Zane and Cos. "Fixin' on a year now."

"A year . . ." Zane shook his head, the ice turning brittle in his eyes. "Those two weeks you disappeared to visit some gal back east?"

"I visited her while I was there." Which wasn't exactly a lie. He had visited Alyssa, which had been every bit as uncomfortable as the memorial and the two weeks of funeral arrangements.

"You're full of surprises."

Zane's flat, cold comment stung, but Rawls shook the bite off. He didn't regret keeping his friends out of that personal and painful intrusion from his past life. His teammates, for all their closeness, didn't know who Seth Rawlings was. Hell, they didn't even know his real name. Shrugging off his old life had been the entire purpose of joining the navy, of qualifying for the teams, of convincing HQ1 to let him join a platoon as a corpsman, rather than sticking him in the bowels of some naval hospital removed from the action. He'd been determined to erase that clueless, pampered child, determined to make sure he'd never face such helplessness again, and he had developed the skills necessary for survival.

If he'd told Zane and Cos about his dad's death, they would have insisted on heading out to Columbia, South Carolina, with him, where they would have heard far too quickly about William Crosby Seth Rawlings—the self-absorbed son of one of South Carolina's oldest families—and how his pathetic, ill-prepared, good-ol'-boy lifestyle had gotten his baby sister tortured and murdered.

"Please, make them stop, Will. Make them stop."

He flinched at the memory. Forced it down into that pit of shame that never quite scabbed over.

Sure, headquarters had known his full name, but they'd been as eager to bury his story as Rawls had been. He could just imagine the headlines if some enterprising reporter ferreted out the ugly details—*Southern socialite rescued by US Special Forces, turns Special Forces himself.* Of course SEALs weren't Special Forces, but none of the original articles had gotten that little detail correct anyway.

"Your brothers joinin' your father at the camp?" Rawls asked, recognizing the irony in the question as soon as it hit the air.

He knew everything about Zane—from his four brothers, right down to his quest for his life-mate, which he'd found in Beth. Zane on the other hand? Hell, his best friend didn't even know Rawls had once had a sister.

"Dane, Chance, and Webb are out on rotation, but Gray's going to meet the bird and haul everyone out to Dad. God knows how long he'll be able to stay."

Rawls simply nodded. Zane stared at him for a couple heartbeats too many, as if he was waiting for him to come clean, waiting for him to step back beneath the umbrella of team life and team camaraderie.

When Rawls remained stoically silent, Zane swore beneath his breath and turned, heading for the door.

"You know they have eyes on Amy's kids. They'll be waitin' for her to pick those boys up. Y'all will be walkin' into a trap," Rawls said, raising his voice as Zane approached the door.

"That's the consensus," Zane acknowledged, stopping with his back to Rawls.

While he understood Amy's urgency to collect her kids and get them to safety, moving too early gutted their most effective snatch-and-run strategy. The biggest advantage a SEAL team had was strike hard, strike fast, strike while the enemy was unprepared and unaware. Zero dark whenever was their closest ally.

This mission, on the other hand, was going down in broad daylight with plenty of prior warning. A blueprint for casualties.

All of which Mac, Zane, and Cos knew, but it never hurt to issue a reminder. "Why can't this wait until midnight? Under cover of darkness."

"Because there's too many damn civilians in the mix. Amy's parents, her kids, her brother. And two of those civilians will be armed." Frustration sharpened Zane's voice. "Since we can't shoot on sight, it leaves us and everyone in that house vulnerable."

Nor could they warn Amy's family that they'd be coming. In all likelihood there were ears on that house.

Rawls nodded his understanding, his unease increasing. "What about those handy-dandy premonitions of yours? You gettin' anything?"

Zane shook his head. "But hell, the visions don't always kick in when I need them."

True. Zane's psychic warning system was glitchy at best. Nothing you wanted to count on to cover your ass. "You'll need the med kit. I—"

"Wolf's second has medical training. He's bringing his kit," Zane interrupted. "You know damn well we can't bring you in on this. Not with your head in its current scramble." He waited, one beat . . . three beats . . . five, and then rolled his shoulders. "When you're ready to tell us what the fuck's going on, you know where to find us." Without looking back, Zane walked out the door.

Dead silence blanketed the room. After a moment, Rawls turned back to the amber bottle sunning itself on the windowsill.

"I'm no expert on you boys," Pachico said, his voice a cross between dry and smug. "But sounds like he's losing patience with you. I've got just the song to cheer you up, though. You ready to make that call? No? Five hundred bottles of beer on the wall—" Pachico's voice broke into song as Rawls lifted the bottle of Tennessee Honey and twisted the cap. "Five hundred bottles of beer. Take one down, pass it around, four hundred and ninety-nine bottles of beer on the wall."

Rawls took a pull straight from the bottle, wishing the smooth, slightly sweet fire burning down his throat had more of a bite to it.

Because sweet Jesus, he was looking at a long, long night.

Faith waited until the helicopter carrying Amy Chastain and her self-appointed rescue squad took to the skies before turning to the kitchen counter and picking up the plastic-wrapped plate with its thick roast beef sandwich. She paused at the front entrance of the main lodge, letting the dust devils settle before thrusting open the door. Trotting down the plank stairs, she headed across the earthen courtyard toward the largest cabin. Originally the rustic bungalow had housed all four SEALs. But then Lieutenant Cosky had set up house with Kait Winchester, and Zane with his fiancée, Beth. These days, Lieutenant Rawlings shared the place with Commander Mackenzie, alone—which was reason enough for commiseration as far as Faith was concerned.

From the discussion she'd eavesdropped on earlier, Zane had tracked Rawlings to his bedroom. With luck, he'd stayed put after his commanding officer had left. Waving away a swarm of mosquitoes, she hurried up the three plank steps and knocked hard on the rough-hewn door. Silence greeted her from within the cabin. She knocked again, hard enough to bruise her knuckles. More silence. If he *was* in there, he had no intention of admitting it. Sympathy stirred; she understood the need for solitude. Indeed, she'd often felt it herself while growing up. Sometimes you just needed to get away, to escape the fear in loved ones' eyes—or in his case, his teammates' eyes.

There was nothing worse than knowing someone was worrying themselves sick over you. It hadn't mattered how often she'd reminded herself that the situation wasn't her fault, or how many times her therapists had told her that she wasn't responsible for her parents' fear—she'd still felt accountable for the deep crevices that constant worry had etched into their faces.

The guilt had been bad enough prior to the first transplant, but when the initial heart had failed and she'd ended up back on the transplant list with diminishing chances of receiving a second heart in time . . . She flinched, shying away from the memories. The stress had killed what love remained between her parents—miring them in cold silence or endless arguments. The only reason they'd stayed together had been because of her, because of the care she'd required.

After the second heart transplant had returned her to health, she'd hoped they'd seek happiness for themselves, even if it meant being apart from one another. But by then they'd become so fixated on her health they'd let it define them and had hung her heart condition around her neck like some macabre charm meant to ward off death.

She'd chosen a university clear across the country, and remained there after graduation, to escape their obsession over her mortality. After the lab explosion, when the medical examiner had released the news of her death, she'd thought long and hard about whether to contact them with a "Surprise! Look who's on their fourth life!" But caution had stayed her hand. What if someone was monitoring her parents' calls? What if her stalkers tracked her location through the phone records?

In the end it hadn't been fear of discovery that had stilled her fingers on the untraceable cell phone she'd picked up at the mini-mart around the corner. It had been imagining their reaction to finding out she was alive. That familiar guilt had settled thick as quicksand inside her. A reaction made stronger by the knowledge that her parents wouldn't even be mad that she'd kept them in the dark so long. They'd be so overjoyed to find out she was alive they wouldn't have room for anger. But eventually their relief would shift to fear, and they'd urge her to return to Augusta, Maine, and when she refused, they'd insist on moving out to the West Coast and that whole passive-aggressive obsession would start again.

Frowning, she glared at the heavy wood door barring her entry. Obviously her quarry didn't intend to respond to her knock. If she wanted to talk to him, she'd have to run him down herself, which meant ignoring protocol and letting herself into his current haven.

Waving off another swarm of mosquitoes—heavens, the little beasts were thicker than water—she pushed open the door to Rawls's cabin and invited herself across the threshold. Nerves tightened her belly and tiptoed up her spine one itchy tingle at a time. Like the cabin she shared with Amy, the front entrance opened into a moderately sized room with a sparse kitchenette tucked into the left corner. Thick planks of wood marched across the bare floor and up the bare walls. Tilting her head back, she studied the ceiling, unsurprised to find wood planks there as well. From the furniture choice to the pictures on the walls—or lack thereof—the cabin Rawls shared with Mac, as well as the one she shared with Amy, suffered from a man's touch.

The furniture, which consisted of a long, lumpy leather couch and two wide, lumpy leather recliners, was old and battered and grungy brown. The coffee table was simply a huge log that had been split in half, sanded smooth, and fitted with stubby log legs. Cheap plastic blinds covered the windows. Rather than rustic charm, the room screamed rural apathy.

The bright sunlight and pine-scented fresh air that streamed through the open blinds and open windows were the cabin's saving graces. It still surprised Faith how different the air smelled up here tucked, as they were, in the pristine foothills of the Cascade Mountains. Unspoiled. Crisp. It was the clean, pine-tinged scent that countless air freshener companies sought to replicate—with limited success.

And if she allowed herself to spend any more time procrastinating, she'd still be standing here when the helicopter returned with Amy's kids.

She glanced down the shadowy hall to the right of the kitchenette. The place looked like a duplicate to her cabin, which meant Rawls's bedroom was somewhere down that hall. His bedroom . . . with his bed . . . What if he'd lain down to take a nap? What if he slept naked? Or . . . what if Rawls had migrated to the bathroom to take a shower, and all those long, lean muscles were streaming with soap and water? An image of wet, soapy, tanned flesh took root in her mind. A prickle started in her scalp, marched down the nape of her neck, and infiltrated her arms.

Heat flashed through her, raising her temperature at least a degree or two. A swollen, moist pressure settled between her thighs. She ignored her endocrine system's exasperating flailing, something she'd become an expert at since finding herself cornered by a tall blond god in her lab six days earlier. Who would have guessed that the sexy stranger she'd been discreetly salivating over all those months ago at gate C-18 while waiting to board her flight to Hawaii would be the same man to drag her out from beneath Big Ben, and then step between her and her would-be kidnappers when the bullets started flying?

Even in the midst of danger, her hypothalamus had enthusiastically signaled its attraction to the hot, hard muscles protecting her from danger. Good lord, her memories of that night revolved around butterflies, tingles, and chills—along with all the other renditions of sexual excitement. Any fear she felt had taken a backseat to lust, and God help her, that hormonal flooding worsened with every second she spent in his company.

Thankfully, he hadn't picked up on her intense sexual attraction. Or, his good-ol'-boy Southern manners were ignoring her hormonal meltdown out of politeness. The second possibility was all too real considering he was a Navy SEAL. From what she'd read, SEALs were ultra-observant. He *should* have picked up on her attraction to him.

And here she was, procrastinating again. Shaking her head in disgust, she eased up to the kitchenette and hovered in the shadowy mouth of the hallway. "Lieutenant Rawlings?"

Silence greeted her. She listened hard. Was that faint whisper the sound of water running behind a closed door, or the wind teasing plastic blinds?

"Lieutenant Rawlings, I brought you lunch," she said, lifting the plastic-wrapped plate in her hands as an offering, which was absolutely ridiculous considering he couldn't see the movement.

Okay, this was just silly. Squaring her shoulders, she headed down the hall.

"Leave it on the kitchen counter," he said from somewhere down the hall and to the left.

She passed a small bathroom as his voice reached her, and she relaxed. At least she didn't have to worry about stumbling in on him in all his naked glory—regardless of how much her endocrine system would have enjoyed the show. She followed his voice to the end of the hall and the open door on the left.

"I brought you a sandwich," she said, darting a quick look at the bed, with its bunched, tangled sleeping bag, before seeking out the bed's current owner.

He sat staring out the window, a clear warning in the rigid length of his spine that he didn't want to be disturbed. She glanced at the empty glass and capped bottle of whiskey sitting on the windowsill in front of him. The golden liquid still climbed most of the bottle, so he'd abstained from drinking himself into a stupor. Thank goodness . . .

"Just leave it on the table," he said, his voice so polite there was no question he was masking some strong emotion—probably irritation at her unwelcome intrusion. But at least he harnessed his anger, rather than unloading it on the world like Commander Mackenzie did.

Frowning, she shuffled her feet, trying to force her appeal out. Why was the request so difficult to make? It was a no-brainer, damn it. Her life depended on getting more of her meds. She couldn't afford to procrastinate, yet here she was doing just that.

He twisted in his chair, scanned her face, and slowly unfurled to his full height. "What's wrong?"

"I need some prescriptions filled." The words burst out. "Can you help me with that?"

The drawn flesh across his forehead knitted. He scanned her again, this time a full-body sweep. A quick up-and-down skim that took in everything from her hot face to the hands clenched around the edges of the plate. As his gaze lingered on her hands, she forced her fingers to relax their grip. Crossing the room, she carefully deposited the sandwich on the small table next to the bed.

"What kind of prescriptions?" he asked, his blue eyes as intense as the laser beam in her lab.

"Cyclosporine, mycophenolate, and Cordarone."

"Cyclosporine . . ." His voice trailed off. He scanned her again, longer this time, more intently, as though looking for symptoms. "Cyclosporine and mycophenolate are immune-system suppressors. What condition are they treatin'?"

Well, he knew his medications. The fact that he'd questioned why she was on the prescriptions was a clear indication he knew the drugs were used to treat many diseases, including psoriasis, rheumatoid arthritis, and lupus, along with organ transplants.

She hesitated before squaring her shoulders. He did need to know her medical history. Her heart condition could have a direct effect on him, as well as the rest of the people in this camp.

"They're suppressing an organ rejection."

Dead silence greeted that informational bomb.

"What organ?" he finally asked in a far too quiet voice. A muscle started to twitch in his jaw.

She considered sidestepping the question, after all, the precise organ wasn't of importance.

"Which organ?" he asked again, louder, the determination in his voice a clear indication the specific organ mattered to him.

She hesitated before shrugging. "My heart."

"You've had a heart transplant and you didn't reckon it was advisable to warn anyone about your condition?" His voice remained soft for all of three seconds before the lazy glide to his vowels hardened. "How long have you been off the suppressors?"

"Since you dragged me from my lab and over to the Sierra Nevadas." She forced herself to hold his disbelieving gaze. "If you'll remember back, you guys didn't give me a chance to grab my stuff from the motel."

Although that wasn't quite fair. She hadn't asked them to swing by her motel. At the time, she hadn't been sure she could trust them, so she'd decided to keep her motel room quiet in case she needed to escape. She'd had her emergency stash of cash there, along with her meds, so that, if she needed to, she could go to ground for at least a couple of weeks.

"A heart transplant, sweet Jesus, Faith." He broke off and she could almost see him counting numbers off in his head. Exactly six seconds later he took a deep breath and let it out slowly. "You should have told me about this before now."

Considering his reaction, it was a good thing he didn't know that her current heart was her second transplant, and the odds of receiving a third anytime soon were . . . tricky at best.

"Rejection is a slow, drawn-out process," she told him instead. "There's a two-week window before I even need to worry about it. As long as I get back on my meds as soon as possible, I should be fine."

"Should be?" His voice sharpened, his gaze narrowing.

"The transplant happened years ago. When I was fourteen." At least the second one had. She'd received her first transplant two weeks after her thirteenth birthday, but it had failed within the first year. "I've been stable for fifteen years. That's in my favor."

Of course, her heart was also four years past the mean survival for a transplanted heart, but he didn't need to know that.

"You were fourteen? . . . Jesus." He looked oddly shaken for a moment before his face stilled. He cocked his head slightly and studied her closely. "What about the Cordarone. It's an antiarrhythmic. You have arrhythmia?"

"Ventricular tachycardia—the donor heart was damaged during its removal. But I had an emergency stash of Cordarone in my pocket." She rushed the last sentence out, suspecting he'd understand how dangerous tachycardia was. "So I've been taking those meds."

"A stash in your pocket?" he repeated slowly, his face tight. "Why? In case the tachycardia hits unexpectedly even though you're on medication?"

Well, he'd figured that out way too fast for her liking. "Arrhythmia can be brought on by stress, so before leaving the motel for the lab the night your team found me, I grabbed the old vial of Cordarone and shoved it in my pocket—just in case the adrenaline of sneaking into the lab brought on an episode. There's still some pills left, but I'll need more soon."

"How soon?" His question hit the air like a demand.

"I've got four doses left." She winced at the thunderstorm that swept across his face.

"You take a pill twice a day?" He didn't wait for her nod. Just shook his head, disbelief wrestling with the thunder on his face. "Sweet Jesus, Faith. That's only two days' worth, and that's assumin' you don't need an emergency dose in between. What were you thinkin'?"

She set her jaw. "I was *thinking* that I needed to ask you how I could refill my medications without anyone being the wiser since I'm supposed to be dead, and I have some super-secret, nasty organization on the lookout for me. I've been *trying* to track you down to ask for help."

"You could have—" He broke off to take another series of those obvious deep breaths. "Okay, let's back up. I'll talk to Wolf as soon as he returns." Another breath and the darkness lifted from his face. "What doses are you takin'?"

He didn't write down the dosages Faith rattled off, but she didn't doubt he committed them to memory. She relaxed—he was so much easier to talk to than Mackenzie, or even Cosky and Zane.

"I'll need to up the dosage for a few weeks, though. So we'll need to account for that." This wouldn't be her first fight against organ rejection, if she followed the previous dosage protocols, she'd be fine.

"Okay, darlin'," he said, his drawl back in full force. "Don't fret, we'll get you hooked up with your meds." He paused to eye her cautiously. "I reckon I should have a listen to your heart. Make sure your ticker is working all proper."

She backed up a couple of steps, swarms of butterflies erupting in her belly. "That's not necessary."

"I disagree," he countered firmly before making an obvious effort to lighten his tone. "And who's the doctor here?"

When she took another long step back, he took a matching one forward.

"I am," she announced, knowing her PhD in alternative energy wasn't the kind of doctor's degree he was talking about. "In fact"—she took another cautious step back, her pulse spiking as he followed her— "since you didn't finish your residency, I believe I'm the only doctor in the room." When the retort hit the air, it was laced with a snide superiority she hadn't intended, and she stopped dead in mortification. "I'm sorry, I didn't mean that the way it came out."

"Darlin'." The solemn, slightly hurt tone of his voice was belied by the twitch to his lip. "Y'all done demolished my mas-cu-lin-ity."

After studying his straight face for a moment, she lifted her eyebrows. She suspected nothing anyone said or did could dent his self-confidence.

"Let me guess," she said dryly. "My reparation somehow ends with you listening to my heart."

He grinned and waggled his eyebrows. "Well now, that does sound like an apology I can live with." When she continued to hesitate, he dropped the humor. "You want to tell me what's kickin' around in that head of yours? After fifteen years, you must be an old hat at checkups by now."

She frowned. Granted, more men than she could count had listened to her heart over the span of her life. But none of them had given her chills or tingles or launched a fleet of butterflies in her belly. Her physical reaction to Rawls was out of control. If he leaned in close enough to listen to her heart, it just might stop beating to savor the moment.

He tilted his head, his gaze narrowing. "Talk to me, darlin'."

She sighed and girded herself for the inevitable. All this stalling was just making him suspicious. "It's a waste of time, that's all." She shrugged, trying to project nonchalance. "But fine, if you want to listen to my heart, be my guest."

He studied her face for a moment before offering an encouraging smile. "Why don't you take a seat?" Pivoting, he headed for the table against the wall, across from the foot of the bed, and grabbed an oblong black bag. "This will be easiest on the bed."

On the bed . . . oh goodie . . .

She swallowed to lubricate the sudden desert parching her throat and settled on the mattress with stoic acceptance. A minute tops, and she could escape. She could handle a few minutes of personal contact. No problem.

He followed her to the bed, set the black bag on the mattress beside her, and opened it up, rummaging around inside. Removing a stethoscope, he settled on the mattress next to her with his left leg drawn up until his calf was braced against the mattress. He shifted to face her.

"Why don't you turn toward me?" he said as he plugged the ear pieces of the stethoscope into place.

She scooted around as he'd requested, and the heat of his big body toasted her from shoulder to thigh. His warmth loosened something inside her, something urgent and hungry.

Leaning forward, he lifted the disk of the stethoscope and pressed it against her chest. Faith caught her breath and held it. Even with her blouse shielding her breast from his hand, she was unbearably aware of his closeness, his warmth, of the clean, soapy scent of his skin and hair. She felt torn between pressing closer and wrenching herself away.

Seconds later a frown touched his forehead, and he pulled back, lifting the metal disk. "I need a better seal."

Without giving her a chance to protest, he lifted the hem of her blouse and slid his hand underneath. His fingers were hot and scratchy, the metal disk icy and smooth—the erotic juxtaposition sparked a trail of fiery shivers as he guided the instrument up her abdomen. Her breasts swelled. Her stomach flipped. Her muscles weakened. Goose bumps gathered at the nape of her neck and marched down to the base of her spine.

He bent his neck and tilted his head, his moist breath caressing her bare forearm, as he nestled the disk under the left cup of her bra. Helpless, she quivered, his humid breath bathing her sensitive skin, his fingers burning against the swell of her left breast. Heat bloomed, a slow lazy sprawl through blood and bone.

"You can breathe anytime now, darlin'," he said, a hint of humor in the roll to his vowels.

Breathe, yes—she needed to breathe. Lack of oxygen would account for this sudden fit of dizziness. But when she tried to wrestle in a breath, his clean, soapy scent flooded her lungs, paralyzing her.

"Come on, sugar." His calloused fingers slid to the right an inch or so, prickling against the swollen underside of her breast, and then pressed the disk firmly against her aching flesh. "No need to hold your breath, I can hear your ticker fine."

She drew in a raspy breath, and prayed her rigid lungs would know what to do with it.

"Relax," he said in such a soothing voice she wanted to curl up in an embarrassed ball and roll on back to her cabin. "Everything sounds just dandy in there." He tilted his head to the right. "No need to get all—" His voice simply broke and stopped as they locked eyes.

He froze, his fingers still burning against her breast. The laser-blue eyes darkened and dilated. And then slowly, oh so slowly, they dropped to her lips.

Chapter Four

THIRTY-FIVE MILES NORTHEAST OF BELLINGHAM, WASHINGTON, MAC watched the Jayhawk that Wolf had loaned them bug out. Once the dust cloud settled, he shifted his attention to Jude, the big, braided Arapaho warrior taking Rawls's place. Twisting slightly, Mac scanned the equipment strewn across the landing strip. Supposedly the guy was a medic, although how he intended to treat injuries without a med kit was open to question. Son of a motherfucker—he should have checked the bastard's gear before they hopped off the chopper.

"Jude, isn't it?" Mac asked after waiting until the helicopter crested the hill looming in front of them and disappeared from view, where it would touch down, settle in, and wait for recall. "Wolf said you're his team's medic?"

An abbreviated nod of the regal head sent Jude's long, graying braid swaying.

Mac eyed him closely. The guy looked a hell of a lot like their host. Same square face and hawkish black eyes. Same massive, muscled build tucked into a light green T-shirt and olive Flex-Tac pants. Same impassivity—although from the looks of it, the bastard had an extra twenty-five years on Wolf.

"Where's your med kit?" Mac fought to keep the words a question, rather than an accusation.

Jude lifted his eyebrows and patted a small square pouch hanging against his side from an ancient leather shoulder strap. The bag was made from worn leather and embossed with a spider's web in vibrant red and yellow.

Gritting his teeth, Mac turned away. That damn pouch was maybe four inches by four inches, barely big enough to carry a couple packages of QuikClot, a spool of gauze, and a suture kit. Sure as hell not much else.

In the distance, the Jayhawk's rotor slowed as the pilot began the shutdown procedure. Mac swore beneath his breath. While Zane's internal psychic alarm hadn't sounded—yet—that didn't mean much. Over the past fourteen years, numerous insertions had blown up in their faces without any warning from Zane's emergency broadcasting system.

They'd better watch their p's and q's and pray they didn't take a hit. Even with the chopper on site, it would take a good ten minutes to evac the wounded to the nearest emergency room. And that was after the rotor warmed up and the bird climbed into the air.

Still, the Sikorsky MH-60T was their ace in the hole—few organizations could afford the thirty-million-dollar price tags these babies carried, which raised some serious inquiries as to who Wolf worked for . . .

Mac shook the questions aside, grim satisfaction rising. Party crashers wouldn't expect an ambush from the air. Or a rescue for that matter. But since the beat of its blades could be heard for five to six klicks, the machine had to be shut down. Which meant a cold start when they needed it, and that meant several minutes of limbo.

Lives could be lost in those minutes—hell, forget minutes. Lives could be lost in seconds.

Shoving his unease aside, Mac turned in a slow circle, surveying their rendezvous site. Cosky had chosen the perfect terrain. The Jayhawk had dropped them into a bowl. Steep hills dotted with scraggly brush and smalls stands of Douglas fir rose from every direction. The single access point—a rutted dirt road—cut through the smallest hill to the north and dead-ended in the middle of the bowl. Once they climbed the hills and settled in on top, they'd have a bird's eye view in every direction.

With a soft grunt of satisfaction, he relaxed slightly and turned toward Cosky. "What's on the other side of those hills?"

"Acre after acre of trees," Cosky said with a slow, sweeping survey from the right to left. "Besides the entry point, the closest road is an abandoned logging trail ten klicks to the east."

"We'll have eyes in every direction. Nobody's slipping past us." Zane signaled his approval with a hard thump to Cosky's shoulder.

Mac slowly pivoted for one last scan of the surrounding hills and got down to business. As he started his third and final weapons check, Zane and Cosky silently followed suit. Once satisfied their weapons were good to go, Mac nodded toward Amy's silent, tense figure. "Take positions and test her gear. Make sure the signal carries."

During the flight out, Cosky had fitted her with a mic that fed into their headsets, but they hadn't been able to test the device's range. The ridge was a good three hundred yards uphill—they needed to make sure they could hear Amy's conversation with her brother from their posts.

"Can I call Clay now?" Amy asked, her tone flattened by extreme patience.

"Not till I'm sure you're hooked into our headsets," Mac said with a quick sidelong glance at her rigid, athletic figure.

The tension in her limbs and shoulders announced her anxiety. This rendezvous with her brother and children had the woman tied in knots, a clear indication of how important her boys were to her. Mac's chest tightened in sympathy. Amy rarely exhibited emotions. Hell, she was an old hand at locking down uncertainty or fear, an expert at projecting controlled competence. No doubt her ability to compartmentalize and bury her anxiety had been partly responsible for her meteoric rise through the bureau. Prior to her marriage she'd been on the fast track to taking the SAC's chair of the white-collar crimes division in the Seattle field office.

Not that he'd gone to the trouble of checking the woman out—at least no more than was necessary when dealing with an unknown ally.

"Once we've taken our positions and tested your feed, I'll signal you to call your brother," Mac said, holding Amy's shadowed gaze. He ignored the urge to assure her that everything would turn out just fine. He couldn't promise her that. Nobody could promise her that.

Frowning, he swept Amy's tense figure. The plan had been to let Amy handle the rendezvous herself while they provided cover from the ridge, but the woman was edgy as hell. It wouldn't hurt to give her a partner, someone to step in if the situation went south. They could afford to lose the extra set of eyes; they'd still have plenty of scopes keeping watch from above.

"Cosky, stick around and watch her six," Mac ordered, answering Cosky's double take with a slight nod. "Zane, Jude—head up and into position."

Amy squared her shoulders and pivoted until she faced Mac. "Jude should stay with me. Cosky should take to the ridge."

The sympathy he'd been feeling for her withered. The woman liked countermanding his orders way too much. "Cosky stays."

Her chin rising, Amy held his eyes firmly, which would have been admirable if her penchant for stubbornness wasn't so damn infuriating.

"Look, Mackenzie. Clay's a federal law enforcement agent and you and your men are at the top of every agency's BOLO. You're probably at the top of the bureau's most wanted list by now. If he sees you, any of you, he'll try to arrest you, that's his job. It just makes sense that Lieutenant Simcosky should provide cover from the ridge, while Jude—who isn't on a watch list—backs me up on the ground."

Her arguments made sense. Except having Jude and Cos swap places left her under the care of a virtual stranger. A stranger whose competence was in question considering his lack of a field kit.

"Cosky stays," Mac said. "End of discussion."

"Mackenzie—"

"It's Mac." Where the fuck had that come from? He didn't care what the hell she called him. Suddenly off balance, he scrambled to get his head back in the argument. "Cosky wasn't at the lab. He won't be on any BOLOs."

Looking more determined than ever, Amy set her jaw. "He's a known associate of yours. Clay will haul him in for questioning."

Cosky smiled. "He can try."

Amy blew out a frustrated breath, which locked Mac's attention on her pink, unpainted lips.

Sonofabitch. He wrenched his gaze away.

"I'm just trying to make this as easy as possible on the three of you. Having Clay hound you is only going to increase tensions."

Another fair point, which Mac ignored. No way in hell was he trusting her life to a stranger. He turned to Zane. "I'll take north, you take east." He shot a hard glance at Jude. "That leaves you with the west ridge."

"I'm telling you this is a mistake. If Clay sees Cosky, he'll know the rest of you are here too." Amy's voice shed its patience and climbed into robust irritation.

Mac grunted an acknowledgment, mostly because he knew the response would annoy her as much as her constant questioning of his orders irritated him.

"Fine." Blowing out another frustrated breath, she shimmied her shoulders and squared her stance, which cast a faint jiggle across her high, firm rack.

Mac's attention splintered between her lips and her chest. His skin tightened. So did his crotch. His lungs sped up, trying to keep pace with his accelerating heart. Just fucking perfect. It wouldn't be long before his men questioned why he was wheezing before the action even hit.

There was a time and place for arousal and it sure as hell wasn't on the cusp of a mission in the middle of a crowd.

He should give some serious thought to getting the old boy neutered.

Shifting the MK20 sniper rifle and the MP5SD submachine—two of the weapons he'd handpicked from the compound's arsenal—until they hung against his back, rather than his side, he caught Amy's eye.

"Wait until we've tested your gear before calling your brother," he reiterated.

Her lips tightened, but she nodded an acknowledgment.

With one last glance down the rutted dirt road, he struck out for the north ridge. At least the steep climb would give his libido something besides Amy to focus on. It was hard to maintain an erection when strenuous activity required a constant flow of blood to the brain, heart, and lungs. Not to mention the arms and legs.

By the time he reached the small stand of maple trees he'd chosen for camouflage, he was panting harder than ever. A sad commentary on his naval career. Somehow, through the years, he'd become nothing more than a desk jockey. Since his heart was pounding hard enough to interfere with his breathing, he waited a few seconds for his circulatory system to recover.

"Alpha one, copy." Zane's calm, cool voice came over Mac's headset.

Mac grimaced at the lack of breathlessness in his LC's voice. Definitely time to start using the base gym again.

"Alpha one in position." Mac carefully regulated his breathing. "Alpha three?"

"Copy," Cosky said.

"Alpha four?" Mac dragged the sniper rifle over his head and aimed the scope toward the west ridge, but there was no sign of Wolf's warrior.

"In position." Jude's measured voice came over the air.

"Amy?" Mac asked.

Fuck, was it his imagination, or had his voice actually softened over her name? He tried to convince himself the unusual bout of gentleness was simply a latent round of that earlier, frustrating breathlessness.

"I hear you loud and clear, Mackenzie."

Amy's voice flowed smoothly through his headset. In stark comparison to *his* query, her voice was cold and flat and bristling with irritation. Apparently she hadn't shed her annoyance over their earlier tussle.

"Alpha two? Four? You copy her?" Mac asked, nodding in satisfaction at the instant affirmations that hit his headset. He trained the scope on the east ridge. No sign of Zane either—he'd faded into the landscape as expected. "All right, boys and girls," he said, turning the rifle back in Amy's direction. "Time to get the ball rolling."

Through the rifle scope he watched her dig into the pockets of the gray pants that hugged her ass far too intimately for his peace of mind. Somehow the tactical flex pants looked a hell of a lot better on her than they did on him, or Zane or Cosky for that matter.

She jabbed at the screen a couple of times and lifted it to her ear. Mac absently listened to her side of the conversation as she methodically passed on detailed directions to their rendezvous point.

Her brother was waiting for directions at upper Whatcom Falls Park, thirty minutes out. Which gave them plenty of time to get the lay of the land, and to identify problematic points of entry. He scoped out the hillsides and relaxed after a thorough sweep. His vantage point was damn near perfect. He had a clear, 180-degree view from his position on the ridge. The terrain he couldn't scope fell within Zane's and Jude's positions. Nobody would be able to crash their party unannounced.

They settled down to wait. Thirty minutes after Amy's call, a thick cloud of dust churned into the sky over the access road.

"Our guests have arrived," Mac announced quietly into his comm.

The dust boiled thicker and taller as it closed on Amy and Cosky, and then a blue Ford Expedition broke into the open. He caught the flash of red hair from the driver's seat, which fit the description Amy had given of her stepbrother. He swung the scope to the rear of the SUV, but all he could make out from his angle were two small, dark heads hanging low against the backrest.

"Alpha two, you got a visual?" Mac asked as he swept the dust-veiled road behind the SUV.

If their adversaries were going to attack, it would be soon, but there were no new torrents of dust rising into the air signaling a second vehicle.

"Affirmative. Three subjects. All identified," Zane responded.

The Expedition rolled to a stop in front of Amy and Cosky, and the back doors flew open. Two children with dark close-cropped hair exited the SUV from opposite sides. The smaller boy left his door wide open and raced toward his mother, his small sneakered feet kicking up thin puffs of powdery earth with each stride. Amy stepped in front of two plastic retail-store sacks on the ground and knelt. Mac watched her arms and shoulders tense as she braced herself. A soft "oomph" traveled over the headset as her son hurled himself into her arms.

Something hot and achy, like heartburn, spread through Mac's chest as he watched her fiery head bow and her arms tighten around the child. He wrenched the scope away and focused on the older kid. The second boy had exited with much more decorum, stopped to close his door, and then walked around the rear of the Ford to close his brother's. When he headed toward his mother, not even a hint of dust rose from his feet. He stopped a foot or two from Amy. She glanced up and reached for him. Latching on to the hem of his T-shirt, she dragged him into her hug.

For several long moments the three clung together and that hot, acidic rush in Mac's chest climbed his throat. Scowling, he yanked his obsessed gaze from the tender tableau on the ground and scanned the access road again. The dust storm the Expedition had launched was settling. Judging from the lack of new clouds, Amy's brother hadn't been followed.

An uneasy feeling wormed through him. Those bastards after them should be making their move—he twisted to scan the hillside behind him, but there was no sign of party crashers.

The driver's door swung open as the cluster on the ground separated. Amy rose to her feet and shifted, watching her stepbrother approach. Mac settled the scope on her face, or at least what he could see of it, which was mostly her profile. From this angle she looked more neutral than welcoming.

Frowning, Mac studied the fed. Although they were stepsiblings, surprisingly they looked enough alike to be twins. What were the odds of that? The pocket-sized Venus look suited Amy—but her brother? Not so much. His lack of height combined with his slender frame imbued him with an air of ineffectuality.

Great.

Mac lowered the rifle and scowled. In his vast experience of dealing with assholes, size did matter. Far too often guys built like Amy's stepbrother tried to prove their masculinity in the most inconvenient way possible.

"Thanks for meeting me here," Amy said, her voice as flat as her face.

"Momma!" Her youngest kid grabbed a handful of Amy's polo shirt and tugged. "What do you have on your head?" His gaze skated over Amy's headset before settling on her face. He lowered his voice, but not by much. "Uncle Clay said the really bad words all the way here."

Apparently the aforementioned bad words were much more interesting than Amy's headset and mic. Mac grinned. What, exactly, did Amy consider to be "the really bad words"? Probably everything in Mac's vocabulary. It wouldn't hurt to watch his language around her and her boys. When he realized the direction his thoughts had taken, he froze in shock. When the hell had she become important enough to him to justify modifying his behavior? He was so busy backpedaling in his own mind, he missed her stepbrother's initial reply.

". . . I could have done without the theatrics," Clay continued in the thin nasal tone associated with pretentiousness.

Mac grimaced and shook his head. It was hard to believe these two had been raised in the same household, under the same set of parents. Amy's voice was matter-of-fact, with a side of cool. Her brother sounded like he'd taken acting lessons to get the diction and delivery just right. Where Mac came from, that was called putting on airs . . . or being an ass . . . or both.

"Momma," the youngster said, tugging determinedly on his mother's shirt. "A deer jumped in front of us and Uncle Clay said—"

"Give me some credit." Clay raised his voice, drowning out the childish chatter. "I've been on the job for twenty years. I know what a damn tail looks like." Clay shook his head, disgust sharp on his face. "You're acting paranoid as hell, you know that, right? Nobody is after you or your kids."

While he spoke, the fed turned his head and locked on to Cosky. Mac groaned beneath his breath. Amy had been right about one thing—the asshole was about to become aggravating.

"Momma," the little guy said, still yanking on Amy's shirt.

"Not now, Benji. Let me talk to your uncle."

But the bastard had already turned his shoulder on her in favor of confronting Cos.

"You're Lieutenant Simcosky, aren't you? We've got some questions for you. If you'll accompany me back to Seattle, I can offer you immunity and free you from this mess."

"Considering the lack of progress the bureau has made on our case, I'll pass on your *generous* offer," Cosky said, his voice drier than the dust surrounding them. "I stand a better chance of straightening out this *mess* without your help."

"But *Momma*—" Benji's voice lifted determinedly.

The fed scowled. "That wasn't a request. You will—"

"Don't push this," Amy broke in, her gaze locked on her step-brother. She caught her son's impatient hand and anchored it against her side. "Cosky's here as a favor to me."

Her sigh echoed through Mac's headset as her son resumed tugging on her shirt with his free hand.

Clay's head swung in her direction. "What the hell? Tell me you aren't bunkered down with these clowns. There are warrants out on all of them."

Mac snorted. While he didn't doubt there were warrants out on him, Zane, and Rawls, the feds had nothing on Cos. The bastard was lying through his teeth.

"Considering the evidence against them is manufactured, you'd do well to separate yourself from this *mess*." Amy's voice skated between cool and dogmatic. "When the truth comes out—and it *will*—someone will have to answer for the bureau's incompetence. I'd hate for that someone to be you."

"Let me guess, they told you they were innocent, they weren't at the lab, and they weren't the ones who killed those security guards." Contempt filtered through each word.

"No. That's not what I'm going to tell you." Amy's voice flattened.

Mac broke into an appreciative grin as he peered down the rutted lane leading into the bowl. He was all too familiar with that cool, flat, I've-had-enough-of-you tone of voice. It was a novelty to have it directed at someone else for a change.

But the humor soon faded, and that itchy sense of warning prickled again. He scanned the hill behind him. Nothing. And from Zane and Jude's silence, they weren't picking up on anything either.

What the fuck? Where are the bastards?

He was rarely wrong in his predictions. And this had been a no-brainer. He scowled, that earlier unease back in full force. Maybe their adversaries had decided to tag the kids instead of crashing the rendezvous. If they had tagged the boys, they could track them back to camp and take out everyone at once. If that was the case, they were in for a hell of a disappointment.

"Momma, I'm telling you something." Indignation swam in the youngster's voice.

Another sigh hit his headset, and Amy settled her hand on the boy's tousled, dark head.

"Let's move this along," Mac said quietly into his mic. He grunted softly in satisfaction as Amy turned away from her brother, backtracking to the plastic bags sitting on the ground.

"Mooooomma—"

"You can tell me everything in a minute, Benji. But first, I have a present for you." She picked up one of the plastic bags, peered inside, and handed it to her eager son. "There's a complete change of clothing in the bag—everything from shirt to shoes. Take off everything you're wearing—that includes your underwear—and put the new clothes on." She handed the second bag to the older boy and glanced toward the SUV. "You can change in Clay's car."

"Oh, for Christ's sake." Clay's voice was loud enough for Mac to hear it even though he stood a good ten feet from Amy and her mic. "You think someone bugged them? Who would have gotten close enough to do that? Me? Dad? Your mom?"

Amy's hand latched on to her youngest son's shoulder, who was standing with his head bent as he peered into the plastic bag. She steered him toward the SUV. The older child headed over under his own steam.

"I'm not taking chances," she said without looking back. "I was there, at the lab. I know what happened. The identification of the men who attacked us as unarmed security guards is a complete and utter fabrication. The men in question were well-trained mercenaries armed with AK-47s. They fired on us first. Which means that the entire investigation into the incident is corrupt."

Dead silence followed that announcement. Mac studied the fed's face through the scope and frowned. Her brother didn't look surprised.

"You were there?" Clay repeated, staring at his sister's back. "You weren't on the tape."

Something about the bastard's expression sent a chill down Mac's spine—there was a predatory cast to his brow and chin. Plus, he was lying. Mac was certain of it. He knew Amy had been there, so why the fuck was he playing dumb?

"No, I wasn't on the tape. And Mackenzie and his team did not fire first *or* on unarmed civilians. Which means the footage was doctored and the SEALs are being set up." Amy opened the back door to the Expedition and lifted her son inside. "There's something screwy going on." She stopped talking for a moment, and her shoulders rounded. She stared into the SUV. "John"—her voice stumbled over her murdered husband's name—"told Mackenzie that the men who kidnapped me and the boys had demanded seven of the first-class passengers in trade if John wanted to see us alive again."

"I'm . . . Mackenzie's . . . no evidence . . . support . . ." Clay's reply was indistinct.

"That's where you're wrong." Amy turned to stare at her brother, which gave Mac a perfect view of her determined face. "Seven of the scientists from the company whose lab exploded were booked into first class on that very flight. And just a few months after the aborted hijacking, their lab is incinerated and armed mercenaries show up on their doorstep? There's your evidence."

Clay followed her to the SUV, well within mic range again. "A coincidence, admittedly, but there's no proof indicating the film footage was doctored or that the men killed were more than security guards."

"I was there," Amy reminded him very quietly. "I know exactly what happened."

"Forgive me, Ames. But you're not exactly a credible witness these days. The men you're defending rescued you from hell. This paranoia you're exhibiting? It's a classic sign of PTSD brought on by your kidnapping and rape."

A haunted expression touched Amy's shadowed face.

Motherfucker.

Mac rubbed his chest, trying to ease the sudden, vicious ache digging into his heart. The ache burned as anger stirred. *The bastard.* There had been no reason besides spite to remind her of what she'd endured during her captivity. He resumed his grip on the rifle and focused on Amy, fighting the urge to swing the rifle in the fed's direction and let his finger tighten around the trigger. Not that he wanted to kill the bastard, maybe just hurt him a little . . .

Suddenly the shadow vanished from her face and her chin took on that familiar stubborn tilt. "And this attitude of yours is exactly why Mackenzie and his team are better off pursuing this case on their own. It's clear you have a traitor in your office, yet you're too shortsighted and tied to bureaucracy to admit it."

An explosion of rage touched her stepbrother's face, but it vanished almost immediately.

"Oh cool. So cool!" A childish voice broke the sudden tense silence. "These are the flashy shoes. The ones I wanted for my birthday, but you said they were too expensive." The youngster flew out of the backseat of the SUV wearing nothing but his underwear and his new tennis shoes. And sure enough, his shoes were flashing the entire color palette of the rainbow one hue at a time.

Christ. Why the hell would Amy buy something that lit up the entire countryside and gave their pursuers a glowing beacon to follow if they had to make a run for it?

"They come with an off button."

Her voice came clear and wryly through his mic. Either she'd read his mind, or he'd asked the question out loud without realizing it. He wasn't sure which possibility was more disconcerting.

"Benji, back in the car. Let's get the rest of your clothes on." Turning her back on her brother, she climbed into the SUV after her son.

As a constant stream of childish chatter filled his headset—Christ, that kid could talk up a storm—Mac turned the scope on the fed. The asshole was approaching Cosky, determination in every taut stride. Like he was going to get any answers from that quarter.

Jackass.

With one final sweep down the empty entrance road and the scrubby terrain surrounding him, Mac keyed his mic.

"Time to bug out," he said quietly, knowing the chopper pilot was monitoring their frequency.

"Copy," the vaguely familiar voice of Wolf's pilot said. "ETA five minutes."

The timing should be perfect. From the constant stream of babble flooding his headset, Benji was more interested in talking than dressing. But by the time the bird had warmed up and took to the air, Amy should have him bundled into his new clothes.

"You have five minutes to get that kid dressed," Mac said.

The pilot's ETA would have traveled down her headset as well, but with the kid talking a mile a minute, it was pure guesswork whether she'd heard it.

"Copy."

"Copy what?" the youngster asked as the thump-thump-thump of the rotor sounded in the distance.

Amy's stepbrother cocked his head, obviously listening. "A helicopter?" he asked Cosky. "How the hell did you manage that?"

Cosky ignored the question, and the fed stepped closer, his face hardening.

Yep. Mac grimaced. He'd called that one right, the asshole was about to become annoying.

"I'm not fucking with you, Simcosky. You and your buddies need to turn yourselves in. You aren't doing my sister any favors by dragging her into this mess alongside you." He reached for Cosky's arm, but lowered his hand before making contact. "We're looking into your commander's claims—"

Mac snorted beneath his breath. *Sure you are.*

Cosky stared back, his face as hard as concrete. "The FBI has had months to investigate the attempted hijacking of flight 2077 and the events it spawned. Instead, you appear more interested in pinning everything on us. We'll clear our names on our own."

"Then you leave me no choice," Clay said, reaching beneath his jacket for the weapon holstered at his side.

Instantly the sharp crack of a rifle sounded. A small circle of dust puffed up from the ground several feet in front of the asshole. The report echoed across the hillside and—surprise, surprise—the shot hadn't come from him, or from Zane's direction. Instead it had come from the ridge Jude was covering. Maybe the big Arapaho warrior wasn't quite so unprepared after all.

Amy's stepbrother froze, his hand slowly lowering. "You just fired on a federal agent. Which adds a whole new world of hurt to the charges you're facing."

Cosky raised a brow. "I didn't fire on anyone."

The fed's voice climbed. "Amy—"

"Saw nothing," his sister said flatly from inside the car.

The fed's face set. "It won't matter what either of you claim. As a federal officer, my word will be enough for a warrant."

Cosky snorted. "In other words, you're gonna add this new lie to the list of fairy tales you boys have drawn up."

Mac grinned slightly at that, before swinging his rifle to the left. Amy had gotten the little guy dressed, and both children stood by her side all spiffy in their new clothes. Which was perfect, since the helicopter was approaching in the distance.

"Time to catch our ride," he said, rising to his feet.

It took a fraction of the time to get down the hill that it had taken to get up.

"I should arrest you four right now—" Frustrated rage twisted Clay's face, but there was no surprise as Mac and Zane joined Cosky.

"Good luck with that," Jude said without bothering to look at the fed.

The *whop-whop-whop* of the chopper blades was much louder and closer. Thin trails of dust spiraled into the air.

"Momma!" Amy's youngest went back to tugging on her T-shirt. "That's a *hellcopper*."

"Indeed it is," Amy said in an easy voice. "How would you like to go for a ride in it?"

Mac studied her composed face. Did anyone else sense the stress beneath the veneer of calm?

"We're taking a helicopter back?" the older, quieter kid asked, glancing up at Zane for confirmation.

"That's right." Zane settled a hand on the boy's thin shoulder and gave it a squeeze. "You ever been on a chopper before?"

Before the older kid had a chance to respond, the younger boy let out a squeal and bounced a couple times. "Really? Really? We're gonna ride a *hellcopper*? Can I—"

The beat of the rotor as the bird closed on them drowned out the boy's question. Dust began to fly. Through the gray film he saw Amy press her youngest son's face against her abdomen. Zane drew the hem of the older boy's T-shirt up over his mouth.

The Jayhawk settled to the ground twenty feet ahead. Jude jogged over, crouched as he neared the blades, and dragged the cargo door open. On high alert, Mac and Cosky covered the bird while Zane and Jude boosted Amy and her two youngsters inside. Once their civilians were stowed safely away, Jude and Zane boarded. Mac followed suit, with Cosky right behind him. The bird lifted as they pulled the cargo door shut. After one quick glance to make sure Amy and the kids were settled, Mac took a seat next to the cargo door and stared out the window.

Amy's brother grew smaller and smaller as the dust bowl and hillsides spread out beneath them. He scanned the entry road as they flew over it. Nothing. It and the surrounding hillsides sat in frozen, unoccupied stillness. No vehicles. No men waiting to ambush them as they exited the rendezvous site.

He exchanged confused glances with Cosky and then Zane. Unless the kids' clothes had been bugged, they'd massively overestimated the interest in Amy and her children, which left an unsettled, sour feeling spinning around in his gut. As well as the distinct feeling that the other boot was about to drop in some unknown direction with devastating consequences.

Chapter Five

"Now darlin'." Rawls caught Faith's gaze and shot her an encouraging grin, but the smile faltered at the emotions boiling in her eyes. The uncertainty and awkwardness he'd expected—he intended to tease that out of her. But the desire and sexual awareness . . . hell, those caught him totally off guard and tied his tongue up good and proper.

A burst of sticky heat swept him. Coughing the sudden dryness from his throat, he dropped his gaze. Big mistake, since it latched on to her mouth. Her moist, slightly parted, far too enticing mouth. Her bottom lip was naked and plump, with the sexiest indentation in the middle. The urge to taste it, suck it—tame that sassy dip with the tip of his tongue—hit hard and fast. When the fit of his jeans tightened, he groaned beneath his breath and wrenched his eyes to safer territory.

The safety lasted all of three seconds, which was how long it took him to wonder if those cinnamon freckles stretching from cheek to cheek tasted sweet or spicy. The impulse to lean down and trace the light brown flecks with his mouth damn near swamped him.

He pulled back, his heart drumming in his ears, the tempo building with each throb of his cock. As he dragged his gaze from her face, it fell on her chest and the milky white crescent of skin between her waistband

and the hem of her blouse—beneath which his hand, along with the tubing and diaphragm of the stethoscope, disappeared.

It wasn't his heart beating a mile a minute, it was hers.

He could feel it pounding beneath his fingers, hear it throbbing in his ears. Unable to stop himself, he lifted his head and zeroed in on her face. A dusky rose invaded her cheeks, but it wasn't the red of embarrassment, rather the sultry heat of sensuality. Her eyes simmered with hunger, and as he watched, her blue eyes darkened until they looked black.

A web of sexual tension enveloped them, cinched tighter and tighter, while they sat there, staring at each other, his hand pressed to the warm, satin smooth skin above her galloping heart.

"Jesus fucking Christ, Doc. The bed's right there. She's asking for a good hard screwing. What the fuck are you waiting for?"

It took a second for the words to hit home, but when they did, he recoiled from the bed like he'd just discovered he had hold of a black mamba rather than a stethoscope. Pachico's raucous laughter followed him as he took a few giant steps back for good measure.

What the hell is wrong with you, hoss?

Besides his reluctance to entertain his obnoxious troll of a ghost, this wasn't the girl to get down and dirty with. Innocence and awkwardness rode her like a threadbare blanket. He didn't want to hurt her. But getting involved with her, while his head was good and scrambled, *would* end up hurting her—for sure emotionally, possibly physically. Hell, it could end up killing her.

He was smarter than this. He was—damn it.

"I'm gonna—" The words were raspy and borderline breathless, so he coughed to clear his throat and tried again. "I'm gonna go wrestle up your meds."

Avoiding her face, and what he might find there, he backed right out the door.

"Smooth, Doc, really smooth," Pachico said dryly, following him down the hall and across the cabin's living room.

Rawls ignored his mouthy shadow as he shoved open the cabin door and took the steps in such a hurry it felt like he was in full-blown retreat.

"Probably for the best, all things considered." Pachico continued matching Rawls's breakneck pace across the courtyard. "In her condition, who knows whether she'd survive the horizontal tango. And having a gal die while you're doing her, well it just kills the mood, if you know what I mean."

Pachico's comment hit Rawls squarely upside the head and started to fester. All sorts of questions crowded his mind. Like, were there limits to Faith's physical activities?

From what he remembered during medical school, organ transplants offered patients a normal, healthy return to life. But Faith had said her donor heart had been damaged during the harvest. How damaged? Bad enough to turn sex into Russian roulette?

Not that he had any intention of making love to her. But still . . .

It wouldn't hurt to do some research into her condition, refresh his memory on heart transplants and preventative maintenance. There was a computer next to the sat phone with full Internet access thanks to Wolf's ultra-sleek tech setup and satellite service.

As luck would have it, the command center was empty. He grabbed a couple of chocolate chip cookies off a rack on the dessert-laden kitchen counter as he passed.

"Man, those suckers look good." Pachico stopped next to the counter and hovered there, his translucent feet several inches off the floor. He swiped at the stacks of cookies. "Fuck," he said morosely as his hand sliced harmlessly through the towering, chocolate-studded, golden-brown stacks.

Just for spite, Rawls stopped, backed up a few paces, and grabbed a couple more cookies. Ignoring the grumbling rising behind him, he headed for the computer desk tucked in the far corner of the room and settled in the wheeled chair behind the screen while munching on one of his prizes.

First things first. He dialed Wolf's cell phone from the command center's sat phone.

A burst of static sputtered through the phone, followed by a garbled, terse "Speak."

More static crackled from the sat phone. Rawls waited for the noise to clear and quickly recapped Faith's medical crisis and required prescriptions.

"Ten-four . . . next chopper out."

Rawls released a relieved breath. Jude could have gone for the meds once he returned from picking up Amy's kids, but it was a useless trip without a prescription. His shoulders tightened at the thought of his teammates and the danger they were in. He forced his muscles to relax. His teammates were old pros at these kinds of missions. They'd be fine. Everyone was going to be just hunky-dory.

He glanced toward Pachico, who was hunched over the cookie tray, trying to pick one up.

Except . . . maybe . . . me . . .

Time to grab hold of his balls and ask the other question he needed to talk to Wolf about. He shot Pachico a quick look. His troll was staring morosely down at the tray.

Now was the time, while his stalker was distracted, to question Wolf about ghosts, what he knew about them, if he'd had anything to do with Pachico's disappearance . . .

"Hey, Wolf," he said quietly into the phone's mouthpiece.

An earful of static answered him. He waited a few seconds . . . a minute . . . but the static grew louder. Disconnecting the call, he dialed Wolf's number again. More static.

Damn it.

He shoved the phone back in its charger. Apparently his questions would go unanswered for the time being.

A quick glance toward the counter proved that Pachico was still trying to assuage his cookie craving. Relieved at the uncommon peace, he booted the computer up and got to work on his research assignment.

His relief was short-lived. After several Internet searches on organ transplants, worry crested. According to the data available online, the average viability for a pediatric heart transplant was listed as just eleven years.

Faith had said she'd received her transplant at fourteen, fifteen years earlier, which put her current heart well past the average lifespan. Even if they got her back on her meds early enough to avoid complications, she'd still be living on borrowed time. Her heart could start failing at any moment. It wouldn't be long before she'd have to go back on the transplant list and wait for another donor match.

A match that could take years, assuming it even happened at all. According to his research, on average, twenty-one people died every day while waiting for an organ to become available.

Or . . .

Kait and Cosky kneeling beside his prone body, their hands pressed hard against his still chest, as a dense bubble of silver cocooned them, flowing out of their hands and plunging into his chest, where it advanced in a glowing puddle until it infused every inch of his inert form.

Or . . . they could try some of Kait's magic on Faith's heart. Kait's gift had healed his multiple chest wounds, and wrenched him back from the dead.

Okay, so maybe he hadn't come back alone. Or maybe he hadn't come back sane.

But Kait's touch had given him another shot at life. It could do the same for Faith.

"Jesus Christ, Doc. What the fuck are you moping around here for? You got a camp full of gorgeous women. Maybe the little brunette is damaged goods, but there're still the two blondes."

The comment proved how attached the asshole was to loyalty to think Rawls had any interest in straying in that territory. Cosky was in love with Kait, and Zane with Beth. Both women were off limits. His mind veered to Faith, but he wrestled it back and fought to concentrate.

Frowning, he drummed his fingers against the wood grain of the computer desk. Of course asking Kait for her help meant breaking his patient-doctor confidentiality with Faith. Except that he wasn't a doctor, and he hadn't exactly promised to keep her condition private. Besides, breaking any implied confidentiality was for her own good.

Decision made, he shoved back the desk chair and rose to his feet. He'd have to track down Kait first, make sure she was willing to give this new healing a try, but he didn't foresee her refusing. Kait had a good heart.

As it turned out, he didn't have to do the hunting. The door opened and Kait entered the room before he'd made it halfway across the floor. She stopped short when she saw him, surprise sharp on her face.

"Now that's what I'm talking about!"

Pachico's voice was so loud Rawls almost flinched, but he locked down the impulse just in time.

"Rawls!" Relief lifted her voice as she flew across the room and hugged him hard. "I was just about to hunt you down. Sit." She tugged him toward the table. "I'm going to make you something to eat."

Rawls's lips twitched. Apparently Faith wasn't the only female determined to feed him.

"Faith brought me a sandwich earlier." Which was still sitting on the table next to his bed. He kept that bit of info to himself.

"They say the way to a woman's heart is through words," Pachico said, appearing beside him and eyeing Kait with a lewd expression. "But speaking from experience, I'd say it's through their cunt. Hell, I'd trade every one of those cookies for a stab at her."

"Look, sweetcakes," Rawls said, concentrating ferociously on Kait's face and trying like hell to ignore the asshole by his side. "I need to run somethin' by you."

She pulled back to scan his face. "What's wrong?"

Sudden humor kicked in. His shrug came with a quarter smile. "What ain't?"

She skimmed his face again before returning his pained smile.

"Do you have any idea how worried everyone has been about you?" She laughed and threw up her hands at the dry look he leveled on her. "Okay, okay, I'll admit that was a stupid question. Of course you know. That's why you've been hiding out in the woods." The humor faded from her eyes. "Is this about the healing I did on you?"

The question brought him up short. "No. Why?"

He hadn't gotten around to questioning her about the healing she'd done on him. He'd been a tad distracted by his unwelcome roommate and far more freaked than curious until now.

"Because something went wrong. I can feel it. You're different." Her eyes brimmed with guilt and worry.

So she'd picked up on something, but what exactly? "How so?"

"You're way too tense and jumpy and well . . . " She looked away as her voice trailed off, red claiming her cheeks.

She was thinking about the humiliating shouting match his LC and Cosky had walked in on. That was the problem with hauntings. Nobody else could see the damn ghost, so it looked like he'd been shouting at empty air. But everything she'd mentioned was symptomatic of the underlying problem—the big one she apparently hadn't identified.

Thank Jesus.

"This ain't about me—it's about Faith. She's got a medical condition I'm thinkin' you might be able to fix."

Kait's eyes narrowed. "Did her cuts get infected?"

"No." Rawls hesitated, guilt stabbing him. Faith wouldn't be thrilled with his wagging tongue. But damn it, this wasn't about gossip. He was looking out for her best interests. "Faith had a heart transplant, and the donor heart was damaged durin' the surgery," he admitted at Kait's crinkled brow. "Plus, she's out of her rejection meds. Wolf's gettin' a line on her prescription, but until he can ferry them in, she's courtin' disaster. What are the odds you can fix her up with that nifty trick of yours?"

"The odds are much better if we wait until Cosky returns," she said after a moment, the skin across her forehead tightening beneath her frown.

"Cosky? What's he got to do with this?"

"His touch amplifies my healing. Together we can heal injuries much faster. That's how we managed to save you."

Her words echoed in his ears and that strange waking dream took root in his head. Kait's hands had been pressed to his chest, while Cosky's hands had covered hers, and that liquid pool of silver had flowed through their joined hands into his chest. Was that how they'd managed to yank him back from the dead? They'd joined forces? How, exactly, did that work?

Hell, he'd missed some crucial information by hiding himself away with his head stuck up his ass.

"Well, she's in no immediate danger," Rawls said, pulling back slightly to study her face. "We can afford to wait for Cos to return."

As an added bonus, the delay gave him time to sell Faith on the idea. Considering her hard science background, he doubted she'd put much faith in metaphysical healing, so convincing her to participate might take some major persuading.

Of course, to sway her, he'd have to talk to her. He grimaced. Looking back, he'd bolted from his bedroom, and that tempting bed, and the even more tempting woman on top of it with all the zeal of a man who'd stumbled upon a leper colony. In his experience, women didn't appreciate being treated like lepers, so before he could even start the persuading, he'd have to do some heavy apologizing and even more soothing.

"Okay . . . " Kait paused, her focus zeroing in on Rawls again. "So how about we talk about you?"

How 'bout not.

Her eyes narrowed as though she sensed his resistance. "What happened to you out there? What's going on?"

"Go ahead, Doc. Tell her. I dare ya," Pachico said, smug amusement in his voice.

"Nothin'." Time to make a speedy exit. "Look, darlin'. I need to fill Faith in on your talents."

"You fucking coward."

Pachico's voice was farther away, but Rawls didn't dare glance at him to see what the bastard was up to. Not with Kait in the room. Besides, in his current translucent condition, his ghost wasn't much of a threat.

"Rawls!" Her foot started tapping.

How the hell was he supposed to fill her in on something he didn't even understand himself? What if he admitted to Pachico's haunting only to realize that the whole damn experience was a hallucination manufactured by his oxygen-deprived mind? No—he'd wait until he'd had a chance to talk to Wolf and find out what the man knew before he made an admission he couldn't retract later.

"Not now," he said quietly, relaxing as her eyes softened.

A loud, metallic clang echoed behind them. Startled, he and Kait swung around.

"I'll be damned." Pachico's voice thinned, wavering in and out of range. " . . . changes . . . the game." His translucent form faded until it was barely visible.

Rawls walked over, dread congealing within him. On the other side of the counter, a good three feet from the sprawling cookies, sat the metal tray. Chocolate chip cookies surrounded it.

"How in the world . . ." Kait shook her head, a dumbfounded expression on her face. "Maybe the stack toppled." She shook her head again. "But that doesn't explain how the tray ended up way over there. It's almost like someone threw it, but there's only me and you in the room."

Oh, there was another person in the command center. She just couldn't see him. Rawls glanced toward Pachico's transparent form, only to do a double take. At least up until a second ago there had been three of them in the room, but just like he'd done when Wolf had approached them out by the stream, Pachico had vanished.

Chapter Six

*F*ROZEN ON THE BED, FAITH STARED AT THE DOOR RAWLS HAD JUST bolted through—the key word being *bolted*. He'd vacated the room with all the finesse of a virgin fleeing the scene of an orgy.

Well, that was unexpected.

What exactly was she supposed to make of his reaction? He'd fled with such intensity he'd left the stethoscope behind, still tucked beneath her shirt. Absently, she removed the instrument and laid it on the mattress beside her.

He'd been as caught up in the passionate moment as she'd been. It was easy enough to identify the signs of desire. His pupils had dilated. His face had hardened. A hooded, predatory expression had touched his eyes. Thick ribbons of red had delineated his cheekbones. And then there'd been his mouth. Those thin, mobile lips had even swelled slightly. He'd broadcasted his hunger with every inch of his face. There was no doubt in her mind he'd wanted her, craved her as much as she'd craved him. Nor did she doubt he'd recognized the indicators of arousal on her face.

Although you wouldn't guess it from his awkward flight from the room, the man was sexually experienced. That had been abundantly clear all those months ago while she'd been swooning over him at the airport. He'd returned numerous admiring feminine glances with good-natured silent flirting. The man was comfortable around women.

So why had he scrambled off the bed and fled?

It had been so sudden too. One second he'd been as mired in the moment as she'd been, and the next he was gone.

With a confused shrug, she slid off the bed and straightened her rumpled white blouse and smoothed the wrinkles from her linen slacks. It was rather amazing how Wolf had managed to replace her abandoned wardrobe with clothes so perfectly in line with her tastes, yet without asking her for her size or personal preferences.

Had he had the same success with Amy, Kait, and Beth? From what she'd seen so far, he'd brought the other three women a different array of clothes—although mostly jeans and T-shirts. How had he known she'd preferred a different style? Just one more question to add to her growing unanswered list.

Blowing out a frustrated breath, she headed out the door. The cabin was quiet and cool as she passed through. Apparently Rawls had abandoned his home away from home entirely. But then, the satellite phone was housed in the command center. As far as she knew, none of the individual cabins had access to a line outside the compound. Although she suspected Wolf had a second phone in his cabin. It made sense that the person in charge of the camp would have access to a private mode of communication with his superiors.

If Rawls had gone after the sat phone as he'd claimed, he was probably still at the command center. There went her plans for getting an early start on dinner. Faith hesitated before changing directions and heading for her cabin instead of the main lodge. She had plenty of time to get the roast in the oven—might as well give him time to clear out.

Forty-five minutes later she left her cabin and approached the main lodge from an angle. Peering through the windows, she scanned the room for Rawls. While she wanted to get a start on dinner, she didn't relish the thought of tiptoeing around residual tension.

Her spying served her well. Not only was Rawls in the lodge, so was Kait. The two were wrapped in each other's arms, pressed so close their blond heads blended together.

An uncomfortable burning seared her chest. A sensation she'd never experienced, yet immediately recognized at a visceral level. Jealousy—which was insane. She had no claim on the man. He could hug anyone he pleased. Besides, Kait was committed to Cosky, which meant the hug was likely platonic rather than romantic.

Some of the acid bile climbing her throat settled. She eased back from the window. It would be just too humiliating to be caught peering inside the lodge like some seedy Peeping Tom. As she backed away from the glass, the couple inside broke apart and commenced chatting.

Once clear of the window, she tiptoed around to the back of the lodge. The thought of returning to her cabin and waiting for Kait and Rawls to vacate the command center—and more importantly, the kitchen—didn't sit well. The silence and boredom would give her way too much time to overthink. During moments of stress she had a habit of blowing gopher hills into mountain peaks. But taking a walk would leave her with just as much free time, which presented the same opportunity to overcomplicate things. What she really needed was that kitchen, and the soothing effects of cooking.

By the time she'd infused some steel into her spine and girded herself to march around the corner and take command of the kitchen, Kait and Rawls were leaving the lodge.

Perfect.

Faith waited until they'd disappeared into their respective cabins before emerging from her hiding place. As she'd expected, her haven stood empty. Relaxing, she got down to the business of seasoning the fifteen-pound pork roast taking up half the shelf in the industrial-sized refrigerator. It would take somewhere around six hours to cook, which would put dinner at six p.m. Mackenzie and his crew, plus Amy and her boys, should be back by then. She'd make the dough for the biscuits as soon as the roast was in the oven, but wait to bake them until the meat was out and cooling. It wouldn't hurt to combine the applesauce, brown sugar, vinegar, and cloves for the basting either. Plenty of time to take care of that after the biscuits were made.

She'd preheated the oven to 350, peeled and sliced several cloves of garlic, and cut slots in the roast to insert the garlic, when the door to the lodge opened. Faith froze with her back to the intruder. There were four possibilities as to the identity of the interloper—Beth, Kait, Wolf's watch dog, or Rawls. Her money was on Rawls, and sure enough, when she turned around, that's exactly who was eyeing her warily from across the kitchen counter.

"Hey," he said, after a noticeable hesitation, discomfort and caution darkening his blue eyes.

"I just started dinner," she blurted the information out—only to silently cringe—as though he couldn't see that fact for himself.

This current of unease was exactly what she'd wanted to avoid. With a deep internal sigh, she stiffened her shoulders. Things couldn't get much more strained between them, might as well clear the air and bring the invisible pink elephant into the open.

"Look. It's obvious I'm attracted to you and you're attracted to me. That's plain human nature, and nothing we need to tiptoe around." Look at her, being all grown up and mature about the situation when six days earlier she'd refused to allow him near her wounds for fear he'd realize how attractive she found him. "What happened in your bedroom was perfectly natural and nothing to get all bothered about." She floundered, feeling like she'd lost her point somewhere. "Just because we feel the attraction doesn't mean we have to act on it." She stumbled into silence, all platituded out.

His eyes lost focus and his head started to turn.

Faith glanced in the direction he was turning, but didn't see or hear anything. "What's wrong?"

He froze and jerked back to face her, a mask sweeping over his face.

"Nothin'." He hesitated and then his face softened. "Look, this has nothin' to do with you. The timin' sucks, you know? I mean to start somethin' up . . ."

His voice suddenly picked up speed and strength like he was trying to talk over the radio, even though the room was silent. She could tell the moment he realized what he was doing, and forced his volume back down.

"Things are kinda . . ." He frowned, and looked down. "I'm not in a place . . ." With a slow shake of his head, he ran a tense hand through his blond hair, leaving it rumpled and sexy. "Yeah, the timin' just sucks."

Why in the world would his halting explanation spark regret instead of relief? Since she didn't want to examine that question too closely, she concentrated on a question she did want an answer to. "Did you get hold of Wolf?"

"That I did. Your medications will be on the next chopper out," he said, his eyes losing focus again.

She smiled in relief at the good news, but the emotion soon faded. From the tension on his face, and the nerve twitching in his cheek, something was wrong. "Then what's the problem?"

That brought his attention back to her again, at least for a second. But then the stack of chocolate chip cookies suddenly mesmerized him. He just stood there, totally still, and stared at them.

Okay, this is weird. Is he in some kind of cookie-induced trance?

"They're for eating." She intended the comment as a joke, but it came out entirely too soft and serious.

He started, as though he'd forgotten she was there. But he instantly rallied, an expression of determination descending on his face. "I did some lookin' into heart transplants online after talkin' to Wolf."

Uh-oh.

From the shadow building in his eyes, he hadn't liked what he'd found.

"Okay . . ." She rolled the word out cautiously.

He ran his hand through his hair again, rumpling it even more. "You said you had your heart transplant when you were fourteen—fifteen years ago."

"Actually . . ." She caught herself and dragged her eyes from the gleaming mop of blond hair. In her appreciative daze she'd almost corrected him. She'd had the second transplant at fourteen, the first one had been the year before. However, that information wasn't necessary for him to know. "That's right."

He grunted. An honest-to-God grunt that somehow managed to sound disapproving.

"Accordin' to every article I found, the average viability of a transplanted pediatric heart is eleven years."

Faith cocked her head and eyed him with curiosity. Where was he going with this? "I'm aware of that."

"Your transplant was fifteen years ago. You're four years past the average lifespan now." He reminded her tightly, shoving his hand through his hair again.

"I'm aware of that too." She shot another glance at his gleaming white-gold head. Maybe this constant scalp massage was his secret to such a thick, sexy head of hair.

"Sweet Jesus." The words broke from him softly. He caught her gaze and held it, then gave an oddly resigned shrug. "Then you have to know you've reached the end of your heart's viability."

She frowned slightly, scanning his face. "Of course I know. But there's no benefit in obsessing over something I have no control over." A transparent truth she'd never been able to convince her parents of. "I've done everything possible to keep this heart healthy and to prolong its lifespan. Now it's a waiting game."

Waiting for her heart to fail. Waiting to get back on the transplant list. Waiting for a donor match. For as far back as she could remember, her life had been a game of wait and see. Even these last—relatively healthy—fifteen years had been marred by a sense of wariness . . . of expectation . . . the certainty that at some point her heart would act up again . . . and the stressful, frightening cycle would start for a third time. Only this time she might not come out the other end alive.

She cut off the cold shadow of fear and focused on the here and now. "It's best to concentrate on what you can control, not what you can't."

She offered the rationale as much for her benefit as his. It never hurt to remind oneself of universal truths.

"What if there were somethin' you could do, now, to increase your heart's sustainability?" Rawls asked slowly, back to choosing his words with extreme care.

Just what the heck was he hinting at? Faith studied his shadowed face for clues. "You mean exercise? Diet? Been there, doing that."

"Nah, I mean—" This time he ran both hands, in tandem, through his hair hard enough that she could hear the rasp of his nails scraping his scalp. "Look, this is gonna sound crazy, so hear me out, okay?"

Intrigued, Faith raised her eyebrows. It cost her nothing to listen. "Okay."

"I'm guessin' you haven't realized this yet, or you would have said somethin' . . . asked about it . . ." He rolled his shoulders and rocked from foot to foot, looking increasingly uncomfortable. "Kait's half-Arapaho—son-of-a-bitch!"

He suddenly flinched and jerked his arm hard to the right. Cradling his elbow against his chest, he scowled, his head turning from right to left, as though he were looking for something . . . or someone.

What the heck was wrong with him?

"Are you okay?" she asked, watching him with concern.

"Just a . . . just a cramp in my arm," he said in a tight voice.

Okay . . . so why don't I believe him? Besides . . . "What does Kait's ethnicity have to do with my heart?"

He jerked back to face her, but his gaze continually flitted to the left, toward the cookies.

"If you want one that bad, just take one," she said.

He growled something nasty under his breath, and she could actually see the struggle between his fixation on the stack of cookies and his willpower. Why was he so determined to resist the craving? He'd eaten her cookies before. After several uncomfortable seconds, he finally wrestled his full attention back to her.

"It's through her Arapaho blood that she's able to heal." He dropped the words slowly and deliberately into the conversation and let them just hang there, echoing in the silent room.

It took a second for his meaning to register. "What did you say? Surely you don't mean . . ."

He had to be teasing her, but . . . the expression on his face was all too serious. Faith took a cautious step back, which was silly since the kitchen counter still separated them. "Heal?"

"Kait has the ability to heal with her hands. It doesn't work all the time—maybe thirty percent—but when it does work, she can do some pretty incredible things."

"Thirty percent of the time . . ." Faith repeated. How convenient.

Apparently Kait's healing ability came with an escape clause. If the patient wasn't miraculously healed after Kait's laying on of hands—well, heck, she'd just claim they fell into the seventy percent that couldn't be treated. What an ingenious excuse for failing.

Disappointment struck. She'd gotten to know the other woman fairly well over the past five days, even liked her. It burned to find Kait was capable of such dishonesty and callousness. Which just went to show how terrible she was at reading people.

"I know what you're thinkin'," Rawls said.

"I sincerely doubt it." Faith's response emerged crisper than she'd intended.

"You're wonderin' how I—a man of science, a man who went through four years of medical school, and three years of surgical residency—could believe in something as unsubstantiated as metaphysical healing."

Okay . . . he did know what she was thinking. But that didn't make him a mind reader, any more than Kait was a "metaphysical healer." He was just skilled at reading body language and facial expressions. Obviously, Kait was skilled at something else entirely.

"I believe in her ability because I've seen her heal people," he said, his voice flat, certain.

Faith paused, feeling her way carefully. She didn't want to argue with him—but seriously—metaphysical healing?

Give me a break.

"My understanding is that such healings are staged, and the person being healed isn't actually sick," she offered cautiously, although really, how he'd managed to fall for something so predictable was both a surprise and a disappointment. "So while the session looks authentic—"

"One of the people was me," he broke in, lifting a challenging eyebrow.

Okay, that did change things considerably. She scrambled for another explanation. "The placebo effect can be quite powerful. If you expected her touch to heal you, perhaps your body and mind worked in concert to manifest the expected results."

His lips twisted, but the expression on his face looked more haunted than amused. "I was dead at the time. Lights out. So my mind wasn't exactly orderin' my body about."

"Dead." The word erupted from Faith on a startled breath. "I don't believe it. You're here. You couldn't have—" She mentally backed up and sought a more compassionate approach. He'd obviously undergone something traumatic, and convinced himself Kait had saved him.

"If you were unconscious, you couldn't have seen what actually happened."

The strangest stillness gripped him, he followed it up with a feigned casual shrug.

"True enough. I didn't see what happened. I was out of it. You, however, saw every minute of it." He cocked his head and watched her closely. "So tell me, sweetheart, was Kait fakin' it? Was Cosky?"

"What are you talking about?" Faith whispered, but she suspected she already knew. Something about that moonlit night in the forest had been needling her.

His long, lean, absolutely still body stretched across the ground. Cosky and Kait kneeling beside him, their hands pressed against his motionless chest. The anguish on Zane and Mac's faces. The ethereal play of moonlight silvering his glowing, frozen form.

He'd been glowing . . . so had Kait and Cosky.

He shook his head and tsked her. "Come on, darlin', don't play dumb on me now. Why don't you tell me what you saw in the woods that night?"

There was an equal measure of curiosity and challenge in the blue eyes locked on her face.

Faith swallowed hard, regrouping. "You're saying you were dead? That Kait healed you and brought you back to life?"

"In a nutshell." He shuffled his shoulders and frowned slightly. "Although I hear Cosky had somethin' to do with it too."

"But if you were unconscious, you don't know what happened."

"I reckon I remember enough. Like gettin' shot. Like bleedin' out. I remember that." The laconic, lazy drawl didn't match the tight look in his eyes, or the tension on his face.

Shot . . . bleeding out . . .

He had been drenched in blood, lying there so still . . . she'd been certain he'd been killed.

"Kait, Cosky, and Zane said you were just stunned. That your protective vest caught the bullets," she repeated their explanation slowly, even as doubt swelled in her mind. She'd sensed something odd in their account, had been puzzling over it for days.

He tilted his head and considered her, curiosity eating at the tension on his face. "How'd they explain the blood?"

"They said you'd fallen on top of one of those . . . those men and that the blood was his, not yours."

"Blood transfer, clever." There was admiration in the comment.

Faith stiffened her shoulders and pushed aside her doubt. That weird glow arcing between the three of them had just been the play of moonlight illuminating their bodies in the dark. There was absolutely no proof that he'd been shot, let alone that he'd died and Kait had healed him and then dragged him back to life.

"Everything they said makes sense. I'm sure that's what happened. You probably just had a bad dream, and events got mixed up in your head." Which reminded her of his earlier excuse about why he couldn't have a relationship with her. "You said yourself that your head's all scrambled."

"I wasn't wearin' a bullet-proof vest."

He tossed the words at her like hot wax, where they hit and clung and burned into her mind. She froze, but just for a second. "But they said—they told me you were wearing a vest. The bullets hit the vest."

"They lied. They gave you the most plausible explanation, one you'd believe. I wasn't wearin' a vest. None of us were. The blood was mine. Most of it, anyway, I reckon." He paused to study her face, and whatever he saw softened the sharpness in his voice. "Kait doesn't want her gift made public. We promised to keep it quiet when she healed Cosky." He nodded slowly, emphatically, as her mouth opened in shock. "Yep, she did. She healed Cosky. I was there. I saw it. And guess what? There's absolute proof in Cos's case. X-rays indicatin' a radical improvement in a twenty-four-hour period, which led to a confused and curious orthopedic surgeon."

"There has to be some rational explanation." Metaphysical healing? Really?

"There is—it's called faith healin'."

She wasn't aware she had spoken the objection out loud until Rawls responded.

Rawls shrugged and absently picked up a chocolate chip cookie. "But it doesn't matter whether you believe it's possible or not. There's no harm in tryin'. Worst-case scenario is status quo. Best-case scenario— you won't have to worry about your heart's viability for a very long time. Think of it as an experiment. You can measure the data, study the effect. You know the condition of your heart. You'll know whether Kait is successful or not."

Well, he obviously knew her better than she'd realized, since he was appealing to her scientific curiosity.

As Rawls raised the cookie to his lips, his hand suddenly jerked hard to the right. The cookie went flying, hitting the wall to Faith's left with so much force it shattered.

Stunned into silence, Faith stared at the wall and then stumbled over for a closer examination. Four feet up from a sprawling pile of golden crumbles, a smear of brown grit was embedded in the wall. The cookie had hit the wood with enough force to embed some of its remains.

She shook her head in disbelief. What in the world was going on with the man? It was past time to find out. Pivoting, she turned to face him.

His face had turned white, as bleached as bone, and tension emanated from him like a static charge. The frustration that carved his face into deep ridges and valleys softened the demand in her voice.

"Okay, enough of this. Tell me what's going on."

Chapter Seven

RAWLS GRIMACED, HIS HEAD POUNDING. SHE HADN'T BELIEVED IN metaphysical healing. How likely was it she'd believe in ghosts or that he was being haunted? Yeah—not very likely. At least he had proof that his translucent troll wasn't a result of his oxygen-deprived mind since the results from Pachico's experimentation were noticeable to other people.

"It was an accident. A muscle spasm," he said, surreptitiously scanning the room for his ghostly stalker, but Pachico had vanished.

While Pachico's ability to manipulate physical objects was rapidly improving, the effort appeared to drain him. After each incident, he'd disappeared. Too bad the departures didn't last long.

Faith pressed her lips together and shook her head emphatically. "I know what a muscle spasm looks like, Lieutenant Rawlings, and that wasn't one. You deliberately threw the cookie at the wall. Why?"

"Look, it was an accident. Leave it at that." Turning, Rawls headed for the door. He needed to get out of there before his ghost reappeared and directed its animosity toward Faith.

They'd been lucky so far. Pachico's test objects had been harmless. But there was a block of kitchen knives next to the cookies. How long before Pachico grew bored with the innocuous experimentation and graduated to something more lethal? The camp was full of weapons—everything from guns and knives to flash grenades and explosives.

"Rawls!"

He kept walking.

How the hell was he supposed to protect the camp from an enemy that nobody else saw or heard? His only advantage was that invisible connection leashing Pachico to his side. At least this tie between them prevented the bastard from roaming the camp at will, wreaking havoc left and right.

To keep the camp and the people in it safe, he needed to distance himself. Avoid everyone. He'd grab some supplies and hit the woods, deprive the bastard of the opportunity to harm anyone. Pachico wouldn't appreciate the isolation, which was bound to make the excursion uncomfortable, but hell—the damn ghost could hardly kill him. He'd lose his ride into the physical world.

Maybe . . . or maybe not.

Rawls frowned. He shouldn't assume anything. He had no clue what the parameters of this situation were. For all he knew, his death would dissolve the tether anchoring Pachico to his side, leaving the bastard free to harass people at will.

His best bet was to wait for Wolf to return and hope like hell the big bad Arapaho knew how to drive Pachico back to that translucent otherworld. Which meant he needed to hang out close enough to the helipad to intercept their cagey host the moment the chopper landed, but far enough away so that Pachico couldn't target any of his unsuspecting friends.

"Running away won't solve anything." Faith lifted her voice.

It would solve one thing. It would keep Faith safe. It would keep everyone in the camp safe until he came up with a better idea.

"Now, Doc. Don't go getting all hot footed on us," Pachico said from behind him.

Damn it . . . he'd hoped to be gone before the bastard reappeared.

"You can talk to me. I might be able to help." Faith's voice rose entreatingly.

"Go ahead, tell her what's going on. Better yet, I'll do it."

The ugly undertone in the raspy voice turned Rawls around. Pachico was floating there next to Faith, the block of knives within reach.

Son of a bitch. Rawls spun and launched himself at the door. The sooner he got the hell out of here, the sooner the phantom rubber band would retract and drag his ghost back to his side—away from Faith.

"Rawls!"

Except, Faith's voice didn't sound fainter. Hell, it sounded louder.

Footsteps sounded behind him and he glanced over his shoulder. She was following him.

Sweet Jesus, he wouldn't be able to keep her safe if she insisted on tagging along. To protect her, he needed to kill any interest she had in him. Make sure she avoided him. Regret swelling, he pivoted, ready to go on the attack—no matter how much he hated it—only to find Pachico floating along beside her. The ghost's intent expression as he studied Faith sent alarm bells peeling through Rawls's gut. He flashed back to the moment Pachico had tried to hit his arm, only to sink into it instead.

The pain had been immediate and horrific—an acidic burst that had seared through muscle and bone. Why in hades it had hurt that time was an excellent question, one he still hadn't figured out. Zane hadn't reacted when Rawls's hand had pierced his shoulder, or when Rawls had Caspered through his legs.

But damn it all, Pachico's last punch had hurt. Hurt like hell.

And suddenly Rawls knew exactly what the bastard had planned.

"Son of a—" Rawls launched himself toward the pair.

Separating himself was no longer an option. There wasn't time for that tactic. Somehow, in the here and now, he had to stop Pachico from piercing Faith's body.

"What's wrong?" Apprehension touched Faith's face. She half turned, as though to look behind her.

"Oh, this is going to be fun." On a deep-throated laugh, Pachico stepped to the left, directly into her. His translucent form merged with Faith's body and vanished.

"No! Goddamn you!" Rawls roared, watching helplessly as the asshole he'd dragged back from death disappeared into Faith's body.

Faith froze, her muscles locked and trembling. Her face contorted. Her pupils dilated. And then she screamed. And screamed. And screamed. One long, endless shriek of agony.

The pain when Pachico's hand had plunged into his arm had been overwhelming, but it had also been localized and fleeting. What the bastard was doing to Faith was worse. Much worse. His entire translucent form had merged with her flesh and bone, so the pain was likely widespread, rather than restricted to a specific area. Plus, he'd already been in her twice as long, with no sign of retreat.

Cold, greasy clamminess broke out as her screams reverberated through the room. *Ah shit . . .*

Not knowing what else to do, he swept her up in his arms and cradled her against his chest, gently rocking her while her screams reverberated through the room.

Jesus, Jesus.

The most god-awful sense of helplessness swamped him. An emotion he hadn't experienced since the events leading to Sarah's death—an emotion he'd promised himself he'd never feel again. Except his SQT was useless against an enemy with no physical form.

How do I get the bastard to vacate her body? Demands won't work.

His arms froze around her. But bribes might.

"All right," he shouted, uncertain if Pachico could hear him through Faith's screams. "I'll call your parents. Hell, I'll call anyone you want. *If* you get out of her—*now*."

For a moment nothing happened, and then the acidic burning from before swept through him. He turned in a circle, Faith's screams still pounding him, and scanned the room for his ghost's transparent form. Nothing. If Pachico had vacated Faith's body, he'd vanished again.

Suddenly Faith collapsed in his arms, her screams snapping off in midshriek. From her hoarse, ragged breathing he knew she was alive. Relief flooded him. His legs weak, he carried her to the kitchen table, dragged a chair out with his foot, and sat down, cuddling her on his lap. He checked her pulse, it was rapid and irregular beneath his fingers.

Sweet Jesus, tachycardia was often brought on by stress. Where were her pills? In her pocket or in her room?

He adjusted her limp body and slid his hand in her pocket, exhaling in relief as his fingers touched something small and oblong.

Thank you, Jesus. The pill was in reach if she needed it.

"Shhh, shhh. I got you, baby. I got you," he crooned in a rough voice, his heart pounding as hard and fast as it had the last time he'd sprinted five full klicks to catch the evac chopper. "You're okay. I got you."

She stirred against him, a cross between a whimper and a groan breaking from her.

"Shhhh." His arms tightening, he dropped a gentle kiss on top of her soft, silky head. "You're okay. I've got you."

Her strangled breathing eased. Her arms stole around his waist and clung, and with something close to a sigh, she nestled closer, tucking her head beneath his chin.

He checked her pulse again. This time the beat was slower and more regular beneath his fingers.

Relaxing slightly, he tightened his grip on her and tried like hell to concentrate on the fear still emanating from her, rather than the sweetest, softest ass this side of the Dixie line. Christ almighty, her butt fit his lap like it had been handcrafted for him alone, sculpted to match him perfectly. Each rock of his arms rubbed those softly curved cheeks against his crotch. Jesus H. Christ, he was the biggest ass alive to get all hot and bothered right now. This was the *last* thing she needed.

He fought to keep his movements gentle and soothing, to ignore the tension ballooning in the lower quadrant of his body and the prickles and chills that erupted as her humid breath bathed the bare skin of his neck.

With another of those soft, shaky sighs, she eased back in his arms and stared at him. "What . . . what happened?"

Her face was so close he could see the pinpricks of silver shining in the gunmetal blue of her eyes.

"Just rest, darlin'." He stopped rocking her long enough to check her pulse again and breathed a sigh of relief to find it slow and steady. Much more of that friction and she was bound to notice that he was getting all lumpy down there—which was not the reaction she needed at the moment.

But sexual urgency wasn't the only tension rising. Pachico could pop in any moment. He needed to be gone before that happened—get as far away from her as possible—yet he couldn't leave just yet. She was still shaky and traumatized. She needed the company, not to mention the cuddling.

"But what happened to me?" While a breathless rasp still roughened her voice, the unfocused haze was rapidly fading from her eyes.

He didn't want to lie to her, but hell, she wouldn't believe the truth.

"Did I have a seizure?" she asked, staring at him with huge fragile eyes.

"I'm not sure," he hedged. It could have been a seizure. A possession-induced convulsion . . . He doubted that knowledge would provide any comfort.

He could clearly see the fear in her eyes, the uncertainty, and his chest tightened, guilt hitting hard. This was his fault. He'd brought that *thing* back. She'd been attacked because of him, and every second he sat there left her vulnerable to another attack.

He needed to leave . . . *hell,* he had to leave—*now.*

Reluctantly, he opened his arms, letting them drop to his side, silently urging her to vacate his lap.

Unfortunately, she couldn't read minds. Instead of scrambling off and putting some distance between them as he'd hoped, she frowned and studied his face.

"That wasn't my heart. I know what tachycardia feels like," she said slowly, her eyes still clinging to his face. "And that wasn't tachycardia. That was different." Her eyes lost focus again, like she was remembering. A shudder traveled through her and fear glossed her eyes. "What if it happens again?"

The small, fragile undercurrent in her voice constricted his throat. Before he even realized he'd moved, he framed her worried face with his hands and pressed a comforting kiss to her forehead.

"Nothin's gonna happen," he said in his most soothing voice. He pressed another satin-soft kiss to her right cheek and then her left.

"But what if it does?" she asked, a slight flush climbing her cheeks. The fear drained from her eyes, and her gaze dropped, focusing on his mouth.

He wanted to promise her that nothing would happen to her, assure her he'd keep her safe. But that promise wasn't his to make. He had no control over what Pachico did, other than making sure the bastard wasn't close enough to attack her again.

And damn it, he needed to get moving. Sitting here cuddling was just asking for trouble and not just from his obnoxious troll of a ghost. He liked the warm, soft weight of her ass snuggling his cock too damn much.

One last kiss and he'd evict her from his lap and get the hell out of dodge. He'd intended for this final kiss to be in line with the first three. Gentle, calming, a comfort. But sweet Jesus, that luscious bottom lip of hers, with its sassy dip in the middle, had been tempting him since that moment on the bed, so it wasn't exactly surprising that his good intentions got all scrambled up. Rather than dropping a harmless, asexual caress on her upturned lips, his mouth closed over that sexy bottom lip and suckled. Hardly soothing, definitely not comforting, and a little too rough to be considered gentle.

Even so, he could have salvaged that moment of insanity, if she hadn't responded—if she hadn't pulled her lips free so she could press them against his mouth. Hell, he could even have withstood the feathery caress of her lips, if she'd left her tongue out of it—out of him.

But sweet Jesus, the minute her tongue took matters into his mouth, the tide swept out, dragging him into dangerous water. Deep, dark, sensuous depths fraught with undertows and wicked currents.

Her lips were soft beneath his and seasoned with chocolate, like she'd helped herself to one of those cookies Pachico had flung against the wall. His arms lifted, circling her slender frame. As they tightened around her, anchoring her to his chest, his belly clenched, hunger digging in. Holy hell, he'd just discovered the aphrodisiac to end all aphrodisiacs.

Nothing, absolutely nothing compared to Faith's lips spiked with chocolate. She was the dessert he hadn't even known he was craving.

Their mouths clung, their tongues explored—rubbing, dancing, tasting—fanning the fever higher and higher until the fire raged through him into her and back through him again.

Christ, he wanted her. More than he'd ever wanted anyone before.

Which was why he needed to get the fuck out, now, while he still had the discipline to do so. Much more of this kissing and he'd have her naked and on her back. Hell, the table was looking better and better by the second.

Still, it took every ounce of self-control, along with a massive surge of strength, to rip his mouth away, stand up, and deposit her on the floor.

"What's wrong?" She wavered on the ground, her dark brown hair tangled. Her blue eyes smoky with arousal.

He dropped his gaze from the sensuality in her eyes. Big mistake, since it locked on that swollen, moist mouth of hers and refused to budge.

With a strangled groan he wrenched his eyes away, let go of her waist, and took a giant step back. Then to be safe, he just kept going. With each step his legs threatened to mutiny and reverse directions.

"Rawls . . ." Her hand lifted entreatingly. "*Please*, tell me what's *wrong?*"

Rawls's heart clenched. He needed to drive her off. Make sure the last thing on her mind was following him out to the woods.

"Nothin's wrong. There's just a time and place for"—he hesitated and then forced the word out—"fuckin', and this ain't it."

"A time and place . . ." Her voice trailed off as her brows knit. She cocked her head slightly and scanned his face.

Christ, he needed to get out of here. But she didn't look all that hurt by his explanation. There was bewilderment more than anything in her eyes. He needed to hit harder. Confusion wouldn't keep her away.

"I mean it didn't mean nothin', right? You were on my lap, and it's the nature of the beast to wanna scratch an itch. Maybe later if—" He broke off when she straightened and rolled her eyes. Jesus, he was making a mess of this.

"Let me guess, maybe later, if the itch is still there, we can scratch it," she snapped, straightening her shoulders with a sharp twitch.

"Well, yeah." He backed up until the door struck his back. "Maybe, if the timin' is right."

"You were the one who kissed me," she said, dry challenge in her voice.

Like he needed the reminder. He shuffled forward slightly, his hands behind his back, fingers fumbling with the door handle.

He didn't apologize, because he wasn't sorry. Hell, he fully intended to do it again, under different circumstances. If she'd let him anywhere near her lips again.

Since there was nothing left to say, and every second he lingered increased the danger of Pachico's reappearance, he pivoted and yanked open the door.

"How did you know?" she asked, her voice rising. "How did you know something was going to happen to me?"

He froze with his back to her, his hand rigid on the doorknob. "I didn't."

"You did. I saw it on your face. You knew something was going to happen to me well in advance. How?"

"You're imaginin' things." Forcing his legs to move, he escaped.

"Liar."

The accusation followed him through the door and down the stairs. He expected the thud of footsteps on the wood steps to sound behind him, but the courtyard remained eerily silent.

He gave in to the urge to look back, once he reached the safety of the tree line. But the courtyard was empty. The main lodge sat squat and stoic, the windows shuttered.

There was no sign of Pachico anywhere.

Eric Manheim studied Dynamic Solutions' sprawling company retreat as the helicopter banked over Wilkes Island, skimmed the tops of the towering evergreens, and began its descent to the stone helipad below. Bright sunlight gave way to shadowy feathers of green as the trees closed around them. From the air, the retreat looked perfect for their agenda. Remote. Secluded. Empty.

According to Link, the small island, one of the smallest in the San Juan chain in Puget Sound, was completely self-sufficient and sequestered, accessible only by boat or air. As a company cresting the wave of technological breakthroughs, privacy was of paramount importance to Dynamic Solutions. A technological leak could cost the company millions of dollars. To keep their research safe, Leonard Embray, Dynamic Solutions' chief stockholder and CEO, had outfitted the island with multiple privacy shields. Unwelcome eyes and ears found it impossible to access the compound. Listening devices picked up nothing but static, while digital images were fragmented and warped.

This confidentiality was essential to the success of their current project.

Link emerged from a white-pebble-studded path and halted at the edge of the stone circle, waiting for the helicopter to settle.

"You're good to go, sir," the pilot said into Eric's headset.

Eric pulled the headset off and set it on the dashboard, wincing as the scream of the rotor sank into his ears. With a light shove, the cockpit passenger door opened and he climbed out, joining Link at the edge of the stone pad. Sunlight washed the helicopter silver as it took to the sky again.

"Everything went as planned?" Link asked once the helicopter had traveled enough distance to make hearing possible again.

"As far as I'm aware," Eric said, stretching. "With the exception of your pilots, nobody knows I'm here."

"The staff is paid extraordinarily well to protect the company's interest, which includes preserving our guests' identities." Link turned, moving to the side of the white-pebble path so Eric could walk beside him. "What of your man? Has he made contact yet?"

"The meet-up should happen soon. He'll alert us once Amy Chastain takes possession of her sons."

He glanced at the tall, thin man beside him. Was it his imagination, or had Link lost even more weight since their last consultation—which had been a mere three days ago. His trousers and Fendi blazer hung from his skeletal frame like donated fashions in a thrift store.

Was the weight loss guilt induced? Regret over betraying Embray, the legend who'd pioneered Dynamic Solutions, and by all accounts Link's closest friend since childhood? Was the treachery eating at him, or more accurately preventing him from eating? At what point did the council need to worry whether their associate's guilty conscience would bring repercussions down upon all of them?

It was a fine line to navigate. Link was privy to reams of incriminating information. Material that wouldn't just take down the council, but would spell disaster for everyone tied to the endeavor. They couldn't allow a guilt-induced return to morality to sway him from their agenda. They'd have to excise such cancerous possibilities from their ranks well before it metastasized into dangerous territory.

However, it behooved them not to jump the gun. Link had proved damn near indispensable over the past year. The cutting-edge technology he'd provided had reeled their agenda forward by years. Bloody hell, even the tracking technology they were employing to catch Mackenzie and his crew was Link's baby. Finding the SEALs without it had proved impossible.

He frowned. While it was in the council's best interest to keep a close eye on their Dynamic Solutions partner, it would be wise to keep his suspicions to himself for the time being. Coulson, for one, would act precipitously if he suspected Link of backsliding.

"Is the data stream still live?" His future rested on Link's biological tracker performing as expected.

"It's working at a hundred percent efficiency," Link assured him. "However, the signals have been stationary—or rather, the deviance in the signal has been minimal for the past hour."

Eric nodded. "Our contact was told to wait at a park for directions."

"Ah, that explains it," Link said absently. He increased his pace slightly and stepped in front of Eric to open an ornately carved wood door.

They stepped into a cool, shadowy hall with banks of windows running down the left side, offering a tranquil view of huge moss-covered boulders and large knotted tree trunks.

"If you're hungry, the housekeeper left us a plate full of sandwiches before leaving for the mainland."

"I ate on the plane," Eric said, curbing his impatience.

Link shrugged as they stepped into a large room with leather couches and armchairs facing a television riding the mantel of a rock fireplace.

Eric glanced around the room for the electronic tracker. "The device?"

"In the library." Link led him through a door to the right.

Like the room they'd just passed through, a huge stone fireplace covered the entire north wall. But the couches had been traded for a glossy mahogany desk, and the walls were lined with bookshelves full of paperbacks, hardbacks, and racks of magazines.

A slender laptop sat on the desk, its screen up. Eric headed for it, walking around the desk to get a better view. An irregular red dot hung in the center of a screen surrounded by latitude and longitude lines.

"Where are they?" Eric asked. To him, the latitude and longitude lines meant nothing.

Link circled the desk from the opposite direction and leaned over the laptop. Two keystrokes later and a map of Whatcom County in Washington State popped up. Eric cocked his head, studying the red dot that was dead center on a section of the map identified as Whatcom Falls.

Purcell said that he'd been instructed to wait at a park until Amy Chastain called with specific instructions to their rendezvous site. While the directive had infuriated the fed, it had had the opposite effect on Eric. Pure relief had coursed through him during Purcell's tirade. The caution evident in the instructions was pure Mackenzie. He was sure of it. The paranoid demand was standard operating procedure for the interfering bastard. Which meant that not only was Amy Chastain with those damnable SEALs, but they were aiding in the retrieval of her boys.

Exactly as he'd predicted.

What a bloody relief.

Once Amy had picked up her children, they'd be able to track them back to the SEALs' lair and neutralize the whole lot of them.

"Whatcom Falls," Eric murmured, fishing his cell phone from his trouser pocket.

"It's a park. The map indicates it has restrooms. I imagine this would be vital considering he's escorting two children and may have a lengthy wait."

Eric nodded in agreement and punched in the number to his contractor's burner phone. One ring and a voice answered.

"Yes?" A faint European inflection glossed the cold question.

Eric frowned slightly. He'd been working the accent over in his mind for months now, but still hadn't placed it, something that annoyed him considerably. But considering the parameters placed on their arrangement, questions weren't welcomed. On either side.

"Your unit is mobilized?" Eric asked.

"We're scrambled," the icy voice confirmed. "Awaiting coordinates."

As were they all. "Excellent. I'll contact you with the coordinates once the units are moving."

"We'll need enough lead time for team one to take up positions before team two moves in with the fireworks."

"Understood," Eric said before ending the call.

It was too bloody bad Remburg's second in command hadn't possessed their newest contractor's common sense. If the bastard had surrounded the Sierra Nevada cabin before sending the helicopter in, Mackenzie and his men would be awaiting burial right now.

"Problem?" Link asked, pulling the thickly padded leather chair back from the desk and taking a seat.

"No." Eric turned back to the laptop screen. "You're certain this thing has the range to track the distance we need?"

While the technology had tracked Robert Biesel from Seattle to the Sierra Nevadas with no problem, the distance had only been nine hundred miles. What if Mackenzie and his crew had holed up some-where thousands of miles away this time? He couldn't afford to lose that signal.

"During the testing phase, a gray whale was tagged in Mexico and tracked all the way to the Bering Sea, a twelve-thousand-mile trek. The researchers never left their lab on Kauai, yet the data rolled in clear as day." He glanced up with a shrug. "The latest rounds of testing indicated the range is likely much greater than twelve thousand miles. Closer to twenty-three thousand." He paused a beat, held Eric's gaze, only to frown slightly and look down. "We'll find them." He sounded almost regretful.

Eric let the hint of remorse slide. Link was as complicit as the rest of them. They were long past the point of second-guessing.

The minutes ticked by so slowly it felt like time was sliding back-ward. A quarter of an hour into their endless, all-but-silent wait, Eric dragged one of the thickly padded armchairs facing the south window up to the desk and settled back to wait in comfort. Link mixed them cocktails. And then a second round.

An hour and twenty minutes after his arrival, the laptop beeped. The screen flickered, and the red dot began to inch across the map of Whatcom County. Both he and Link leaned in for a closer look, watch-ing the red dot scroll across the screen.

"They appear to be heading away from all major roa—" The shrill ring of Eric's burner phone cut Link off.

Eric thumbed the green OK button and lifted the phone. "Yes?"

"They're in the air," Clay Purcell said into his ear.

"The air?"

"The bastards showed up with a helicopter."

Interesting. "Is it a Bell Huey 205?"

Which had been the helicopter the bastards had disabled the tracker on and absconded with after the Sierra Nevada incident.

"No," Clay snapped curtly. "It was a Jayhawk. What the fuck difference does it make?"

Eric's lips tightened. The federal agent had the foresight of a rhinoceros. "The helicopter they flew off with five days ago was a Bell Huey. Which means they are using a different machine, which means someone is arming them, which means they have supporters." He paused, cocking his head to the side. "Could they have acquired it through their contacts in HQ1 or 2?"

A thoughtful pause hummed down the line.

"It's doubtful," the fed finally said, the earlier curtness absent from his tone. "Too much red tape. With the current allegations surrounding them, loaning them a twenty-five-million-dollar bird would be career suicide for anyone with access to such an aircraft."

Exactly what Eric had been afraid of. "Which means they have some very well-heeled benefactors."

Silence strummed down the line.

Eric glanced at the red dot on the laptop screen. It was traveling south by east. "Mackenzie was there?"

"Yeah. Along with Winters, Simcosky, and some Indian dude."

Indian . . . ?

Eric's fingers tensed around the plastic casing of his phone. *It wasn't possible . . . no . . . it couldn't be . . . there was no way those two factions could have linked up . . .*

Except . . . a Jayhawk cost a pretty pound, and Mackenzie didn't have that kind of cash or influence. On the other hand, those Goddamn interfering, basket-weaving—

He broke the thought off and took a careful calming breath. He almost asked the fed which kind of Indian had been with Mackenzie—a Native American or someone from New Delhi—but he hauled the question back before voicing it.

It would be a mistake to appear too interested in that question. A big mistake.

A couple of deep breaths later and he managed to force his unease aside. He was being foolish, jumping to conclusions. The addition of an Indian to their team, whether native or imported, was purely coincidence. Besides, according to the dossier they had on Kait Winchester, her father had been full Arapaho and her brother, Aiden, was the spitting image of their father. He relaxed. Of course Kait Winchester would recruit her brother to assist them. No doubt he'd been the Indian operative mentioned.

Nothing to get all wrung out over.

"My untrusting sis had the boys change clothes before hopping aboard the chopper," Purcell said after a minute. "She brought a complete change for each of them, right down to their tighty whities." He laughed, but an ugly shadow dampened the humor. "Ain't she in for a surprise? You got the trace on her brats?"

Eric's eyebrows bunched in distaste. The woman was his sister. The boys he'd so callously dismissed, his nephews. Didn't he have even a modicum of regret?

"Is the tracer activated?" Purcell's voice sharpened, but it wasn't in repentance. Instead, anticipation thickened the raspy vowels.

"It's active. We're tracking them now," Eric said.

"I want to know when it's done."

"Of course." Eric jabbed the End Call button and tossed the phone on the table.

It had been quite clear from the beginning that Clay Purcell's feelings for his sister were far from brotherly—rather, they verged on sociopathic.

But then according to the info he'd collected on the pair, the two weren't actually siblings. They were the product of a blended family, courtesy of the marriage between Purcell's father and Amy Chastain's mother.

Still, the two had been raised as brother and sister from the age of seven—on Purcell's part anyway, Amy Chastain had been a couple of years younger—but the point was, they'd been raised as family.

Purcell had been best man at John and Amy Chastain's wedding. He was the godparent to their oldest child. How the bloody hell could the bastard play best man and best friend to John Chastain only to gut him in an airport closet? Or sign on as Brendan Chastain's godfather, only to orchestrate the child's murder?

Eric shook his head, staring at the red dot as it headed toward the Cascade mountain range. They'd never intended to extend their partnership with their FBI liaison after the hijacking. Agent Chastain's death and the SEALs' interference had bought Purcell a few additional months.

But once the SEALs were neutralized, it would be his pleasure to make sure the bastard didn't waste any more of the planet's resources.

If ever a man needed killing, it was that sociopathic, disloyal, two-faced weasel.

Chapter Eight

WITH A BEWILDERED SHAKE OF HER HEAD, FAITH STEPPED BACK AND closed the door, blocking the swarm of bloodthirsty mosquitoes trying to squeeze through the thin netting of the screen. From the window, she studied Rawls. Or at least what she could see of him, which was the tense line of his back and even tenser set of his shoulders. He was headed across the compound at a swift clip, apparently determined to put as much distance between them in the shortest amount of time as possible.

She watched him for another second or so before dragging herself away. Her heartbeat was settling and with each second, the threat of tachycardia diminished. Time to turn her mind to other things, soothing things. Luckily she had plenty to keep her busy. The roast wouldn't prepare itself. She needed to get it into the oven soon or chance the helicopter landing with a horde of hungry people and nothing to feed them—nothing substantial anyway. But as she went to work studding the roast with the rest of the garlic cloves, her mind circled back to those sensual moments on Rawls's lap.

Hard to believe the man hotfooting it across the compound was the same man who'd kissed her silly only minutes before. Or if not silly, at least into mindlessness. Although, that term didn't quite fit either, not when her brain had been fully engaged, every synapse aware and focused—on him. A more apt term might be lustfulness.

Maybe the whispers were true. Maybe the man was borderline crazy. His behavior had certainly indicated some kind of mental tic. There'd been that bizarre obsessive focus on the cookies, the way he'd thrown that cookie at the wall. The loud talking, like he was competing with some kind of noise even though there was no radio or television on the premises. There'd been no distractions in the kitchen . . . unless the noise was in his own mind . . .

And then there'd been that final bit, his sudden premonition that something was about to happen to her. Because that's what it had seemed like—an advance warning. He'd known something was about to happen several seconds before it did. Why else would alarm have descended on his face? Why else would he have shouted that peculiar warning and sprinted toward her? A person didn't behave in such a manner unless they knew—or at least believed—something terrible was about to happen.

Acidic, all-consuming pain flashed through her mind.

She flinched from the memory. Never before had she experienced such agony, which said a lot considering her medical history. But that consuming volcanic burn had been new. Unexpected. And beneath the burn had been the strangest sensation of compression. Like something was squashing her bones and flesh and nerves together, squeezing her into a small ball of pure agony.

What had happened? Had that horrific, internal burn been a seizure? It was the only thing that made a modicum of sense, yet even that didn't explain much. She'd coexisted with her medical conditions—not to mention all the medications she was taking—for fifteen years. In some cases, even longer, almost three decades. Seizures had never been a side effect or symptom she'd had to worry about. Could going off the suppressors have triggered something?

Except the burning hadn't originated in her brain, and seizures were the result of electrical impulses misfiring in the synapses of the brain.

The sound of the front door opening pulled her from the chaotic circling of her thoughts. Expecting Rawls, she turned, only to find Kait stepping into the room. From the uncomfortable expression on her face, the other woman knew something.

"Rawls said you could use some company," Kait said as she crossed the room.

"You saw him?" Faith glanced up, and then went back to inserting cloves of garlic into the roast.

"No. He called on the two-way radio." Kait held the short, square radio up as though offering proof.

Since cell service didn't work up here, everyone had been given a walkie-talkie, or two-way radios as the men called them. The devices operated from radio to radio on a fixed frequency and didn't require cell tower service, so they'd proved remarkably handy for keeping everyone connected. While the range of the instruments was restricted—up to thirty miles according to Wolf—the limitations hadn't had any effect on the radios' reception, but then everyone was hanging out within shouting distance of each other.

"How did he sound?" Faith bent and slipped the roast into the oven, before crossing to the sink to wash the stink of garlic from her hands.

"Fine." Kait closed in on the counter with its array of baked goods. After a quick glance at Faith, she lifted her shoulders and reached for a knife, slicing off a hunk of zucchini bread. "He didn't say much, though. Just that you weren't feeling well and could use some company."

The cold knot inside her stomach she hadn't even been aware of prior to this moment loosened and warmed. He'd been concerned for her. Still, she didn't particularly want the companionship.

"I appreciate the thought, but I'm fine." At the lift to Kait's eyebrows, she forced a smile. "Honestly. I'm fine."

Which was actually the truth. Her heart rate had slowed to normal, and the threat of a stress-induced attack of tachycardia was well behind her now.

And she suspected she'd remain that way as long as that strange malady didn't strike again. Had that been Rawls's reason for sending Kait over? To make sure she wasn't alone if that awful burning agony struck again? Or had he hoped to facilitate a discussion between her and Kait on the supposed benefits of metaphysical healing?

When it came right down to it, it didn't matter why Rawls had sent Kait over. The woman's mere presence brought a distinct sense of discomfort now that she knew about Kait's claims of hands-on healing, and the fact that Kait knew she knew added to the tension. If he'd just been concerned about her being alone, Beth would have been a better choice. The fact that he'd reached out to Kait, rather than Beth, indicated he'd had dual purposes when choosing his proxy.

"Did Rawls happen to tell you what's going on with him?" Kait finally asked while slathering a thick gloss of butter on the bread. She set the knife down and inhaled the slice in three bites.

Some of Faith's suspicion eased at the other woman's obvious appreciation of the zucchini bread. It was difficult to remain distant when your adversary appreciated your baking.

"No. He's been annoyingly closemouthed about everything," Faith said.

"Too bad. He doesn't say much, but I know Marcus is worried about him."

It took a moment for Faith to remember that Cosky's given name was Marcus.

"I'm sure he'll talk to someone when he's ready," Faith said, uncomfortably aware her voice sounded wooden.

Kait simply nodded. "Well, if you're okay with it, I'll stick around for a while."

Faith started to insist, again, that she was fine and didn't need the company, when a third reason for Kait's sudden presence occurred to her. Maybe Kait was the one in search of companionship. After all, her lover was one of the men on that helicopter, immersed in a dangerous situation and quite possibly under fire. Maybe Rawls had known Kait needed a distraction and provided her with one.

If that were the case, it was too bad he hadn't run his plan by her first, because she sucked at providing emotional support. Invariably, she always said the worst possible thing and made the recipient of her ineptness feel even worse than they had before.

Or she fumbled about in uncomfortable silence without the first clue as to what to say . . . rather like she was doing at the moment.

"You know that no one expects you to do all the cooking, right?" Kait dragged one of the counter stools back and took a seat. "We could make up a schedule, give everyone a day, and take the pressure off you."

Relieved that the conversation had drifted away from the missing men and their mission, thereby disrupting any feeble attempts at reassurance on her end, Faith smiled more naturally.

"I love cooking," she admitted. "I find it quite soothing. Besides, can you imagine Commander Mackenzie cooking us dinner?"

They shared an amused smile at the thought. But soon the worried furrow returned to Kait's forehead. Faith fussed with the dish towel, straightening it out and lying it across the edge of the sink with painstaking obsessiveness while the silence built.

"I'm confident the mission went as directed. They definitely planned for any contingency," Faith finally mumbled, compelled to fill the weighty silence.

Kait's smile looked forced. "I'm sure you're right." Except she sounded far more worried than certain. "Are you packed and ready for our new home away from home?"

Ahh, Cosky must have told her about the safe haven they were sending all the civilians to. Maybe that news was partially responsible for her obvious misery.

"I haven't even started," Faith admitted. Not that she had much to pack anyway, just the two changes of clothing and other essentials Wolf had picked up for her. "When is this happening—do you know?"

While Mackenzie had informed her that she'd be accompanying the rest of the women and arriving children, he hadn't bothered to tell her when that would be.

"Tomorrow sometime. Zane's brother is meeting the chopper and escorting us to our new refuge, but he can't make the drop-off point until early afternoon." She sounded tense, but resigned.

Curiosity stirred. Faith had expected frustration and arguments from the other women, not grudging acceptance. "You seem okay with this . . . ?"

Kait blew out a long breath, which must have released some of her tension because her face smoothed. "Not exactly okay with it, but I understand their reasoning. Civilians underfoot increase the danger significantly. If we're attacked, the team's focus is fractured. They have us to protect. They'll be safer without us handicapping them."

Faith nodded slightly. That made sense. No doubt things got even more tangled when emotions were involved, like the obvious love between Zane and Beth, and Cosky and Kait. The men would be focused on keeping their lovers safe. Still, it had to be hard for Kait knowing the departure was coming, since nobody could predict how long the separation would last.

Not that Kait needed to think about that right now; they needed a change in conversation. "If I timed this right, the roast should be out of the oven and cooling by the time the chopper arrives."

"Just tell me what to do and I can help," Kait said, with a subtle straightening of her shoulders.

"As of now, there isn't much to do," Faith said. "The potatoes don't need to go on for hours yet."

"Okay. I'll go check on Beth, but I'll be back in a bit." After one last thorough scan of Faith from head to shoe, Kait headed off.

Faith got back to work as soon as the door closed, and silence descended on the room. While it was hours too early to cook the biscuits, she could make the dough and set it in the fridge to chill until the helicopter landed.

As always, the act of mixing and measuring calmed her mind, and it didn't take long for questions about that frightening episode earlier to plague her.

How had Rawls known it was going to happen?

Had he sensed it somehow?

Certain animals could sense the advent of seizures. Indeed, several canine breeds were utilized as service dogs to warn their owners of impending attacks. Was that what had happened? Did Rawls have some extra sense that allowed him to predict the onset of seizures, or whatever that event had been?

Her hands stilling, Faith stared at the half-mixed contents in the bowl. If Rawls had the ability to foresee medical crises, as his behavior implied, why hadn't he admitted it to her? She thought back over their previous conversation and her reluctance to buy into the possibility that Kait could heal with her hands. Had her disbelief about Kait's "gift" prevented him from admitting to his own talent?

She nodded slightly, and went back to mixing. That made sense. And if she was brutally honest with herself, she wouldn't have believed him—at least prior to her unwilling participation in the experience.

But the episode had convinced her to consider more unconventional possibilities with an open mind. If animals such as dogs and cats could sense looming medical crises, some people might have similar abilities. Humans were animals after all, and it was certainly possible that some people had more acute senses, thereby picking up fluctuation in body chemistry or electrical currents—minute fluctuations within the human body itself that signaled impending medical problems.

She glanced at the computer tucked in the corner at the back of the room. There was plenty of time to do some research before everyone descended on the lodge for dinner. If she could identify that crippling pain, maybe she could prevent it from happening again.

However, by the time the helicopter sounded overhead, she was more baffled than ever. While two of the symptoms she'd endured could indicate a heart attack, most of the common markers were missing. She'd experienced no nausea, no sweating, and no dizziness, none of the symptoms that had beset her previously when her heart had acted up.

And while the sense of compression, of her flesh and bones being squeezed out of her body, could indicate a heart attack—that symptom didn't quite track either. The sensation hadn't just struck her upper body, as was common. It had struck from her toes to her scalp. So had that acidic, overwhelming pain. Both symptoms had been diffused and uniform, rather than localized, which didn't fit the markers for heart attacks at all.

Yet based on the symptoms associated with seizures, it was unlikely she'd had one of those, either. There had been no buzzing in her head, no strange smells or circling thoughts, no confusion and loss of short-term memory. Nor were the symptoms she had had associated with any of the case studies she'd found.

Apparently she hadn't had a heart attack or a seizure. So what the hell had happened to her, and how likely was it to happen again?

She needed to see a doctor, but the closest substitute was currently hiding from her.

Migrating to the window, she watched the helicopter disgorge its passengers. The men were all tall, with wide shoulders and dark close-cropped hair, and dressed enough alike that from a distance she couldn't tell who was who. At least until the two women, blond hair tangled and gleaming in the sunlight, pounced on their men.

An uncomfortable twinge of . . . something . . . pierced Faith's stomach as Zane cupped Beth's swollen belly and leaned down for a kiss. The rumbling in her stomach had nothing to do with envy—no sir, no way—it was just hunger pains. Even though her appetite had been nonexistent over the past week.

The twinge struck again, stronger, as Cosky dragged Kait into his arms and swooped down until their mouths met.

Okay, maybe she was a little envious. Like microscopically. But it wasn't because of the kissing, although she liked kissing as much as the next woman. It was the instant, unconditional support so evident between the couples. It would be so comforting to have someone to depend on like that: a solid, unflappable fixture bolstering her through life's turbulence. Someone like Zane. Or Cosky.

Or Rawls . . .

She instantly shook the stray thought away. Where had that come from anyway? From the man's actions over the course of the day, he hardly fell into the category of unflappable, or even supportive. He had, after all, abandoned her twice now, and when she could have used his reassurance too. Hardly the kind of steadfast companion she was looking for.

Her gaze narrowed on the two couples headed toward the lodge, each with their arms around their partner's waist. A soft-bodied older woman with flyaway silver hair took Kait's arm, tilted her head up, and leaned into the tall blonde as they walked. Behind the threesome was Amy, a dark-haired child on either side, followed by Beth and—

Suddenly it occurred to her that the horde was descending and she hadn't put the biscuits in the oven yet, or started mashing the potatoes. Turning, she fled back to the kitchen. She'd just set the timer for the biscuits as the door slammed open and loud footsteps and even louder voices claimed the lodge. As the room filled with people, Faith identified at least four distinct conversations. From the relaxed voices and laughter, the rendezvous and reunion with Amy's children must have gone as planned.

"Faith," Kait said, lifting the soft white hand of the older woman standing next to her. "This is Marion, Marcus's mom."

"Nice to meet you," Faith offered politely, only to stiffen as the older woman bustled around the kitchen counter and approached her with wide-open arms.

"Oh my poor, poor lamb!"

Faith took a giant step back but found herself enveloped in a soft, fragrant embrace anyway.

"What an awful, awful thing to survive. But don't you worry—" Marion said, punctuating her sentences with pats on the back and slow, circular massages. "My boys will keep you safe."

Boys?

Faith's gaze skidded from one hard masculine face to another. Nothing about the three men dominating the interior of the lodge resembled a boy, and the reference to the stern-eyed warriors as boys added to the sense of unreality shrouding her.

Just as she prepared to extricate herself from the other woman's floral embrace, Marion let go and nudged her aside. It took Faith a few seconds to realize Cosky's mother was lifting pot lids and taking inventory.

"Mashed potatoes?" Marion asked as she picked up the carving fork and speared one of the potatoes. "Looks like they're soft enough." She stopped talking long enough to take an appreciative sniff. "And whatever you have in that roaster smells divine."

"Pork roast," Faith managed faintly, watching helplessly as she lost control of the kitchen.

"It smells delicious, darling. And oh my, look at all those goodies on the counter. I can already feel my pants getting tighter. Now you go catch up with everyone and take a load off your feet while the girls and I finish up. You deserve a break after putting this together for us."

"But . . . but . . . but . . ." Her protest came too late and too low, and Faith found herself expelled from the kitchen.

She hovered in the mouth of the kitchen, listening to the laughter, chatter, and flurry of final dinner preparation between Beth, Kait, and Marion. The three women moved in sync, a well-choreographed machine, as though they'd been cooking together for years.

Feeling oddly abandoned, she sidled forward, preparing to slip back into her haven and reclaim at least one of the last-minute tasks.

"I rode on a hellcopper," a voice shrill with childhood said from behind and below her as a surprisingly strong tug dragged the hem of her ivory blouse down.

Faith turned. The smallest and youngest of the children Amy had returned with stood staring up at her with excited, shining eyes.

"You did," Faith said, forcing a smile, which she just knew was unwelcoming and stiff. "I hope you had a good flight."

I hope you had a good flight?

Really? Really? That's all you could come up with? You're not a damn flight attendant.

And you're going to share a house with these children for the night?

Luckily the boy didn't take offense. He didn't appear to even notice her discomfort.

"It was grrrrrreat." He rolled the description out like Tony the Tiger. "It went like a gabillion miles fast." Unable to contain his enthusiasm, he bounced repeatedly on his heels.

"A gabillion?" Faith said with a straight face and level voice. "I'm unfamiliar with that unit of measurement." When the delight didn't dim on his face, she relaxed slightly. This wasn't nearly as difficult as she'd feared. Maybe it wouldn't be so unsettling sharing the cabin with Amy's children after all. "Is that faster than a million miles per hour?"

"Like a gabillion times faster," he assured her, his small face blazing with zest.

Before Faith had a chance to respond, Amy appeared with the second dark-haired, dark-eyed boy in tow.

"I see you've met Benji, my youngest." Amy's face had shed twenty years, along with most of the deep crevices brought on by stress. She rested a hand on the shoulder of the older child. "This is Brendan, my oldest. Brendan, this is Faith Ansell."

"Hello," Faith said, accepting and shaking the hand the older boy solemnly held out while her earlier discomfort reared up to strangle her. "Very nice to meet you." Which was a little better than *I hope you had a good flight* but not by much.

"Have you been on a hellcopter?" the little tyke asked, tugging on Faith's blouse amid another round of heel bopping.

"Helicopter," Amy corrected him.

A confused expression crossed his face. "That's what I said."

While Amy and her son had a pronunciation moment, Faith studied the children. She would never have guessed they were Amy's kids. Both boys sported dark hair and dark eyes, rather than their red-haired, hazel-eyed mother's coloring. Since the darker coloring was predominant in the boys, she could deduce the coloring of their father. Genetics at work. Fascinating.

"Boys, help me set the table," Amy said, which sounded like a fine idea to Faith as well.

As she gathered silverware and napkins, she kept an eye on the door. There'd been no sign of Rawls since he'd fled the lodge that morning, which meant he'd gone all day again without eating. But it would be useless to call him to dinner—he'd simply ignore the summons as he'd done every night since they'd arrived.

She glanced around the table, soaking up the laughter and cacophony of voices, as everyone took their seats and began passing around platters of food. It was odd how, even amid the clatter of dishes and the rise and fall of voices, she still felt so isolated and alone.

The window across from her was getting darker by the second as night fell. Where was Rawls? Did his mind keep circling back to that kiss, like hers did?

Had it meant anything to him at all?

Chapter Nine

RAWLS ROLLED ONTO HIS SIDE IN THE SLEEPING BAG AND SCANNED the silent compound. Overhead the ashen tint of dawn grayed the sky and tinted the tree trunks, pine needles, and shrubby brush surrounding him a brackish maroon. He'd set up camp between two downed pine trees, flanked by a four-foot scraggly bush. The spot was several yards past the tree line to the east of the complex, but close enough to the helipad to allow for a quick interception when Wolf returned.

He had a good visual of the entire compound thanks to the angle of the two tree trunks he'd sheltered within. After dragging the end of the first tree closer to the second until they formed a V, he'd hollowed out the soft earth between them until the space would accommodate his six-foot-four-inch frame.

After piling pine boughs along either side of the trunks, he'd crawled inside his sleeping bag. By dragging the stockpiled branches across the trunks and over his head, he'd formed a rudimentary shelter of sorts. One that shielded him from both the elements and unwelcome eyes.

Not that his makeshift accommodations would fool his teammates if they got close enough for a good look, but from a distance—particularly at night—he'd blend into his surroundings. But the structure might fool Faith's more inexperienced eyes if she came looking for him. Although why would she seek him out after the ass he'd made of himself follow-ing that kiss?

As though thinking about her had conjured her, toward the far end of the compound, a woman wrapped in a dark coat came into view. Judging by her black hair and thin frame, the early riser was Faith. From her course, which was on a direct intercept with the lodge, she was probably getting a start on breakfast.

His hunch proved correct when she climbed the steps to the com-mand center and went inside. Seconds later a slew of lights blinked on. He imagined her starting the coffee with her hair tangled, her face sleep-flushed, and her body warm and soft. When his stomach tightened, he wasn't sure which image had sparked the response—the thought of piping-hot black coffee . . . or her tangled hair and soft, unpainted lips.

It took far more effort than it should have to wrench his atten-tion away from the lodge, or—if he was honest—the woman inside it, which sent a frisson of alarm through him. All told, he'd barely spent an hour in the woman's company. Not nearly long enough to have forged this intense connection with her, even if that connection was—strictly speaking—physical. The decision to back off may have been for the wrong reason, but it would put things back in perspective.

Grimacing, he settled into the hollow he'd dug between the tree trunks. The sleeping bag was surrounded by earth on three sides. That, along with the pine boughs overhead, had shielded him from the crisp air as the night wore on and the temperature dropped. Even without a fire to warm him, his camp had proven surprisingly cozy. Hell, it would have been downright comfortable if it hadn't been haunted by a venge-ful troll of a ghost.

Long before Pachico had reappeared, Rawls had grabbed the sleep-ing bag from his bed in the cabin, stuffed several water bottles and his jacket into a rucksack, and climbed out his bedroom window. The win-dow escape had been a precaution. If Faith, or anyone for that matter, came looking for him, they'd come to the door.

His bedroom was on the opposite side of the compound, and right next to the tree line, which made it easy to slip in and out via the window while using the forest for cover. It was a tactic he'd been using since his arrival to avoid his teammates.

Pachico hadn't been impressed with his ingenuity. Instead, the ghost had been furious to find himself banished from camp. Unfortunately, Pachico's attempts to enforce his agenda had graduated from annoying to excruciating. Each time the slimy bastard drove his transparent hand into Rawls's shoulder or chest, a tightlipped white-out of agony followed. Luckily the torture didn't last long, seconds at most, and then Pachico would blink out and disappear. After the third incident of teeth-clenching, stomach-rolling pain, followed by a blessed twenty minutes of relief, Rawls had reached a critical realization. Each time Pachico plunged his arm into Rawls's body, he depleted his energy stores a little more. Or at least he disappeared for longer periods of time.

The knowledge had made it easier to grit his teeth and withstand the seconds of volcanic agony. Hell, maybe the bastard would eventually wear himself down to nothing and disappear for good.

At some point during the night, his ghostly stalker must have realized he was depleting himself for nothing, because he'd switched back to the singing. Regrettably, the noise factor didn't seem to require excess energy, which meant the bastard didn't vanish. Still, Rawls had been able to block him out enough to get some actual shut-eye now and again. Not enough, but it was a start.

"Look," Pachico said from somewhere outside Rawls's shelter. "I promise to leave your gal alone. I swear on my mother's life. I don't know what else will convince you."

Since nothing would convince him, Rawls ignored the question. From his behavior, Pachico had obviously realized that he had no leverage if Rawls kept them out of camp.

"So you're just going to ignore me, you asshole?" When Rawls remained silent, Pachico's voice took on an ugly undertone. "You can't stay away from people forever, you stupid fuck. Sooner or later someone is gonna stumble into range, or you're gonna have to return to camp."

Rawls grimaced. He'd already come to the same conclusion. Unless Wolf had some mystical Arapaho remedy to turn the situation around, he—along with whomever happened to be within range of his vengeful hitchhiker—was well and truly screwed for the foreseeable future.

Apparently his continued silence infuriated Pachico past reason, because volcanic, burning agony plunged into Rawls's back and penetrated into his chest. Locking a groan behind clenched teeth, Rawls closed his eyes and waited the attack out. It lasted five seconds. Five endless, agonizing seconds, and then the pain vanished as suddenly as it had struck.

Shaking, his stomach rolling, and nausea climbing his throat, Rawls slowly relaxed in his sleeping bag. He wasn't certain why the attacks on him were so much shorter than the one on Faith. Or why Pachico hadn't attempted to walk inside his body, like he'd done to her. Maybe it was a simple matter of energy reserves. If Pachico was depleting his energy at a faster rate than he was replenishing it, he wouldn't have the power necessary to penetrate a body fully, or even partially, for an extended period of time.

Which meant it was in Rawls's best interest to egg him into these constant small-scale attacks in order to prevent him from storing enough energy to launch a full-body penetration.

Sighing as his muscles unclenched, Rawls released a long, slow breath. If this post-attack lull followed the pattern of the previous ones, he had at least fifteen minutes of peace before the bastard showed up again. Rolling onto his side again, he scanned the quiet compound.

Judging by the silvering of the landscape, and the fact that Faith had already escaped to the kitchen, it had to be close to six thirty. Which meant it wouldn't be long before the compound stirred. He'd watched from the safety of the tree line the afternoon before as the chopper settled, and his teammates, along with Marion, Amy, and her two boys, had disembarked. The whole lot of them had ambled toward the lodge, where the mouthwatering scent of cooking originated.

Zane had held back in order to radio him. Their conversation had been short. After giving his sitrep, which included Faith's condition, and a recap of his emergency call into Wolf requesting a refill on her meds, Rawls informed his LC he'd be going dark for the foreseeable future. Zane responded with a succinct four-letter curse and demanded an explanation.

An explanation that Rawls couldn't give. He suspected he wasn't going to have a choice much longer. Judging by his LC's icy reaction to his hedging, there was a good possibility that Zane intended to track him down and force the confession out into the open.

His teammates were losing patience.

Grimacing, he rolled his head, and a flicker of movement caught the corner of his eye. Instinctively he froze. The morning was still, which meant no wind to rustle a branch or wave a twig. So the movement was either animal or human. Animals were always a possibility in the woods. But then, so was Zane. After that terse conversation the night before, he had no trouble imagining his LC hitting the woods at dawn in the hopes of catching him bedded down and slow on the uptake.

With painstaking care, he rolled his head in the direction of the flicker. His eyes landed on a pair of thick brown boots. Slowly, his gaze crawled up two legs clothed in the green and gray of camouflage.

Not Zane. Or Cosky. Or Mac.

The figure was standing maybe eight feet in front of him, at an angle, just behind one of the larger trees surrounding the compound. A sniper's rifle hung from a strap across camouflaged shoulders, a pistol was holstered on the left hip, and a knife staged just below the pistol on his thigh.

He'd moved into place silently, so silently Rawls hadn't heard him, which pegged him as an operator. The position of the pistol and knife indicated he was left-handed. Maybe Jude? He assessed the figure again, but remained perfectly still. Nah—the height was off. And the stance was unfamiliar.

A chill prickled the back of his neck.

His eyes slid up. An NVD attached to a helmet covered the top half of the guy's face, leaving only a tight mouth and hard chin visible.

The guy had obviously come in from behind them, through the forest, not via the Jayhawk as Wolf and his men had arrived. Plus—he was in camo and full battle regalia, which Wolf's team wouldn't need, and then there was the fixed focus on the compound. Yeah . . . this wasn't one of Wolf's boys.

. . . *they'd been found . . .*

The faint sputter of a radio reached his straining ears. Not his. He'd dialed the volume way back on his until he could barely hear it so his team couldn't track him through the crackle, but his hadn't squawked all night. Inch by inch he slid his hand down until it touched the plastic casing of his own radio and carefully nudged the dial to off. One inopportune crackle and he'd be dead.

He'd been damn lucky so far. The asshole in front of him was obviously more interested in the compound and the people occupying it than he was in the terrain at his feet. But if he looked back and down . . .

Too bad he'd left his Sig stashed in the cabin. But damn it, he hadn't wanted to give Pachico access to the weapon. Sure, his ghost couldn't manipulate the weapon for more than a second at a time, but that second was enough to blast a hole through him. Or someone else.

He needed to take this guy out, but silently. Which was going to be difficult thanks to his current situation. For Christ's sake, he was trussed up in his sleeping bag like a caterpillar in its cocoon and just about as easy to squash.

Yet he could hardly remain lying there either. Sooner or later the bastard was bound to notice him. He'd prefer that moment coincided with the Tango's demise.

"Goddamn it," Pachico said from above him. "I'm getting—"

Rawls locked down his reaction as Pachico's voice boomed overhead. At least he didn't have to worry about his ghost alerting the bad guys to his presence. The Tango in front of him hadn't even flinched.

A low laugh sounded above him, followed by an amused, "Now this is an interesting development."

Sweet Jesus. Rawls's eyes shot to the rifle hanging from the Tango's shoulders. Pachico had proved repeatedly through the past twenty-four hours that he could manipulate physical objects. If he went for that weapon and managed to knock the safety off and compress the trigger—the resulting ammunition spray would bring all hell down on them.

Son of a bitch.

As though his ghost had read his thoughts, the translucent bald-headed figure advanced on their new camp mate and took a swipe at the dangling rifle. The weapon slammed against the Tango's hip, and Pachico's form dimmed. Galvanized into action, Rawls started to shove his way out of the sleeping bag as his unwelcome visitor jolted and turned.

Hell, he wasn't going to get mobile in time to subdue the bastard before the Tango got that rifle up and the bullets started flying. Except Pachico unwittingly came to his aid. The ghost's second swipe at the gun went right through it and into the Tango's side. The man seized up like he'd been pierced with a red-hot poker. Luckily the guy had some top-notch training behind him—rather than squealing and giving his position away, he locked the agony behind tight lips and rode it out.

From experience Rawls knew he had five seconds tops to get out, up, and take the Tango down while he was still occupied.

Rawls was out of the sleeping bag before Pachico removed his hand and blinked back out again. On his way to his feet, he snatched up one of the drier branches beside him and snapped it at an angle so the break was jagged and sharp.

The guy simply teetered there on his feet, his breath coming fast and uneven, before shaking his head and turning toward the sharp crack of the branch breaking. Rawls was on him before he finished the motion. One hand jerked the helmet off and clamped around the compressed mouth, while the other hand drove the jagged end of the stick into the Tango's neck, right above the carotid artery, and then jerked the stick back out again.

As the poor bastard struggled urgently against his grip, Rawls bore down harder on the hand across the guy's mouth, ignoring the teeth that dug into his palm, and the blood raining down on the ground. Raw, animalistic sounds, muffled by his hand, grew fainter and fainter. He counted the seconds off in his head. The Tango would bleed out in under two minutes, but he'd fall into unconsciousness in half that time.

Once the guy stopped moving, Rawls lowered him to the ground and knelt to take a quick pulse. Slow and thready. The poor bastard wouldn't be getting back up again. Locking down regret—God knows the bastard wouldn't have hesitated to take his life—he stripped the rifle and the pistol along with its holster off the limp figure. Then he quickly unbuckled the knife holster, with its fixed-blade knife, from the guy's thigh.

The blade would come in mighty handy.

Undoubtedly Pachico would make a play for the weapons upon his return—but it was just one more thing to guard against. He couldn't afford to be weaponless in the coming battle. Although how he was going to warn his team about the danger of their weapons going momentarily berserk for no apparent reason . . . *yeah.*

Locking his frustration down, he backtracked to his sleeping bag, shoved his filthy socks into his boots, and laced them up in record time. Then he grabbed the radio. He couldn't afford to use it yet to warn his team. At least not unless he ran out of options.

Too likely his voice would carry and alert the wrong people. Even if he concealed the message in some fashion, just the fact that he'd radioed from the woods would give the game away and send the rest of the Tangos, who were holding on the perimeter, swarming into camp. What they were waiting for was unclear. Maybe for the entire team to assume positions, or—his mind flashed back in time, to the helicopter hovering over the driveway while Wolf's Sierra Nevada home exploded.

Alarm lifted the hair on his arms. If the Tango he'd taken out was part of the mop-up team, and a chopper was on the way . . .

Sweet Jesus . . .

He needed to alert his team pronto.

He kept the radio in hand, in case he ran out of time, as he eased back into the woods and silently made his way toward the closest cabin, which happened to be the one he shared with Mac. He could access the structure through his bedroom window. It struck him as ironic that the window he'd left unlatched to facilitate his return or departure from his bedroom in the hopes of avoiding his teammates might just end up saving all their lives.

Assuming he could get there without notice. He had no clue how many Tangos stood between his current position and the cabin.

As it turned out, that number was two. The team hunting them had taken up position along the tree line, which made sense for monitoring and targeting. But the tactic left them at a clear disadvantage from the rear. They had no one guarding their sixes. No doubt they considered that vulnerability negligible. They were attacking at dawn after all, while everyone lay sleeping. There shouldn't have been anyone in the forest for them to worry about. Hell—there wouldn't have been, if it hadn't been for a bitchy ghost.

Taking advantage of their vulnerability, Rawls fell back, easing from tree to tree. The second Tango blended into the shrubbery, but Rawls's experienced eyes picked up on him immediately.

With the element of surprise on his side, and his visitor's blade in his hand, Rawls had the second guy limp and on the ground in seconds. The third Tango was posted several yards to the right of the cabin. Another few seconds and his path to the window was clear. He wiped the blade on a tuft of grass and holstered the knife.

So far the team members had been positioned every fifty feet, give or take. Which meant he *should* have easy access to the window. Should being the operative word. You couldn't count on logic or patterns, and leaving cover for open ground was always a gamble.

Still, it had to be done. So he crouched and rushed the window. With each abbreviated stride, the muscles of his back twitched in anticipation of a bullet or a blade.

Behind him the forest remained silent. Tranquil.

Reaching the window, he crouched and carefully pushed it to the left. So far so good . . . one last quick scan behind him, and he hoisted himself up and swung his feet inside. Carefully he eased himself back down, simultaneously shifting the rifle to the front so it wouldn't get hung up on the window seal.

"What the fucking hell, you stupid motherfucker," a harsh raspy voice growled as Rawls's boots touched down on the wood floor.

Rawls raised his head and found a fully clothed and booted Mac glaring at him from the open bedroom door.

"The fucking window? Are you shitting—" His tirade cut off at the finger Rawls held to his lips. Mac's dark eyes dropped, completing a quick up-and-down scan that took in every smear of blood on Rawls's clothes.

Pivoting, Rawls eased the window closed again, and when he turned back, Mac was inches away.

"How many?" Mac asked in a low rumble.

"Every fifty feet." Rawls calculated the length of the compound and doubled it. "Twenty-five—give or take."

"How the hell did they get past the sensors? Wolf has this place wired to the gills," Mac growled.

Rawls shrugged, but he could guess—Pachico. The bastard must have done something to the security system. Damn it, he should have expected something like this, took steps to prevent it. Instead, he'd let his preoccupation with Faith and his current situation blind him.

Mac glanced at the bloodstains.

Rawls shook the frustrated guilt off. Wallowing in regret wouldn't help them. "I dropped three. We're clear from here to west of the helipad."

With a curt nod, Mac snatched the radio from Rawls's grasp. "Zane and Cos can get their women into the tunnels. We need to grab Amy and her kids. Faith is in their cabin too. We'll grab all four of them and hustle them below."

"Faith's in the kitchen," Rawls said. He glanced at the radio and raised a brow. "They'll be monitorin' the channels."

"No shit." Mac grimaced. "Let's hope Winters and Cosky are as smart as they think they are." Mac's voice turned grim. He shot a glance at Rawls. "You'll need to get the doc underground. Grab the sat phone while you're there. We'll rendezvous in the hub." He stared down at the radio for a moment and grimaced. "Let's hope like hell those bastards circling us are monitoring the channels. We don't have time to take the tunnels to grab the gals." He glanced toward the window and lifted the radio to his mouth.

"Alpha two, three, and four." Mac keyed the radio. "Jude's taken a turn for the worse. We can't wait for the medevac, that appendix needs to come out now. Doc will do the surgery, but we'll need all hands on deck. Rawls is on his way to the lodge to get the med kit. The rest of us will rendezvous with Amy in the hub." He paused. "Copy?" A static crackle followed by two calm affirmatives. "Amy? You copy?"

At Amy's quiet confirmation, Mac tossed Rawls the radio and waved him away.

The Tangos outside were holding off their attack for a reason. Mac's ruse had been clever enough. It gave them a good reason to be crossing the compound like bats out of hell so early in the morning. Maybe it would convince their uninvited visitors to resist turning Mac and him into bloody sieves. Assuming the Tangos were monitoring the channel, assuming they bought Mac's excuse, and assuming they didn't open fire just for the sheer hell of it.

He burst through the cabin door and leapt down the front steps in one bound. As he sprinted for the kitchen and Faith, he heard Mac's boots hit the earth behind him, and charging footsteps take off toward the right—in the direction of Amy's cabin.

That earlier icy prickle as he had climbed through his bedroom window didn't hold a candle to the glacier currently encasing his spine. With every step he expected the hot agony of metal to pierce his flesh and bones.

And unlike his annoying troll of a ghost's attack, those rifles locked on him as he raced toward Faith wouldn't vanish after five seconds. Nor would the pain and damage to his body be phantom and fleeting.

Mac glanced toward his bedroom as he followed Rawls down the hall. It would take a quick three seconds to pivot and retrieve his radio, but he opted to save the time. Those seconds might well be the difference between arriving at Amy's cabin whole and mobile versus sluggish and bleeding out. Besides, Amy had a walkie-talkie, not that there was much sense in using it under the circumstances. They had to assume the channels were being monitored.

At least he had his weapon. He'd grabbed the pistol before heading out to investigate the subtle scrape of the window sliding back in Rawls's room. The walkie-talkie hadn't been a priority since he'd been certain the noise was indicating his corpsman had returned.

Without a backward glance, Rawls shoved open the screen door and took off in the direction of the command center and kitchen. Mac tensed, expecting gunfire to light up the compound. They had no clue whether the men scoping out the camp had overheard his transmission or, if they had, whether they bought into the ruse.

If the situation had been different—meaning if they'd been alone, unhampered by a camp full of defenseless women and children—he and Rawls would have slipped back into the woods and taken out as many of the bastards watching them as possible. But to do that in the current circumstances chanced some of the motherfuckers attacking before they could be neutralized.

Which left them with only one option. Get the women and children to safety before gearing up for the counterattack. With that in mind, he followed his corpsman down the steps and veered off toward Amy's cabin.

Sixty feet stretched ahead of him . . .

Of all the women, Amy was fully capable of defending herself. But she was also responsible for her two children. One of whom appeared to be a handful. Contrary behavior in a battle situation was the quickest way to get a person—or a child—killed. Hence the race to her rescue.

Fifty feet stretched ahead of him . . .

With each thud of his boots, his scalp prickled and the flesh down his spine crawled. He could sense the scopes locked on his back, itchy fingers caressing the trigger as the bastards surrounding them watched him run.

Forty-five feet . . .

The compound remained quiet . . . still . . . the only sound disturbing the calm was the thunder of his and Rawls's boots.

Thirty feet . . .

For whatever reason, the motherfuckers on the perimeter were holding their fire. If he were lucky—damn lucky—that decision would last until he and Rawls reached their targets and the cover provided by the cured whole logs that made up the compound structures.

Fifteen feet . . .

He strained to hear beyond his own pounding feet and deep breathing. Their current fucked-up situation just proved what he'd been saying all along—they had no Goddamn business cohabitating with a bunch of Goddamn civilians.

Five feet . . .

The three steps to Amy's cabin loomed in front of him. He took them in one leap, while the muscles in his back twitched and the absolute certainty rose that those bastards were just playing with him, and planned to punch him full of lead as he reached the door.

And then the door was within reach.

He wrenched it open and shot through, letting it slam loudly behind him. Relief surged through him, and his legs went weak and shaky.

Son of a bitch!

He could barely believe he'd actually made it across the compound without losing half his blood supply.

What the fuck were those motherfuckers out there waiting for?

Could Rawls have hallucinated the forthcoming attack?

He immediately dismissed the question. There'd been too much blood staining his corpsman's clothes—real blood—for the danger to be imaginary.

A bolt of adrenaline shot through him. The tunnels were reinforced concrete about twenty feet beneath the surface. Even so, if a missile penetrated the ground above a weak spot in the web of connecting catacombs, the tunnels could end up being their tomb rather than their salvation.

No help for it, though. Based on Rawls's estimate, there were too many Tangos out there to neutralize when they had all these damn civilians to worry about. At least Rawls had given them a head start. Maybe his corpsman's mind wasn't as scrambled as they'd assumed.

Adrenaline spiking through his veins, he scanned what he could see of the cabin. All empty.

Where the fuck were Amy and her kids?

Toward the back of the cabin came a soft snick. Mac took off in that direction. At the far end of the hall, a previously locked door stood ajar, the keypad that provided access to the staircase beyond flashing red. Apparently the woman had decided to forgo an escort and descended into the tunnels on her own. Torn between irritation and admiration, he paused on the staircase landing long enough to drag the door shut behind him, and then took the long, narrow line of stairs two at a time.

Behind him a click sounded as the lock engaged again. As he neared the bottom of the staircase, a high-pitched childish voice drifted up to him. Amy's youngest from the sound of it.

A few more steps and he could make out the kid's words.

"A tunnel? Like in *National Treasure*? Is there a treasure, Mom? I bet there is! We're gonna be rich!"

Mac reached the bottom of the staircase as the child squealed in excitement.

"Look at all the guns, Mom! Can I have one?"

The trio must have reached the staging room at the entrance to the tunnel. They'd stashed several pairs of NVDs as well as weapons and boxes of ammo on the steel shelves lining the room.

"Benji, you stand right here. Don't move a muscle," Amy said, her voice calm and commanding.

"I've got him," the older boy said, his voice as calm and adult as his mother's had been.

Mac turned the corner and entered the staging area to find the older boy dogging his younger brother while Amy shoved pistols and equipment into a duffle bag. She turned her head long enough to scan Mac as he crossed the threshold, and then turned back to the shelf.

"How many?" she asked, as she shoved boxes of ammo and bottles of water into the bag.

After a quick glance at the two boys, he shrugged. "Nothing that we can't handle," he said in an easy voice. No sense in alarming the youngsters.

Although any handling, and/or mop-up, would have to wait until after they stashed the civilians someplace safe. Too fucking bad the bastards hadn't attacked later in the day, after they'd loaded the women and children onto the helicopter and removed them from harm's way.

He punched the access code into a second keypad—the one that allowed access into the tunnel system itself. After a loud click, a hiss of escaping air sounded and the door eased open. He shoved it the rest of the way, revealing the concrete tunnel.

"Here." Amy handed him a flashlight. As she passed it to him, she leaned forward and dropped her voice to a whisper. "How many are out there?"

Chills shot from his scalp down to his ass when her warm, tooth-paste-spiked breath brushed his ear. He jerked hard, forced down his instinctive urge to retreat, and stayed put.

"Unknown." Something sweet and clean teased him. He drew in a deep breath before realizing the scent was drifting from the bright red strands of hair almost brushing his cheek. He locked down the impulse to lean in closer and fill his lungs with the fragrant scent again.

Her hair? He wanted to smell her hair? Jesus Christ, he was pathetic.

Grimacing, he accepted the NVD she handed him. "Rawls estimated twenty-five, but he took down three."

Amy shot him a surprised look. "Rawls?"

"Yeah. He stumbled across them this morning." He shrugged at her questioning look and took a casual step back. "He slept out there last night."

And damned if that decision, which he'd been so disgusted about twelve hours earlier, hadn't saved their collective asses.

"You ready?" He turned the flashlight on and aimed it into the gaping black maw of the tunnel before waving her boys over. "I'll lead, you bring up our six."

He waited for her to turn on her own flashlight and guide her youngest into the steady beam of silver before stepping inside the mouth of the tunnel and dragging the door shut behind him. It sealed with a heavy click and the hiss of escaping air as the lock engaged.

A thick, claustrophobic pressure cinched around them.

It didn't occur to him, until he turned around, that he'd made one hell of a mistake.

The tunnel was six feet tall, which meant he had to hunch slightly to avoid scraping his scalp. No big deal there. But widthwise, there was only room for one adult at a time. He'd have to squeeze past Amy and her children to take the lead. The kids? Piece of cake. But the woman . . . hell . . . he'd be rubbing against places he had no business rubbing. Tantalizing places.

He shut that line of thought down fast and scrambled for a distraction. Luckily there were plenty of questions on hand. Like why hadn't Wolf's perimeter alarms sounded once their camp had been breached? Wolf had run through the exterior alarm system at the same time he'd shown him the catacombs and given him the access codes. The alarm systems were state of the art. All the bells and whistles. And a perfect example of why it was never wise to depend on someone else for one's personal safety.

As he started the excruciating process of sliding past Amy's petite, sturdy frame, which involved far too much rubbing of chests and thighs, his concentration fractured.

Christ . . . she felt good. Too good. All taut, toned muscle and warm flesh. And then there was that clean fresh scent he'd noticed earlier. It reared up to fog his mind and mess with his reason. He held his breath, sucked in his gut, and pressed harder against the concrete wall. Even so, he couldn't avoid physical contact. Hell, while the brush of his bare arms against hers was light, more skim than caress, the contact was enough to send sparks cascading through his blood and launch an electrical sizzle in his belly.

He happened to catch her eyes as he squeezed past her, his chest rubbing across hers, and he saw something in the hazel depths he didn't want to see. Something hot. Something sensual. A molten shimmer that told him clear as hell that she was feeling the same charged attraction he was feeling.

Son of a bitch . . .

It was the very *last* thing he wanted to know. It was hard enough keeping his own lust in check. But to know she shared it—fuck. That's what he was—fucked.

Frustration surged as he wrestled his mind back in line. They needed a major distraction, and he had just the topic. It was sure to spark a reaction and send her backpedaling all the way down the mountain.

"You do realize that your boys are tagged, right?" he told her. His voice emerging rougher and more confrontational than he'd intended. He frowned and tried to modify his tone. "The camp's been secure for days. We bring your boys in and, boom, twelve hours later security's been compromised. Your boys were followed. It's the only thing that makes sense."

Amy waited until he'd squeezed past before responding. "They changed clothes completely. Right down to their skin. There was nothing that could have been chipped. The timing's a coincidence."

But her voice lacked confidence. She didn't sound like she believed it herself.

"Then it's a hell of a coincidence," Mac countered. "And too damn convenient if you ask me. If they shucked everything, then the tracking device has to be beneath their clothes."

Hell, it was common practice to insert identification chips in pets, how much harder would it be to insert a tracking chip beneath someone's skin? Not difficult, for damn sure. But if that were the case—then they had a huge problem on their hands.

If the device was still transmitting their location—and why wouldn't it be?—then they were leading their assailants directly to the rendezvous site, thereby jeopardizing everyone.

Chapter Ten

YAWNING, FAITH LEANED AGAINST THE KITCHEN COUNTER AND watched the coffee level creep up the glass decanter. Dawn barely brushed the sky, but her camp mates were early risers and big coffee drinkers. As morning rolled into afternoon, she'd be measuring coffee grounds and filling the machine with water at least three, possibly four more times. The only two people in camp who didn't overdose on coffee every day were her and Rawls. But then, her hot beverage of choice had always been tea. As for Rawls, he was rarely in the kitchen, and when he was, it wasn't to eat or drink.

Turning, she stared out the window, scanning the lightening landscape. Where was he? From eavesdropping on Zane and Mac the night before, she knew he'd abandoned camp to bed down in the woods.

Why? Was it because of her? Because of what had happened between them? She glanced at the kitchen table. He'd held her on his lap over there, stroked her hair, and caressed her back. Even kissed her.

Of course, he'd rejected her there too.

Surprisingly, the rejection didn't sting. Maybe because it had been so strange. Plus, it had been obvious that he was interested in her. He couldn't hide the bulge pressing against her bottom, clear evidence that he'd been as aroused as she'd been. She hadn't been wrapped in that fog of sensuality by herself. He'd been caught in the spell right alongside her.

And she was almost certain she hadn't been the one to drive him away. Something else had done that. Apparently it had driven him from his friends as well—clear out of camp as a matter of fact.

When the teapot whistled, she lifted it from the stove and poured boiling water into the cup on the counter. As the tea steamed, she turned off the burner and absently dunked the tea bag—chamomile, to calm her nerves—into the hot water.

Too bad Rawls wasn't here so she could force some of the chamomile tea down his throat. If anyone's nerves needed soothing, it was his. Which was so odd, considering his career choice. Navy SEALs were rumored to have nerves of steel.

What was equally odd was that she was worrying about him. She was even considering searching the woods in the hopes of tracking him down and verifying for herself that he was okay.

Stupid. Stupid. Stupid.

Seth Rawlings is not your problem. His problems are not your problems. Let it go. Let him go. You have enough problems of your own without taking on his.

With luck, her immediate problem would be resolved today when Wolf arrived with the refill on her meds. Of course, that still left her newest problem unresolved. While she'd only experienced the one attack, it made her nervous not knowing what she was dealing with, or when it might strike again. Not that there was anything she could do about the situation. At least not until she identified what the episode had been. Her best hope at the moment was remaining calm as she tracked down the new symptoms so her old nemesis tachycardia didn't swoop back in to wreak havoc.

Hence the tea, and the soothing ritual of cooking—breakfast this time.

The loud thud of boots on the front steps leading up to the lodge provided a welcome distraction. She turned to face the command center's entrance as the door flew open. Rawls entered the building at a dead run, the door banging shut behind him. He slowed to a jog. Intense blue eyes swept the room and fixed on her face. Surprise locking her in place, she simply stared back. Apparently he was bringing his problems to her . . .

Barely breaking stride, he headed for the desk tucked in the corner of the main room and snatched up the satellite phone, tucking it beneath his waistband at the small of his back. "You get Mac's message?"

"What message?" she asked.

His face was hard, tight, yet somehow seething with tension. She didn't realize she'd taken a step back until she felt the edge of the kitchen counter against her back.

"On the radio."

He swept her frame as he strode toward her, as though he were looking for the walkie-talkie, which he wouldn't find since it was sitting on the dresser in her bedroom.

"I'll explain on the way." He beckoned her forward, the motion urgent.

"On the way? On the way where?" As she pushed slowly off the counter, her gaze was drawn down to a series of ruddy smears glistening on his shirt and jeans.

Glistening as in wet . . . and ruddy as in . . .

"Is that blood?" Her voice rose as her pace picked up. "Are you injured?"

His face tightened even more. "We have a situation. I'll explain on the way."

"On the way where?" she asked cautiously, slowing her pace to a crawl.

He didn't sound like he was in pain. He sounded impatient. And urgent. She studied the ruddy smears again. They hadn't gotten any bigger or wetter, so he must not be bleeding. In which case the blood must be someone else's . . .

Whose?

Her feet screeched to a stop. "Uh, Rawls, whose—"

He was on her before she finished the question. A huge hand clamped over her mouth. She was too stunned to struggle as his mouth dipped toward her neck. The quiver that shook her as his warm breath tickled her ear had little to do with fear. At least until his words registered.

"The camp's surrounded. We need to get into the tunnels *now*. No questions. We may have unwelcome ears listenin' in."

They were surrounded? By whom?

Stupid, stupid question, Faith.

She nodded her understanding and he released his grip on her mouth, transferring it to her arm. He towed her forward, along the outside of the kitchen counter, heading toward the hall at the back of the lodge. As the log walls flashed past, she glanced at the ruddy smears streaking his chest.

It had been pretty clear for days that something was misfiring in Rawls's brain. Something like hallucinations, if his teammates' hunches were correct. She wanted to discount his urgency now, discount his insistence that the camp was surrounded, convince herself that he'd imagined whatever he'd seen . . . except.

Except he was smeared with blood—blood that didn't appear to be his own.

Which meant something must have happened out there.

Her heart skipped a beat and then made up for it with a few seconds of double time. She groaned beneath her breath and worked to calm her breathing and nerves. She only had one Cordarone tablet left. If the camp really was surrounded and Wolf couldn't land, that one tablet might have to last her for a long time. She'd best save it for when her heart rate got completely out of whack. As her heart settled back into its normal, strong rhythm, she breathed a sigh of relief and glanced at Rawls, relaxing even further to find his attention fixed on the far end of the hall. At least her momentary health scare hadn't distracted him.

He drew her to a stop in front of the last door on the right, its security panel glowing red. She'd been given the grand tour of the lodge as well as the cabin she and Amy shared when they'd first arrived—so she knew about the tunnel system beyond this door and how to gain entrance to it. While each of the individual cabins had its own entry into the tunnels, the access panels shared the same security codes. On the other hand, while each cabin had its own stash of weapons in case of an emergency, the only building with access to the main weapons locker was the main lodge. From the weapons locker, one could enter the tunnel system.

Wolf had given her the code to the security system within hours of their landing, even made her recite the encryption repeatedly until he was satisfied that she'd remember it during an emergency. She repeated the numbers silently as Rawls punched them into the panel. As soon as the click sounded, indicating the lock had released, Rawls dragged the door open and propelled her inside. The door swung shut again, sealing behind them with another slight tick.

Bright light from the fixture above their heads spilled down a steep staircase. Rawls headed down the steps at breakneck speed. Luckily, the space was too cramped for the two of them to travel abreast, so he had to drop her arm, which allowed her to descend more cautiously. He'd already punched the access code into the second steel door that guarded the weapons locker and had it propped open by the time she reached the bottom.

After a quick glance at his face, which hadn't lost any of its earlier tension, she silently preceded him into the concrete, steel-shelved room. But as soon as the door swung shut behind them, she turned to face him. With two steel, impenetrable doors between them and their would-be captors—or killers—they should be safe enough for a quick discussion.

"Is any of that blood yours?" she asked as Rawls pulled a canvas bag off the bottom rung of the steel shelving to her right.

"No." He shot her an indecipherable look before unzipping the duffle bag and dropping the satellite phone inside. "The camp's surrounded. I had to neutralize a few of our uninvited guests on my way back in."

Neutralize?

Faith flinched and avoided examining that description too closely.

"Mac called for a rendezvous." He straightened with the bag in hand and started filling it with guns and ammo from the shelves above. "Which you would have known, if you'd had your radio." The glance he shot her was full of admonishment.

Faith grimaced. He was right. She should have brought the radio. If Rawls hadn't come back for her, she wouldn't have known she was in danger. She would have been merrily cooking away while a band of killers swarmed the compound.

The other women wouldn't have been as ill prepared. But then, they had their own personal SEALs to provide protection. Or at least Kait and Beth and Marion did. Amy, on the other hand, was in the same predicament as Faith—only worse, since she had her kids to worry about as well. And from the micro amount of time Faith had spent with the family the night before, it was clear Amy's youngest child was a handful.

"Amy's going to need help getting her kids into and through the tunnels," Faith said, watching Rawls add more guns and boxes of ammo to the canvas bag. They certainly weren't going to run out of weapons or ammunition anytime soon.

"Mac was headed toward her last I saw." Rawls stretched up on his toes to drag down an oblong black plastic box with a huge red X stretching from corner to corner across the plastic top.

"Mackenzie?" Her voice rose with incredulity. The bad-tempered, woman-hating, chain-cursing commander had raced over to help Amy and her boys? And under his own volition? Wow . . . just wow.

With a snort, Rawls shoved the black box into the duffle bag, added several devices that were similar to binoculars but mounted on plastic headpieces, and then zipped the bag up. "Mac's not nearly as surly as y'all are convinced. Push comes to shove—he's the first to jump between a civilian and a bullet. That goes a hundredfold for women and rug rats."

Faith raised her eyebrows. "I find that hard to believe."

With a light chuckle, Rawls lifted the duffle bag and slung it over his shoulder. "I'm not sayin' he doesn't make misjudgin' him downright easy. But actions speak louder than words, and he's over there protectin' Amy and her rug rats right now."

They'd have to agree to disagree on that particular cliché. In her opinion, words carried as much weight as action, and she had plenty of empirical data proving that Mackenzie's loud and often nasty vocalizations marked him as a misogynistic jackass. Not that they had time for such an argument.

"I can carry something," she offered, deliberately changing the subject.

"You sure can." He handed her a heavy-duty metal flashlight and picked up a second one for himself. "I've grabbed some NVDs in case we need them, but the flashlights will do us for now."

"NVDs?"

"Night vision devices. They'll give our vision back if the torches go dark." He paused to scan her frame, his gaze lingering on her face. "How you holdin' up? That ticker of yours behavin'?"

She schooled her face into sincerity, held his gaze, and nodded. "It's ticking away just fine."

Which wasn't a complete lie. At the moment it was beating normally. And he hadn't asked about earlier incidents . . .

Instead of easing, the tension on his face intensified. He frowned. "How much Cordarone you got left?"

The pill count wasn't something she could exaggerate. Not when he needed to know where the pill was in case her heart flatlined and she lost consciousness or couldn't get to the tablet herself.

"I've got one left. It's in my right pocket." She offered him a tight smile. "I guess we can't count on Wolf making a medicine drop under the circumstances."

A moment of concern touched his face, but he quickly buried it. His blond hair flashed beneath the overhead lights as he shook his head.

"Not the original drop. But we've got the sat phone. After we rendezvous with the others in the hub, we'll call him. Fill him in." He offered her a reassuring smile. "Hell, knowin' Kait's big bad friend, he'll probably grab the closest chopper and mount a rescue."

It was doubtful the phone would work in the tunnels, let alone the hub—where the various tunnels intersected. The hub was a natural stone cavern seven hundred feet or so from where they currently stood. The rock would block the satellite signal, making the phone ineffectual.

But she swallowed her reservations and tried to project confidence. There was nothing they could do about their lack of outside communication at the moment. At least they had the phone on them. Worst case, someone could sneak outside and send off an SOS.

"Flashlights on," Rawls said, lifting the duffle bag from his shoulder and easing the strap over his head until it hung from his upper back. "Stay on my six. Yell if I go too fast."

He didn't wait for her confirmation, just turned toward the steel shelf beside them and pressed a lever on the inside of the top rung. He stepped back as the metal unit jerked and slid out from the wall, revealing a thick, black hole. Once it stopped moving, he dragged it back another foot.

"Pull the door shut behind you." He grunted with satisfaction as the beam from his flashlight ruptured the profuse darkness.

With a deep breath, Faith followed his bent back and the jiggling canvas bag into the tight enclosure. Bending slightly herself, she stopped just inside the tunnel, her flashlight beam bouncing across water-streaked concrete walls. The thick metal door with its attached shelf slid back into place with remarkable ease and hardly any effort on her part. She aimed the flashlight at the door's bottom, it had to be mounted on some kind of roller.

"You need help?"

A hint of impatience sharpened the question. Apparently she wasn't going fast enough for his liking.

"I got it," she said, turning to follow him.

This obviously wasn't the time to let her curiosity get the better of her. Not that they were in any real danger being twenty feet beneath the ground and protected by a multitude of locked, electronically sealed steel doors.

She studied the walls, floor, and ceiling of their current tunnel as they struck out for the rendezvous point. It looked like some kind of huge concrete pipe—the thick, round ones used for sewers or flash-flood drainage. It was tall enough for her to stand upright, although there wasn't enough room for the two of them to walk side by side.

The cylinders must have been difficult to handle, considering how huge they were and the fact that they were buried so deep in the ground. Installing them would have required excavation equipment, which must have been brought in by helicopter since the camp was so removed.

"You okay back there?" Rawls's voice broke into her thoughts.

"I'm fine," she said, looking up. A metallic shimmer drew her attention toward his left hip.

She squinted to get a better look in the murky light.

That was odd . . . it almost looked like the rifle hanging from his shoulder beneath the duffle bag had drifted up and was pointing at her. It had to be a trick of the flashlight beam bouncing off the concrete at her feet. Lifting the torch, she aimed it toward his side and the offending rifle, which was quite visibly hovering there—in midair—pointing directly at her. With a stifled shriek she jerked hard to the right, colliding with the wall.

He stopped hard, and turned, the duffle bag scraping against the concrete. "What's wrong?"

"That wasn't funny!" she snapped, aiming the flashlight at his face. Her heart skipped a beat, only to take two in rapid succession. Groaning beneath her breath, she fought to get her breathing and heart rate back under control. "Is that thing loaded?"

Of course it isn't loaded. There's no way he'd point a loaded gun at you!

Then again, it wasn't like him to point an unloaded gun at anyone either. What's gotten into the man?

Her heart stuttered, then resumed business as usual.

With a deep, tension-releasing breath, she relaxed.

"What are you talkin' about?" A scowl slammed down over his forehead, and his eyes looked burningly blue.

"The rifle," she shot back. "I don't appreciate the joke."

"What joke?" His voice rose to as close to a shout as she'd ever heard from him.

"Pointing the rifle at me. It's not funny. If anyone should know how dangerous aiming a gun at someone can be . . ." She trailed off to glare.

He froze, his expression falling perfectly still. A fraction of a second later an explosion of pure rage lit his face. The blue of his eyes burned so bright they looked almost incandescent.

"Pachico!" he roared, turning in a slow circle. "Goddamn you!"

Pachico?

The name—somehow she knew it was a name—echoed in the tight confines of the channel. She puckered her forehead, repeating the word beneath her breath. It was so familiar, lingering there at the back of her mind. She knew it from somewhere . . .

And then it burst into her head like the flashlight beam had illuminated a deep, dark, repressed memory.

Pachico . . .

A bald head wrapped in a bloody bandage . . . a long face . . . muddy brown, resigned eyes . . . a huge knife sticking out of a thin chest. A thin trail of crimson trickling down a white dress shirt . . .

Pachico.

The man Jillian had killed at Wolf's Sierra Nevada home six days earlier. The man whose body had been cremated courtesy of a helicopter-to-house missile. *Six days?* Good lord, it felt like sixty.

She shook her head in disbelief. Pachico was dead. So why was Rawls bawling the man out. Because that's what the tone of his voice sounded like. Not to mention he'd swung around as though searching for the culprit. He was reading someone the riot act. Only the man he was searching for was dead. Very, very dead.

A chill winnowed through her, and it had nothing to do with their current predicament—running for their lives, twenty feet beneath ground.

"Why are you shouting a dead man's name?" The question tumbled out as her flashlight beam fluttered over his face.

It seemed to take a second for her query to register, and then his face went blank again. But she knew the answer.

"A ghost? You're seeing ghosts?" It was the only thing that made sense. The only reason he'd be yelling a dead man's name.

This was his problem? His hallucination? A ghost? He was seeing dead people? Every single comedic rip-off of *The Sixth Sense* reeled through her mind. Hysterical laughter bubbled up her throat and tried to escape out her mouth.

Except . . . there wasn't an ounce of levity on his face. Instead, it looked frozen, almost fragile. Which was crazy when describing a six-foot-four hunk of muscle and strength. But yeah, he looked vulnerable, as though the wrong reaction from her could shatter him into a billion pieces and nothing would ever be right between them ever again.

The urge to laugh vanished.

"That's what's going on, isn't it? You're seeing ghosts." She couldn't quite bring herself to call them dead people—even though that was what they technically were. "Talk to me."

Blue eyes scanned her face, lingered, and the intensity softened. "Ghost. Singular."

She nodded, trying to maintain an open expression, even though every synapse in her brain had warped straight into denial. *Ghosts? Seriously?* "Pachico?"

It made sense that if he were suffering from a psychotic break, his delusions would center on the last person he'd tried to save, only to helplessly watch die.

"That would be the one." He shot her a wry glance. "Relax. I don't expect y'all to believe me." He stared at the ground for a moment before running a tense hand through his hair. "Hell. I wouldn't believe it myself if it wasn't happenin' to me."

Okay, so her open expression must not be so open after all. "I'm sorry . . . it's just . . . there's no scientific evidence to support the existence of ghosts."

His head pulled back. After a nanosecond, his eyebrows rose. "You don't say. Well, *I* wasn't touchin' that rifle. So if it was pointin' at you, as *you* claim, I reckon that's about as scientific as it'll get." He stroked a palm down his lean face. "The bastar—" He caught himself with a grimace and shot her an apologetic glance. "*Pachico* has been manipulatin' objects in the physical world, and he's gettin' better at it each time. We're damn lucky he hasn't pulled a trigger yet."

"The physical world?"

A fleeting expression of annoyance touched his face, as though he'd said more than he'd intended.

"He's incorporeal. A regular Casper. At first he just passed through everything. But now that he's figured out how to manipulate physical objects—" He broke off with a shrug hard enough to lift the duffle bag up his back.

Manipulate physical objects . . .

His explanation echoed in her mind. Was he talking about the cookies? Or the cookie rack? Had he built a bunch of delusional scenarios around simple accidents? Or even unconscious actions on his own part?

The rifle had been pointing at her. She was certain of that. But his hand or elbow could have been manipulating it outside of her line of sight.

Another chill sliced through her. There were plenty of cases where people in the midst of a psychotic break experienced delusions, hallucinations, and memory lapses.

She jolted as he barked out an unamused laugh.

"And this is exactly why I haven't told anyone. You're afraid of me now." Beneath the exasperation in his voice lurked that earlier vulnerability.

"I'm not afraid of you." The reassurance came unbidden, but she realized it was true.

She wasn't afraid of him. Looking back, he'd done everything possible to protect the camp from his perceived threat—even to the point of abandoning his comfy bed for the cold, damp forest.

Curiosity stirred as his actions started to make sense. "Was that why you left camp? Why you avoided everyone? To protect us from this ghost? How does that work? Why doesn't it just harass us at will, whether you're there or not?"

"Because it's tethered to me somehow," he snapped, a harried expression settling over his face. "And we need to move. If the time frame holds true, it'll be gone ten, maybe fifteen minutes. Time enough to reach the hub."

"It's gone?" What fascinating, intricate scenarios had his mind built around this delusion? "It just periodically disappears? Why?"

He ignored the question in favor of turning and stalking off. Faith followed, watching the stiff line of his spine, or at least what she could see of it below the canvas bag. He obviously didn't want to talk about his ghost. But maybe that's exactly what he needed. A chance to examine the inconsistencies inherent in his delusion through an outside perspective.

"So when did he appear?" she asked.

Although he didn't respond, from the catch in his stride, he'd obviously heard her.

"We might as well talk about it," she offered after a few minutes of pregnant silence. "It will give us something to concentrate on while we're making our way to the hub."

"We're not on a damn nature hike, Faith." The chill in his voice was enough to frost the air surrounding them. "Nor do we know what kind of listenin' devices they have topside. Less chatter, more speed."

Well that certainly shut down any chance of conversation. Although he did have a point. Maybe she had been a bit premature in her assessment of the danger facing them. Her heart jumped into double time, but quickly dropped down to normal again. Her hand reached for her pocket and the little white pill nestled within, but she hesitated. Normally she'd have taken an extra dose when her heart got this erratic. But this was her last pill. If she took it now, and later in the day things got worse . . . Scowling, she dropped her hand and increased her speed, paying close attention to her heartbeat.

They approached a section of the tunnel where the concrete walls and ceiling leaked dirt through thick cracks. Thick, fibrous roots squeezed through the fissures. They must have reached the tree line.

From above, a muffled explosion sounded. The ground rolled beneath Faith's feet, and the concrete walls to her right and left shook. A low groan rumbled from the ceiling, and the trickle of dirt and crumbling concrete increased to a stream.

"Son of a— The ceiling's giving," Rawls yelled. Half turning, he reached out and snagged Faith's arm. "Move!"

The deep moan above them shifted to a shriek and then a crack.

"Move! Move!" Rawls bolted forward, dragging her along.

Another crack. A chunk of concrete slammed into her shoulder. Rawls yanked her arm—hard—jerking her out of the sudden avalanche of dirt. She felt, rather than heard, the pop as her shoulder separated. Her heart jumped into rapid, irregular spasms. There was a second—maybe two—of gravid numbness from her chest into her shoulder and down her right arm. And then raw, burning agony swallowed her from the inside out.

Vaguely, she heard the scream break from her. Heard Rawls's frantic swearing. Somehow his cursing was important, but her foggy mind couldn't quite pinpoint why. Her vision blurred, black squiggles and pinpricks shrouding her sight.

The agony consumed her, restricted her chest until her lungs refused to draw breath. Turned her head heavy and thick. Incapable of thought or reason.

"Faith." An urgent voice drew her back to consciousness. "Come on, baby. Stay with me."

Baby?

Distantly she felt something thick and hard, driving into her pocket. His hand. In her pocket. Searching for the Cordarone.

Her heart. Ah this was bad . . . very bad.

Fear swelled.

She had to be awake to swallow the pill.

She tried to focus, to drag herself up from the whirlwind sucking her into the darkness. To remain awake long enough to swallow that one tiny pill. To swallow her one chance at life.

"Goddamn son of a motherfuckin' bitch."

She must have already lost the battle, because she was dreaming. They were Mac's words, but Rawls's raw voice.

And then that dusky whirlwind caught her, dragging her into the smooth, velvet blackness.

Chapter Eleven

THE FIRST MISSILE STRUCK THE COMPOUND WITHIN FIVE MINUTES OF them entering the tunnel, by Mac's estimation. He spun to face Amy and her kids as the muffled explosion shook the terrain above their heads. The ground heaved beneath his feet.

At the youngest child's shrill cry, he lunged forward, grabbed both boys, and pressed them to the ground. Crouching over their small bodies, he tensed—waiting. But the walls and ceiling held.

After the ground stopped shaking, he dragged the boys back up and tossed an urgent glance their mother's way. "Let's move."

More detonations rocked them.

The kids must have been scared shitless as they didn't even squeak. Even the youngest, and they all knew how much that kid liked his voice.

He didn't have to tell Amy twice. As he hustled the boys forward, his flashlight beam illuminating their path, he heard her footsteps and heavy breathing behind him. At least she was keeping up.

On the one hand, it was reassuring to know that Rawls hadn't hallucinated the attack force surrounding them. On the other hand, if the assholes above continued to hammer the compound with air-to-ground missiles, there was a good chance the tunnel would collapse before they could reach the hub. In which case, bye-bye to all of them.

Fuck . . . if those assholes' intentions had been to incinerate the compound, why bother bringing in the ground crew?

The obvious answer was that they'd learned from their mistakes. This time around, survivors wouldn't find refuge in the woods. Whoever escaped the missiles would be picked off by the snipers surrounding the camp. It would have worked too—if they'd taken to the woods.

Thank God—or in this case, Wolf—for the tunnels. His foresight had proved to be a lifesaver. Hell, multiple lifesavers.

Assuming his men and the civilians they protected had made it into the tunnels. And assuming the aforementioned tunnels hadn't collapsed on anyone.

He scowled, tension locking his muscles tight. The cabins were gone. He had no doubt of that. From the sound of the fireworks over-head, those motherfuckers were blowing every fucking building in the compound. He could track the destruction by the location of the explo-sions. First the lodge, then Zane's cabin, followed by the one he'd shared with Rawls.

Motherfucker.

If anyone had been stuck aboveground when those missiles hit, they'd be dead by now.

He shoved that worry aside and concentrated on their immediate predicament.

So far the tunnel they were in was holding up remarkably well. No doubt its stability had much to do with the fact that the concrete cylinder was buffered by twenty feet of soil. With luck, they would make it to the hub, and its natural rock protection, before the stress started to show.

Slowly the explosions above dwindled. Several minutes of heavy breathing and pounding feet followed. Christ, they were making more noise than a crowd of panicked civilians. He strained to hear anything from aboveground.

Had the chopper left yet?

"Do you think the helicopter left?" Amy rasped from behind him.

His skin tightened as an eerie chill worked its way through him. Her question was identical to his. Apparently they'd been wondering the same thing at exactly the same moment.

Doesn't mean a damn thing.

A milky, wavering light down the tunnel brought a welcome distraction.

"Wait." He slowed, easing his weapon from his waistband. "We've got company."

"Our people?" Amy asked in a low voice from behind him.

"Probably." But it never paid to take chances, and they couldn't be a hundred percent certain the tunnel system had remained secret. He sighted his flashlight and Glock on the bouncing circle of light.

If the kids really had been physically tagged, and the tracking devices were still transmitting, then the bastards above them knew their targets were belowground. Hell, maybe someone had gotten lucky, stumbled across an outside entrance in the woods, and come looking for them.

In which case they were about to be welcomed with a couple rounds to the chest.

"Sweet Jesus."

The horrified whisper leaked around the flashlight in his mouth as Rawls stared down at the fresh mound of dirt—the dirt that had buried Faith's last dose of Cordarone. He'd had the pill out and on the way to her lips when a section of the ceiling had sheared off, dropping a fresh load of earth on top of them and knocking the capsule from his fingers.

Even if he had the time, sifting through that mound of dirt in the hope of finding one small pill was a useless endeavor. And he couldn't afford the time.

Partially buried beneath the flash flood of soil and chunks of concrete, Faith released the softest of sighs and slumped against her makeshift bed. The sound jolted him from his disbelieving stupor. He lifted his chin until the beam of light caressed her face, and pressed his fingers against the side of her neck. Her pulse was thready. But she was alive. Thank Christ for that at least.

But they needed to get out of there. The crumbling concrete would weaken the ceiling even further—it wouldn't be long before the whole damn thing came down.

He started to reach for the duffle bag beside him, when another series of detonations rocked the compound above. The tunnel rocked and rolled, and that ominous groan rumbled above.

There isn't time to grab Faith and the bag.

He switched directions in midswoop and dragged Faith's good arm over his shoulder. Lifting her into a fireman's hold, he shot to his feet, flashlight still clenched between his teeth. Dirt cascaded down on him like a waterfall, burying his legs up to his thighs.

His muscles hot and fluid beneath a burst of adrenaline, he drove forward, pushing the earth to the sides and front, carrying Faith's silent, still body along with him. He broke through the front of the dam as another explosion rocked the world above.

Those bastards sure do love their explosions.

The tunnel shuddered, the walls and floor contracting and then expanding beneath the shock wave.

The first two detonations had almost buried them alive; they might not survive this third one. With every ounce of strength he possessed, he plowed forward, his arm a vise around Faith's legs, straining to catch the slightest sound from the limp body atop his shoulders.

Nothing.

Crackcrackcrackcrackcrack—

The series of sharp pops overhead plunged ice into his veins. He lunged forward, his flashlight beam bouncing from undulating wall to undulating wall.

The cracks gave way to groans, which escalated to a deafening roar. Thud after thud sounded behind him, followed by an eerie sibilant hiss. A cloud of dust rolled over and past him, the gray flecks swirling within the halo of his flashlight beam. Silence fell. Shrouded the tunnel in stillness.

Deep. Dense. Stillness.

His lungs laboring to find air within the thick, dry mist, Rawls milked another burst of speed from his heavy legs. The explosions had stopped. So had the rocking and rolling under his feet. Beyond the drifting dust particles, the tunnel walls were hazy, but motionless.

He concentrated on Faith's dead weight atop his shoulders. Her lifeless, silent body. No movement. No sound. He needed to assess her condition. But while the imminent threat of burial had faded, it hadn't vanished completely. One more blast directly above could jolt the structure into collapse again. If he stopped to assess her condition, he could be sacrificing both their lives.

They needed to navigate the rest of the tunnel and get into the safety of the caves ASAP. Their lives might depend on it.

Gritting his teeth, he kept moving.

But the body he was rushing to safety showed no signs of life. What was the use of escaping to the hub if Faith didn't survive the journey? His scalp tightened. Burned.

Fuck. Fuck. Fuck.

Against every deep-seated instinct, he dropped to a walk and then stopped completely. He crouched, bending forward, easing her off his shoulders and onto the ground. Her face looked blue, almost frozen beneath the harsh white stream of the flashlight. Her pulse was weak. Erratic. Barely there.

Her best chance of survival without the Cordarone was a shot of adrenaline. Which was in the med kit, in the duffle bag.

Jesus. Don't let it be buried.

Ripping the flashlight from his mouth, he shot to his feet and raced back down the corridor, praying the collapse hadn't been as bad as he feared. Praying he could locate the duffle bag and get back to her in time.

Around the first bend the flashlight illuminated a wall-to-ceiling blockage of soil and concrete.

Jesus. Jesus. Jesus.

He spun and sprinted back to Faith. The duffle bag was somewhere past that blockage. Likely buried as well. Unattainable.

He'd have to work with what he had . . . which wasn't much.

Sweet Jesus, Kait. I could sure use you now.

Faith lay where he'd left her. He checked her pulse.

Nothing.

Checked her breathing.

Nothing.

Fuck.Fuck.Fuck.

His hands and legs suddenly shaking, he knelt, set the flashlight on the ground, and pressed his ear to her chest.

Nothing.

Fuck.Fuck.Fuck.

A chasm opened in his chest, threatened to suck the hope from him.

Tilting her chin back, he opened her mouth, made sure her tongue was out of the way, and blew steadily down her throat. Her lips were soft against his, supple.

Heartbreakingly lifeless.

Lifting his head, he stared at her inanimate face and started chest compressions. "Come on, baby."

His chest aching, memories flooded him.

The sweetest little ass rubbing against his crotch . . . luscious, chocolate-chip-seasoned lips matching his mouth kiss for kiss . . . hot, moist breath bathing his neck . . . solemn, gentle eyes caressing his face. "I'm not afraid of you."

She was the oddest mixture of strength, spunk, and fragility. Curiosity and intellectual stubbornness. Sultry hunger and innocence.

And he wasn't going to let her go.

He bent to breathe into her mouth again. "Come on, baby. Come on. Don't leave me, now."

"Mom! Mom! There's someone coming," Benji all but shouted from behind Mac. Apparently the absence of bombing had brought a return to confidence, which equaled a return to volume.

"Brendan, watch Benji," Amy's calm voice said from behind him.

"I got him," her equally calm son said.

Her *eleven*-year-old son. It was odd how mature for his age one of Amy's kids was, while the other child acted so damn young.

A breath later Amy squeezed into the space next to him, her gun braced over her flashlight. He considered ordering the flashlight off. But hell, the glare might prove blinding and provide some protection if that beam bouncing toward them didn't belong to one of his men.

He shifted slightly to the right, giving her more room, trying not to breathe, so he didn't draw any of that damn fresh scent into his lungs. He'd been in similar situations more times than he cared to remember, shoulder to shoulder with a teammate, watching an unidentified Tango creep closer. But motherfucker, he'd never paid attention to the smell of his teammate's hair, or waited for the brush of their bare skin against his arm.

He sensed the pressure invading the slim body beside him, but doubted it sprang from the same emotion constricting his muscles.

He recognized the tight, clipped stride within the brilliant halo of light before the face registered. Amy's sudden exhale proved she'd recognized Cosky as well. He straightened and stepped forward—relieved to escape the warmth of Amy's body.

His kryptonite turned to address the darkness behind them. "It's okay," she called softly. "It's Lieutenant Simcosky."

And Kait, Mac realized, as another figure, slightly shorter and much more slender, trailed behind his lieutenant.

"But we're hiding," Benji yelled back, pure enthusiasm in his voice. "They're supposed to find us!"

Ah, Brendan must have told the little guy they were playing hide and seek. Good call, turning the crisis into a game. But Christ, it made him feel old to see how quickly the kids had recovered.

Mac moved forward, meeting Cosky midway. Since the pair was coming from the direction of the hub, they must have already been there. At least he'd be getting a sitrep.

"You made it to the hub?" he asked once Cos was in hearing distance. At his lieutenant's nod, Mac grunted in satisfaction. "Who's accounted for?"

"Now that we've located you four—everyone but Rawls and Faith."

Mac scowled. Rawls had been headed to the main lodge from their cabin. But what if the doc hadn't been there? He could easily imagine his corpsman's Southern honor getting him into trouble if he had to track the damn woman down.

He turned to Amy. "Any idea where that roommate of yours disappeared to?"

"She said she was going to the kitchen to get a start on breakfast."

Which was where Rawls had been headed.

Mac froze, as the next possibility struck. He exchanged grim looks with Cosky. "How did your tunnel hold up during the raid?"

Cosky frowned. "Fair. We had some leakage where the tree roots had invaded the concrete, but not enough to pose a problem."

There hadn't been any roots in this section of the tunnel. What if Rawls and the doc hadn't been so lucky?

Son of a bitch.

From the grim mask stamped across Cosky's face, he shared Mac's concern.

"Kait and I will backtrack. Look for them," Cosky said on a sharp turn.

Mac started to follow, eager to remove himself from his current uncomfortable partnership, but—motherfucker—he couldn't just abandon her twenty feet underground with two rambunctious boys.

"Problem?" Amy asked in a low voice, apparently picking up on something in Mac's tense silence.

"Nah, they're headed back to look for Rawls and the doc. The hub's up ahead. We'll wait for them there." He fought to keep the frustration out of his tone.

"I'm perfectly capable of protecting myself and my children," Amy pointed out in an edgy voice. "Go look for Rawls and Faith. The sooner you find them, the faster we can get out of here."

Well, she'd sure as hell picked something up from him. Something she didn't appreciate.

Too fucking bad.

But he bit back the immediate bad news.

Until they figured out how their hidey-hole had been located, they couldn't afford to take the kids anywhere. Not if there was any chance they were bugged and transmitting their location.

With a ragged exhale, Rawls straightened, drawing in a deep breath to refill his starving lungs. Ignoring the raw ache in his lower back and the sweat trickling down his cheeks and stinging his eyes, he started the next round of chest compressions.

He stared into Faith's peaceful face as the heel of his hands pressed hard against her chest and then lifted, repeating the rhythm over and over again. A dull blanket of defeat dragged at him, tried to smother him beneath exhaustion and loss. While he'd managed to jolt her heart into action a couple of times, the beat had been too erratic to sustain any rhythm on its own. Within seconds it had stalled. Again. And again.

While he'd been giving her the standard two breaths per thirty compressions for a one-person rescue scenario, it was doubtful she'd received enough oxygen to supply the depleted stores in her brain. Not without breathing on her own. Even if he could get her heart started and keep it pumping, in all likelihood she'd never wake up.

In all likelihood, she was already gone.

Sarah's bleached, empty face loomed in his mind. He'd failed Faith as clearly as he'd failed his sister.

He should have tried to reach Kait . . . But Kait was Christ knew where. To find her meant leaving Faith alone. *Alone*—for Christ knew how long.

Long enough to die. That was for certain. To die all alone, in a dark, cold tunnel.

He hadn't been able to tear himself away. Instead, he'd promised himself that someone would come looking for them when they didn't show up at the hub. Someone would find them and then leave to get Kait. Kait would fix her. Kait would fix everything . . . he just had to keep Faith's heart beating and her lungs full of air long enough for Kait to arrive.

He groaned out a shallow breath. A dull roar of defeat vibrating through him.

. . . Wrong decision. I should have left her. Found Kait. By refusing to leave, I killed her. Just like I killed Sarah.

He'd lost people before. On the field of battle, it happened. You learned to live with it. But this . . . this was different. It sheared at his soul. Not just the loss of life, but the loss of hope and possibilities and the chance at a future he'd sensed but hadn't had a chance to explore.

Yet.

He hadn't explored it yet. But it had lingered there in the back of his mind. Something to pursue after he'd exorcised his ghost and got his life back on track. A bright shiny possibility waiting for him in the future.

She'd wanted him. He'd known that. She hadn't tried to hide it. Hadn't pushed it, but hadn't hid it either. And he'd noticed. Sweet Jesus, had he ever noticed. And been tempted, only to haul back because of the circumstances. She'd wanted him. And he wanted her. They could have started with that.

Not that it mattered anymore.

Turning his face toward his shoulder, he rubbed his stinging eyes on his shirt. But the cloth was soaked with sweat and did nothing to absorb the trickles of perspiration or liberate the sting from his eyes.

Might as well stop the compressions. She's gone. It's too damn late.

He lifted his hands, but leaned down, opened her mouth, closed off her nose, and gave her two more lungfuls of air.

He straightened to the sound of footsteps behind him.

"Rawls?" It was Cosky's voice.

"Yeah." A puddle of light closed over him as he started back in with the chest compressions. "Kait with you?"

His question was lethargic. Without hope.

Too late. Too late. Too late.

The lament pulsed in time to the beat of his hands on her chest.

"I'm here." Kait squeezed past him, stepped over Faith's limp body, and knelt across from Rawls. "What happened?"

"Her heart stopped." The dullness graying his world echoed in his voice.

"How long has she been . . . out?" Kait asked, her tentative voice ripe with concern. "If it's been too long, I might not be able to help."

She meant dead. How long had she been dead?

Too damn long.

"I know." He forced his palms to relinquish their claim on her chest and sat back, watching Kait's slender hands with their long, tapered fingers replace his as Faith's guardian against that silvery, transparent world he'd escaped.

"Cosky. I need you on this," Kait said, settling onto her knees and pressing her hands against Faith's still chest.

A vague memory stirred in Rawls's mind. Kait's voice.

"The odds are much better if we wait until Cosky returns. His touch amplifies my healing. Together we can heal injuries much faster. That's how we managed to save you."

His mind warped back to that eerie otherworld. He hadn't been simply injured. He'd been dead. Kait and Cosky had dragged him back. Why not Faith as well? Hope swelled as he shuffled to the side and pulled back, making room for Cosky's taller, wider frame.

Abruptly he remembered Faith's dislocated shoulder. Best to fix that before Kait got cranking so the healing could work its magic on her joint as well.

"Hold this," Cosky said as soon as Rawls had taken care of Faith's shoulder. He handed over a flashlight and knelt across from Kait, covering the top of her hands with his palms.

Rawls directed Cosky's flashlight toward the drama taking place on the ground. The beam from his own flashlight, still upright and propped against Faith's knee, ricocheted down from the tunnel's ceiling, intensifying the spotlight haloing Faith's prone form.

His mind flashed back to his stint on the ground, with Cosky and Kait hovering over him. Beneath the backdrop of a gloomy liquid night, they'd been glowing. A bright current of white running from their arms into their hands and plunging into his chest.

He frowned, the tension expanding, pressing against the hope. The flashlights were so bright they drowned any supernatural glow. If Kait and Cos were glowing, he couldn't tell.

"Is it workin'?" The question finally burst from him.

"I think so." Kait sounded drugged.

Another minute ticked past while Kait's face and Cosky's hands turned redder and redder. He stared at Faith's chest so hard his eyes burned. No movement. At least none that he could see.

Come on, baby. Come on.

He concentrated, willed life into her.

Still nothing.

The dullness from earlier returned, started to compress the hope.

Come on, sweetheart. Come back to me.

Cosky's hands lifted slightly. Rawls's gaze locked on them, his breath caught in his tight throat.

Come on, come on, come on.

Had it been his imagination? Wishful thinking? But no—there. Another flutter of movement and then a steady rise and fall of hands and chest as Faith's heart and lungs went to work again.

The breath locked in his throat escaped in a whoosh.

She was breathing. Breathing on her own.

The seconds ticked on again.

"That's enough." Cosky pulled Kait's wrists away.

"What the—" Rawls jolted forward. Faith needed more time beneath Kait's hands. While it looked like the combined healing had healed her heart, what about her brain? Had it reversed the damage caused by oxygen depletion? "Let her keep goin'."

"No," Cosky snapped, still holding Kait's hands. He rose to his feet, taking Kait with him. "She'll drain herself completely trying to help."

"Maybe you should let her make that decision," Rawls snapped back, shooting a quick look at the easy rise and fall of Faith's chest.

"I said no. Kait's done." Cosky's voice hardened.

But Faith needed more time, damn it. He crowded closer to Kait and rustled up a coaxing tone. "Darlin', just a bit more . . ."

His voice trailed off at the sight of her face.

Her brown eyes were glazed. Exhaustion carved deep crevices into the hollows of her face.

She looked as drained and sick as she had way back in the parking lot when she'd healed Cosky's trashed knee. The memory morphed into déjà vu as her legs folded and she started to collapse. He leapt forward, catching her before she hit the ground.

"Son of a bitch." Cosky's voice rose grimly. He all but ripped her from Rawls's arms. "You take care of your charge. I'll take care of mine."

Rawls surrendered his grip, guilt rising. Cos had been right. Kait wasn't in any condition to continue the healing. He could only hope that Faith had received enough of whatever magical elixir flowed through Kait's hands to heal her brain as well as her heart.

Chapter Twelve

THE HUB WAS EXACTLY AS MAC REMEMBERED IT. JAGGED ROCK WALLS, bumpy rock floor. Fifteen by twenty feet in diameter. The tunnels fed into each other, until eventually, a single corridor spilled into the hub. At the moment, the rendezvous point looked smaller than it actually was. But then, a multitude of clustered bodies and flickering flashlights tended to have that effect on any given space.

Mac scanned faces as he entered the cavern. As Cosky had indicated, everyone was accounted for except Rawls and the doc. He frowned. He hoped like hell Cosky had found the pair, and not under the dire circumstances they'd both assumed.

He nodded toward Zane before beckoning him over. With their rock fortress encasing them, they were safe enough for the moment. They could afford to take a breather, figure out where the hell to go from here, and how the hell to get there.

Once Cosky returned, with or without Rawls, they'd discuss heading topside to take those bastards on. Do some damage of their own.

They could sure use a fountain of information—even a reluctant one.

Of course, someone would have to stay with the women and children, provide some protection in case the motherfuckers above found their way below. Not that there was much chance of that—although . . .

He scowled as Amy's youngest pushed past him and made a beeline for a jagged edge of the rock wall. If he was right, and the boys were tagged, those bastards might know they were underground and start looking for a passageway.

"Look how much it sparkles, Mom! I bet it's a diamond. Grampa says they come from the ground."

Zane joined him. "Glad to see you guys made it out in one piece." He glanced over Mac's shoulder.

"Cos went back to look for Rawls." Mac acknowledged the implied question.

Zane simply nodded. He glanced at the child enthusiastically prying at the sparkling chunk on the wall. "You realize they must have been followed."

"No shit." Mac rolled his shoulders, lowering his voice as well.

"They changed clothes, right down to their skin," Amy pointed out from behind them in that flat, conversational tone of voice that annoyed him profoundly. Why the hell it affected him so adversely, he had no clue, but he gritted his teeth and swallowed his instinctive retort.

"Then the tracking device must be somewhere on their bodies, not their clothes." He managed to remind her in an even voice.

"Which they haven't noticed? And I didn't notice when I helped them change." Amy's voice flattened even further.

Zane glanced between the two of them and scrubbed a palm over his head. "Maybe they were drugged, and the device was inserted while they were out. If it's small enough, it could be inserted in a filling, or injected directly into their skin."

She snorted, rolling her eyes toward the ceiling. "Or maybe it's just a coincidence. They haven't been out of my brother's or my parents' sight. Believe me, if the boys had been injected with something, we would have known about it."

Zane traded a cautious glance with Mac, before tilting his head and facing off against their redheaded momma bear. "Maybe . . . but it won't hurt to check the boys out."

Mac had no clue what Amy's response would be. Normally she was the most reasonable, calm-headed woman he knew—until, apparently, her maternal instincts kicked in.

"Could it have been inserted during a flu shot?" Brendan broke in.

"A flu shot." Amy's voice sharpened. "Did someone give you one recently?"

"Yeah, some doctor friend of Uncle Clay's." Her son turned a considering look on his left forearm. "It hurt too, swelled way up."

"You had a flu shot before school started." Amy's eyes narrowed. "Did Clay say why you needed another one?"

Because those bastards had needed a means of injecting a tracking chip, and a flu shot made the perfect cover. Mac stirred restlessly. Was the woman really so dense she didn't see that? But he immediately jettisoned that conclusion. Amy wasn't stupid. Far too loyal maybe, particularly to family—but hardly stupid.

"The doctor said there'd been an outbreak at school, and they wouldn't let us back in without the current inoculation against it." He paused to cock his head as though he was thinking back. "Uncle Clay stayed with us to make sure there wasn't any funny business."

Amy raised her gaze to Mac's face.

"There've been a lot of flu strains this year, so it's possible," she said, but her eyes were troubled. "Clay wouldn't do anything to hurt the boys. He may not always show it, but we're family. He loves us."

Mac swallowed his snort. From what he'd seen in the quarry, *Uncle Clay* was a rat-asshole. Not that he was going to tell her that.

"Of course, it's possible there was an actual flu outbreak." Zane calmly took the reins of the conversation. "It's also possible a microchip was inserted during that shot."

"Okay." Her chin lifted, her gaze shifting back to Mac. "What are our options?"

There was only one option, and she wasn't going to like it. "We know where the shot was given. We take a look. See if something's in there."

The words just hung there, echoing in the thick, dusty air.

And then her chin tightened and tilted. "And how, exactly, do you suggest we do that?"

She already knew, of course. There was only one fucking way to see inside flesh without an MRI or X-ray machine.

"We cut into the spot and look. If there's something there, we remove it." He hardened his face and tone. It wasn't like he wanted to cut into the kid's arm. Regardless of what she apparently thought, he didn't enjoy torturing children.

"Without a doctor? Or sanitary conditions? Or the necessary equipment? Absolutely not."

"He's right, Mom," Brendan said, stepping up beside them and instantly dissolving the standoff.

There was no way that adult tone had come from an eleven-year-old—more like a seasoned warrior with numerous campaigns under his belt.

Brendan shifted to face Mac, holding his gaze with steady dark eyes. The expression on the kid's face was as old as his voice. "The shot left a scab. It will be easy to find the injection site."

Respect stirred. Christ, if the kid was this self-possessed at eleven, what the hell was he going to be like at thirty? At forty?

He was going to be pretty damn formidable, that much was certain.

Amy's face tightened, she glanced at her son's calm, resolute face, but before she had a chance to countermand him, Jude stepped forward.

"This will not be necessary. Wolf comes. He will take us to *betee3oo hohe'*. We have the facilities there to remove such devices."

Mac scowled. *Betee3oo hohe'*? *Where the bloody fuck is that?*

And then the first part of Jude's speech hit him. Wolf was coming? When the hell had that happened, and how did Jude know? Had he called Wolf somehow? If so, how? The radios didn't have enough range . . . and the sat phone was in the kitchen. Rawls wouldn't have had time to contact Wolf above the tunnels, and there wouldn't have been enough reception below—besides, how would he have gotten the info to Jude? If it had come via radio, everyone would have heard it—including the assholes attacking them. A third possibility struck. Did Jude have a sat phone? Had he called his CO prior to escaping into the tunnels?

He shot a questioning look at Zane, who shrugged.

With an irritated roll of his shoulders, Mac dropped the questions. From past experience, he knew the impassive bastard wouldn't answer unless it suited him.

"If the boys are tagged, our enemies will follow you back to your base," Mac said. Not that the Arapaho badass needed the reminder. Jude had damn well understood the implications of his suggestion.

Jude folded his muscled forearms and lifted heavy black eyebrows. "They can try."

Faith awoke slowly, vaguely aware of a strong, rhythmic throb against her ear. Heat cocooned her, rocked her in a firm embrace. She sighed, a low hum of satisfaction, and snuggled closer to the warmth toasting her right side from cheek to hip.

The rocking stopped.

"Faith? Open your eyes for me, sugar."

The entreaty in the deep, Southern-spiced voice forced Faith's eyes open. Not that she could see much through the shadows surrounding her. But what she did see was confusing—like a band of arms encircling her and a broad chest against her cheek.

"You awake, baby?"

She would have thought she was dreaming, except for the tension in the smooth, rich voice rumbling against her ear. She recognized that voice. Responded to it.

"Rawls?" She started to stretch, but the bands of steel encircling her constricted, holding her in place.

"How you feelin', baby?" The normally smooth voice was rough, raspy.

She frowned slightly, unease jiggling. Why did he sound so raw? But the disquiet was impossible to maintain when she felt so wonderful—warm, cozy, cared for.

"I feel great." She sighed again, nuzzling her cheek into his chest. And it was true. She did feel great. Better than she could ever remember feeling. Which begged the question. "Why are you carrying me?"

There was a noticeable lift and fall to his chest, as though he'd taken a deep breath, followed by an even bigger exhale. And then the rocking started again.

"Do you remember what happened?"

She thought back, images unfurling in her mind.

Explosions overhead. The ceiling cracking and tumbling down. Dirt and concrete plunging through the gaping holes. Fleeing. Agony in her arm and chest. The inability to breathe.

Her heart must have acted up. Hardly surprising considering they'd faced the very real possibility of being buried alive. She glanced up, relieved to find the concrete above her head intact. Rawls must have hauled her to safety. At least they didn't have to fend off that particular danger at the moment. The first time had obviously put enough stress on her heart to trigger the tachycardia. Thank God she'd saved that last dose of Cordarone.

"Thank you," she mumbled on a deep contented breath. The earlier crisis so dim and dreamlike, it didn't have the power to pierce her current serenity.

"For what?"

His voice sounded closer, and she could swear something was nuzzling the top of her head.

"For getting the Cordarone into me. I would have died without it." An unwelcome realization scratched at the contentment. She must have been totally out of it, because she didn't remember taking that pill.

"Yeah . . . " That odd rasp was back in his voice. "I couldn't get to the pill. I didn't save you. Kait did."

"Kait?" She raised her head, trying to make out his face in the shadows surrounding them. Where were the flashlights? But then the renewed tension in his arms and the rawness to his voice distracted her. There was more to the story than he was telling her.

"She healed you." Thickness ironed out his drawl.

"Healed? Why did I need healing?" She tried to remember. But her recollection stopped when the ceiling had given way. "What happened?" She forced the question out, even though she was pretty sure she didn't want to know the answer.

"Your heart stopped. I couldn't get it goin' again." There was a world of dark, gritty anguish in his stark reply.

My heart stopped? I died?

She shook the possibility off.

No way. I'd know if I died.

"I'm awake. Alert. So you must have gotten it going again." She tried for a teasing tone to lighten his mood, because it was impossible to take his account of what had happened seriously. Not when she felt better than she had in—well—ever.

"I didn't. Kait did."

So they were back to that again, were they? Faith shook her head. "It was probably beating, just so faintly you couldn't hear it without your stethoscope. It must have recovered on its own, given time."

"Sure." Pure dryness condensed the words. "I reckon all that CPR I did was just for show."

He'd done CPR on her? Faith focused on her chest. If he'd done CPR, there should have been some lingering sense of pain. Bruising or aching. She sure as heck wouldn't feel like she'd spent the last month at a spa.

He must have picked up on the skepticism in her silence.

His voice cooled. "Have you forgotten I'm a medic?"

"Of course I haven't forgotten. It's just—"

"—easier to believe I couldn't find your heartbeat than Kait healed you?"

Well . . . pretty much.

But guilt stirred. By everyone's account, he was a very good medic. Which made sense since he'd gone through medical school and into his third year of residency. Not to mention all those years keeping his teammates alive on the battlefield.

Against her will, common sense stirred. Someone with those kinds of credentials *would* know if a heart was beating. It wasn't fair to just dismiss his opinion like that.

No wonder he hadn't appreciated her disbelief.

"Okay. Let's agree my heart did stop. Maybe your CPR took effect at the same time Kait arrived." She offered the alternative tentatively.

With a snort, he picked up his pace. "Anythin's possible."

While he didn't sound like he believed her new explanation, that earlier tension seeped out of his muscles.

Faith relaxed against him again. He appeared to carry her with no effort, but it wasn't fair to let him do all the work. She was perfectly capable of walking—even if she didn't want to. Even if she'd much rather lie here and wallow in the pleasure of his closeness and the feel of his hard, warm muscles rubbing against her body. Drown in the hot, musky scent swirling around her head.

Good lord, did the man ever *feel* and *smell* delectable.

"I'm perfectly capable of walking," she finally forced herself to admit.

"I'm sure you are." He stopped long enough to give her a sub-tle hug. "Just kick back and relax. No sense in tuckerin' yourself out. Everyone's waiting for us just up ahead."

She glanced down the dusky tunnel, for the first time realizing there was a flashlight beam bouncing around up ahead—leading the way. Which explained why the area around them was dusky rather than dark. Some of the light ahead must be filtering back.

"Who's up there?" she asked. All she could make out was a bulky shadow.

"Cosky and Kait."

Oh . . .

Her mind shifted gears. "Was anyone hurt? Did everyone make it out of the cabins okay?"

"Everyone else is fine."

Everyone *else*, as in *she* wasn't fine. Possibly her willingness to remain in his arms was giving him the wrong impression.

"Honestly, I'm fine. Put me down."

"No." His arms tightening, he continued walking.

Well, fine then. She'd just enjoy the ride. With that in mind she looped her arms around his neck and settled back down to enjoy his muscles and scent. Her momma hadn't raised a fool.

The silence that fell between them was easy. Comfortable. She gave in to the impulse to close her eyes and doze.

"Faith."

"Hmmmm."

"Do you remember anythin' from when you were out? When your heart stopped?"

That question brought her head up. "What do you mean?"

He was quiet for a moment. And then a shrug lifted the arms curled around his neck. "You have any weird dreams? Any stray memories? Anythin' odd happen back then?"

She frowned. "Like what?"

Stillness fell again, only this time it lacked the ease of earlier.

"Any . . . you know . . . out-of-body kinda experiences?" he finally asked after the silence had dragged on far too long.

She raised her eyebrows at the combination of curiosity and discomfort in his voice. "You mean like an NDE?"

"Yeah, like that."

"No. There was nothing like that."

What an odd question. Why in the world would he ask about near-death experiences? But his question elicited another memory.

The rifle lifting. Rawls spinning in a circle shouting a name. Pachico. Pachico—who was dead and apparently acting as Rawls's ghost.

Suddenly the question about NDEs made sense.

And just like that it was her turn for curiosity. She tried to frame her question as tactfully as possible. "Is that what happened to you that night you were shot in the woods? Is that where you picked up your ghost?"

He'd told her in the kitchen the day before that he'd been mortally wounded and Kait had healed him. Maybe he'd experienced something akin to a near-death experience while he was out, and the experience had paved the foundation for his delusion.

"My ghost," he repeated beneath his breath in a disgusted voice.

Who was that irritation directed at? Him? Her? Pachico? All three of them?

Nor did it escape her notice that he hadn't answered either of her questions. Obviously he didn't want to talk about what he'd gone through. She swallowed her brewing sermon on the scientific veracity of near-death experiences. As someone with wide experience in the medical profession, he would have heard all the competing theories.

His ghost, on the other hand, that was just too tempting a subject to ignore. "Is Pachico here?"

A slight twitch of his shoulder was the only indication he'd heard the question. But once again he refused to participate. Apparently the topic of his ghost was off limits too.

Well, that was just too bad.

However, her plan to pester the information out of him vanished beneath a wave of exhaustion. Apparently, her body recommended immediate sleep to offset its recent ordeal. It didn't help that his arms were warm and comforting or that with each step, he rocked her. Her eyes drifted closed . . . she'd just rest for a while . . . plenty of time to ask about his ghost later.

Eric Manheim scowled as he dropped his cell phone on the breakfast table.

Breathing deeply, he counted to ten while sitting perfectly still. Damn it. Another delay. Another fuckup. They'd found their targets, even had the camp surrounded. They'd had every fucking thing in place. Was it too much to ask that things go according to plan?

"Problem?" Esme murmured, commiseration warming her pale blue gaze.

He focused on her face. Breathed in her light, breezy scent, and the frustration eased. Her eyes never failed to fascinate him, shifting as they did between pale icy-blue and brilliant azure, depending on the whim of the lighting or her emotions of the moment.

"The signal's gone underground," Eric told her tightly.

"How far and where underground?" Esme folded her newspaper in half and set it neatly on the glass table beside her cup of tea.

"Twenty feet, give or take, within a thousand feet of their camp. Apparently, the campsite was built over some kind of rabbit's warren."

He hadn't taken any chances this time. He'd surrounded the camp with snipers before calling in the air strike. He'd covered every angle—except the damn ground.

Irritation flared. If he were lucky, eventually the signal would simply cease, indicating that the boys had died beneath ground. With the compound exploding above them, there was a good chance the tunnel had collapsed, burying them.

But he couldn't count on luck.

"Are you sure the SEALs are with them? From the satellite images, their camp is a cluster of small cabins. What are the chances they're all living in the same space? Or that Chastain's widow is staying in the same one with them. As a mother with young children, she'll want her privacy."

Eric nodded absently. The men could have been staying in different cabins. But it didn't matter. If Mrs. Chastain and her kids had been able to escape into the tunnels, the frogs could have too.

"We'll just have to wait them out. Eventually they'll surface to find food or water. When they do, we'll move on them. If Mackenzie and his men are in the tunnels, we'll take them out at the same time as we hit Chastain's family." He relaxed and smiled across the table at her.

He saw the flash of regret cross Esme's face and reached for her hand, squeezing it comfortingly. His wife had a soft heart. While she understood that the deaths of Amy Chastain's children were for the greater good, an absolute necessity, she didn't like it.

For her sake, if there had been a way to kill the SEALs without involving the two boys, he would have taken it. He didn't derive pleasure from the slaughter of innocent children either. But the SEALs had gone to ground, and there'd been no other way to flush them out.

So for the sake of the millions of lives he'd be saving in the future, he'd see Amy Chastain's sons die in the now.

And he'd bear that black mark on his soul with no regret.

But then he froze. His whole plan rested on the kids exiting the tunnels at some point. But what if they didn't need to? Mackenzie's men were seasoned veterans. They'd have prepared for a retreat. Stocked for it. They'd have food and water stored in the tunnels. His best bet was to call in another air strike. Hit the bastards with a lot more firepower, enough to blast a twenty-foot hole in the ground. Make sure they never emerged from those tunnels.

Of course, it was also highly possible, probable even, that the boys would remain in the safety of the tunnel, while the men snuck aboveground to clear the camp of intruders. They were SEALs after all. Trained warriors with years of battle experience behind them. They weren't going to wait belowground while their enemies destroyed everything.

They'd join the fight. Or even take the fight to Eric's crew.

He swore beneath his breath and reached for his phone. Last time one of his teams had tangled with Mackenzie and the rest of those bloody sods, they'd paid for it with their lives. Every last one of them. He'd lost an entire team, along with their chopper, and those bastards had escaped without a scratch.

True—he was using a different contractor, one who'd provided his own team, but it wouldn't hurt to remind the man of the results from the first skirmish with this group.

Or what the consequences would be if it happened again.

Chapter Thirteen

CLEARLY, LACK OF OXYGEN HADN'T DAMAGED FAITH'S MIND.

Torn between relief and rankling irritation, Rawls blew out a frustrated breath. She'd awakened with her intellect fully intact, along with her stubborn refusal to consider anything that didn't fit neatly into her scientific mindset.

The discovery that Kait had completely healed her—sweet Jesus, even retrieved her from the dead—had kicked off a full-blown chorus of hallelujah in his head. The euphoria had lasted right up until Faith opened her mouth to contradict everything he'd told her. It was the first time in his life he'd wanted to kiss a woman and shake her simultaneously.

A steady glow appeared ahead, intensifying the closer they got. Cosky and Kait melted into the brilliance.

Looks like they'd officially reached the rendezvous point.

"Hot damn." A transparent shape slipped past him and approached the hub at full-speed ahead.

Just . . . perfect . . .

Rawls scowled.

His ghost—as Faith insisted on calling it—had returned immediately after the healing. It had been remarkably docile since its reappearance. Holding its tongue and antics in check. Of course, Rawls hadn't taken any chances. He'd removed the ammunition from the SCAR PD assault weapon and the Glock 17. Pachico might have succeeded in manipulating the rifle, but he'd find it a lot more challenging removing the rounds from Rawls's pocket and inserting them into the guns.

Erring on the same side of caution, he'd hung way back from Cosky too. Effectively creating a lengthy barricade between his transparent troll and his teammate, or rather his teammate's weaponry.

At least for the time being.

Dread building, he paused, watching as Pachico abruptly stopped as well. The time had come to admit to his hitchhiker and warn everyone. Now that Pachico had mastered the ability to lift and point weapons, it was only a matter of time before he figured out how to compress the trigger. Trapped, as they were, in such a small space, someone was bound to pay the price.

Frustration swelled, a thick clout of tension in his chest. Yet avoiding the hub was a false hope. If he didn't show up, his teammates would come looking for him. Likely Kait and Beth too. As much as he'd tried to avoid it, to protect everyone, his mere presence would place everyone in immediate danger.

Even more maddening was the fact that they wouldn't believe him any more than Faith had. At least until the first shot was fired.

His best bet was to drop Faith off, and get the hell out of there. Return to his original plan of avoiding everyone in favor of lurking in the woods. But to do that, he needed to pass through that cave. It was the only passage to the outside world now that all access points behind him had been blown.

He stared at the radiant cavern and the shadowy figures drifting around within. Knowing his teammates and company protocol, the damn place would be bristling with weapons. A virtual treasure trove to a disgruntled ghost.

Swearing beneath his breath so as not to awake Faith, who'd taken to dozing against his chest, he backed up, dragging Pachico away from that shiny beacon of peril.

It made more sense to let his buddies come to him. It would be easier to monitor a couple of weapons rather than dozens of them. He would explain the situation to Zane and Cosky—maybe Mac—and let them explain it to the rest.

Jude stepped into the mouth of the cave, his big body blocking the spill of light, his silhouette a hulking, menacing shadow.

Wolf and Jude shared similar ancestry. Did that mean he'd be as open to the possibility of ghosts as his gruff commanding officer?

"Goddamn you," Pachico yelled as he stumbled backward. "How about you stop being a fucking jackass, and I'll leave your girlfriend alone?"

Faith stirred, her head lifting.

Jude's hand went to his chest. Suddenly he stepped out of the cavern and headed toward Rawls.

"I'm serious, you fucking shithead. Don't think I won't—"

Pachico abruptly disappeared.

What the . . . ?

Rawls froze, scanning the tunnel ahead. No, it hadn't been a trick of his beleaguered imagination. The bastard really was gone. And the dematerialization had been sudden too, without any of the normal triggers.

Except . . . his mind flashed back to that moment at the stream with Wolf. Pachico had blinked out then too.

He turned his head and stared at Jude, who was rapidly approaching. *What the fuck?* Did the Arapaho nation possess some secret weapon that jettisoned ghosts?

"What's wrong?" Faith asked, her voice thick and sleepy and sexy as hell. "You look angry." She turned her head, following his gaze to Jude, and stiffened slightly in his arms. "You can put me down now."

When her demand penetrated his mind, Rawls's arms instinctively tightened. The most absurd fear had struck at the thought of letting her go, as though the only thing anchoring her to life was the strength of his arms. Which was ridiculous—her heart had been beating on its own when he'd picked her up.

He hadn't been the one to drag her back into the land of the living—Kait had done that.

"I'm serious, Rawls," she hissed, jabbing him in the chest with her elbow. "This is embarrassing."

When he didn't release her, she struggled in earnest, which raised the alarming question of whether his hold was bruising her. His stomach twisted at the possibility of hurting her, so he reluctantly released her and lowered her to the ground. She wavered there for a moment under his steadying grip, and then her legs took control.

Her relieved sigh when her muscles kicked in was loud—hell, probably loud enough for Jude to hear—and then she got to work straightening her clothes. The smoothing, tucking, and tugging went on so long it got downright amusing. His irritation dissipated beneath the rising humor.

"Darlin'," he said around the edges of a grin. "Much more of that and your knickers are liable to file harassment charges."

Her hands froze. Bright red swarmed her cheeks. She looked so uncomfortable and lost standing there, her hands clenched at her sides, uncertainty swimming in her eyes, that the urge to laugh vanished.

"Hey!" He framed her face and kissed her forehead, the tenderness rising so thick and fast he thought he might drown beneath it. "You're perfect the way you are. No need for fussin'."

She relaxed beneath his hands and leaned against him, pressing her mouth against his throat. Her lips were soft against his skin, silky . . . hot as hell. They burned the tenderness right out of him. His hands dropped to her hips and pulled her hard against his crotch.

As his head lowered, his mouth searching out hers, a loud cough sounded beside them. Faith broke away with a startled gasp, as though they'd been caught doing something shameful.

Well, hell . . .

Rawls looked up with a scowl. Looks like he had two bones to pick with the Arapaho warrior. He got right down to the first one. "You want to tell me why Pachico vamooses when you or Wolf show up, but not when anyone else is nearby?"

Faith twitched at the question. She obviously hadn't expected him to publicly admit to his ghost.

Jude's face tensed. The lines bracketing his mouth deepened in disapproval and discomfort. "It is not wise to speak of the *biitei*. Acknowledging it brings it much power."

"You didn't answer my question," Rawls snapped. He had no intention of being led down an Arapaho rabbit hole. "Why did it disappear when you approached?"

His face impassive, Jude tugged up the thin leather cord draping his neck, and lifted it from beneath his T-shirt. Dangling from the bottom was a tiny, circular weaving.

"Okay." Rawls leaned in for a closer look. It resembled a primitive sun, with eight triangular spokes circling the outer edge. Upon closer look, the spiked sunburst was repeated again and again within the weaving—the pattern stacked in on itself in rich reds and blues. "You want to tell me what that is?"

"Protection," Jude said succinctly.

From ghosts, apparently. Which made sense considering Pachico had vanished as Jude approached.

"Wolf have one of these things?"

Jude tucked the weaving back under his shirt and rearranged the cord around his neck. "We all wear a *hiixoyooniiheiht.*"

Wolf had known about Pachico. He'd known Rawls was being haunted.

"No shit," Rawls said, fury rising. "Why the hell didn't Wolf tell me about this thing? Loan me one? Help me out just a fuckin' bit?"

Faith shot him a surprised look as the f-bomb broke loose, but sweet Jesus, he'd been going certifiably crazy over the past few days. Not to mention how dangerous his transparent troll had become recently. Someone could have been seriously hurt. Wolf could have saved him a boatload of frustration and worry if he'd just opened his damn mouth and explained about this ghost-protection amulet.

Jude shrugged. "*Hiixoyooniiheiht* are created specifically for an individual, using the individual's blood. They are not interchangeable."

Blowing out a frustrated breath, Rawls regrouped. "How's it work?"

Jude's face collapsed back into its normal fountain of inscrutability. "That is the *notonheihii's* domain, not ours to know."

Rawls took a deep breath and counted to ten. The bastard had to be deliberately trying to piss him off.

"Did you see it?" Faith interrupted, sharp interest in her eyes.

"Only one who has dwelled in *hiihooteet* and walked the other side can see a *biitei.*"

Faith's eyebrows crinkled. "Then how do you know it was there? How do you know ghosts even exist?"

Jude turned an indulgent look on her. "How does one know the wind exists?"

Faith's eyes widened and pure exasperation flooded her face. "That's not the same thing *at all!*" She leaned forward, her body practically vibrating with irritation. "I can quantify the wind. I can measure its velocity with an anemometer. I can see its effect on vegetation or kites or birds with my own eyes. I can capture it to power a sailboat or a windmill. I can measure everything about it from direction to miles per hour."

Rawls choked back a sputter of laughter and hauled her back, anchoring her to his side. Sweet baby Jesus, she looked like she wanted to go after the man with her bare hands.

"I reckon the wind wasn't the best comparison," Rawls drawled.

Faith tipped her head back, gazing up at him with wide, earnest eyes. "I'm just saying there are plenty of scientific experiments that prove the existence of wind. However, there isn't one that proves the presence of ghosts."

He reached out to stroke her cheek. "You may not be able to see Pachico, Faith—but I can. I have."

"Well, you might think—"

"Let's table this discussion for now," Rawls interrupted before she had a chance to launch an attack on his credibility or mental stability and get him all disgruntled again.

After a small hesitation, Faith nodded.

Rawls turned back to Jude. "So as long as you stick close to me, we can keep my invisible hitchhiker at bay."

Jude frowned, looking uncomfortable again. "This *biitei* is bound to you. Only a *hiixoyooniiheiht* created for you, from you, will keep it at bay. Nor is it wise to allow it access to my or Wolf's *hiixoyooniiheiht*. It will test the protection spells. Adjust to them, weakening your own *hiixoyooniiheiht* once Wolf arrives with it."

Well that was news. "Wolf's bringin' me one of those things?"

Jude simply nodded.

"You said it had to be made from my blood—"

"Created, not made," Jude corrected.

Yeah, well, same difference as far as Rawls could tell, not that it mattered in the grand scheme of things. "How'd he get my blood?"

But he suddenly knew. Wolf had asked about his shirt, the one Rawls had been wearing when he'd taken the bullets. He frowned, shook his head. There was no way Wolf would have had time to swing by the cabin Rawls shared with Mac, grab the bloody shirt out of the garbage, and then abscond on the helicopter before Rawls had even reached the helicopter pad. He hadn't been that far behind the big bastard. So what had Wolf used?

An even more important question hit him. Why hadn't Wolf, or Jude, told him what was happening and how to combat it?

Anger rushed him. Someone should have told him.

"Wise or not, you're gonna have to stick to me like butter and keep that thing away as long as possible. My *biitei*"—he stumbled over the word, mangling it in the process—"has learned to manipulate objects in our world, which is dangerous as hell considerin' all the weapons ahead. Plus"—he broke off, shooting a quick glance at Faith. He hadn't told her this part yet. Not that she would believe him—"there's this possession thing he's got goin'."

A jolt vibrated through Jude's body, shaking the impassiveness loose. Alarm tensed his face and tightened the skin around his eyes. "It has skin-walked?"

Skin-walked . . . interesting term for that nightmare in the kitchen.

Rawls nodded, glancing meaningfully toward Faith.

It was Faith's turn to jolt. "Oh come on, I would know if—"

"The kitchen," Rawls reminded her, dismissing the disbelief on her face. He'd already known she wouldn't believe him.

"This . . . this . . . is not good." Jude shook his head, obviously struggling to regain his mantle of eerie calm. "One does not expect such escalation from a fledgling."

"So you'll stick close to me?"

Although he looked royally unhappy at the prospect, Jude agreed with a brusque nod.

And just like that the tension whooshed out of Rawls.

Finally, *finally* he had the means to protect his people. A thick, pervasive blanket of oppression lifted, and he emerged a thousand pounds lighter.

"Rawls," Mac yelled from the cavern's entrance, beckoning him forward.

Rawls nodded an acknowledgment and took hold of Faith's elbow.

From her behavior, it was obvious she didn't need his help, but he wasn't ready to let her go yet.

Every head in the hub turned their way as they walked into the room. Zane broke away from Cosky, who had settled on the floor with Kait curled in his lap.

Concern rose at the heat and exhaustion evident in Kait's face. Changing directions in midstride, Rawls detoured toward her. Kait had come close to overheating that first time, when she'd healed Cosky's leg back in the parking lot. Best to make sure it hadn't happened again.

Zane intercepted him, his calm green eyes scanning Rawls's face. "Glad to see your ugly mug. Mac and I were about to go look for you. Dig you up if we had to."

There was enough residual tightness on Zane's face to tell Rawls his best friend and teammate wasn't simply razzing him. And from the relieved glances spreading through the cavern, Zane hadn't been the only one worried.

"Yeah." Rawls shrugged, aiming for a casual expression and tone. "The tunnel turned a mite possessive." No sense in broadcasting Faith's medical condition to the rest of them.

From the sudden relaxation of the arm he held, Faith obviously appreciated his discretion.

Zane simply nodded. But from the assessing look he turned on Faith, he knew the circumstances of their delay. Cosky must have filled him in.

"How you holding up, Dr. Ansell?" Zane asked, his tone cordial rather than concerned. As though he were merely exercising good manners.

But Rawls knew better. The sharp look of assessment his LC had leveled on Faith's face was a clear indication that Zane was calculating how much her condition was going to cost them. Apparently Faith picked up on that as well, because her arm stiffened beneath his fingers.

"I'm just fine," she said, her tone stiff with challenge.

Zane scanned her again and shot Rawls a quick glance. "When you get her settled, come find us. We've got things to discuss."

Well, how about that. They'd decided to let him back in the big boys' club.

Zane stepped back and Rawls continued toward Cosky. If Kait *was* overheated, the stone would be their best bet of cooling her down—which meant Cosky had to stop cuddling her and lay her out on the floor. Stone retained cold, which just might suck the heat from her. Without water, it was the best they could hope for.

Cosky caught sight of Rawls and scowled. His heavy shoulders tensed. Chips of ice swam in hostile gray eyes. "Kait's not doing another damn healing."

Rawls raised his eyebrows at the welcome. "I'm not expectin' one. I'm here to see how she's doin'."

He was keenly aware of Faith beside him, her warmth, her stillness, the intensity with which she was studying Kait's red, fatigued face.

"How the fuck do you think she's doing? She's hotter than hell and I've no water to cool her down."

"You have the stone floor. Use it."

Cosky froze for a moment. His eyes narrowed and absolute disgust slammed down over his face. Apparently his worry had shut his common sense down.

"Shit." He straightened and eased Kait off his lap and onto the bare stone.

With a sigh of relief, she rolled over onto her stomach and stretched out. Cosky pulled her tangled, golden braid from beneath her hip and laid it next to her body. After a gentle swipe over the back of her head, he glanced up.

"Thanks." The acknowledgment came grudgingly, and there was still a fair bit of hostility in the gray eyes.

Rawls shrugged. He wasn't going to waste a second of guilt on what had happened there in the corridor. Of course he'd wanted another healing for Faith. He'd wanted the best possible chance of ensuring her recovery. At the time, he hadn't realized how much the first healing had cost Kait. If he'd known, he would have backed off.

He didn't regret his actions in the slightest. Under the same circumstances, he'd make identical choices.

He wasn't going to apologize for that.

Beneath Cosky's watchful gaze, he crouched to press two fingers against Kait's still neck. Her skin was hot and moist against his fingers. But her pulse was steady and strong.

"Her heart sounds good. So does her breathin'." He glanced around the cavern, skimming face after face. "Nobody brought water?"

He'd had some bottles in his rucksack, but it was buried back in the tunnel.

"Mom's asking people," Cosky said gruffly. But some of the tension had left his face.

"Rawls," Mac barked impatiently from across the hub.

"Go," Faith said, with a light squeeze to his arm. "I'm fine, really. I'll wait for you here."

With a nod, Rawls glanced at Cosky. "You comin'?"

Cosky shook his head and settled on the ground next to Kait. "They don't need me."

Frowning, Rawls headed toward Mac and the cluster of people surrounding him. Nobody looked hurt or incapacitated. Hopefully the situation he'd been summoned to rectify wasn't critical.

When he reached the group against the wall, Mac rested a hand on Amy's eldest child and steered him toward Rawls. "Would you be able to tell whether a chip was inserted in Brendan's arm?"

Rawls froze for a second.

That's how they'd been found? He shook the surprise off.

"How was it inserted?" Rawls asked. Getting down to business, he accepted the narrow, surprisingly muscular arm Amy's son presented him.

"By injection, right here," Brendan said, brushing his finger across a slightly raised, rough patch on his arm.

Rawls carefully probed the thickened blotch of skin with his fingers. After a moment he shook his head.

"I don't feel anythin'." He lowered his hands. "But if they inserted it deep enough, its presence wouldn't be identifiable by touch."

Nobody looked surprised by this news.

"I still say we should check the spot out now. Make sure we won't be followed to our next safe haven," Mac said, looking straight at Amy, his voice the oddest combination of defensiveness and conviction.

Check the spot out . . .

Rawls winced, doubting Max was referring to hands and eyes. Sure, he'd operated on plenty of people in the field. But not a kid. And not without some kind of painkiller.

"And I *still* say no." Amy's voice was just as determined. "Not in these conditions. Not when Wolf is on his way to take us to their base camp."

"Their base?" Rawls asked. He obviously had a lot of catching up to do.

"Our Arapaho friends' home," Mac said, staring flatly at Jude. "Apparently we've been invited to visit."

"For a time," Jude agreed, staring blankly back.

Rawls casually scanned the cave, relaxing when he didn't catch site of his translucent hitchhiker. At least the Arapaho was fulfilling his obligation and sticking close by. Maybe Jude's charm really would keep Pachico away.

Mac blew out a thick breath and rolled his shoulders. Rawls could almost feel the frustration heating the air around him.

"Now that the women and kids are safe, how do you two feel about stepping outside? Taking care of business?" Mac suddenly asked, his gaze shifting between Rawls and Zane.

"I'm looking forward to it." Icy anticipation chilled Zane's face, glittered in his green eyes.

Rawls, well, he wasn't quite as eager. Yeah, he was all for leveling out the playing field and taking some of those bastards down—but there were Faith and Kait to consider. He needed to be on hand if they took a turn for the worse. And then there was his ghost. If the bastard made a reappearance, out there on the battlefield, there would be even more weapons for him to play with, and ways for him to interfere.

Best not chance it.

"Get Cosky," Mac told Zane. "We'll head out in five."

Rawls had opened his mouth to man up and inform his commander that he wouldn't be embarking on the mission with him, when Jude chimed in.

"No." The refusal was emphatic.

Mac stiffened. Slowly his head turned. Thick black eyebrows shot up. "I don't remember asking you."

"My brothers are out there. Clearing a path for you. Leaving now endangers you both."

Mac's eyebrows collapsed into a scowl. "Wolf and his men are here? Now? Outside?"

Jude simply nodded.

"Son of a bitch . . . " Mac's grim voice trailed off.

"I'm all for taking the initiative for a change, but with Wolf and his team already in the field . . . " Zane shook his head, frustration and regret flashing through his eyes. "It's ripe for friendly fire."

"No shit." Mac looked even less happy than Zane. He turned his scowl back on Jude. "We need to grab one of those bastards who attacked us. Preferably someone up the food chain. Someone with answers." He paused, pinned Jude with a hard look. "It's the best shot we have of tracking these bastards down."

Jude's expression didn't alter. "What you seek already walks among you."

Rawls rocked back on his heels in surprise. The ambiguous warrior had to be referring to Pachico. But just how the hell did he expect them to pull answers from the surly ghost? Pachico was hardly in an accommodating mood.

"What the *fuck* does that mean?" Mac exploded. "And while you're at it, you want to explain how you even know your buddies are out there? You have no radio. No sat phone. No motherfucking technology to contact your brothers, but you somehow—by osmosis, apparently—know where they are?"

Jude simply shrugged, that enormously annoying aura of serenity surrounding him again.

But the question niggled at Rawls.

How *did* Jude know his team was out there? What mystical technological advances did their new allies have up their sleeves?

Chapter Fourteen

"IS SHE OKAY?" FAITH ASKED, HOVERING ABOVE KAIT, TORN BETWEEN wanting to help and not wanting to get in the way.

"She'll be fine," Cosky said gruffly. He glanced up, his face tense, his left hand resting on the back of Kait's head. And then his gaze sharpened. After a quick up-and-down scan that took in Faith from head to toe, he raised dark eyebrows. "How are you holding up? You had Rawlings pretty damn freaked out back there."

She had?

"I'm fine," Faith assured him.

"Good to hear." He turned his attention back to the woman beside him. There was a world of worry in the gray eyes watching the blonde goddess lying so limply on the rough-cut stone floor.

Judging by the glimpse she'd caught of Kait's face earlier, he had reason for his concern. His girlfriend had looked awful—bright red, sweaty face, exhaustion evident in the curve of her shoulders and limpness of her muscles. She'd barely been able to hold her head upright. And then there was the condition of her shirt. It was soaked with sweat down the length of her spine, as well as under her arms.

The woman was obviously running a fever. She must have been hit with a nasty flu. What terrible timing. Running for your life was bad enough, doing so with a high fever and dogged by the flu had to be even worse.

Suddenly Rawls's account of what had happened earlier burst into her mind. He'd claimed she'd died and Kait had healed her. But Kait had been in a different cabin, with separate tunnel accesses. Which meant she must have doubled back in the tunnel system to look for her.

Even burning up from a fever, exhausted to the point of collapse, she'd still braved a collapsing tunnel system to find and help a virtual stranger? Granted, they'd spent the past week in somewhat close proximity, but they'd hardly interacted enough to become friends—mild acquaintances at best.

Would a con artist do that? Driven by self-interest, a con artist wouldn't put their own life and health in jeopardy to help someone else, would they? Not when they had a perfect excuse to stay put and avoid additional danger.

After that talk with Rawls in the kitchen, she'd been convinced that Kait was playing everyone—although *how* had been uncertain. According to Rawls, she refused monetary reimbursement for her self-proclaimed healings. But maybe she received other benefits from her con.

Faith glanced at Cosky as his mother came bustling over with a bottle of water. The lieutenant didn't seem the type to fall prey to a con artist. He appeared far too guarded and intelligent for that. But then, beautiful women had been beguiling men for thousands of years. He wouldn't be the first wary, smart man to fall for the wiles of a temptress. He wouldn't be the last either.

"Here you go, sweetie," Marion said, leaning down to pass her son a bottle of water. "Amy brought a bunch, so there's more if you need it." She straightened with a hand on her back. "I just don't understand it. The poor dear was fine when we reached the hub." A confused shake of her head sent her silver bob flying. "I've never seen anyone get so sick so fast. She was fine when she left with you to find the stragglers.

You weren't gone even fifteen minutes. What made her so sick? The flu wouldn't attack that fast."

. . . left to find the stragglers . . .

Marion's words echoed in Faith's mind. She'd been one of the stragglers. Was Marion referring to Kait's trip down the tunnel to find and supposedly heal her?

"She overdid it, that's all," Cosky said, dragging his shirt over his head. He used the knife sheathed at his belt to slice the material and then tore off a broad strip. After soaking the cloth with water, he recapped the bottle. "She'll be fine once she rests."

Overdid what? Was he referring to the healing?

Faith absently watched Cosky pick Kait up and cradle her against his shoulder. He held the water bottle while she drank and then went to work running the cloth over her red, fatigued face.

She didn't look as bad as she had before. Some of the tomato-soup color had faded from her cheeks, and the lines of exhaustion didn't cut as deep.

If Cosky *had* been referring to the supposed healing Kait had done—how in the world did one overdo the simple laying on of hands?

She was still turning that question over in her mind when Beth arrived with a second bottle of water. "How's she doing?"

"I'm fine," Kait said, opening her eyes. The smile she offered took obvious effort. "You better hang on to that bottle. There's no telling how long we'll be here. We should preserve what we can."

"We'll make do with conserving the rest. It's more important to get your temperature down. It's too bad there isn't a glacier-fed lake handy, like there was with Rawls," Beth said as she set the plastic bottle on the floor next to the wall, where it promptly fell over and rolled a few inches.

"With Rawls," Marion repeated, a shrewd gleam to her gray eyes. "What happened with Rawls, and what does it have to do with Kait's fever now?"

The woman obviously suspected that there was more going on than she'd been told.

"I'll explain later, Mom," Cosky said. He lifted the water to Kait's lips again, refusing to remove it until she'd swallowed a good share of the contents.

Beth shot Cosky an apologetic glance and stepped back. "If you need anything, I'll be right over there." She nodded across the room toward Zane.

Faith glanced between Cosky and his mother. Apparently, Marion was in the dark about Kait's supposed healing powers, otherwise Cosky wouldn't have to "explain later." Why had he withheld the information from her?

When Beth left, Faith started to follow, only to turn back. No matter what, Kait had risked her life out there for her and Rawls. That alone deserved appreciation.

"Hey." Faith shuffled her feet uncomfortably. "Rawls says you came back for me . . ." She glanced uncertainly between Cosky and his mother. To avoid additional questions, it would probably be best to keep her thank-you vague. "Anyway, I wanted to thank you."

Kait smiled as her eyes drifted shut. "You're welcome."

Left with nothing else to say, and the strong impression that Kait and Cosky wanted some privacy, Faith turned away. But she had nowhere to go. Rawls was involved in some intense discussion in the corner with Zane, Mac, and Jude, and judging from the explosive frustration on Mac's face, she'd do well to avoid that corner of the hub.

"I'm so sorry!" Beth suddenly appeared by her side to grasp her hand. "I was so focused on Kait, I completely forgot what you'd gone through out there."

"Perfectly understandable," Faith assured the pretty, pregnancy-plumped blonde. "She's your friend. Besides, I'm fine, really. I was apparently out of it, so I don't remember anything." She offered Beth a polite smile.

"Well, you must have been pretty bad off, otherwise Kait wouldn't be in the condition she's in," Beth told her absently, only to freeze and flush. "Oh my God. I didn't mean it like that! It's not your fault. Honestly! It's just that fatal injuries or illnesses require a lot more energy during the healing. So they really wipe her out."

Fatal injuries . . .

A chill prickled her scalp. "Why do you say it was fatal?"

"Cosky told Zane." Beth suddenly stopped, blushing even worse than before. "Oh man. I obviously need to stop talking. I assumed that Rawls had told you what kind of shape you were in."

"He said my heart had stopped," Faith said slowly, the chill spreading down her spine. It was much harder to dismiss two accounts of her death, than one.

"Oh good." Relief softened Beth's face. "Anyway, for what it's worth, I'm really glad Kait was able to bring you back."

Interesting . . . Beth completely believed in Kait's abilities. So did Cosky and Zane, from the sound of it.

She'd already known that Rawls bought into Kait's ability. But to find out Cosky, Zane, and Beth did too raised a serious question. Rationally, it didn't seem feasible that Kait could have fooled all four of them. Particularly the men. SEALs were schooled in scrutiny and strategic thinking. They were taught to rely on their logical mind. Maybe Kait could have fooled a SEAL lover by tangling his intellect with emotion. But Zane wasn't in love with her. Neither was Rawls . . . they would have seen right through her . . . wouldn't they?

The oddest doubt rose. The SEALs wouldn't believe in Kait's abilities so completely unless they had personal experience with it . . . as Rawls claimed to have.

Faith turned to Beth, the question breaking from her without thought. "Have you actually seen her heal anyone? I mean actually watched her, with your own eyes?"

Beth's mouth dropped open in surprise. "Well, sure. So have you. Back in the forest when Rawls was shot."

"They told me it wasn't his blood. That he was just stunned. That he'd been wearing armor plating and it stopped the bullet." The words tumbled out of her.

Beth looked even more surprised. "You were there, Faith. You watched them take off his shirt. There was no armored vest. Don't you remember? You saw the healing glow. You even mentioned it."

I did?

Of course she remembered the weird glow, but after contemplating the memory, she'd convinced herself it had simply been the light of the moon hitting the trees and refracting downward. Or even the moonlight bouncing off the lake. Except . . . the forest would have blocked the reflection from the lake, and the treetops would have shielded the forest floor from most of the moon's glow.

So where had that strange glow come from? She focused. Thought back to that night six days ago.

Cosky and Kait kneeling over Rawls's limp, bloody body. An eerie silver sparkle cocooning them.

Unconsciously, Faith shook her head. What the silver radiance had been, she couldn't say. But it hadn't been moonlight. That she remembered with certainty. It hadn't reflected from the lake or filtered down through the treetops. The platinum shimmer had originated within Kait's chest and flowed down her arms, into her hands, and from there into Rawls . . . and maybe Cosky . . . his hands and arms had been glowing too.

Amy pushing up Rawls's bloodstained shirt, exposing the steady rise and fall of his bloody chest. "He's not bleeding . . . I can't even find any wounds . . . "

She reeled as the memories exploded in her mind. He hadn't been wearing a bullet-proof vest, or armor plating, or whatever else they wanted to call it. The only thing between his chest and the bullets had been his shirt. His bloody, bullet-riddled shirt.

A shock wave traveled through her. She swayed, more off balance than she could ever remember feeling. How in the world could she have buried something so critical? She'd always been so contemptuous of scientists who steadfastly ignored any evidence that didn't corroborate their own conclusions. Yet she'd done the exact same thing when it came to Kait's unusual healing abilities.

"Are you okay?" Beth asked, worry in her voice.

"I'm fine," Faith said automatically, only to swallow a bubble of laughter. At least as fine as someone could be who'd just had their entire world view incinerated.

"Maybe you should sit down." Beth steered her toward the cavern wall.

Faith sat. When it came right down to it, she was nothing but a hypocrite. She winced at the realization. Take the Thrive generator. While they'd been working on a new energy generator first and foremost, once they'd stumbled onto the prototype's side effects, she hadn't denied they existed. Not like she had with Kait's gift—even though she'd witnessed the miracle of Kait's touch firsthand.

But then again, they'd experimented like crazy with the machine once they realized its capabilities. Or, at least they'd experimented as much as they were able to while maintaining the project's confidentiality. They'd run double-blind testing on both the machine and its test subjects. Before long, they'd had reams of scientific data to extrapolate from. So yeah, while the Thrive generator had interfaced with certain subjects' brains to produce supernatural-like abilities—talents that were somewhat similar to Kait's healing ability—there was one big difference.

She knew what powered their machine's pseudosupernatural effect. She didn't know what powered Kait's.

Once this was over, and the bad guys were behind bars and no longer interfering with her life, maybe she could talk Kait into undergoing some testing. If Kait really did have the ability to heal, there was bound to be a scientific or biological explanation for her gift. They just had to find it.

Of course, there was always the possibility that Mackenzie planned on doing some testing of his own—or at least the navy did. It didn't take much imagination to envision the military's interest in weaponizing Kait's talent. If her touch could heal, it must have the potential to kill as well. Had any of the men broached the subject to her?

She frowned, staring absently at the wall. It might prove useful to nudge Kait aside when the opportunity arose and ask. The answer might tell her whether she could trust these men enough to fully disclose the Thrive generator's secondary effects. They'd need to know this information if they located her team and launched a rescue.

She was so caught up in her thoughts she flinched when Rawls suddenly squatted in front of her.

"Hey," he said, scanning her face. "How you doin'?"

She paused before answering to assess her heart's beat and rhythm. Both felt stronger and more regular than they had before.

"I'm fine." She groaned beneath her breath. She sounded like a broken record.

"How 'bout I have a look-see for myself?" With a reserved smile, he loosely circled her wrist, pressing two fingers against her pulse.

There was a distance to him that she hadn't felt in a while. Not since the kitchen when she'd come to her senses to find herself sitting on his lap. She flushed slightly as images and sensation rolled through her, delineating all the other things they'd done while she'd been sitting on his lap.

"Your heartbeat feels strong. But you're flushed," he said, some of the reserve giving way to concern. "Maybe you should lie down. Rest for a while. Accordin' to Jude, their base has a full medical facility. They'll be able to check your heart out and refill your prescriptions."

"Okay," Faith said, watching the detachment solidify on his face again.

A sharp sting of loss rose. It was so strange—she'd only known the man for a week, and until yesterday, she hadn't spent any time alone with him. There was nothing between them except a fragile friendship. There was no reason to feel like she'd lost something special.

Yet, she did.

"Although, I don't think I need any medical attention. I feel pretty phenomenal considering I died less than an hour ago." She held his gaze, willing him to recognize the apology. Which was beyond cowardly. He deserved the words. "I'm sorry. I should have believed you."

He rocked back on his heels, intently studying her. And then his face softened. Heat flared, burned blue in his eyes.

"I promised myself somethin' if you came back to me," he said, his tone a cross between haunted and determined. His focus dropped to her mouth and his blue eyes started to glitter.

"What?" she asked, although from his intense concentration on her mouth, she could guess. A flush scorched her cheeks. "Reserved" certainly didn't describe him now.

"This." Rough hands rose to cup her hot cheeks and he lowered his head.

His lips were tender against hers. Gentle. Like she was breakable. Or fragile—to be handled with care.

She didn't want gentle. She didn't want temperate. She wanted that fiery rush of sensation he'd given her before. She wanted to feel him. Every aspect of him from tenderness to lust, and every shade of hunger between.

Her surroundings fading away, she offered a soft moan and opened her mouth, inviting him inside.

"Finally, it's about fucking time. I don't get what you see in the broad, but Jesus, just get her into a dark corner and out of those clothes already."

The disgusting comment crashed into Faith's head, disrupting the tantalizing, sensuous haze.

"Excuse me!" She jerked her mouth from Rawls's and planted her palms against his chest, shoving him back. Twin volcanoes of embarrassment and fury spewed inside her.

Although the voice hadn't sounded quite right, the asshole who'd ruined the mood had to be Mac. Nobody else was so loud and mouthy and grossly unpleasant.

"Faith . . ." There was the oddest look on Rawls's face. Shock, only a hundredfold stronger.

"Look, I don't care if he is your commander. I don't have to put up with that kind of crap from anyone. Not even him," Faith snapped, shooting to her feet.

"What the hell are you talking about?" Mac asked from across the hub. He sounded baffled. "I didn't say, or do, a damn thing to you."

Okay, maybe she'd jumped the gun a bit there. The two voices weren't the same at all.

"Faith." Rawls snagged her hand and drew her to his side, motioning Jude toward them with his other hand. "Sweetheart. That's not Mac."

"I know that now," she told him impatiently. "But that doesn't make the asshole who said it any less an asshole."

Rawls choked on a shout of laughter and gave her a hard, quick hug. "That you got right, darlin'."

"What the hell are you two yammering about?" Mac growled, stomping toward them, Jude hard on his heels.

Rawls released Faith and nudged her to the right until a thin man, his forehead sheathed in a bloody bandage, came into view. She froze, her mouth dropping open in startled shock. She could see the cavern wall, and Zane and Beth, through his translucent frame.

"Would you look at that?" An ugly smile spread across his transparent face and sank into vicious, muddy brown eyes. "We got a new member in our exclusive club."

The cavern went eerily silent. A hollow pit opened up in her belly. Her legs went weak and shaky. And then an electrical buzzing took over her brain.

Her gaze dropped to the big black knife sticking out of his chest, and her legs shook harder.

The ghost laughed, his bald head gleaming wetly beneath the reflection of multiple flashlights.

"Boo!" It lunged at her and laughed harder as she shrieked and cringed back.

A howling, spinning storm spun through her mind. Slowly an image took shape. A memory.

A wood-grained kitchen . . . a man bound to a kitchen chair, his bald head gleaming beneath the dim lights . . . shouting . . . raging . . . blood pooling on the floor.

"Looks like you remember me," Rawls's ghost said with a smirk.

Of course she remembered him. She'd watched him die. That wasn't something a person forgot.

"What the hell's wrong with her?" she vaguely heard Mac ask.

Maybe she was simply dreaming, because she could swear she heard concern in his voice.

"This will be so much more fun with you in the mix." Pachico grinned, his teeth sharp and menacing in the flickering light. He took a threatening step toward her. "Look how much fun we had in the kitchen yesterday. You remember that, right? Remember how hard you screamed?"

"—there's this possession thing he's got goin'."

Alarm flared across Jude's face, pulled the muscles of his face tight. "It has skin-walked?"

Possession. Skin-walking. That agonizing acidic pain flashed through her mind.

Oh . . . God . . . her stomach heaved. Revulsion rolled through her. This . . . this thing had been inside her? She'd never feel clean again.

Drinking a dozen gallons of bleach wouldn't come close to washing away the loathing.

"Yeah, well you're not so peachy yourself, you condescending bitch," the thing that used to call itself Pachico said. Its muddy, inhuman eyes promised retribution and agony. It took an ominous step forward, the hub's stone walls shimmering within its translucency.

Possibly she should have tried to mask her revulsion and horror.

"Rawls?" Faith stumbled backward, a film of sweat, cold as ice, slicking her skin.

"Jude!" Rawls's arms slid around her, dragging her tight against his chest.

"Here." Jude's voice, much closer.

Pachico's expression darkened with rage. "You—"

His transparent image flickered, in and out, like a hazy satellite image. And then it was gone.

Still shaking, Faith turned her head. Her gaze locked on Jude's tight, uneasy face. Slowly, her eyes dropped to his chest. A slight bulge against the fabric of his T-shirt hinted at the location of the weaving that carried his ghost-protection spell.

The *hiixoyooniiheiht* that had protected her too.

"You want to tell me what the hell just happened?" Mac asked, his sharp question echoing through the chamber.

How odd . . . the commander's voice—which until now had always sounded too loud and hard and twitchingly angry—sounded comforting. Familiar. Safe. Downright trustworthy.

"What happened"—Faith's voice climbed shrilly. She scanned the cavern for a translucent monster—"is that I tapped into Rawls's hallucination."

And she wanted to believe that. She wanted to believe that so bad. Shared delusions existed after all. They'd been studied. There was plenty of empirical evidence to back them up.

"You tapped into my hallucination . . ." Rawls repeated dryly. He tilted her chin and stared into her eyes, a combination of amusement and irritability on his face. "You're not gonna seriously go with that."

"Hey, it happens. Read up on Point Pleasant back in 1966. Shared delusions are an accepted psychological phenomenon." She tried to interject rock-solid certainty into her voice—but alas, it faltered.

"Which you don't believe in." Rawls's voice was impossibly gentle.

"I want to," Faith whispered, scanning the hub again.

"I bet you do." His arms tightening around her, he leaned down to kiss the top of her head.

"Does anyone have a fucking clue what these two are talking about?" Mac sounded more confused than angry now.

With a sigh, Faith straightened in Rawls's embrace, and realized for the first time that everyone was watching them. Everyone. She glanced from curious face to curious face.

Uh-oh. She'd just exposed Rawls's secret to everyone. Well, not the exact secret, because nobody knew they were dealing with a ghost—except for Jude, of course—but now everybody knew Rawls was seeing something invisible to the rest of them.

So was she for that matter.

"I'm sorry." As hard as he'd tried to keep this information from his teammates, she should offer him more than an apology. Maybe cooking for him for the rest of the month would make it up to him.

He shrugged good-naturedly. "You didn't tell them anythin' they didn't already suspect."

Okay, that news surprised her.

"They already knew about Pachico?" It didn't occur to her until the name had hit the air and he'd grimaced that he'd meant they'd known he was hallucinating, not that he was being haunted.

I'm so sorry. She mouthed it this time, feeling like a complete and utter idiot.

Maybe they wouldn't identify the name.

Please don't let them recognize the name.

"Pachico," Zane repeated, sudden stillness on his face. "Pachico's dead." He'd figured it out. Faith could see the realization spreading across his face.

"I know he's dead." Rawls paused, shrugged, ran a tense hand through his short, thick platinum hair. "But that hasn't stopped the bastard from fuckin' with me."

Dead silence fell, hummed through the cavern for the count of five.

"A ghost?" Cosky said, his voice neutral. His face flat. "You've been seeing a ghost?"

"Pretty much."

His answer might have been laconic, his attitude careless, but Faith could feel the tension vibrating through him. Their reaction was important to him—vitally important. Stepping closer to him until their arms brushed, she slipped her hand into his and squeezed, and felt, more than heard, the uneven breath he released. His fingers tightened around hers.

Cosky's eyebrows beetled. He studied Rawls's face intently before turning his head slightly and pinning Faith with implacable gray eyes. "And you? You see it too."

God help her, but she wanted to say no. No, she didn't.

Instead, she squared her shoulders and took a deep raw breath. "Yes. Yes, I did. I do."

For a moment it felt like she'd stepped off a ledge and her body was in free fall, no sense of gravity to cradle her. But then Rawls's hand contracted, stopping her midflight.

The tension vanished from Rawls's muscles and a hoarse breath sounded in her ear. That's when she realized her reaction had been as important to Rawls as his teammates' had been.

Maybe even more important.

With Faith's hand held tight in his and her admission that she'd seen Pachico warming his chest, Rawls faced off against his teammates. So far the revelation had gone exactly as he'd envisioned—blatant disbelief from Mac, questioning and concern from Zane, and frozen neutrality from Cosky. While the timing of the disclosure could have been better, such as not in front of the entire damn camp, it could have gone much worse too. At least his ghost hadn't grabbed one of the rifles hanging off his teammates' shoulders and sprayed the cavern with semiautomatic gunfire. Talk about a brutal introduction to Ghosts 101.

Bracing himself, he waited for the avalanche of questions to resume. The fact that someone like Faith, a scientist driven by logic and empirical data, had admitted to seeing the ghost too, might have bolstered his position—assured everyone he wasn't crazy. Assuming his teammates didn't simply pin her with a crazy tag too.

"A ghost," Zane repeated slowly, his forehead crinkling. His eyes narrowed, as though he were measuring the possibility. "That's what's been going on with you? A ghost?"

Rawls shrugged, using his free hand to scratch his forehead. "I'm surprised y'all never figured that out, what with all the shoutin' at empty air."

"That's because we were holding on to the hope you hadn't gone fucking crazy," Mac interrupted, his voice surprisingly calm. He ignored the quelling look Zane shot him. "You do realize that ghosts don't exist."

"What I realize," Rawls fired back, "is that most people can't see them."

"No shit." Mac's voice rose, along with his eyebrows. "So you and the good doc just happen to be two of the lucky ones? Why's that?" His eyebrows climbed even higher as he crossed his arms across his chest and rocked back on the heels of his boots. "From that earlier kiss, it's obvious you two are involved. Let me guess. That's the secret? Since you're intimately involved, you two can see the ghost while nobody else here can?"

With a snort, Rawls shook his head. "Don't be an ass, Commander. If intimacy had anything to do with it, Zane and Beth and Cosky and Kait would see the damn thing too."

"Then why you two and nobody else?" But it was Cosky's flat voice that asked the question.

"Because they have walked the other side and returned. You have not," Jude said coolly.

"Walked the other side?" Zane asked, his attention skipping between Jude and Rawls with periodic trips toward Faith.

Rawls ran a hand over his head and shrugged. "He means Faith and I both died and then returned to our bodies, while the rest of you managed to avoid that particular nasty journey."

"Died?" Zane shot a glance at Cosky. "Admittedly, from what Cosky and Kait said, Faith didn't have a pulse back there in the tunnel, at least not until Kait did her thing. But you—" He shook his head, his green eyes almost regretful. "Sorry buddy, you had a heartbeat."

"Did I?" Rawls turned his head to stare at Cosky. "I watched every-thin' you and Kait did from outside and above my body. Watched you two heal me. Felt myself sucked back into my body. That's how I ended up with Pachico, he hitched a ride back into this world when you healed me."

Silence fell, and every eye turned to Cosky.

"Hell." Cosky stirred and shook his head. "I don't know. I thought I felt a pulse, but it was faint, erratic. There one moment, gone the next. It could have cut out when I lifted my fingers."

A memory slipped through Rawls's mind.

"What the hell do they think they're gonna do?" Pachico asked. *"Bring you back from the dead?"*

Cosky hissed. "I got a pulse."

Pachico laughed again. "Wishful thinking on your buddy's part. If you had a pulse, you wouldn't be all floaty beside me."

His heart had stopped beating several seconds before Cosky's arrival on the scene, as evidenced by Rawls's front-row seat in that silvery otherworld. He wouldn't have been watching the drama, all disembodied there beside them, if his heart had still been beating—would he?

He frowned, the question a sharp itch. Hell, he couldn't make the assumption that he'd been dead. Maybe Cosky had felt a pulse. Despite the fact that he'd spent several minutes there, he didn't know much of anything about that eerie netherworld. Maybe a borderline pulse was enough to get the soul—or essence, or whatever the hell people called that transparent, incorporeal state—ejected from the corporeal body. And then there was Faith. She didn't have any recollection of dying or playing voyeur outside her body, yet she'd still seen Pachico.

Who the hell knew what the rules were? As Pachico had complained, death didn't come with a manual.

"Look," Rawls said after a few seconds of uneasy silence. "All I'm sayin' is that I was outside my body, in a transparent state, watchin' everythin' that was happenin' there on the ground. I heard everythin'. Saw everythin'. At least until I was dragged back into my body . . . everythin' gets hazy after that."

"Take us through what you saw and heard," Zane said calmly.

"Oh, for Christ's sake," Mac snapped, disbelief flashing across his face. "We're wasting our time with this shit."

Zane shot Mac another of those quelling looks. "We were all there. There's no harm in comparing his version to ours."

Cosky nodded in agreement.

Well . . . hell . . . Rawls rocked back slightly in surprise. They were actually taking his story under consideration . . . maybe.

With Faith's hand still warming his palm and fingers, he briskly recounted what he remembered from that night, a week earlier, when he'd died. He skipped telling them about the weird snake of energy that had impaled his transparent chest and pulled him back into his body. From what he remembered of the conversation back then, as they circled his splayed, still body, they'd seen the energy as a glow, or a shimmer, but nobody had mentioned that weird tentacle. If they'd seen it, sure as hell someone would have mentioned it.

After he finished, an edgy hush seized the cavern.

"What he described is pretty much what I remember," Zane finally said. He shifted to scan Mac's and Cosky's faces, as though looking for confirmation.

A round of uneasy agreements lit the tense silence.

"Which doesn't mean shit," Mac interrupted, although a troubled expression had settled on his face. "He could have heard everything we said."

"While unconscious?" Zane asked with raised eyebrows.

"We don't know that he was unconscious," Mac fired back. "But hell, even if he did step out of his body like he claims, to play voyeur on us, that has no bearing on the damn ghost he claims tailed him back."

Rawls locked his instinctive protest down. Arguing wouldn't convince anyone that he was sane.

"Your belief holds no weight," Jude announced in his habitually expressionless tone. "The *biitei* existence is not conditional on your acceptance."

Another thick silence fell.

Once again Zane was the one to break it. *"Biitei?"*

Rawls turned to Jude, but the big Arapaho had stilled and was staring at the ground, his long, graying braid dangling over his right shoulder and swaying slightly. As paranoid as he was about the whole ghost thing, he must have decided to go back to ignoring the topic under discussion.

"Ghost." Rawls finally translated the Arapaho word.

Jude suddenly straightened. "Wolf comes."

As distractions went, it immediately shifted everyone's focus—although from the censorious look Zane directed at him, the ghost conversation was far from over.

."Come," Jude said, pivoting and heading toward the back of the cavern and the rock passageway that penetrated deep into the heart of the hillside.

"What the fuck," Mac growled, slamming his hands down on his hips. "He could spend a few fucking words filling us in."

Faith beside him, Rawls weaved his way between people as he headed for Jude. He had no clue how much range that amulet had. He couldn't afford to let his ghost protection get too far ahead. But just before he joined the gray-haired warrior, a huge body dressed in camo stepped out of the darkness behind Jude and joined the older Arapaho in the mouth of the cavern.

Wolf.

Rawls picked up his pace.

After a brief conversation with his second in command, Wolf shifted, his dark eyes landing on Rawls. He beckoned him forward. When Rawls reached him, Wolf passed him a wad of leather.

"Don't take it off," Wolf said flatly, and brushed past him, advancing on Cosky and Kait.

Rawls unwrapped the leather and found a small weaving attached to a leather cord. The new amulet carried the same stacked starburst pattern as Jude's charm, but in vibrant purple and blue.

Relief whooshed through him. He slipped the thin cord over his head and lifted his T-shirt, slipping the weaving beneath it. It rasped against his skin, itchy and annoying, but at least he didn't have to count on someone else's shield now. With this *hiixoyooniiheiht* he could protect himself and Faith and everyone else for that matter.

"Does it feel . . . I don't know . . . weird? Strange?" Faith asked him, curiosity shimmering in her eyes.

"Just itchy," Rawls said absently. He turned to find Wolf, Mac, Zane, and Cosky in a huddle maybe ten feet behind him.

"Can I see it?" Faith asked.

Rawls tugged the weaving up by the cord, dropping it into her hands when she reached for it. Since the cord was still around his neck, she had to lean in to inspect it, until she was so close her head was tucked beneath his chin and the sweet scent of her hair tickled his nose and libido.

To distract himself, he sought out Wolf again and found the huddle breaking apart.

"Listen up," Mac said, stepping into the center of the hub and raising his voice. "We're moving out. Wolf, Jude, and I will lead the way. Rawls, Cosky, and Zane will bring up the rear."

As people stirred and lined up, Cosky headed toward Kait and lifted her to her feet. He held a water bottle to her lips, and once he was satisfied with her intake, he gave her a swift hug and handed her off to Marion, who wrapped an arm around her waist. Zane kissed Beth and joined Cosky. They wove their way through bodies toward the back of the hub.

"It doesn't feel any different," Faith said, disappointment in her voice. She gave the rough starburst one final rub between her fingers and dropped it.

"How you doin'?" Rawls asked quietly as he tucked the weaving back beneath his shirt. He reached for her wrist to check her pulse. It beat steady and strong beneath his fingers.

She'd be safer in the middle of the flock, guarded by the front and back flanks. But, if her heart was even the slightest unstable still . . . procedures be damned . . . he'd glue her to his side.

"I'm fine. Honestly." She pulled her wrist away and made a shooing gesture. "Go. Go."

Rawls gave her one final, thorough scan from head to toe. Her color looked good. Her eyes clear. She was breathing with ease.

"I'll be right behind you if you run into trouble," he told her softly and leaned down, brushing her lips with his. Her mouth was soft beneath his. Satin smooth.

Intoxicating.

Stifling a groan, he forced himself to lift his head and step back. The soft cloudy look in her eyes followed him as he headed back to Cosky and Zane.

"Mac has a point," Cosky told Rawls and Zane in a low voice, as they slowly followed Amy and her two boys through the hub and into the rock-cut passageway. "How the hell *did* Jude know Wolf was on the way?"

"You think he's lyin'?" Rawls asked.

"No. Fuck. Wolf's here, right?" Cosky slowed, letting Amy and her chattering son increase the distance between them. "But there's something weird there. Jude showed up at our door before Mac's nine-one-one hit the radio waves. He said Wolf had contacted him, warned him to get everyone into the tunnels immediately."

Zane shrugged. "He's Wolf's second. Probably has the CO's sat phone."

Cosky frowned. "He didn't have it on him when he showed up at the cabin. And he didn't have it when he told us Wolf was here."

Okay. That was odd.

"So what are you thinkin'?" Rawls asked, craning his neck for a glimpse of Faith, but the bounce of flashlight beams ricocheting off the rock walls blinded him.

"Hell, I don't know." Cosky scrubbed a hand through his hair and picked up his pace. "Just keep your eyes open." But then he slowed again and glanced at Rawls out of the corner of his eye. "So this ghost? He around now?"

"Nah, we're good." Unconsciously Rawls's hand climbed, grazing the slight bump lifting his T-shirt where the weaving burned slightly against his skin. "Where we headed, anyway?"

An odd silence greeted the question.

And then Zane gave a bemused laugh. "To the elevators." At Rawls's double take, he snorted. "I'm not shitting you. They have a helipad on top of this hill and two elevators from the tunnels to the helipad."

Two elevators. It would be a hell of a lot quicker to the top of the mountain by elevator than stairs. But what the hell powered them this far from their compound?

"They have a chopper waitin'?" Rawls asked, although he was pretty certain of the answer.

"Two birds," Cosky corrected him dryly. "And according to Wolf, his team neutralized our visitors and took out *their* helicopter."

"Mightily accommodatin' of 'em." Rawls drawled.

"No shit," Zane said, his voice a cross between suspicion and admiration.

But the same question weighted the air between the three of them. *Who the hell are these guys?*

"What?" One rigid finger at a time, Eric Manheim forced his grip to relax around his cell phone.

"An unidentified squad of highly trained mercenaries slipped in behind my men and took them out." His new—and widely acclaimed contractor—delivered the news evenly.

In the midst of a battle, either in the boardroom or out in the wilds of Washington State, one prepared for every foreseeable possibility. Considering his current contractor's reputation, Eric couldn't believe the fucking imbecile hadn't prepared for this one.

"You didn't post guards? Mackenzie and his crew got the jump on you?" Eric didn't smooth the edge from his voice.

"Negative. The targets were holed up in their cabins. This was an unidentified team."

Eric's jaw tightened until his entire head throbbed. "How the fuck would you know? You said you never saw the men who struck."

His soon-to-be-deceased contractor had the intelligence to remain silent.

Forcing himself to rein in his anger—strong emotions were so unproductive, often blinding you to the possibilities inherent in the moment—he regrouped, and looked for a means to salvage the mission.

"The Chastain boys' signals are still broadcasting. They're moving up the mountain. Likely there's a second entrance into this tunnel system somewhere on top of the mountain and they'll emerge there"—some of his anger slipped out—"along with those fucking SEALs. So how about getting your bloody helicopter into the air? Target them from above when they emerge from the tunnels."

It was so damn simple he couldn't believe the idiot hadn't considered it himself.

"Our chopper"—this time the even tone tightened—"is no longer in play."

Eric froze. "What the fuck does that mean?"

"It means it was taken out."

There was a hint of a snap to the voice, as though the man it belonged to didn't appreciate the scolding. Which was too bloody bad and justification for terminating his contract.

"By what?"

"Some kind of experimental aircraft."

"The hell you say? You lost your helicopter and most of your men and didn't find that news worth reporting?"

This time he didn't bother to relax his fingers when they started to cramp. The pain gave him something to concentrate on, something to combat the urge to throw his coffee cup across the room and watch it shatter.

"I'm reporting in now. And FYI, these SEALs are hooked up," his facilitator said, his accent thickening. "Much more than you indicated."

Really? Really? The bloody fuckhole was blaming him?

In an effort to calm himself, he stared out the rain-beaded window of the penthouse's breakfast nook. Central Park, in all its sprawling, wild glory, sparkled like a glistening emerald beneath the misting rain.

For once, the view failed to soothe him.

It was too bad there was so much time and distance between him and the man on the other end of the line. The bastard had talked himself into a painfully slow execution. His family as well.

"No excuses. I don't care how you do it. Just get it done." Eric cut the call, knowing the man wouldn't be calling back.

"Problems, darling?" Esme asked, looking up from the business section of the *New York Times*.

With the rage still trying to break free, he focused on the beautiful woman who shared his table, his bed, his life, and his vision of a new world order. Her normally sleek cap of blond hair was slightly rumpled, her blue eyes soft and languid: a slight flush still rode the crest of her cheekbones. She looked like a woman who'd just climbed out of bed after a night of thorough loving—which she had. His hands unclenched as that unquenchable hunger she never failed to unleash in him stirred. Beneath the silk nightshirt obscuring her slender figure, she wore nothing but warm soft skin. His fingers tingled, itching to slide the shirt up and explore every inch of that sleek body . . . again.

But regrettably, duty beckoned.

Crossing to her, he leaned over to place a gentle kiss on her upturned swollen lips and then picked up her teacup.

"Looks like we're in the market for another freelancer," he said as he set her cup in the marble sink. "Perhaps it's time to contact Coulson's man. At least Coulson's tactics produce results."

"They escaped? Again?" She cocked her head slightly, her hair fluttering around her ears.

"For now. But the signal's still broadcasting. We'll track them down." He frowned, staring down at the brilliant diamond pattern etched into the teacup's glass as unease brewed in his mind.

They were dealing with an unknown variable. And in his experience, unknown variables tended to prove disastrous. "It would appear that our SEALs are better connected than we realized. They have access to reinforcements, at least one experimental aircraft, and some major artillery."

"Could the reinforcements be coming from Coronado?" Esme asked, reaching across the table to stroke his hand. He caught it and carried it to his lips.

"Possibly, but doubtful. Most of their buddies are out on deployment." He'd made sure of it. "Besides, they couldn't acquisition an experimental helicopter from the navy." He shook his head and frowned. "Or the kind of firepower it took to shoot down team B." He turned to stare out the breakfast window again as more of those uneasy chills peppered his spine.

His instincts were usually dead-on, and at the moment, they were clamoring that those damn SEALs had hooked up with someone with major resources and the ability to do serious damage.

If he wanted to survive the oncoming storm he sensed looming on the horizon, he needed to find out whom they'd climbed into bed with, and take immediate steps to neutralize the whole damn lot of them.

Chapter Fifteen

MAC SETTLED AGAINST THE PADDED WALL VIBRATING AGAINST HIS back. The average military-grade chopper could travel 150 knots an hour, and six hundred kilometers on a tank of fuel. They'd been in the air for five hours now, which meant this bad boy shuttling them to Christ-knew-where was far superior to any military bird he knew of. He estimated it was going faster than 150 knots an hour too. A hell of a lot faster—which made it one pretty sweet ride.

He smoothed his palm down the sleek, almost metallic sheen of the wall beside him. The surface didn't feel like metal, or fabric, or anything he'd encountered before. He'd bet his pension on this craft being experimental.

Assuming you still have a pension.

He sighed, envy rising. What he wouldn't give to have one of these babies sitting on the tarmac at Coronado.

Whomever Wolf and his team worked for, they were well funded.

Impressively funded, impressively connected too—experimental aircraft weren't handed off to every Tom, Dick, or Harry. Nor were mysterious compounds with intricate tunnel systems, which included elevators in the middle of fucking nowhere.

Elevators, for Christ's sake. Mac shook his head.

And oh, the surprises hadn't stopped there. When they'd stepped out of the elevator, they'd found themselves on the top of one of the bluffs surrounding camp. And two of these bad boys had been waiting to bug them out. He glanced around the blinking ruddy interior. A Blackhawk cost a cool thirty million plus some good-sized change. Considering the fuel capacity and speed on this baby, it had to run more. A lot more.

And Wolf had two of them.

The first had easily taken all the passengers, along with Wolf's crew. The second was likely a guard dog. On hand for counterattack and intercepting enemy fire. Not that there was anything currently in use that could keep up with this baby. Or at least in current public or military use.

Somebody was obviously engineering this new aircraft. Christ knew who else they'd sold them to.

This bird was a working one, though. Used for combat. It was set up for insertions, with benches along the back and side, and a matted open interior to carry extra men and equipment. The straps at arm's length along the wall were a dead giveaway that this chopper had seen some action. You needed something to grab hold of to stabilize yourself when the pilot banked hard to the right or left.

At the moment, rather than ferrying a team into battle, the chopper was full of sleeping civilians. Amy Chastain had taken the back bench. She was sitting in the middle, her head tilted back against the wall, with a child curled on either side using her thighs as pillows. Someone had handed out blankets, and periodically she'd stir, check on her sons, and drag the blankets back up to their necks. Not that her ministrations did much good; within seconds the vibrations traveling through the walls and floor rattled the cloth back down the slope of their shoulders. But he had to hand it to her. At least she tried to tend to her kids—she tried over and over again. She was determined to keep her kids warm and safe.

Something softened in his chest, went disgustingly gooey.

Scowling, he dragged his gaze away and scanned the rest of the refugees. Because that's what they were now, fucking refugees. Estranged from their government and country. The country that he'd given the best years of his life to.

He nipped that line of thought in the bud, since all it did was lead to heartburn.

At the moment, Marion and Kait were sound asleep—Marion curled on the side bench and Kait on the floor beside it, her cheek pillowed on Cos's shoulder. He, along with the rest of the men, sat along the walls, either dozing or stoically waiting with eyes closed and bodies relaxed.

Oddly, the atmosphere inside the bird was eerily familiar. It had the same sense of exhausted relief and anticipation that accompanied an evac after a mission. The relief that you'd made it through one more mission alive, relatively unscathed. The anticipation of returning to base, sleeping in your own bed, eating something that wasn't out of a tube or a pouch.

Not that they were returning to his base, or that he'd be sleeping in his own bed.

And that was the whole fucking problem, wasn't it? He had no Goddamn clue where they were headed. The tension inside him tightened a notch. It would be nice if he could see out a damn window and pinpoint what direction they were headed: east, west? Were they over water? Land? Mountains?

But like all working birds, this one's windows were reserved for the cockpit. From his current position, all he could see was the dense black of night out the windows in front.

Wolf was sitting across from him, his back against the wall, head back, eyes closed. He looked like he was getting a nice nap in. Mac rolled onto his knees and crawled across the matted floor. Once he was close enough, he kicked the warrior's huge boots and settled next to him. The big bastard didn't open his eyes, but Mac caught the sudden tension in previously loose muscles, indicating consciousness.

"Near as I can figure it, we're closing in on five and a half hours in flight. I won't ask what kind of speed and fuel capacity this bird has." Mostly because he knew the annoying bastard wouldn't satisfy his curiosity. Mac wouldn't if their positions were reversed.

"Wise of you," Wolf murmured without opening his eyes.

Asshole. Mac's mouth quirked.

"You could at least fill us in on where we're headed."

"I could . . ." Wolf agreed, his voice trailing off.

Mac grunted in irritation. He considered kicking the asshole again. It wouldn't loosen the guy's tongue, but it would give Mac some satisfaction. "How much longer?"

Christ, I sound like one of Amy's kids.

"As long as it takes."

Which could mean anything from a minute to a fucking week. Knowing he wouldn't get anything more from the bastard, Mac settled back against the wall to wait.

It turned out that Wolf's "as long as it takes" boiled down to ten minutes. Suddenly the chopper's speed subsided. After a few seconds it slowed even further and banked to the right, straightened out, and dropped.

Wolf's men stirred and stretched. Mac could hear the pilot talking into his comm, but the words were garbled by engine vibrations and the beat of the rotor. He stretched up against the wall, trying to get a glimpse out the cockpit windows. But all he could see was a ring of mountain peaks breaking through the milky glow of dawn. Without any reference points, those peaks were impossible to identify.

There wasn't much sense in standing and losing his balance if the bird suddenly banked, not when his boots would be hitting the ground soon enough anyway. He'd wait until the ground was stable beneath his feet before launching a recon and identifying where the hell they'd been taken.

As the bird settled on the ground, he expected Wolf's men to rise in anticipation of departing the cramped interior. But nobody moved. The rotor slowed, slowed even more. Still no movement from anyone in the bird. The engine died, and blades went still.

But nobody moved a fucking muscle.

What the hell?

Cosky shifted, shook Kait awake, and started to rise to his feet, only to slowly settle back with a puzzled frown as Jude turned his head and said something to him.

As his lieutenant's gaze searched out his own, Mac could read the same questions in those flat gray eyes. Where the hell had they taken them and what the fuck were they waiting for?

Wolf suddenly rolled his head toward Mac and opened his eyes. "We aren't there yet," he said, as though he'd read Mac's mind.

Okay . . .

"We're refueling?" he asked. It was the only thing that made sense, but he didn't hear any people or machinery outside.

"Not exactly," Wolf murmured, facing forward again and closing his eyes.

Oh, for Christ's sake. The asshole was just fucking with him now.

Suddenly an intense whining hum came from outside. The bird started to drop. The sensation was unmistakable. They were sinking. He stretched again and looked out the cockpit window. Sure enough, he couldn't see the mountain peaks anymore, just a wall of green trees in the distance. Frowning, he pressed his palm against the wall, but the vibrations from the engine were gone. So was the roar from the rotor. The chopper wasn't descending under its own power. Shifting slightly so he could see out the cockpit windows without craning his neck, he watched the bank of trees give way to pitch black.

That blackness obscuring the windows wasn't coming from night, more like a glossy wall. They were sinking into a tunnel or shaft or something similar, and from the hum beneath them and the sensation of moving, they were obviously still descending. It was like being in another elevator.

The drop down seemed to take forever, a minute at least. Maybe two. And then a clang sounded. With a jolt, the bird stopped moving. More clanging from outside, along with the roar of laboring equipment and the shout of voices.

The men camped out along the walls came alive. One of them unlocked the sliding door and forced it open. Mac winced as bright light flooded the dark interior of the craft, temporarily blinding him. By the time his eyes adjusted, Wolf's men were lined up and disembarking. All he could make out between the huge bodies bristling with weapons and equipment was the dull gray of concrete.

He waited until the last of Wolf's men hopped off the chopper before rising to his feet and following them to the door. Before disembarking, he took a moment to survey his new surroundings.

He'd been right about the concrete. Apparently Wolf had flown them to a garage. At least that's what the facility looked like—a giant, cavernous, domed, underground parking facility . . . for aircraft. Slowly he dropped down to the concrete floor and stepped aside so Cosky could disembark.

The place was huge—absolutely immense. It needed to be, considering the size and volume of the aircraft it housed. Not just helicopters either. Hell no—there were plenty of planes too. He spotted a C-12F Huron light transport/evac plane as well as a Raytheon for surveillance. And Jesus Christ, that looked like a motherfucking Grizzly 11 airbus in the far corner.

Whomever the hell Wolf worked for, they were armed to the teeth.

Vaguely aware that Cosky had hopped out beside him and then stopped to stare, Mac took a couple of steps forward. As far as he could tell, there didn't appear to be any hangar doors to this place, so how the hell did they transport the planes to the runway?

The memory of that mechanical hum flashed through his mind, along with the accompanying sense of sinking. They'd obviously landed the helicopter onto some kind of lift, and then the lift had retracted, lowering the craft underground. It would be easy enough to employ the same technology on the planes. They must have a runway nearby; from there they could taxi the planes onto their lifts. He looked up to find the ceiling was intact. A door must swing into place once the machine was lowered.

Jesus Christ, the engineering behind this facility was astounding.

Cosky let out a long, low, appreciative whistle. "I guess we're not in Kansas anymore."

A kid with bright orange hair and a thunderstorm of freckles bustled over to them. His stained overalls were at least two sizes too big for his thin frame and marked him as a grease monkey.

But what he lacked in size, he made up for in attitude. "Hey, Commander, good to see you didn't blow this one up too. *Beniinookee* is threatening to deduct the last one from your paycheck."

At first Mac thought the kid was talking to him, but it quickly became apparent the guy was focused on Wolf.

So the big bastard was a commander too, but from what branch of military? Or was he even with the military?

It was past time to get some of his questions answered. And he'd start with the simplest, but most crucial one.

"Where the hell are we?" he demanded, the question directed at the orange-haired kid since Wolf had proved annoyingly vague in the helicopter.

The grease monkey turned to him with lifted eyebrows and something close to a smirk. "Mackenzie, isn't it?" But he immediately turned back to Wolf. "You know a pool started on whether you'd actually bring them back against direct orders, but the pool was dropped after a day or so because nobody would take the odds against it."

Which didn't tell Mac a fucking thing—other than the people here had too damn much time on their hands.

"Where"—Mac asked again with cold deliberation, far too aware that Amy and her kids had stepped up next to him—"are we?"

The orange-haired kid smiled at Amy, and Mac went rigid. There was far too much male appreciation in the grease monkey's eyes—he had half a mind to pound that masculine interest out of the little punk.

"It isn't so much where you are, as what you're in." The kid smiled conspiratorially at Amy, and it was all Mac could do to not flatten him right then and there.

His internal explosive reaction sent up warning flares. All this fucking proximity to the woman had escalated the intensity of his hunger—and apparently his possessiveness as well. Time to take a long, permanent step back. Reconfigure. Avoid the woman as much as humanly possible.

"Okay . . ."Amy said slowly, apparently deciding to play along. "What are we in?"

But Wolf was the one to answer. "Shadow Mountain."

Rawls stared at the computer screen displaying the Doppler echocardiogram of Faith's heart. Like the EKG printout, it indicated a healthy, completely regenerated muscle. Full function of the left ventricle—with a normal ejection fraction of over seventy-five percent. The speed and strength of the electrical pulses passing through the cardio muscle on the electrocardiogram had been well within the normal range too. The electrical pulses had been strong, steady, with no suggestion of tachycardia. The ultrasound hadn't picked up any abnormalities in the organ's musculature—exterior or interior.

Unbelievable.

Every test showed a perfect heart, in prime condition.

No evidence of a heart transplant. No indication of ventricular tachycardia—sweet Jesus, no sign of tachycardia at all.

"As you can see," Dr. Kerry said, reaching out to slide a finger down the computer screen, "the left ventricle and atrium show no sign of the previous atrophy or damage."

With a slight nod, Rawls switched his attention to the second monitor with an image of Faith's heart taken almost a year earlier. The image showed distinct diminishing of function of the left ventricle. If he hadn't known the films were of the same heart, he would have thought they'd been taken from two separate people.

He didn't ask how they'd managed to acquire a copy of Faith's medical history, including all the results from her latest physical, or how they'd managed to get their hands on the file so quickly—for Christ's sake, they'd had it on hand before Faith had even stepped through their medical-bay doors. The medical facility, along with the impressive array of equipment it housed, was positive proof Wolf's people could get their hands on pretty much anything they deemed necessary. Including Faith's prescriptions, as her meds had been waiting for her too.

They'd stepped off the helicopter into a huge aircraft-parking zone, and from there, he and Faith, along with Amy and her kids, had been shuttled across the massive facility to the medical wing. The last two hours had been one round of tests after another. He hadn't seen Cosky, Zane, or Mac since disembarkment, and when he asked, Dr. Kerry had said they were with the *beniinookee*. Further explanation had identified the word as one meaning a high-ranking officer, which could mean Wolf—or whomever Wolf reported to . . . if he reported to anyone.

Faith's hand slipped into his and clung. She cleared her throat. "I don't understand. How can it be completely normal now? This doesn't make sense. They sewed that heart inside my chest. There has to be evidence of that."

You'd think so . . . but there wasn't.

Far too aware of the warm, soft weight of Faith's hand cradled in his, Rawls tried to concentrate on the conversation. She sounded shell-shocked. He didn't blame her.

Admitting that her heart may have stopped and that Kait might have gotten it beating again had been hard enough for her.

But this . . . sweet Jesus, this took Kait's ability into an entirely new realm.

Intellectually, he'd known there had to be some insanely strong mojo in Kait's hands. She'd healed the damage from those bullets to his chest, after all. Even dragged him back from the dead.

But seeing the miraculous results of her healing power on the screen took it out of the abstract and into the here and now.

"Now that we have a baseline for your heart, we can move on to the exertion testing," Kerry said, pushing his glasses up with his forefinger. He turned from the bank of computer screens to smile at Faith. "Later today we'll get you on a treadmill and hook you up for monitoring, take a look at that heart of yours in action. But so far everything looks normal."

He turned back to the screen to survey both sets of images before shaking his head, an expression of awe creeping across his face. "It's remarkable, Commander, the strength of your sister's ability. She's markedly stronger than Will or One Bird."

Commander? Obviously the doctor wasn't addressing him. He turned, unsurprised to find Wolf standing behind them, his huge body swallowing what little space remained in the computer room.

And then Kerry's comment registered.

Sister? Kait was Wolf's sister?

Well shit, of course she was. How could he have been so obtuse? The facial resemblance was strong, now that he'd thought to look for it.

After a second of studying the two computer screens, Wolf appeared to dismiss them. Shifting slightly, he caught Rawls's eye. "Walk with me."

The words weren't a request, but Wolf wasn't his priority. He turned back to the radiologist.

"When are you doin' the stress test?" He'd make certain he was there when they strapped those sensors to Faith's chest and cranked up the treadmill.

Faith's hand, which had been still as a frightened bird within his own grip, stirred and squeezed his fingers.

"Later this afternoon?" The lift in the man's tone turned the words into a question. "I'm sure Dr. Ansell would like to get some rest. And I have a couple of patients I need to check on."

A radiologist making rounds? Rawls reassessed this guy's role at the facility. He was obviously a hell of a lot more than a simple radiologist, as Wolf had introduced him. But then . . . Rawls turned to consider the man waiting patiently behind him. Wolf was a hell of a lot more than a simple commander too.

Maybe taking that walk with their host would give him a better sense of what kind of organization they were dealing with. At the moment, the only thing he knew for sure was their hosts were exceptionally well stocked on everything from weaponry to aircraft to medical equipment.

Hell, the medical bay was as well-equipped as any high-tech hospital. Their ultrasound, X-ray, CAT scan, and MRI machines were all the current incarnations within an ever-changing technology. And from what he'd seen of the lab— Which reminded him . . .

"They find anythin' in Brendan or Benji's bloodwork?" he asked, looking over his shoulder at Wolf.

They'd scanned the children for microchips or implants while he'd been waiting for Faith to return from the last round of testing.

According to Amy, they hadn't found anything inserted into her sons' flesh . . . however, following a routine blood test, they'd found an anomaly in the red and white blood cells.

They'd taken the boys to the lab for additional testing.

A grim shadow fell over Wolf's normally taciturn face. "A genetically modified biological isotope was found in their blood cells. This compound appears to have bonded with every cell in their bodies."

An engineered biological compound?

"They're usin' this compound to follow the kids?"

"It appears so," Dr. Kerry said. He sighed and scrubbed at his forehead. "The isotope is siphoning off the cells' electrical impulses and using them to power a high-frequency signal. If the people who injected the compound know the frequency the isotope emits, theoretically they could locate and follow it."

Considering how quickly their camp had been attacked after the kids' arrival, there was nothing theoretical about it.

"Sweet Jesus." Rawls's throat tightened. "They're just kids. What's wrong with those people?"

You didn't target children. You sure as hell didn't fill their bodies with experimental chemical shit. If the isotope was hijacking the electrical output, the cells would break down much faster. As more and more cells failed, the health of the host would decline.

Those Goddamn bastards had effectively condemned two children to a prolonged and likely agonizing death.

He took a deep breath and forced the rage back. There had to be a way to counteract the compound they'd been injected with.

"Can the isotope be neutralized?" Rawls asked.

"We're looking into that." Kerry's gaze shifted back to the MRI of Faith's heart on the monitor. "Along with other possibilities."

Wolf dropped a heavy hand on Rawls's shoulder. "Walk with me. There is much to discuss."

"Such as?"

"Your *biitei*." Wolf's hooded black gaze dropped to the leather cord circling Rawls's neck.

"The *hiixoyooniiheiht* seems to be holdin' it at bay," Rawls said, feeling the slight burn of the colorful amulet beneath his T-shirt.

Faith fixed determined eyes on Wolf's face. "These charms are fascinating. I understand only the person who mak— creates them, is aware of how they work. I'd like to speak with whoever this person is. Perhaps—"

The shoulder Wolf turned on her was answer enough, and she stumbled into silence.

Rawls remained silent, but he had questions as well. Wearing the thing triggered the strangest sensation, not just the scratchy burn, but the way it vibrated every now and then. When it quivered, the burning intensified, never enough to prove painful, but enough to be noticeable. He hoped that meant it was working and Pachico's reign of frustration was officially over.

Wolf turned back to Rawls. "This *biitei* took orders from your enemy. Is this not true?"

"He worked for them, if that's what you're gettin' at."

"Then it carries answers to many of our questions." Thick black eyebrows rose in a quizzical expression. "Does it not?"

Rawls shrugged. "He's not exactly forthcomin' with what he knows."

Hell, Pachico had bled out without giving up any of his knowledge. And death hadn't softened his disposition. Why would he answer their questions now, when they had nothing with which to entice him or hold over his head in threat?

"Even if the *biitei*"—Rawls said the word carefully—"decided to answer our questions, we couldn't trust what it tells us. He wasn't much help alive; he's even less help dead."

Wolf's smile was slow and deadly. "Your *biitei* will answer the questions you put to it and speak with truth."

"How can you possibly promise that? It just has to say no thanks and vamoose," Faith protested.

Wolf shrugged, his gaze never leaving Rawls's face. "The binding ceremony will give it no choice. It will answer your questions. It will speak the truth."

"The binding ceremony?" Faith repeated with interest in her voice. "Is that along the same lines as this?" She nodded toward the amulet beneath Rawls's shirt.

For the first time, Wolf looked uneasy. It reminded Rawls of Jude's expression in the cavern when he'd quizzed him on how the amulet worked.

"It is best not to speak of such strong medicine," Wolf said. He turned back to Rawls, his expression flat. "The elders are preparing for the ceremony. You will call the *biitei* once the circle has closed."

Yeah . . . Rawls had no idea what the guy had just said or whether this binding ceremony, whatever it was, would work—but what the heck, it wouldn't hurt to give it a try. Besides, Wolf and his people certainly knew a lot more about the workings of ghosts than he did.

"Fine. When do you want to do this?"

"Soon. I will return when they are ready for you." With that announcement, Wolf pivoted and disappeared out the swinging door. When the door swung back open, Zane came through it.

He paused just inside the viewing room and nodded at Faith, but his flat, unreadable gaze never budged from Rawls's face. "You got a minute?"

Faith caught Rawls's gaze, her own eyes soft and filled with sympathy. No question that she'd picked up on how much he'd been dreading this moment.

The fallout from his admission had been postponed by Wolf's arrival and the withdrawal from the hub. But it had been clear a reckoning was in his future. This seemed hardly the time to settle things. But the confrontation was upon him and he wasn't going to bail on it.

Rawls gave Faith's hand a squeeze and let it go. He followed Zane out of the control room and through the medical bay. The electric entrance slid open and then closed behind them with an airy whoosh, expelling them into a diminutive, gun-metal gray parking area of maybe twenty by twenty-five feet. Most of the striped parking slots, which were barely large enough to accommodate the facility's golf carts and ATVs, sat empty beneath the sputtering glow of a malfunctioning fluorescent light. Zane paused to scan the deserted backdrop before swinging around to face him.

Rawls braced himself.

"Mac wants to huddle."

Okay, that wasn't what he'd been expecting. "When?"

"Tonight. After we've had a chance to look things over. Keep your eyes open, and your ears sharp."

Rawls simply nodded. The order was redundant. By now, years into their careers, it was impossible to turn their scrutiny off. Hell, his eyes were open and his ears sharp while snacking at a company barbeque.

"This is why you've been climbing the walls? This ghost?" Zane abruptly asked, his face neutral. Voice calm.

And there it was.

"Pretty much," Rawls admitted, holding his LC's eyes steadily.

Zane frowned, shook his head, a glint of anger sparking in his eyes. "You forget who the fuck I am?"

Rawls pulled back, opened his mouth. How was he supposed to answer that?

"For Christ's sake, you ass. You've trusted my visions for years. Trusted me without question, without corroborating evidence, without proof—why the hell wouldn't you give me the same benefit of doubt when it came to what you were seeing?"

Rawls's mouth slammed shut. He grimaced. Rolled his shoulders. "It's not the same thing."

"Bullshit." There was a glint of anger in Zane's eyes as they touched his face.

"It isn't," Rawls pointed out tightly. "Your visions happen. There's your proof."

"You didn't know that the first time you acted on them," Zane snapped back. "You trusted me. I trusted you. That's what saved our asses back then."

Fair point. But still, Pachico was different. The whole situation was different. "You knew what you were seeing was real. Was about to happen."

Zane cocked his head, reined the anger in. "And?"

"I didn't. Hell, for days I was certain I'd had a psychotic break. Certain the bastard was a product of my broken mind."

The anger faded from Zane's face. He ran a hand over his hair. "You should have told me."

"Hell no," Rawls said flatly. "You're my LC. You'd be obligated to relieve me of duty. Report the incident up the chain. You'd have no choice but to turn me in. I'd lose my spot in the beach boat. Lose my spot on the teams. And you know damn well I'd never get the okay again, even if Pachico had disappeared before I stepped in the head-shrinker's office."

Zane's sharp crack of laughter echoed between the concrete walls surrounding them. "Has it escaped your notice that we don't currently have a damn chain of command to report to?"

That stopped Rawls, but just for a moment. "When we're clear—"

"Have you been paying any attention to what's going on at all? It won't matter if we're cleared," Zane broke in, frustration and anger throbbing in his voice. "We're on fucking national television. Our faces everywhere. When we're cleared, the story will be even bigger than it is now. We've lost any fucking chance of getting back to our squads—period. We're fucking done."

Chapter Sixteen

*I*T DIDN'T OCCUR TO RAWLS, UNTIL HE WAS SITTING IN THE MOTORIZED cart across from Wolf, that Zane hadn't said whether he believed in ghosts. Or more specifically—Rawls's ghost. The conversation had gotten off track, and then their private little chat had been disrupted by a shift change at the medical bay.

Zane had left, without much more said, but they both knew the discussion wasn't over—merely shelved for the moment.

Wolf showed up an hour later to escort him to his first séance. Not that they called it that, but hell, they wanted to summon a ghost . . . wasn't that exactly what a séance did?

He didn't bother to ask any questions as Wolf drove. His escort had proved—repeatedly—that he wasn't much of a talker, let alone an explainer.

Instead, he took the opportunity to check Shadow Mountain out. Not that he could see much. The landscape was comprised mainly of shiny black walls, with embedded caged lights. The corridor Wolf took was wide—two lanes separated by a solid yellow line. White-striped paths to the right and left were designated walkways, or so he assumed from the volume of people they passed walking along them. Corridors branched off the main street, because that's what it was, a damn street— underground, inside a mountain.

They passed a wide section with defined parking spaces along the sides and a wide, almost translucent section of the wall that slid open every few seconds disgorging a steady stream of people, along with the rich, thick scent of cooking. Rawls's stomach growled loud enough to catch Wolf's attention, reminding them both they'd lost dinner and breakfast.

But Wolf pressed on.

They passed a good two dozen golf carts identical to the one Wolf was driving, as well as others twice as long, and then a few with rows of seats for extra passengers.

As one would expect from a facility this size, it bustled with men and women, although far more of the former than the latter. The ages ranged from midtwenties to midsixties. Most wore jeans and T-shirts or sweatshirts. Some wore overalls, others basic green fatigues. The lack of uniforms was a dead giveaway that the place wasn't military.

The army, navy, and air force were damn proud of their regalia.

Nor were all the people he saw Native American—although most looked like they were.

Slowly the maze of corridors grew narrower, and they ran across fewer people. Eventually they reached a walkway the golf cart couldn't navigate and Wolf parked along the wall.

This section of the facility looked old, ancient even, the path carved from damp stone. Rawls followed Wolf in silence. A hundred feet in, his escort suddenly took a hard right and disappeared through the rugged rock wall. Rawls blinked, but he didn't see the narrow, irregular gap in the wall until he was right next to it.

It was a tight fit squeezing his body through the opening, which meant Wolf must have scraped off a layer of skin forcing his considerably larger frame through the hole. More of those caged lamps burned along the walls of another narrow corridor. He could just make out Wolf's big shadow ahead and increased his stride.

The rock passage wound from left to the right, but after the fourth bend, it opened into a large cavern. Rawls stopped in the mouth of the cave and stared. Caged lamps ringed the walls here too, but several were dark. Flickering shadows twisted and twined along the stone, highlighting faded white-and-red images of stick animals and stick people and strange prehistoric symbols that reminded him of cave paintings he'd seen in *National Geographic*.

They looked old, thousands of years old. Reluctantly, he dragged his gaze from the walls to check out the rest of the room. In the middle of the cave, large white rocks, identical in size and color, had been placed next to each other, so close they were touching, and then curved into a perfect circle. Outside the circle of white rocks were four split logs. Each log was braced on more of the white rocks to form a bench.

Rawls slowly stepped into the room.

In front of each bench burned a small fire ringed with smaller white stones. The scent of smoke hung heavy in the air and stung his eyes.

"Come," Wolf said from his left, and Rawls turned.

His escort was standing beside four men with graying braided hair and a patchwork of wrinkles carved into their leathery faces. Each of the elders wore a poncho-type garment made out of hide. Etched on the front was the same layered sunburst symbol that was woven into the *hiixoyooniiheiht*.

Like the amulet that had been given to him and the one Jude carried, each of the elders' ponchos was embossed with dual colors, but in varying combinations.

The elder closest to him wore a sunburst of deep red and vivid yellow. The elder closest to Wolf carried colors of forest and pea green. Another, blue and yellow. The last, flat red and vivid green. Rawls sensed that the colors had some significance, but doubted he'd be told what it was. It wasn't until he got closer that he noticed each of the elders carried a leather pouch with a sunburst matching the design on their garments.

Once he was in front of them, Rawls stopped and shifted uncomfortably. Should he offer a greeting and handshake? Or would touching them be considered an insult?

"They are ready to begin," Wolf said, taking the decision out of Rawls's hands. "Give me your *hiixoyooniiheiht.*" He waited until Rawls had removed the cord from around his neck and handed the weaving over. "You will stand beside me until they give you leave to summon your *biitei.*"

Rawls nodded his understanding. The elders started to chant, their voices lifting and waning in unison. In a straight line, led by the man with the red-and-yellow sunburst, they began a slow, rocking path to the circle of white stones. As they traveled the outside edge of the circle and slowly rocked a chanting path around the white rocks, their hands would dip into the pouches hanging at their sides and toss whatever they removed into the circle.

And sweet hell, with each toss from the pouches, the small fires burning so sedately in front of the log benches would erupt into spitting, hissing, ferocious flames. After two trips around the circle, the elders stopped and shouted. Whatever they said was in Arapaho, so Rawls couldn't understand it, but Wolf did. Stepping forward, he handed Rawls's *hiixoyooniiheiht* to the leader wearing red and yellow and then took three huge steps back.

The elder held the object up and the chanting resumed. The rocking, chanting parade continued with two revolutions to the right, at which point the elders pivoted and did three more to the left. And then suddenly, when each elder was in front of a bench, they simply stopped. Silently, three of the men sat behind their small fires, leaving only Red Poncho to stand and chant. After a few more seconds of chanting and rocking—standing in place this time—the elder dropped the corded amulet into the flames at his feet.

The fire spat, flames leapt, devouring the weaving instantly. Once the fire had settled back into its sedate glow, the elder motioned Rawls over.

"It is time," the man said in perfect English. "Summon your *biitei.*"

Yeah . . . how did one go about summoning a ghost? That wasn't something taught in SQ training.

Wolf picked up on his uncertainty. "Call it by name."

"We didn't know his name," Rawls said, running a hand through his hair. "He was usin' an alias. And he hasn't felt like sharin' his real name since turnin' transparent."

"Did the *biitei* offer you a name before it crossed over?" the elder asked.

"It called itself Pachico. Took a local cop's name," Rawls said.

Red-and-Yellow Sunburst nodded, as though the matter was settled. "This is the name it offered to you, this is the name you will summon it under."

Okay . . . Rawls shifted uncomfortably.

Ah, what the hell. Squaring his shoulders, Rawls lifted his head.

"Hey, Pachico," he said in a loud voice, and waited.

Everyone stared expectantly at the circle, but nothing manifested in the middle. Well . . . he was assuming it was supposed to show up in the circle. He took a slow turn, surveying the rest of the cavern. Nothing. He waited a bit longer.

"Again," the lead elder said. "Concentrate. See his image in your mind and summon him to you."

Feeling foolish Rawls closed his eyes and tried to visualize his ghostly stalker's thin body and bald head. Didn't it just figure that the one time he wanted the asshole to show up he'd turn all contrary?

Once the image was fairly clear in his head, he opened his eyes, focused on the white circle of rocks, and tried again. "Pachico, get your transparent ass over here."

The forceful words echoed in the chamber. For a second it looked like his second command was going to have the same effect as his first— which was to say no effect whatsoever. But then a misty swirling stirred the dirt floor within the stone circle. Slowly, oh so slowly, a transparent form took shape. It wasn't long before Rawls recognized the bald head and black knife sticking out of the translucent chest.

"So now you wanna talk to me." Pachico's hollow voice was filled with condescension. But then he noticed the four elders on their benches, and a surprised look crossed his face. The surprised look gave way to caution. "What is this? A welcoming party?"

Although the question was spoken sarcastically, Rawls could hear the tension in the ghost's voice. Apparently death hadn't stolen his instincts. He knew something was in the works. Something he wasn't going to like.

"Ask the *biitei* its name," Red Etchings said, his face calm and body still.

Rawls turned back to the circle of rocks and the translucent form caged within. "What's your name?"

The ghost laughed, although there wasn't an ounce of humor in his voice or on his face. "Seriously? You want to know my name? What the fuck do you think we are? Girlfriends or some shit?"

In unison the four elders reached into the pouches hanging at their sides, grabbed a handful of whatever was in there, and threw it on the fires burning at their feet. The four fires flared, their reflections glowing in the circle of rocks, and Pachico screamed.

The scream was so unexpected, Rawls jumped, watching in shock as the translucent form that had been tormenting him for the past seven days writhed in apparent agony.

What the hell . . .

"Ask again," the lead elder said as the flames died and the translucent form in the rocks quit squirming.

Rawls cleared his throat. "Your name."

"Fuck you," Pachico snarled, his form going thin and so translucent it was barely visible.

The elders reached into their pouches and their fires flared again. Pachico's scream echoed with agony.

"It has been bound to the circle. It cannot leave."

Once again it was the guy with the red-and-yellow sunburst who spoke. Rawls was getting the distinct impression he was the only one of the four who had a voice.

"Ask its name."

"I'm pretty sure they can do this all night," Rawls told the rock circle, with its barely visible hostage. "Do yourself a favor and tell me your damn name."

A snarl sounded from within the stones, but when the four elders reached for their pouches, a name erupted from the circle. "Robert Biesel."

Well, look at that, they were making progress. He doubted the ghost had lied, because it would be too easy to check out the name. All it would take was a trip to the DMV.

The four men on the benches lowered their hands, but kept them on their pouches in a subtle threat.

"So, Robert Biesel, who were you workin' for?"

Might as well get the big questions out of the way first, from there he could work his way down to the nitty-gritty stuff. When Biesel remained stubbornly silent, the four musketeers dug into their pouches again. Once the screaming stopped, Rawls stepped in with a not-so-gentle reminder.

"You realize, you stupid fuck, they're only usin' a pinch from those pouches. How much more painful do you think a handful would be? So let's try this again. Who were you workin' for?"

This time Biesel's hollow voice sounded a little ragged, and thick with rage. "I don't owe that asshole a thing. So you want to know his name? Fine. Eric Manheim. Good luck touching him, motherfucker."

Eric Manheim.

Of all the names Biesel could have shouted, Manheim's shocked him the most. The billionaire, hell, more like trillionaire, was one of the wealthiest men in the world. Among the one percent of the wealthy who controlled most of the world's wealth . . . except Manheim spread his wealth around. He funded countless charities and nonprofit organizations. His wife was the face and voice of the Focus on Hunger program. His was the least likely name to come up in conjunction with terrorism and blackmail.

"Eric Manheim," Rawls repeated slowly, trying to wrap his head around this news and figure out if the asshole was lying to him. "Why the hell would he be involved in somethin' like this? The prototype Faith and her team were workin' on wouldn't affect him. His money comes from financial institutions."

In fact, the Manheim family trust owned most of the banks in the world. On the other hand, the family also had enough cash and influences to run the kind of operation required to take down an airliner, and frame anyone that got in the way.

Now that Biesel had started talking, he got downright chatty. "His interest has nothing to do with money. It has to do with how it would affect the rest of the world. Manheim belongs to this crackpot conglomerate of Richie Riches who see themselves as the new ruling order. Christ, they even call themselves that. The NRO—New Ruling Order. Humanity's not-quite-so-benevolent dictators."

"The NRO?" Rawls repeated, making a note to remember the acronym, and to do some googling as soon as he got back to a computer.

Out of the corner of his eye, Rawls saw the four elders sitting on the benches, along with Wolf, react to the acronym. Hell, Mr. Stoic, who was standing next to him, actually rocked back on his feet, surprise registering on his hard, normally blank face.

"You know this organization?" Rawls asked, turning to address Wolf.

"It would appear," Wolf said with a tight, cold smile, "that your enemies are our enemies."

Well that was news. Good news too, considering the arsenal of technology and weapons Wolf had at his disposal.

"Where is the NRO located?" Rawls asked Biesel, and knew from Wolf's grunt of approval that he wasn't the only one wanting to know the answer to that question.

"There is no united location. They meet in secrecy, in undisclosed locations, a couple of times a year and plot and scheme to advance their agenda."

"Their agenda of what? Takin' over the world? Sounds like an unsubstantiated conspiracy theory," Rawls said.

There was nothing quite like a conspiracy theory to get many of his SEAL brothers all fired up. Hell, you get a couple of these true-blue believers in the same room and they'd argue the merits of various conspiracies for hours. Generally, there was just enough truth in the telling to make one wonder—which was undoubtedly how the originators of the theories hooked their believers.

"From the sourpuss expression on the Big Bad Wolf's face, I'd say he's run into the living embodiment of this debunked conspiracy theory before." There was a hint of dryness to the hollow voice.

Rawls stole a glance at the man standing so dangerously still beside him. Biesel was right about that. Wolf looked like he'd just swallowed an entire package of Warheads.

"Tell me about the lab we apprehended you in. Were you part of the team that kidnapped the scientists and faked their deaths?" If they could find the scientists and extract them safely, they could exonerate his team and bring Manheim's involvement out in the open.

"Yeah, you have any idea how hard it is to effectively fake that many people's deaths?" The hollow voice dropped to an irritated grumble. "But did the big boss appreciate that? Hell no."

A dizzying sense of unreality swept through Rawls. Sweet Jesus, he was standing here interrogating a ghost, listening to it bellyache about unfair working conditions.

Wolf stirred beside him. "Was this *biitei* involved?"

"Yeah," Rawls said slowly, for the first time realizing that Wolf couldn't hear what Biesel was saying. The Arapaho warrior was reacting to Rawls's responses. Not Biesel's answers. But what about the four elders? "Can any of you see Biesel?"

"No." Wolf's voice was abrupt. "Only those who have crossed over and back within a short time of the *biitei*'s crossing can see it."

Rawls mulled that over. If he understood that answer correctly, that narrowed the field down to him and Faith.

"Many among us can sense them," Wolf continued after a moment, his voice slightly less tense.

"Like Jude? And you?" Rawls glanced at the four elderly men on their benches. "And them?" He took Wolf's grunt as an affirmative.

But after a moment he turned back to the rock circle. He still had plenty of questions left. "Where did you take the scientists?"

Biesel laughed. "Where else? Silicon Valley. Who's gonna notice another lab springing up there?"

Rawls repeated the address the ghost rattled off, and committed it to memory. "They're still alive?"

"How the hell should I know? I'm dead and stuck to you, you moron."

Biesel took him through the layout of the lab where they'd stashed Faith's team, and Rawls committed every room, every guard to memory. All this shit would come in handy when they moved in to rescue the hostages.

After several minutes of questions and answers, there was only one thing left to ask. "How did they track you to Yosemite?"

The smirk was clear on the transparent face. "Through the same shit they dumped into little Brendan and Benji's veins. Poor bastards. They're a walking data stream now."

Rawls's mouth tightened at the bastard's callousness. "How can the compound be neutralized?"

"It can't, far as I know. Or at least that information wasn't made available to us."

Rawls scowled. Unfortunately, the bastard didn't appear to be lying about that. It was more like he simply didn't care. Which was believable since it no longer affected him.

"Who developed the compound?" Whoever had developed it had to have an antidote.

"I don't know. Someone at Dynamic Solutions. Ask James Link. He brought that shit with him when he came on board." Biesel's voice turned impatient. "Look, I answered all your damn questions. You want to let me out of this damn cage?"

"Not my call. I'm just a guest here," Rawls said, although from the Arapahos' reaction to having a ghost present, he'd bet that Biesel wouldn't be getting loose anytime soon, if at all. The interrogation wrapped up soon afterward, and Rawls turned to Wolf.

"It would be handy if we could keep him on ice like this, in case any more questions come up," he said in a low voice.

Apparently Biesel had the ears of a cat. "Ah, come on, man, that's inhumane. This thing's smaller than a fucking cell."

Wolf shook his head. "Too dangerous. *Biitei* grow stronger with age. It must cross back over."

"Now wait one Goddamn minute." Biesel's voice climbed. "I can help you. I know lots of things we haven't even touched on."

With a ceremonial half bow, Wolf nodded to the elders. Four male voices rose in chant. In unison, the men stood and emptied their leather pouches into the fire at their feet. Flames hissed and crackled and shot so high in the air they touched the ceiling.

The reflection of the fires engulfed the rock circle and the translucent figure within it. Ravenous orange tongues engulfed the writhing, gyrating form. This time Rawls couldn't hear the screams. The crackle and pop of the fires drowned the ghost's cries out.

As the fires burned hotter, the figure inside the circle disintegrated, until there was nothing left but flames.

———————————

Her stomach a tight knot, Faith pushed a pair of green beans around with her fork. The tension had started the moment Rawls and Wolf had returned, and it continued to build steadily during lunch. From the reassuring looks he kept sending her, and his comments about how good all her tests looked, Rawls had picked up on her anxiety and assumed it was associated with her heart and the tests she'd undergone, or the tests still to come. He thought she was having trouble adjusting to this miraculous new life Kait had given her.

How to tell him her worry wasn't linked to her health, rather it was driven by fear for his?

For sure the tests had shown a miracle. A completely functional, totally restored heart. The echocardiogram and EKG had given her reason to believe in a new life. A life without restrictions. A normal life. One where she didn't have to worry about organ rejections or replacement. She'd barely had a chance to process this realization, to accept it—when Rawls had returned with Wolf and told her that Pachico had told them where her fellow scientists had been taken.

Just listening to Rawls banter with his buddies during lunch had deepened the dark cloud of foreboding hanging over her. From the suppressed tension and barely leashed anticipation emitted by the four men, they were planning something . . . And then there was this big meeting with the brass of Shadow Mountain the four men were headed to after lunch.

Her belly cramped and a light gloss of perspiration broke out down her spine. She was very much afraid she knew what the meeting was about, and why the men were vibrating with such adrenaline-fueled anticipation.

If they'd located her fellow scientists, then they had all the information they needed to run off and rescue them. Or try to, anyway.

If Dr. Benton had rebuilt the prototype, and it unleashed the same effect on the brain, they'd be slaughtered during the rescue attempt. Every last one of them.

She stared down at her shaking fingers and forced them to stillness. She couldn't let that happen.

"Hey," Rawls said in a low voice from beside her, nudging her with his shoulder. "You okay? You're awfully quiet over there."

"I've been thinking," Faith said. Giving up on the appearance of eating, she pushed the plate aside. "You're going after them, aren't you? After Gilbert and the rest of my team?"

Rawls cast a cautious look down the long steel cafeteria table their group had taken over. Beth and Zane sat hip to hip, their heads tilted toward each other, quietly talking. Cosky and Kait sat across from Marion Simcosky, laughing at something she was saying. The women were upbeat and relieved.

Did they know what their men had planned? Or that they were acting off information provided by a ghost? She doubted Wolf or Rawls had explained the circumstances behind this sudden opportunity.

"How about we talk about this when we get back to the clinic?" Rawls said, bending toward her so his request was spoken directly into her ear. "The doc's doing the stress test in two hours, right? We can talk then."

She quivered as his warm breath caressed the side of her neck and tickled the inside of her ear. She wasn't sure exactly where things were headed between them, which was one more thing they needed to talk about. There was definitely a sense of building intimacy in their interactions. He wasn't pulling away any longer. But what that meant, she didn't know.

The only thing she knew for absolute certainty, at this moment, was that her information couldn't wait until after her stress test.

"When are you meeting again to discuss their rescue?" she asked in an equally quiet but persistent voice.

"Faith." He turned a censoring look on her. "We'll talk about this later."

"No." She half twisted on her seat to look at him. "We'll talk about this now. I want to be in on this meeting."

He smiled at her, a patient, maybe even affectionate smile. "Yeah, that's not gonna happen, darlin'."

It had to happen. It would happen.

She couldn't let them attack the building where her team was re-creating the technology she'd been instrumental in creating—not without warning them of what they were walking into. It was true they were military. It was true there was a possibility that once they realized the prototype's potential, they would move to weaponize it. But she couldn't let them walk into a possible ambush.

She simply couldn't.

If the prototype was working at capacity, they'd be massacred.

"Look, there are things you don't know about the research we were doing. Things that will get you killed."

He studied her face intently, and in some indefinable way, his gaze seemed to sharpen. "What things?"

She released a frustrated breath. "I'll tell you at the meeting!"

"What meeting?"

It was Cosky's flat voice. Faith glanced down the table to find everyone's gaze locked on her. The argument had finally caught the attention of the rest of the table.

"Our nineteen hundred," Rawls said after a moment, still studying Faith's face. A faint frown furrowed his brow.

"That's classified." Mac's tone was clipped and abrupt—like the subject was closed.

"She has critical information to share about her research," Rawls said, shooting Mac a flat look.

"Sure she does," Mac snorted.

"Information," Rawls continued, his voice cold and challenging, "that is essential to any rescue attempt."

Faith's stomach tightened and churned. For a moment it felt like the small amount of chicken and bread she'd managed to force down was about to come up. She glanced down the table at Beth and Kait, wondering how the two women were handling the news that their men were about to throw themselves into harm's way. Neither woman looked surprised. And if they were worried, they had locked the fear behind calm faces.

A wave of shame washed over her at their courage and her lack thereof. She was barely involved with Rawls and the thought of him in danger left her crumbling inside.

"If you have vital information, then tell us now, and we'll pass it on," Mac said impatiently.

Rawls ran a hand over his hair and shook his head. "We're not runnin' this show. Wolf and his team are. And somethin' tells me they're gonna want to hear the information directly from the horse's mouth."

Chapter Seventeen

RAWLS HAD NO LUCK HUNTING WOLF DOWN BEFORE THEIR 1900 strategy session, so when the two men sent to escort Rawls to the meeting showed up in the clinic after Faith's stress test, Rawls took them aside and explained the situation to them. After a moment of conferring with each other, Faith was motioned forward. They were both escorted outside the clinic to where another golf cart waited, but this one had rows of seats for extra passengers.

Cosky, Zane, and Mac were already seated in the back row of the vehicle. Rawls helped Faith into the cart and took the seat beside hers. Once they were settled, the driver took off in the opposite direction from where Wolf had taken Rawls earlier.

Apparently they weren't going to the same office where they'd gone to report the information Pachico had given them . . . curious.

This time the trip through Shadow Mountain was short. Their driver took the first corridor to the right after the medical bay, and drove less than a hundred feet before pulling into an empty parking space against the wall. They followed their escorts through one of those strangely translucent sliding doors and into a web of connected offices and halls.

None of the offices they passed were marked, nor had there been any indication above the entrance to tell them where they were. And now that he thought about it, nothing was marked in this place. The only way you could tell you'd arrived at the hospital was that the people exiting and entering were wearing scrubs, and at the mess hall, by the smell of food.

Nothing about the place shouted operations.

Until their escorts turned a corner and he found himself in front of an open set of double doors.

Behind the doors was a large round table, which could accommodate a dozen men, and a huge freestanding dry-erase board. Dozens of maps ringed the room and a white projection screen swallowed the entire front wall.

Half a dozen hard, watchful faces turned to study them.

Instantly he knew where he was. Instantly he felt at home.

He'd spent thousands of hours seated at similar tables, in similar rooms, eyes glued to wall maps or schematics projected on giant screens. He'd drunk gallons of coffee from identical Styrofoam cups from coffeepots placed in similar unobtrusive, out of the way places.

He'd been in this same room, in dozens of different locales, over the course of his career. It was as comfortable as an old pair of combat boots.

He spotted Wolf across the room and beckoned him over. For a moment it looked like the big warrior was going to ignore him, but then his gaze fell on Faith and a frown touched his face. Without saying a word to the men standing beside him, he headed across the room.

"Dr. Ansell," he said when he reached them, and offered her a formal half bow. After straightening, he glanced at Rawls, his gaze shrewd. "Problem?"

Before Rawls had a chance to explain, Faith stepped up.

"There are . . . aspects . . . of the research we were doing that are classified," Faith said, tugging at the bottom of her T-shirt. "But in light of the rescue, and the fact that my team was kidnapped rather than killed outright so they could repeat the process—" She cleared her throat. "So in light of all that, there are things you need to be aware of. Things you may run into. Things you won't be prepared for."

She went from tugging the bottom of her shirt to smoothing it repeatedly over her hips. It was a nervous tic. She'd done the same thing in the tunnels. A grin threatened at the memory, until he got a good look at the tension on her face.

Wolf studied her face for a moment and then dropped his gaze to the constant smoothing of her hands. "Your insight is appreciated," he finally murmured, his voice unusually gentle. "Sit. We begin soon."

She acknowledged his suggestion with a tight nod and let Rawls take her elbow and escort her to the table. Once she was seated, however, her hands had nothing to smooth, so she started absently picking at her cuticles.

Rawls watched her quietly before covering her restless hands with his. "Everythin's gonna be fine. You just wait. You're worryin' over nothin'," he said, trying to project encouragement and calm in his voice.

She nodded, but without much conviction. Luckily, the side door swung open and four older men with tanned, leathery faces and long, graying hair in immaculate braids strode in. From the way Wolf greeted them, it was obvious he'd been waiting for them, which meant they'd be getting started soon.

As Wolf spoke to the middle elder, recognition stirred. The four newcomers were dressed differently from the four elders in the cave. Rather than roughhewn rawhide poncho-styled garments, they wore loose jeans and button-down shirts, but he'd swear they were the same four elders who'd performed the binding ceremony.

With Wolf still talking, the lead elder glanced at Faith. After a moment he nodded. The four elders took seats at the head of the table, leaving Wolf standing alone. Not that he appeared uncomfortable, but then, Rawls had never seen Wolf look uncomfortable.

"Dr. Ansell, if you would join me," Wolf said, his gaze steady on Faith's tense face.

Rawls frowned; he hadn't expected them to call her to the front of the room like some schoolgirl being disciplined. She didn't seem to mind, though. Without hesitation, she pushed back her chair, climbed to her feet, and walked up front.

"Thank you." She cleared her throat nervously. "I'm not sure how much Commander Mackenzie and his team told you about the research my team and I were involved in."

"We are aware you were advancing the new energy paradigm and created a prototype capable of pulling energy from the atoms in the air," Wolf said. "And that your lab was targeted and your team kidnapped because of this."

"Yes, all of that is true." She coughed, fidgeting, looking more conflicted than ever.

"Dr. Ansell?" Wolf's voice was so quiet Rawls barely heard it.

She glanced up, stared directly at Wolf, and squared her shoulders. "Yes, everything I told Commander Mackenzie is true. However, much of our research is classified, so there were . . . things . . . I didn't mention during that conversation."

"Such as?" Wolf prompted when Faith fell silent.

"Such as the fact that the prototype is capable of connecting with and augmenting certain people's brain waves and expanding their brain's capacity." She seemed to force the explanation out.

An uneasy stir went around the table.

Brain waves? Expanded capacity? Of all the possibilities he'd expected her to spill, this news hadn't even been in the periphery of his mind.

"Augmenting? How?" This time it was Wolf's superior who asked the question. And while all Rawls could see was the back of the guy's head, his voice was the same as the elder who'd worn the red etchings in the cave.

"The machine basically turbocharges certain people's brains. It makes them capable of doing extraordinary things . . . mentally."

"Specify," Wolf said.

From the sharpness in Wolf's voice and the grim expressions ringing the table, he wasn't the only one who saw the ugly ramifications in Faith's news. No wonder she'd been so dead set on addressing Wolf's superiors.

"In one experiment, the subject turned on a microwave just by thinking about it. In another, she blew the same microwave up—just by thinking about it."

Blew something up with just a thought. A chill feathered down his spine. How the hell did you protect yourself against something like that?

Down the table someone swore softly.

"You're telling us"—Zane's calm voice ruptured the stunned silence—"that this machine you developed can turn certain people's thoughts into weapons? They can kill by just thinking about it?"

"Yes." She responded to Zane's question as calmly as he'd asked it. "That's exactly what I'm saying."

She was remarkably collected now, as though letting the cat out of the bag had drained all the tension away.

"And you didn't tell us about this. Jesus Christ, with the hands it's fallen into, this thing could destroy the world. This thing could give one person the ability to control the whole fucking world. And you didn't tell us about this? Jesus Christ." Mac shook his head, stunned disbelief lifting his voice.

"No. I didn't tell you about it," she agreed, her voice empty of apology. "And I wouldn't be telling you now if you didn't absolutely need to know. How do I know you won't use it for yourself? Turn it over to your military and weaponize it? How do I know that what you'd do with it would be any better than what they'd do with it? I didn't know if I could trust you. There's a good chance the people who stole the schematics for the prototype haven't realized its full potential and it could be recovered and destroyed without anyone realizing what it can do."

Dead silence followed her retort. The four elders glanced among each other, and Rawls saw a new respect in the eyes that turned back to Faith.

"You said it affects certain people's brains," Cosky finally reminded her. "What percentage of people does it affect?"

"From the data we've been able to gather, it syncs with certain brain chemistries and brain waves. In the lab and surrounding offices, three out of nineteen were affected. But it wasn't a large enough sampling to foretell what the rate would be in the general population."

Rawls nodded absently. What she said made sense. Brain chemistry varied slightly between individuals. Much of the data would depend on the range of brain chemistries or waves the machine could sync with. Only through sampling hundreds of brains would they have been able to work out an average. Yet sampling the volume of brains necessary to acquire a percentage would have caught someone's attention eventually. Attention they couldn't afford.

In fact, from what he remembered from their earlier conversation, Dr. Benton had destroyed the prototype for fear it would fall into the wrong hands.

The precaution made much more sense now, as did the NRO's interest in the research.

Christ, if this technology got into the wrong hands . . . it was absolutely essential they recover it before the NRO re-created the prototype.

"You said it took years to develop the original prototype, and that Dr. Benton destroyed all the research along with the machine before they were taken," he reminded her.

If it took years or even months to create the machine, they'd have plenty of time to track the scientists down and retrieve them before their invention went online and operational.

"Yes, but Dr. Benton has a photographic memory. He won't need the research to complete the necessary steps. And he'll be able to complete those steps faster since he's done it before. I'm sure he'll try to slow the process down, but . . ." Her voice trailed off and she swallowed hard, her gaze clinging to his.

He could see the pain from the memory of her murdered friends burning in her eyes. And she was right. They couldn't count on Benton stalling. The bastards who held him had proved repeatedly that they were ruthless and deadly.

"How long would you estimate it will take them to re-create the prototype?" Zane asked, his voice thoughtful.

Faith shook her head. "I honestly don't know. But the machine doesn't need to be fully operational before it can sync with the human brain. Last time it started at sixty-nine percent."

Rawls frowned, something niggling at him. "How did you find out about the machine's ability?"

The original intention of the machine had been energy based after all; they hadn't been doing any research on people's brains.

"It started small. Lights turning on or off randomly. Machines as well. We thought the lab had an electrical short. We didn't put it together until Marcy asked Julio to turn on Big Ben and the machine suddenly powered up. Marcy laughed, said, 'Wouldn't it be funny if it turned off just by asking too?' And it just . . . turned . . . off. That's when we started testing her on other machines, the centrifuge, the microwave, the lights, everything. It became obvious fast. All she had to do was think about turning a machine on or off, and it did. But we didn't know why. Not at first." Her face tightened for a moment and she took a deep, calming breath. "We didn't realize her sudden almost-supernatural ability was connected to the Thrive generator until the machine overheated and shut down during our flurry of testing. Just like that, Marcy was normal again. That's when we put it together. The ability was only present when the prototype was on."

Rawls's chest tightened in sympathy. Marcy and Julio had been two of her friends murdered in the lab that day. Apparently two people those bastards hadn't had any use for.

"You said three of you had the ability to sync with the machine. If they do create the prototype, they can use it too—"

"No," Faith broke in. "None of the people kidnapped were able to sync with the machine."

"So they killed those of you who could sync with it?" Cosky asked, a puzzled tone in his voice.

"Not exactly. Whoever attacked us and kidnapped my team didn't know about the machine's side effects. We were very careful to keep that quiet. They must have been after the new energy utilization, or possibly they were interested in repurposing the prototype as a clean bomb. It would take very little rewiring to create an energy distributor." She paused for a moment to frown and then shrugged. "I'm guessing, of course. But if they'd known about the secondary effect, they wouldn't have killed Marcy or Bekka, and they would have tried harder to find me."

It took Rawls a second to realize what she'd just admitted.

Oh hell, no.

His whole body stiffened. He didn't bother praying that nobody else had picked up on that confession because every single person in the room had been trained to zero in on and use such slips of the tongue.

Jesus—Faith had no fucking clue what she'd just brought down on her head.

"Let me get this straight," Mac said slowly. "You were one of the three who could sync with the machine."

Rawls's fists clenched, of course it would be Mac to feed her to the lions.

"I was," Faith admitted with a frown. She glanced at Rawls, and whatever she saw on his face had her eyes widening in alarm.

"Forget it," Rawls snapped. Shoving his chair back, he surged to his feet. "We don't even know if they've built the damn machine."

"But if they have," Wolf said, his dark gaze fixed on Faith's profile. "And Dr. Ansell can sync with it . . ."

"No," Rawls snapped again, his voice rising. "We aren't talkin' about a fuckin' walk in the park, here. You'd be puttin' her life in danger, and for what? For the possibility that she might be able to sync with a machine that probably isn't even erected yet? Her team was grabbed less than two weeks ago. That isn't enough time to build this contraption."

"You don't know that."

He'd expected the cool counterargument, just not from Faith.

"Faith." He paused to calm his breathing. "You don't know what they're askin'. You don't—"

"I think I do." Her voice was very quiet and far too determined. "I think I know exactly what they're suggesting. They're suggesting I come along and sync with the prototype if it's operational."

Okay, so she had picked up on what they were asking of her. But damn it, she didn't know what she was getting herself into. Rawls raked a hand through his hair, shocked to find his heart hammering like he was fighting for his life. Hell, he was sweating like a stuck pig too. He could feel his shirt sticking to his back.

"You don't have CQB trainin', you don't—"

"She will be protected," Wolf broke in, his normally inscrutable face softened by sympathy, except he was looking at Rawls, not Faith.

"You can't protect her from everythin'." He could hear his voice rise, but he was powerless to stop it. "All it takes is one stray bullet. One moment of inattention. She's not trained for this. You have no damn right to drag her into the field."

And for the first time since—well since that other life, when he'd still had a sister and family—panic struck. Strangled him with fear. His breathing hitched, his heart pounding so hard he could hear it in his head.

He'd just found her, Goddamn it. Barely had her back from the dead. He wasn't going to lose her so soon. Fuck, he wasn't going to lose her ever.

What the hell?

Where did that come from?

"What about what I want?" she asked, her gaze locked on his face as though they were the only two people in the room. "Those were my friends they murdered in the lab. My friends are being held by a group of monsters who treat people like disposable objects. Who jeopardize children for the sake of their own agenda. If there's even the slightest chance that my presence could help bring these monsters to justice, then I'm doing it."

Before Rawls had a chance to launch another argument, the elder from the ghost binding stood up. He nodded to Faith, and turned to face Rawls.

"The decision is Dr. Ansell's. She alone has the final say," he said with finality. "She goes."

Chapter Eighteen

*T*HE LAST THIRD OF THE MEETING WITH WOLF'S PEOPLE WAS A BLUR in Faith's mind as she entered the sleeping quarters Wolf showed her to. She'd been too busy having a mental meltdown after agreeing to accompany them on the rescue mission. A very dangerous operation too, judging by Rawls's violent reaction.

Vaguely, she remembered a discussion about some organization called the New Ruling Order, which sounded like a bunch of rich people with too much time and money on their hands. And then Eric Manheim's name had popped up as the force behind the attempted hijacking of flight 2077, as well as the attack on Amy Chastain's family and the murder and kidnapping of Faith's coworkers.

Not that anyone but Rawls, Wolf, and Wolf's people knew the information had come courtesy of interrogating a ghost! When pressed by Mackenzie, Wolf had blandly attributed the intel to classified intelligence. It had been all Faith could do to hold her tongue; Mackenzie and his men deserved to know where the information they were about to risk their lives on had come from.

Except . . . Rawls had been so terribly stiff beside her, furious that she'd agreed to join them on the upcoming rescue mission. She hadn't wanted to chance souring the fragile new relationship budding between them.

Wolf had been utterly confident that they'd have confirmation of the "captives," blueprints of the building, as well as head counts of the people inside, within twenty-four hours.

Twenty-four hours . . .

Which meant what, exactly? That she'd be down in San Jose sometime tomorrow preparing to attack a lab?

A chill washed down her spine and prickled across her scalp. She shivered, but then squared her shoulders and headed for the bathroom. A nice hot shower was just the thing to relax her. It sure as heck beat standing around and stewing about things she had no control over.

The bathroom carried the same bland, unoccupied-motel motif as the bedroom and its tiny attached living room. But at least the shower had a huge round showerhead and wonderful water pressure. She soaked for a long time beneath the spray, letting the beat of the water massage her tight, sore muscles. By the time she stepped out of the tub and wrapped herself in a cotton robe, her muscles were limp.

Her mind on the other hand had revved up rather than dialed down.

Sitting on the edge of the bed, she listened to the strong, even beat of her new miracle heart and fought the sense of isolation.

With the exception of a fling early in her freshman year of college with a grad student, which had ended with summer break, she'd spent much of her life alone, buried in her studies or experiments. But loneliness had never haunted her, until now.

Except, she wasn't lonely for just anyone, there was a specific face attached to this emotion. A specific name.

Rawls.

Somehow over the past two days, his smile, his drawl, his humor, and his patience had filled her mind and heart so full she felt diminished without him beside her.

Empty.

More than anything in the world, she wanted to get up and go to him, step into his arms and lean into his kiss, and explore this hunger simmering between them. The mission she'd agreed to was dangerous. Nobody was downplaying the risk. She knew full well she might not come back, and the thought of dying down there, in San Jose, without knowing the heat and tenderness of Rawls's embrace, the beauty of his body on top of and inside of her . . . the thought of not knowing him in every possible way a woman could know a man was . . . distressing.

Depressing, even.

But the memory of the last time she'd seen his face held her prisoner on the bed.

He'd been icy, detached, and furious. When Wolf had dropped them off in front of the sleeping quarters they'd been assigned, he'd vanished inside his without a word.

She wanted to believe the strength of his reaction to her inclusion on this mission indicated he had equally strong feelings for her. She'd never seen him so angry—or so grim. But what if the emotions driving him weren't as passionate as she hoped? What if he was being driven by a sense of responsibility instead? What if all the recent touching and light kissing meant nothing—or at least nothing serious?

Or even worse, what if she had killed whatever they'd been building toward when she'd ignored his advice and dismissed his wishes?

Her escalating list of what-ifs was cut short by a knock at the door.

With her heart in her throat and her mind full of hope, she got up to answer the summons, only to jump back with a gasp.

"Sorry," Rawls said, his hand still raised and fist clenched for knocking. "I didn't mean to startle you."

"That's okay." Faith's pulse picked up speed again, only the rapid rhythm had nothing to do with fear. At least not fear of his hand, more like fear of his heart.

He took her response as an invitation to come inside. As he closed the door behind him, he cast a quick look over her robe-clad body and heat kindled in his gaze. A moment later he broke eye contact and glanced around the room. "I see we got the same decorator."

She forced a smile along with the small talk. "At least they're letting us stay. I got the distinct impression Wolf wasn't supposed to bring us here."

"Yeah," Rawls agreed.

And that closed that particular topic. An awkward silence fell.

Oh, for Pete's sake.

Faith cleared her throat and took the bull by the horns. "So are you still mad at me?"

"Hell." He raked a tight hand through his hair. "I was never mad at you, Faith. I was concerned, not angry."

She tilted her head and considered that. She didn't doubt for a second he'd been—was still—concerned for her. But there had been definite rage there as well.

"You were angry too," Faith contradicted him quietly.

He studied her, and his face softened. Lifting his hand, he brushed her cheek with his fingertips. "Yeah, but not at you."

She quivered beneath the caress. "Then who?"

"At Wolf. At Mac. At all of them. They're usin' you." He stroked her cheek again and then his fingers trailed down to her chin and tilted her head up. "I won't have you in danger."

She quivered harder, her skin so sensitive it burned beneath his touch, her insides all warm and tingly. There was a hot look in his eyes. A hungry look. She hadn't been with many men, and the last had been a lifetime ago, but she recognized the look he was giving her—and responded to it on the most primitive level. Without giving herself a chance to analyze or quantify, she gave in to instinct and went up on her toes to wrap her arms around his neck.

Instantly his arms locked around her, dragging her against his body, sealing them together from shoulder to thigh. His mouth came down, found hers, and hot, hard lips forced hers apart. The kiss started off rough, marauding, but then he seemed to catch himself, and his mouth gentled. He backed off, brushed her lips with his, and started to pull back.

Except she didn't want him to stop. Somewhere, in the back of her mind, at a subconscious level, she'd been waiting for this moment since that kiss in the kitchen . . . anticipating it . . . wanting more . . .

Instinctively she stretched up, pressing her mouth to his. Driven by some deep, primitive urge, she caught his bottom lip between her teeth and gently bore down.

He jolted against her and then grabbed her butt, lifting her and grinding her against his crotch in the most graphic display of sexuality she'd ever been subject to. Her legs went weak. Her brain foggy. Her skin tightened.

Good lord, that felt so . . . good.

And then he turned the tables on her and caught her bottom lip in his teeth. Only he sucked on it, hard. With each pull of his mouth, she felt a corresponding tug deep in her belly and a flood of moisture between her legs.

In an effort to alleviate the sudden violent ache throbbing between her legs, she rubbed herself against the bulge pressing into her belly. He groaned, and the bulge gained length and width.

Breathing hard, he dragged his mouth away and pressed it against the sensitive skin of her neck.

"Baby," he said in a breathless voice before pausing to suckle at the base of her neck until she squirmed against him. "We need to either stop this, like right now—or get naked and in your bed."

She voted for the naked and in bed.

Eager to show her enthusiasm for his suggestion, she grabbed the hem of his T-shirt and fought to shove it over his head. But the feel of his warm, smooth skin stretched so tight over hard muscles distracted her. Her hands slowed to a long, gliding caress.

He groaned again, arching into her touch, his skin rippling beneath her fingers. And then he grabbed his T-shirt and yanked it over his head. She stared in fascination at his muscled chest, with its thin arrow of golden hair trailing down the tight muscles of his abdomen, only to disappear beneath the waistband of his jeans. Without thinking, she leaned in to press her mouth against his heart. His skin tasted slightly salty, with the oddest tinge of smoke, and so damn good she was quickly becoming addicted to it.

He'd twitched with each stroke of her hands, but the brush of her lips earned a jolt. She smiled at that delightful discovery and slowly slid down his body, teasing the length of his abdomen with her lips, teeth, and tongue.

When she knelt before him, her arms wrapped around his thick thighs, with only the buttoned and zippered waistband of his jeans preventing further exploration—he suddenly came alive.

As she unlocked her arms from around his legs and her hands went to work on the button securing his jeans, a curse exploded from him. Urgent hands slid under her arms, lifting her.

His face was hard as he stared down at her, his eyes dilated, his bottom lip swollen, a flush riding his cheekbones.

"Last chance to call it quits, sweetheart," he said between hard and fast breaths.

Call it quits? Why in the world would she want to do that? She wanted him, wanted him more than she'd ever wanted any man before. Wanted him to be the man she spent her last night on earth with, if tomorrow meant the death of her.

"I say we reconvene in the bed." Her voice was so thick and sultry, she barely recognized it.

He didn't wait for a second invitation. Bending, he swept her into his arms and carried her to the queen-size bed taking up most of the room. He set her down on the foot of the mattress and slowly loosened the tie to her robe.

Deliberately, almost reverently, he spread the garment wide and pushed it off her shoulders, leaving her completely bare. She sat there beneath his glittering blue gaze, her nipples puckering, her breasts tightening, her skin aching for his touch.

Instead of joining her on the bed, he dropped to his knees and smoothed his palms up her legs, from ankle to calf to thigh. His hands were rough, slightly scratchy, leaving the oddest mixture of fire and chills in their wake. He pressed her thighs apart far enough to accommodate his body and leaned in, continuing his gentle assault at her belly, only this time with his mouth.

Boneless, splayed before him, she lost herself in the heated sensation of his mouth and the light scrape of his teeth as he explored her body. He feathered kisses up the old silvered scars on her chest, his mouth so gentle she could barely feel the feathery caress, and then slid over to take a tight nipple in his mouth. As his warm, wet mouth closed over her breast and suckled, she arched into him, her arms stealing around his ribs and up his bare back—savoring the hard, smooth flow of muscles beneath her palms. He felt so good pressed against her, strong and firm, completely male.

But she needed to know how he'd feel inside her.

She skimmed her hands back down his back and slid them beneath the waistband of his jeans and underwear to cup the firm muscles of his ass. The fact that he arched into her touch brought her a smile and the confidence to move her hands around to the front of his jeans for some deeper exploration.

He groaned into her breast and lifted his hips. Unbuttoning and then unzipping his jeans, she pushed them, along with his underwear, out of the way. His penis was thick and smooth, and it actually seemed to arch into her hand. With each long, slow stroke from the base of his penis to its bulbous head, he'd groan—a low animalistic sound. He was so caught up in her stroking, he abandoned her breasts and simply pressed his forehead against her chest, his hips rocking in concert with the stroke of her hand.

But soon the heavy globes at the base of his penis caught her attention and she moved her hand down to explore.

To her amusement, the simple act of cupping the warm, soft weights broke him. With an urgent grunt, he caught her legs, dragged them up and over his hips, and took hold of his penis, guiding it between her thighs.

He looked up as he pushed into her, his eyes so intensely blue they burned like the laser in her lab. "Jesus, you're makin' me lose my mind."

She smiled at that, her chest melting. She couldn't imagine a better compliment than that.

With a deep breath Faith closed her eyes, concentrating on the feel of him pushing inside her, the hot, heavy force of him . . . the almost painful friction of him stretching her . . . She shifted uncomfortably, trying to hang on to that earlier delicious tension. But the sting soon turned to burning pain.

He must have sensed something was wrong, because he stopped pushing and lifted his head.

"Easy, sweetheart," he whispered in a thick voice. Pulling back, he pressed a kiss to her forehead. "How long has it been since—"

Oh God, he'd realized he was hurting her and was stopping. There was no doubt in her mind that once she got past the initial adjustment of his body merging with hers, the pain would ease. It had in the past. Best to do the merging fast, and get on with the adjusting. With that in mind, she clenched her legs around his hips and arched up, impaling herself on his penis.

Only it hurt much worse than she'd expected, or remembered.

"Easy, easy," Rawls said in the grimmest voice she'd ever heard, but the kisses he brushed across her mouth and cheeks were soft and soothing. "I got you, sweetheart. Easy, babe."

That's when she realized the dampness flowing down her cheeks was tears.

"I'm okay." The reassurance had a hint of sob to it, but then the entire length of him inside her burned like molten steel.

"Sure you are." The grimness deepened his voice to a growl. Still, he brushed another kiss across her mouth. "That's why you screamed."

"I did?" She didn't remember that.

"You did." This time his kiss was less soothing and hungrier, but he broke it off and brushed another of those unbearably chaste ones across her forehead. "Hang in there. It'll get better. Just don't move."

Not moving sounded like a great plan. She settled back, her rigid muscles relaxing. Good lord, she'd been as stiff as a board. Slowly the burning pain eased.

After a moment she sighed and smiled up at him. "You're right. It doesn't hurt nearly as much now."

"Good." He pulled back to study her face, and whatever he saw there must have reassured him, because he scowled. "You mind telling me why the fuck you did that?"

Lord . . . she'd rarely heard him use the f-word before, at least not with her. That didn't bode well for the coming explanation. She swallowed hard.

"You were stopping and—"

"I wasn't stoppin'," he interrupted, his voice a little less grim, but maybe . . . exasperated. "I was slowin' it down. I was going back to the basics, makin' sure you were ready for me, makin' sure I didn't hurt you."

Her mouth fell open.

"Oh," she managed in a small voice.

"Yeah, oh." He sighed and kissed the tip of her nose. "So, are you ready to let me handle the penis work now?"

That made her laugh.

He caught the laugh with his mouth and then pulled back enough to whisper, "Don't move. Let me do all the work."

She wanted to snap a salute and ask if that was an order, but one of his hands had moved to her breast and was slowly pinching and rolling the nipple between his fingers. The friction wasn't enough to hurt; instead it sent a landslide of tingles coursing through her body. His other hand slid between her legs and began caressing the soft sensitive flesh, restoking her earlier fire. Slowly, lazily, he stroked her nipple, rubbed her clit, and caressed the inside of her mouth with his tongue.

That lovely, winding tension seized her again. At some point, she wasn't even sure when, the burning pain disappeared, or maybe it simply became unimportant. Her hips began to move in conjunction with the tug of his mouth on her bottom lip.

He moved back from her mouth to search her eyes. "Okay?"

The question was guttural, but at least he managed to speak. She'd apparently lost access to her lungs and could only manage a dazed nod.

His smile held pure satisfaction.

Still watching her face, he pulled back slightly. She groaned in protest and clamped her arms and legs around him.

"No movin'," he reminded her, but the words were thick and teasing. Carefully, he pressed forward again.

There was no way she could follow his directive. Not when every cell in her body was demanding that she match her rhythm to his. So she arched into his next thrust, and then his next and his next, until they were moving in concert.

Somehow the sight of his bunched shoulders, corded neck, and the way his unfocused eyes were still locked on her face as he hammered urgently into her, ratcheted her pleasure to the next level.

The tension twined tighter and tighter and tighter until it simply burst.

Until they both burst.

And floated down to earth with legs and arms still wrapped around each other.

Rawls returned to awareness slowly, utterly content, his spent body stretched across a soft, damp pillow. When the pillow moved, he froze. Instantly his memory and hearing returned.

Faith . . . ah hell—he had to be crushing her.

Wrapping his arms around her, he rolled, keeping her tucked against his body so that when they stopped moving, she limply draped him from thigh to chest. Sheer perfection.

As his body and mind recuperated, an insane need to touch her nagged at him, to keep touching her, to cement this intimacy between them—which was rather redundant considering they were pressed together, naked torso to naked torso, as intimately as two people could possibly get . . . well, almost.

They'd been a hell of a lot more intimately connected a few minutes earlier. He smiled at the memory, the satisfaction so thick inside him it had weight and substance.

It had been a long time since she'd had a man in her. He had no clue why that knowledge filled him with such intense satisfaction. He simply accepted that it did. Hell, the thought of another man touching her made him want to throw the bastard down a flight of stairs—after breaking his legs and arms so he could never touch her again.

He sighed and stroked a hand down her back, more content than he could ever remember feeling. In the past, he'd never cared how many lovers a woman had taken before him—or how many more she'd take after he parted ways with her. This possessiveness was new. Unexpected.

Her skin was cooling beneath his palm as her sweat dried. Grabbing a handful of blanket, he dragged it over her thin frame.

While he'd been vaguely aware of her thinness earlier, the urgency of his hunger had obscured just how frail she actually was. Jesus, her spine was far too prominent, every bump and hollow identifiable by touch. And then there were her shoulder blades and collarbone—they were so pronounced they looked capable of piercing her skin at any moment. The woman needed to eat—a lot.

He was making it a priority to pack some pounds on her.

As he continued stroking her, worry built, tension rose, and something very much like dread unfurled in his mind and clotted in his chest. How the hell could anyone think she was capable of making it out of that damn rescue mission alive?

It wasn't until she lifted her head from his chest that he realized she was awake too.

"What's wrong?" she asked, propping her chin on her hands and staring at him steadily.

She'd probably picked up on the tension invading his muscles. He lifted a hand and threaded his fingers through her hair, gently untangling the thick dark strands.

"You have the most beautiful hair," he said, running his fingers through the glossy strands again before pulling his hand free and stroking a finger across the network of freckles on her cheek. Sometime soon he was going to kiss his way along every freckle on her body. "And freckles," he added. He lifted his head to press a kiss to first her right and then left eye. "And eyes. You don't have a clue how beautiful you are."

Without reacting, she watched him solemnly. "What's wrong?"

His chest tightened as he stared back at her. She didn't believe him. Well, he'd just have to make it priority number two to convince her. But he needed time to do that. A lifetime of it. Starting now.

"Please don't go on the rescue mission." The plea broke from him and then just hung there.

"I have to. Surely you see that? I wasn't exaggerating about what the technology can do, Rawls." She seemed to hesitate and finally sighed. "If anything, I downplayed it. There's no way to defend against what someone can do while under the influence of that machine. You, Cosky, Mac, Zane, Wolf and his team— you'd all be massacred."

His stomach tightened and he shied away from that possibility. "It's likely your team hasn't gotten far enough along in the re-creation."

She shook her head, and her silky hair slid through his fingers to tickle his chest. "It could prove to be a fatal mistake if we banked on that."

"Faith—" His throat tightened, cutting the rest of the protest off.

This time she was the one to stroke his cheek. "I have to," she said again. "If the machine is operational, they'll need me." She paused and leaned up to brush a kiss across his lips. "Besides, you'll be there beside me, right? Keeping me safe."

He flinched, memories of Sarah's empty, dying eyes flashing through his mind. "You'd be wise not to count on me for that."

A frown wrinkled her forehead and her dark eyes sharpened. But she just shrugged. "You've saved my life twice so far. I'd say you're a safe bet."

"My sister would disagree with that." The admission was out before he could call it back.

"Why?" Her voice was neutral, but the palm she pressed against his heart was warm and calming.

"Because she died because of me. I couldn't protect her."

Maybe she expected something similar, because she didn't look surprised, nor did she pull back. Her hand remained warm and encouraging against his chest. And her voice was the epitome of casual. "When was this?"

Somehow her lack of reaction made it easier to force the whole sordid story out. "Just before my final year of residency. Sarah was just startin' medical school, and I knew the gruelin' hours she was facin', so I convinced her to join me and a friend, Carl, on his family's yacht."

"What happened?" she asked, her voice unbearably gentle, as though she already knew what was coming, or thought she did.

"The boat was surrounded and captured by a flotilla of pirates. Those aboard were held for ransom. Carl and I were left alone." Except for constant vicious beatings and the mental torture of watching what was happening to their loved ones, while being powerless to stop it.

"But they . . . used . . . Sarah and Bitsy—Carl's girlfriend—they used them over and over again, by the dozens." His sister's white, frozen face and hunched body as he had cradled her in his arms burst so clearly into his mind he could actually smell the blood in her phantom hair. "And I couldn't stop it." He could hear the hollowness in his voice.

"Oh Rawls—"

He flinched at the tenderness on her face.

"They released you after the ransom was paid?" The question was matter-of-fact, and he relaxed slightly.

"Hell no, that would have been too honorable for those bastards." His grimace was more a snarl. "I'm sure they planned to kill us. But Carl's brother was in the Corps and he had contacts. HQ2 cleared ST4 to take down the ship and rescue survivors. Those malicious bastards never knew what hit them." For a second, the sound of close-quarters gunfire and screams filled his head.

"Your sister?" Her voice was tentative.

"She died hours before ST4 scaled the yacht."

"And you've blamed yourself ever since." But rather than under-standing, her brisk voice was full of . . . exasperation?

What in sweet Jesus's name . . .

He frowned and zeroed in on her face. Yep, definitely exasperation, and she wasn't even trying to hide it. The unbelievability of her reaction banished the ghosts.

"So tell me, Lieutenant Rawlings, how many pirates were holding you hostage?" she asked in that same annoyingly exasperated voice.

"Hell, I don't know, two dozen, but—"

"Two dozen, well then, of course you should have been able to defend your sister and defeat them all singlehandedly at age—what?" He could almost see her doing some quick estimation. "Twenty-four? Twenty-five?"

"Twenty-four," he snapped. "You don't know—"

"What I know is that that's some mighty fine hubris you've got going on there," she shot back.

What the hell!

He jolted upright and since she was lying on top of him, she did too, until they were sitting there, chest to chest, face to face, and eye to eye.

"Well, isn't that what you're telling me?" she asked, not backing down in the slightest. She lifted an eyebrow. "That even as an untrained twenty-four-year-old with no military experience, you could have subdued twenty-four heavily armed pirates? Who are you? Superman?"

"Of course I couldn't . . ." He stumbled to a stop, suddenly seeing the trap she'd set for him.

"Exactly," she said, the exasperation replaced by tenderness. "You couldn't do anything. There were twenty-four armed men between your sister and you. Sometimes we have to accept that things are out of our control."

"Jesus." He collapsed back down to the bed, taking her with him. "That blitz attack was sneaky as hell."

But to his surprise, he could actually feel a slight loosening inside himself, the easing of an ancient ache.

"Yeah, well, I knew you wouldn't listen to reason." The silence that settled between them was contented, rather than confrontational. "I'm sorry about your sister," she said after a few seconds.

"Me too." He forced the words through his tight throat and leaned down to brush his mouth across her forehead. "I'm sorry about Marcy and"—what had their names been?—"Bekka and Julio."

"Me too." Her voice sounded hoarse. She cleared it and slanted him a shrewd look. "When are you telling your buddies this entire rescue is based off information provided by a ghost?"

He'd wanted to respond "never," but yeah, she knew him too well. "Mornin' will do."

They needed to know the circumstances surrounding this mission they'd volunteered for. If the revelation caused them to opt out—so be it. He was done lying, or skirting the truth.

Faith stretched and sent him another of those judicious looks. "Too bad Kait wasn't on that yacht, or in my lab."

The casualness didn't fool him. Cocking his head, he studied her face.

"With Kait's incredible gift, she could have healed them, like she healed you . . . like she healed me." She paused, stared at him steadily. "Think how welcome such a gift would be on one of your missions."

His scowl started back up now that he saw what tree she was headed up. "There's no way Cosky is gonna let Kait come along on the rescue mission."

She smiled back at him, amusement swimming in her dark eyes. "Do you really think Cosky is going to be able to stop her when there's the possibility that he'll be the one in need of her gift? Besides, this obviously isn't your team's call, and my guess is Wolf will want her on board."

He stirred at that, a hand absently rising to drag the blanket back over her bare back. She was right. About all of it. But even having Kait on the team didn't negate the danger to Faith, although perhaps it did lessen it.

"If Cosky is injured and unable to supply Kait with whatever it is he contributes to the healin', her ability will be cut in half. Maybe even in quarter. We can't count on her," he told her.

"True." Faith pressed a kiss to his shoulder, and Rawls felt his cock stir. "But remember this morning? Dr. Kelly mentioned two other healers. Kait obviously isn't an anomaly among their people."

"Maybe," Rawls admitted, his hand sliding under the blanket for another round of stroking. "But judgin' from what the good doctor said, it doesn't sound like they're nearly as strong as Kait."

"Singularly, sure." Her voice grew breathless as his hand grew bolder. "But it would be interesting to see what would happen if they pooled their— ah . . ."

She quivered against him, abruptly losing interest in the conversation. A damn fine thing, since his interest had shifted to other pursuits as well.

"Are you up for a round two?" he whispered in her ear before the perfect little shell distracted him and he circled the edge with his tongue.

He shuddered as her taste exploded in his mouth. Salty and sweet, it sank into his blood and set it on fire like the purest of drugs.

"Definitely," she said, her voice raspy. A soft hand grasped his cock and gave it one firm pump. "I see you're up for it too."

He groaned at the pun, and pulled her down so he could steal a kiss from her lips.

And then his arms wrapped around her, locking her against his chest, until he could feel the strong, steady thump of her like-new heart against his.

Exactly where it belonged.

Chapter Nineteen

ERIC MANHEIM PAUSED IN FRONT OF THE BANK OF FLOOR-TO-CEILING windows to stare absently down at the emerald sprawl of Central Park. "What do you mean the signal's disappeared?"

"I mean the signal is gone. One minute it was broadcasting as it has been for weeks, the next second it vanished." James Link's voice rasped through Eric's cell phone.

Forcing himself to turn away from the window for fear he might give in to his impulse to drive his fist into the glass, Eric paced back to his executive desk, which overlooked the huge bank of windows.

The desk had been a surprise gift from Esme on his thirty-sixth birthday. Custom-built to her specifications from Parnian's exotic-woods collection—with each choice of wood embodying an element of their love and life together—he prized the desk as much for its sentimental value, as its half-a-million-dollar price tag.

It was a rare day that the desk's stunning visual artistry and hidden symbolism couldn't soothe his irritation.

Today was proving to be such a day.

"Could they be dead? You said the signal would cease once the cellular structure broke down." Which was a fancy way of saying once the Chastain boys had ceased to exist.

"Highly unlikely." Link's throaty rasp turned into heavy breathing. "If the cells were deteriorating, the signal would have gradually weakened. It wouldn't just disappear. This appears to be something else."

"What then?" Eric locked his snarl behind his teeth as he stalked behind the desk.

"If I had to guess—"

"You do." Some of the growl escaped as Eric's hand tightened around his cell phone. Silence pulsed down the line.

"Then . . . I'd . . . say . . . the signal's being blocked." The last four words came out in a spurt.

"How is that possible? You said the compound was unremovable. That the signal would be trackable from anywhere in the world, under any conditions." Eric's throat tightened against the desire to yell.

He pulled back the Ares line Xten chair—another gift from Esme. Only for no special occasion this time, other than the fact that the chair—which had been designed by Pininfarina, the same company responsible for Ferraris—was considered to be the most comfortable chair in the world.

Link coughed. "Which is what our testing indicated. But our testing was limited. It's impossible to test it against every condition. I would guess the boys have arrived someplace that blocks the signal."

Slowly Eric sat, relaxing as the Technogel cushions conformed to his frame, cradling him. If what Link had said was true, the signal would resume once the children left the area interfering with the signal. Since Link had been tracking them right up until the signal disappeared, he must know the approximate location they'd gone to ground.

"Where did the signal disappear?" he asked. At the last check-in, the signal had been approaching the Alaska state line.

"In the vicinity of Mount McKinley."

McKinley? The mountain was—he ran a quick Google search on his phone—at least 1500 miles from Seattle. Which meant the aircraft the SEALs and their charges had appropriated was flying at speeds of three hundred miles an hour. At least—he googled typical helicopter speeds—twice as fast as any chopper currently in use by the military.

"Who in the hell are they working with?" he muttered beneath his breath. "They didn't get that helicopter from Coronado."

"Maybe it was a plane. A private jet can fly over six hundred miles an hour."

Eric shook his head. His last team leader had specifically mentioned a helicopter taking out their Jayhawk—the second bloody one he'd lost to those navy bastards, mind you. Too bad he hadn't gotten a description of the aircraft before his spineless, incompetent asshole of a team leader had fucked everything up and then gotten himself killed.

He grimaced and got back down to business. "If there's something blocking the signal, it should resume once they start moving again. Correct?"

A pause echoed through his phone. And then Link cleared his throat. "Assuming they haven't arrived at their destination, or that they haven't transferred to another vehicle that is blocking the signal. If the latter is the case, they could be anywhere."

Bloody hell. Eric scrubbed at the headache behind his eyes. He needed another team. Someone to send up to Alaska and do some poking around, but the fuckup in the Cascades had deprived him of choices. He thought about asking Link if he had anyone they could send, but he swallowed the question at the last moment.

It was pretty much guaranteed that anyone Link recommended would lack the sociopathic, cold-blooded killer instinct the job required. If you wanted to hire an assassin, your best bet was to ask a killer for recommendations.

"Let me know immediately if the signal comes back online." He didn't wait for an agreement. He simply ended the call and dialed David Coulson.

"Thoughts?" Mac asked, looking back and forth between his two officers. The two men in front of him were Rawlings's best friends. Hell, they'd been roommates for years. If anyone knew how bad off the poor bastard was, it would be them.

"At least we know what's going on with him now," Cosky pointed out, lifting the tumbler of whiskey to his lips and taking a healthy swallow.

Zane rolled his shoulders in what might—or might not—have been agreement as a hard knock sounded on the door.

Pushing back the bottle of Jack Daniel's, and then his chair, Mac climbed to his feet. He studied the grim faces across the table before silently turning and heading for the entrance to his quarters.

Since Rawls had been the one to call the meeting, his face on the other side of the door was expected. Mac stepped back, allowing him entry.

"You want a shot?" Mac asked, following Rawls back to the table. He lifted the bottle of Jack Daniel's. When Rawls waved the offer aside, he refilled three of the four empty glasses spread across the Formica surface.

"I have some information y'all need to know," Rawls said, jumping into the subject immediately.

Stiffening, Mac held up a palm, halting the flow of words. "We can't assume this is a private conversation."

It was a safe bet that the quarters he'd been given had come with an extra set of ears. Of course, it was an equally safe bet that they'd have someone listening in on their discussion no matter where they had it.

Rawls's tight grin looked more like a grimace. He shifted from foot to foot, shoving tense fingers through his hair. "Trust me, Wolf and his people are fully aware of everythin' I'm about to tell y'all."

Cosky and Zane exchanged guarded looks.

"Okay," Mac said, and waited.

"All the intel at the strategy session yesterday came from Pachico."

Stunned silence rocked the room, thickening the air until every rustle of clothing or shuffle of feet sounded muffled and languid.

"Pachico," Cosky finally said, his voice neutral. "As in our dead cop impersonator?"

The operative word being *dead*.

"That's the one," Rawls said in an equally flat voice.

Giving himself time to batten down his immediate, explosive burst of disbelief, Mac picked up his tumbler and drained it, concentrating on the furious burn traveling down his throat. He wasn't certain what he'd expected, but it sure as hell hadn't been this.

While the tunnels had brought to light the fact that Rawls was convinced he was seeing ghosts, who'd have guessed he intended to interrogate the damn things?

"I assume this information was collected after Pachico died?" Cosky asked dryly.

"How much of the intel from yesterday are we talking about?" Zane asked, sharp intelligence glittering in his eyes.

"All of it," Rawls said.

"Where the scientists are being held? Who's holding them? Who's behind this whole damn operation?" Mac asked, shooting the questions out like rapid gunfire.

Rawls lifted his shoulders into an exaggerated shrug. "Yes, yes, and yes."

More silence.

Eventually Mac stirred. "You're telling me these morons are gearing up for a major operation off intel provided by a ghost?"

"That they are," Rawls said quietly. "They know exactly where the information came from."

"And they believe it? They're acting on it?" Mac didn't bother hiding his disbelief.

Intel from a ghost, for Christ's sake. What the hell are they thinking?

"Look," Rawls said, staring them one by one in the eye. "I know y'all don't believe me. That's plenty fine. I just thought y'all should know before signin' on board."

Another long, awkward pause and then Zane lifted his glass in a toast. "Appreciate it." He brought the glass to his lips, tilted back his head, and poured the shot down his throat before turning the tumbler upside down and placing it with deliberation on the table. "So let's say Pachico did supply this information . . . can you trust it? Hell, the guy was less than cooperative when alive. You telling us death has opened his mouth?"

Rawls barked out a laugh. "Hardly. But he didn't have a choice." He paused for a moment and frowned, as though not sure how much to admit. "Wolf and his people are much more attuned to this shit than we are. They have a ceremony that forces ghosts to tell the truth."

"Really." The very neutrality in Cosky's voice shouted his skepticism. "They use a ceremony to force truth from ghosts?"

"Yep. As well as to exorcise them," Rawls said, his voice getting progressively tighter.

Mac couldn't help it. A snort escaped. "So you performed an exorcism too?"

For the first time, an honest-to-god emotion flickered across Rawls's face. Pure irritation.

"I don't give a shit if y'all believe me. Just thought you should know." He pivoted and took a step toward the door.

"Are you headed down with them?" Zane asked, his voice flat, but concern tightening the skin around his eyes.

Rawls stopped walking. "Yeah, they got Faith convinced they'll die without her help." Frustrated anger sharpened his vowels. "I'm goin' to keep an eye on her."

"Then I'm in," Zane said simply.

"Me too," Cosky agreed.

"What the hell. Can't let you bastards have all the fun." Mac shrugged. "I'm on board."

"Appreciate it," Rawls said after a moment.

Throats cleared. Mac broke the moment by picking up the half-empty bottle of JD and filling the glasses again. He kicked an empty chair toward Rawls. "How about you get the fuck over here and sit down? We've got other shit to talk about besides ghosts."

Once Rawls had taken a seat, Mac sat down himself. The whole damn ghost thing was a useless distraction.

"Wolf claimed he'd have visuals on the building by tomorrow. Schematics. Head counts, blueprints," Mac reminded everyone absently. "So we'll know soon enough whether they're targeting the right place and people." He didn't question how Wolf would acquire the information. Shadow Mountain obviously had some pretty kick-ass contacts.

"So this Eric Manheim and James Link, those names come through your ghost too?" Mac asked abruptly.

"Yeah." Rawls reached for the bottle of whiskey and poured half a finger into the fourth tumbler on the table.

When he sat back, he jabbed Zane in the side with his elbow. With a grunt, Zane pushed his chair, loosening up some room. The table was so small the four of them were packed around it like sardines in a round tin.

"But Wolf and his boys recognized the names. Apparently they've run into this New Ruling Order before. Wolf didn't say much, but I get the impression the NRO is a major threat," Rawls added quietly.

Zane nodded absently, staring thoughtfully into the amber liquid in his glass. "I did some checking last night. If your ghost isn't fucking with you, we've got a serious problem. Eric Manheim heads up the Manheim-Clifton financial coalition. They own hundreds of banks and financial institutions throughout the world. Hell, as the only child of the Manheim family dynasty and husband to the only child of the

Clifton family dynasty, Eric Manheim controls the national banks of virtually every country in existence—including the Bank of England, the United States Federal Reserve, the Bank of Japan, the Central Bank of Jordan, the Bank of France, and the Central Bank of Austria. He's arguably the most powerful man in existence—untouchable."

Mac frowned. "Nobody's untouchable."

Although it would be much, much harder to level accusations at someone with such an elite stature. And that was assuming Rawls's damn ghost, or more likely their corpsman's fertile imagination, produced anything substantial linking Eric Manheim to anything.

But Manheim wasn't the person he wanted to focus on.

"James Link is the name that interests me," Mac said, leaning far enough back in his chair to bring the front two legs off the ground. "Ghost interrogation aside, with Embray out of commission, Link heads up Dynamic Solutions' experimental department. That shit swimming in Brendan's and Benji's cells is as experimental as fuck, right up Dynamic Solutions' alley. James Link has to know what the hell was injected into Amy's kids. That's where we start looking."

Heads nodded in agreement.

Mac turned to Rawls. "You hear if Wolf's people had any luck neutralizing the isotope?"

Rawls had spent every spare moment in the clinic overseeing Faith Ansell's tests, so maybe he'd run into Amy recently. The last update Mac had gotten had been within hours of arriving at Shadow Mountain. While they'd identified the synthetic compound in the boys' blood cells that was powering the signal, nobody had known how to deactivate the element. But maybe progress had been made in the past twenty-four hours.

"Far as I know, they don't have a clue what to do about it." Rawls's voice was grim.

Cosky leaned forward, bracing his elbows on the table. "Have they tried a healing?" He glanced around the table and shrugged. "Kait says there're other healers in this place. She's all gung ho to try herself, but hell"—he broke off to scowl—"she needs to do some resting and recharging before she burns herself out."

"If doing a healin' is an option, I'm guessin' they would have already tried that," Rawls said, glancing up. "Cos is right. Doc Kerry rattled off a couple of other healers while talkin' to Wolf—" He glanced at Cosky. "He also said she was stronger than the others. In fact, I believe he called her remarkable . . ." He paused, shrugged. "By the by, did you know those two are siblin's? Or half sibs anyway?"

"Who?" Mac's question hit the air at the same time Zane's did. Apparently he wasn't the only one in the dark when it came to the Shadow Mountain's gossip mill.

"Wolf and Kait," Rawls said. "Kerry said she's Wolf's sister."

Mac turned to stare at Cosky, who didn't look at all surprised.

Zane picked up on that as well. "You knew?"

Cosky shrugged. "Wolf was worried for her and Aiden's safety. Wanted to keep the connection private."

"Well that explains why he's been so damn invested in her," Zane said.

"Can't say I envy you having that stony bastard as a brother-in-law," Mac said on a grimace.

With a snort, Cosky settled back against his chair's backrest. "You forgetting all the toys he comes with?"

Mac grinned slightly at that. He'd sure as hell like to get his hands on that little beauty that had ferried them up to Alaska in five hours—give or take a couple of minutes. The trip had taken half as long as it would have taken in a stripped down Black Hawk. Which reminded him. "You realize this damn compound is *in* motherfucking Mount McKinley?"

Shadow Mountain's brass hadn't been nearly as closemouthed as good old Wolf.

"It makes sense. The mountain's sacred to the native population," Cosky said. "What's incredible is the amount of work that must have gone into hollowing it out and constructing the base." He paused to scowl. "Yet nobody noticed? Fuck, fifteen hundred people climb to the summit every year, and nobody noticed what was going on under their feet, or that huge flat tarmac up there where helicopters and planes land and disappear? There's something pretty fucking weird about this place."

Uneasy silence ringed the table.

"Makes you wonder," Zane agreed, his green eyes thoughtful.

Cosky took a generous swallow of whiskey and set the glass back on the table, absently rotating it. "Wolf's got the same handy-dandy trick Zane has." He glanced toward Zane and raised his tumbler in a salute. "Although not quite the same. Wolf doesn't have to touch anyone to get the vision. They just come. It's how he knew our condo was about to blow back in Coronado." He paused to shake his head, a frown darkening the turbulent gray gaze that met Mac's. "He knew the compound was going to be attacked yesterday morning. He sent Jude over to warn us. We knew what was happening before your nine-one-one came over the wire. Hell, I had the radio in hand, was about to warn the three of you, when your call came through."

"Okay . . ." Mac said and waited for the rest of it—because there was a huge "but" in Cosky's tone.

Cosky reached for the bottle of Jack. "Hell, I don't know. It's just . . . there's something fucking strange about this place and the people holed up in here."

Rawls laughed.

Cosky turned to him with a glare. "You find that funny?"

"Yeah, I do." He chuckled, irony clear on his face. "How about we take an inventory? So we have Zane, who's psychic—able to predict a person's death with one touch. We have Cos and Kait—together they can heal life-threatenin' illnesses or injuries—hell, even drag people back from the grave. And then there's *moi*. I see dead people. Or at least I used to. With the exception of Mac"—he lifted his glass of whiskey in a theatrical toast—"we fit right into this place."

Chapter Twenty

*A*FTER THIRTEEN YEARS AND HUNDREDS OF INSERTIONS, RAWLS HAD identified certain similarities no matter the mission. There was the edgy pressure that knotted the belly and shoulders. Not fear so much as a low-grade tension where preparation gave way to anticipation. After all of the planning, monitoring, and assessing, the green light was finally given and all that groundwork was about to be put to the test. There was the cramped, silent flight where legs and feet fell numb, where bodies were buffered by bone-rattling vibrations, where equipment checks were rampant and the smell of jet fuel overpowered everything. There was the deploying into darkness and unfamiliar territory. Sure, the satellite images often provided reference points, but the insertions themselves took place in unfamiliar, often alien landscapes.

Until today . . .

Rawls silently shook his head, his arm tightening around Faith's frail body. Oh, the tension was there, only this time that edgy pressure butted against fear. Not fear for his safety, or any of the other experienced warriors silently stretched out in the helicopter, but fear for Faith.

Although everyone's vulnerability had gone up exponentially when Wolf and Cosky had flatly refused Kait's appeal to join the mission. They'd vehemently opposed Kait's inclusion, insisting that William and One Bird were fully capable of handling any injuries, and that her inclusion was unnecessary and a potential distraction. Cosky and Wolf's intense reaction had reinforced just how dangerous this mission was.

But Faith didn't belong in this dark, dangerous world either. She was as ill-equipped for this operation as Kait was. She had no business being on this helicopter, awaiting the one-minute prep call for insertion.

A couple minutes earlier, Wolf had appeared in the cockpit doorway and held up his right hand, all five fingers splayed. The universal five-minute warning. The interior of the bird was murky, the only light piercing the darkness was the rosy-red digital displays in the cockpit. The ruddy burn had burnished the big Arapaho's hand until his fingers looked rimmed in fire.

Faith had stiffened in his arms even more. With a deep breath he'd pressed a comforting kiss to the top of her head. Rather than the smothering stench of jet fuel, the scent of strawberries and raspberries washed over him.

The scent was coming from her hair. He recognized it from the past two nights he'd spent in her bed. And like any good hound dog, his dick had imprinted on that particular combination of berries as something to celebrate, which it was currently doing with an enthusiastic salute.

Another first—the first time in his military career he'd dropped into hostile territory with an erection. A wry smile curved his mouth even as the tension cinched another notch tighter.

But the big *first* currently topping his list of *Holy Shits*—although it wasn't a first so much as a second—was their insertion point. He was about to drop his boots on United States soil for the second time in his career. Sure, he'd *practiced* warfare on home ground—plenty of training missions took place within US borders. But a true insertion—an actual close-quarters battle—he shook his head in disbelief.

Operating within US borders was a violation of the Posse Comitatus Act—for him, Zane, Cosky, and Mac at least. Wolf and his crew? Hell, they didn't appear to be operating under the umbrella of any branch of the United States military. Which meant that while this operation broke at least a dozen laws, the Shadow Mountain teams didn't need to worry about the Posse Comitatus. Not like he and the rest of his teammates did.

Few soldiers would ever violate the Posse Comitatus during their careers. Yet here he was about to disregard it for a second time. The last time they'd stuck their necks out on US soil, they'd had them all but chopped off. You'd think they would have learned something from that lesson.

But hands down the strangest aspect of this operation was how familiar he was with the territory. He'd recognized the terrain the instant Wolf had put the first satellite image up on the big screen.

Mount Hamilton.

At just over forty-two hundred feet, Mount Hamilton looked out over Silicon Valley. He'd recognized the Lick Observatory on the satellite images. The giant white dome, which perched at the top of the mountain and was surrounded by clusters of smaller white domes and white buildings, was instantly recognizable.

The Lick Observatory—an astronomical observatory operated by the University of California—was twenty miles up State Route 130. Until this morning, he'd only seen the observatory from the ground, up close and personal. Mount Hamilton Road was a popular trek for bikers. The twenty-mile course to the top of the mountain was a gradual and scenic ascent. Once bicyclists reached the observatory, it was customary to break for lunch and a breather before heading back down to their vehicles. He'd pedaled the route half a dozen times, so he was familiar with the overall layout of their insertion point.

Not that their target was the Lick Observatory, or even at the top of the mountain. It was tucked into one of the canyons five miles up.

The satellite image had zeroed in close enough to pick up the security cameras ringing the building's flat roof. The angle and quantity of cameras would give the bastards inside a 360-degree view of the grounds below.

Wolf stepped into the cockpit doorway again. This time he held up his index finger. Translation, one minute until touchdown.

Men stirred, checked weapons, stretched the kinks and numbness out of stiff muscles. Faith slowly sat up.

"One minute to touchdown," Rawls told her, pitching his voice loud enough to reach her over the scream of the engine and whine of the rotor.

She nodded her understanding. He quickly checked his equipment and then hers—although all she'd been given were an NVD and the standard radio. Well, plus the vest and armor plates, which all but swallowed her, even though they'd found her the smallest size possible.

The chopper banked and dropped. The shriek of the motors eased as the bird slowed. One of Wolf's men rose to his feet and muscled back the door, and the roar of the wind merged with the scream of the engine and the shrill *whop-whop* of the rotor. They'd approached from the west, out of the target's line of sight, and were inserting into a meadow two klicks away. The rest of the distance would be covered by foot.

The bird rocked slightly as it settled on the ground—no fast roping this time around. The roar of the wind vanished, and the engine's whine dropped to a hum. Crouching, Wolf's men dropped from the chopper and melted into the darkness. Rawls's teammates followed.

Rawls turned on Faith's NVD and then his, wrapped an arm around her waist, thereby anchoring her to his side, and eased them both from the bird. Head bent, flinching from the pelting of pebbles, grass, and dirt kicked up by the rotor's wash, Faith stumbled along beside him. Once clear of the blades, he stopped long enough to show her how to adjust the scope on her goggles.

"I'm sorry." Her voice was so thin he could barely hear it. Apparently she'd taken all the warning to maintain silence seriously.

"Nothin' to be sorry about," he said in an equally quiet voice. Sound carried, even buffered by trees, and they had no clue whether those bastards had ears out here.

"I'm holding everyone up."

Even as thin and shaky as her voice was, he could clearly hear the self-reproach in her tone.

He gave her a quick, one-armed hug. It was true, she was holding everyone back. But then, nobody had expected anything less.

"Nobody expects you to turn into Rambo, darlin'. You're doin' fine."

A soft snort came from behind them. Mac undoubtedly, since he was bringing up the rear. Zane's and Cosky's crisp, fluorescent-green figures were waiting ahead, about midmeadow.

"Let's head up," Rawls said, giving a final one-armed hug before letting her go and grabbing his rifle, which was hanging—safety engaged—from his shoulder.

Thank Christ he didn't have to worry about Pachico getting all frisky on him. According to Wolf and his Arapaho elders, Pachico had passed—or been shoved—over to the other side. Since his trollish hitch-hiker hadn't put in an appearance since the binding ceremony, he was inclined to believe them. But to err on the side of caution, the *hiixoyoo-niiheiht* still burned lightly against his chest. From the volume of leather cords circling the Shadow Mountain warriors' necks as they'd climbed on board the chopper, he wasn't the only one siding with caution.

Faith kept up with him easily as they crossed the meadow, and with each step, he could feel her nerves settle.

"What are these called again?" Faith whispered, briefly touching the goggles covering most of her face.

"Night vision devices," Rawls whispered back.

"Why is everything such a sharp shade of green?" she asked, curiosity rather than nerves in her voice.

A fist suddenly slammed into his shoulder from behind, shoving him forward a step. Mac, giving him the one-second warning to shut the fuck up.

Rawls half turned to glare at his commander. If the bastard hit Faith, there'd be more than one fist flying.

"Never mind, I'll google it," Faith said. She turned slightly to frown behind her. "No need to get physical, Commander Mackenzie. A verbal warning would have sufficed."

Rawls fought a grin at the censure in her voice. She was certainly getting her nerve back fast.

The trip to the target took less time than he'd expected, and well before he was ready for it, they joined Zane and Cosky and the bulk of Wolf's team at the edge of the forest.

The building jutting into the night sky before them was three stories, square, with a flat roof. Cameras ringed the roofline, and the glowing, barred windows were few and far between. An acre of lawn surrounded the place. To their right, a rutted dirt road emerged from the forest and dead-ended to the right of the building in a large square of gravel and dead grass. He counted eight cars parked there. Which could indicate anywhere from eight to thirty Tangos inside waiting for them—depending on number of employees per vehicle.

Zane leaned in so close his mouth was next to Rawls's ear.

"They scrambled the cameras. And Wolf sent his scouts out." The words were so low they'd be nonexistent a foot away.

Rawls glanced at Wolf. They were right on schedule. The Shadow Mountain strategy had called for scrambling cameras and cell phones prior to scouting for secondary entrances. Once the entrances were secure, they'd bring in the second bird, which carried team two.

A minute passed, then two . . . five . . .

Wolf's men stirred uneasily and then everyone froze, faces tense, heads slightly cocked as though they were listening to something.

Seconds later, a short, vicious-sounding foreign word broke from Wolf—an Arapaho swear word. Rawls had no doubt. The word was repeated by several of Wolf's normally taciturn men. Something had sure shoved a poker up their new allies' asses.

Wolf wheeled on Jude and a spat of urgent Arapaho words crackled between them. Pivoting, Wolf closed on Mac. "Team two's down."

Rawls winced. Christ, of all the bad luck. The bird must have been way behind them. If it had gone down in the vicinity, they would have heard the impact and been able to backtrack to offer support.

Mac swore, sympathy in his eyes. "Casualties?"

"We're assessing," Wolf said, his voice grimmer than Rawls had ever heard it.

Zane and Cosky glanced at each other, and Rawls knew exactly what they were thinking.

How had they known the chopper had gone down? Nothing had come over the comm.

Although Mac didn't react or question Wolf—it was hardly the time for demands and questions—Rawls knew he was silently asking the same questions.

Hell, maybe the Shadow Mountain team monitored two channels.

"For this operation to continue, your team will need to step up," Wolf said, back to wearing his flat, expressionless mask.

Mac nodded, the gesture both an agreement and an acceptance. "What do you need from us?"

Their original instructions via Shadow Mountain Command had been to remain with Faith. Protect her. They'd been assigned guard duty, not a breachers' position. While the order had sat fine with Rawls—he had no intention of abandoning Faith—it had rankled something fierce with Mac. As experienced operators with hundreds of successful missions beneath their boots, he'd felt command should have made better use of their talents.

Wolf glanced at Rawls. "You remain with Dr. Ansell." His gaze shifted, landing on Mac's face. "You, Cosky, and Zane take the ground. My team will take the roof. Give us time to scale the wall." Without another word, Wolf turned and launched himself forward in a crouching run.

Simultaneously his teammates erupted from the tree line, joining him, and together they swarmed the left side of the building. Through his NVDs, Rawls watched a large luminous green bag disgorge a pneumatic grappling gun. The hook went flying, the attached rope unraveling behind it. As soon as the hook caught and secured the line, Wolf's first man started climbing.

The double breach was under way. Wolf's team would access the roof and insert from above. Mac, Zane, and Cosky would breach the building from below. The Tangos inside would be cut off and pinched between the two flanks of attack.

While the insertion hadn't gone quite as planned, and Wolf's team would be clearly visible to anyone who bothered to look out one of the left windows, so far nobody inside seemed aware of, or at least reactive to, the imminent attack. Still, the alert should have been given as soon as Wolf's team took out the cameras and the inside monitors went dark.

Which meant any second now things could go to hell in a hand basket because operations *never* went so smoothly. At least not for long. Some overlooked or unknown detail always stepped in to fuck things up.

"Let's go," Mac whispered, lifting himself into a half crouch. With Cosky three feet to his left and Zane three feet to his right, he advanced on the house in a truncated run.

About halfway across the yard, with the grass spongy beneath his boots, it occurred to him that Zane hadn't had time to do his prebattle ritual of touching everyone in the hopes of psychically pinpointing possible threats. Since the ritual was fucking eerie as hell, and didn't always yield the intended results, he refused to consider the omission as bad luck. They'd survived plenty of insertions blind to what their futures held.

Seconds later their target's front entrance loomed large. From the number of vehicles parked to his right, the place was obviously inhabited. The sudden dearth of cameras should have tipped the Tangos off to the fact that something was wrong. But the place stood silent and still, its barred windows illuminated and shedding bright light into the darkness beyond them.

The lack of a sentry and absence of defensive positioning rang warning bells. Someone should have noticed them by now.

This whole damn setup smelled foul.

Mac took the right-hand position beside the front entrance, while Zane took the left. Cosky waited center stage to breach the door. Mac held up five fingers. Cosky nodded, tried the door handle, which was locked, and on the five-second mark drove his boot into the door just below the knob. The jamb held. The fact that it held indicated some degree of home security, but Mac's internal alarm system continued ringing.

With a muffled grunt, Cosky abandoned brute force in favor of weapons. Lifting his semiautomatic rifle, he riddled the left side of the doorframe next to the handle and locking mechanism with bullets. Wood splinters peppered the air.

If the bastards inside hadn't realized they had company before, they sure as hell knew now. By the time Cosky stopped his assault on the doorframe, the wood strip stood fragmented and warped. Two floors above them, gunfire hammered the night. Wolf and his crew had inserted.

Cosky's second try with his boot laid the door wide open. Already firing in case a welcoming committee was positioned on the other side, Cosky eased forward. Mac fell in behind him and Zane brought up the rear. The hall was empty, narrow, and straight, with four doors on the left and two on the right. Cosky and Zane slipped into the first room, a cramped office with a desk and file cabinets, while Mac stood vigil in the hall.

Within seconds, Zane called "clear." They repeated the process and cleared the first floor offices and conference rooms, while periodic bursts of gunfire stippled the floors above.

The shooting indicated Wolf's team had engaged the Tangos, but the absence of the motherfucking mercenaries on the ground level was a pressurized itch down the back of his neck.

Why the fuck would the whole lot of them camp out above?

Cosky and Zane joined him in the hall, and in unison they moved toward the stairwell at the back.

"Ground level is secure," Mac said quietly into his mic as they closed on the door to the stairs. "We're moving up."

A burst of weapon fire came through the mic and then Wolf's quiet acknowledgment echoed in his ears.

Mac slid into position beside the door leading to the stairs, while Cosky crouched to the side, next to Mac's knees, offering as small a target as possible. Mac eased open the door enough for Cosky to scope the space with his rifle.

"We have a dead body," Cosky said quietly.

Zane, who'd positioned himself across from Mac, reached for the door handle and pulled the door wide open. Cosky shot up the stairs, clearing the splayed, bloody body with a quick leap. Zane swung into the staircase behind him.

After a quick glance around the corner and up the next flight of stairs, Cosky pulled back and settled his shoulder against the wall. "Clear ahead."

From his position at the bottom of the stairs, Mac nodded toward the corpse. "One of the scientists?"

It was a good bet. The body was wearing a white lab coat. As he waited for Zane to identify the body—they'd been shown photographs of Dr. Ansell's kidnapped team—Mac swept the hall behind them. Rawls would have taken out anyone trying to access the building behind them, but it never paid to rely completely on someone else.

"Dr. Benton," Zane said. "He's been dead awhile. The blood's almost dry."

"Son of a bitch," Mac said grimly, sourness rolling in his gut.

There went the rescue mission. If Benton had been killed, the likelihood that the rest of his team had suffered the same fate was exceptionally high.

"Shouldn't we move up?" Faith whispered. "I need to be closer to the prototype to interface with the generator's static field."

"Soon," Rawls whispered back. "Mac will radio when the buildin' is secure."

"But I'm of no help way back here if they run into problems." Faith's voice rose slightly.

Rawls's hand tightened on her arm, holding her back in case she got the insane idea to rush in on her own. Hell, they didn't even know if the machine was operational, or if it was, whether anyone had turned it on. It could damn well be that there was absolutely no need for her to get anywhere near the damn building.

"We wait until Mac gives the okay," Rawls said, his voice flat, unbending.

The strategy they'd collectively come up with during the last meeting had given Faith the best protection possible, but it depended on the rest of his team guarding her, and Faith only accessing the building after the premises had been locked down. But his teammates were currently one hundred yards away and otherwise engaged. No way in hell was he letting her near that damn building until he was certain it was safe.

The soft crack of a branch snapping sounded behind him. Instinctively he shoved Faith down and pivoted, crouching in front of her. The muffled report of a suppressed semiautomatic pistol echoed through the trees, and chunks from the tree trunk behind them rained down on his head.

As he raised his rifle and sighted on the crisp, green, glowing body partially obscured by the luminous shrubbery, he shielded Faith as best he could.

"We've got a Tango wedged in the stairway between levels two and three. Copy?"

Wolf's grim voice filled Mac's headset.

Translation: the motherfucker was playing peek-a-boo with a semi-automatic, and Big Bad Wolf's team couldn't line up a clear shot.

"Copy," Mac said, reading Wolf's request loud and clear.

The motherfucker shooting at them would find it much more difficult to fend off two approaching flanks.

"Zane, stick around down here. Watch our six." He motioned Cosky forward. "Let's head up."

They climbed the stairs cautiously. Christ only knew how many other motherfuckers there were entrenched in this place. Rather than continuing up to the third floor and engaging the Tango immediately, they exited at the second floor for a quick sweep.

The bastard in the stairwell wasn't going anywhere. Cosky, who was stationed at the entrance, would ensure that. And if for some ungodly reason his lieutenant missed—fuck, Zane would take care of him when he reached the bottom of the stairs.

But if there were more motherfuckers hiding on the second floor—hell, missing them could prove disastrous for everyone. As it turned out, the second level—more offices, from the looks of the dented, steel furniture—was clear.

Where the hell is everyone?

He rejoined Cosky at the door to the stairway. Sporadic gunfire filtered out through the heavy, fortified door.

"Remember, we need the bastard alive," he mouthed the words since their best tactic was stealth and silence.

Cosky nodded and gently eased the door open. Mac scoped the stairs going up. No sign of the Tango, but from the sound of that AK-47, he was right around the bend.

They needed a distraction.

"Cover," he said softly into his headset, grunting in satisfaction as a steady barrage of gunfire pounded the stairwell.

Cosky pushed the door open wide, and Mac silently shot up the immediate flight of stairs. He paused at the landing, with his back against the wall, and chanced a quick peek around the corner.

Wolf's distraction was working well. The Tango's back was pressed against the wall, at an angle to Mac. He was facing the stairs going up, concentrating on the men above, totally oblivious to the men below.

Normally he'd go for a kill shot. But damn it, they needed the fucker alive. Mac had a whole slew of questions for the bastard.

The Tango was right-handed according to the way he was holding his gun, so Mac targeted the bastard's shoulder. Best to disable him first, then worry about the interrogation.

His finger steady on the trigger, he squeezed off a shot. The target spun toward him and Mac dropped his rifle barrel, nailing the asshole's hand.

The bastard's gun hit the stair.

Satisfaction swelled, but it was short-lived. As the gun clattered down the stairs, the trigger engaged and the falling gun sprayed the stairwell with bullets. One moment the target was standing. The next he hit the ground with half his face and head missing.

Mac's mouth dropped open in pure disgust.

Son of a fucking bitch.

There went his informant.

"Stairway's clear," he said into his mouthpiece.

"Copy," Wolf responded immediately.

Heading up the stairs, Mac stepped over the dead Tango and joined Wolf on the third-level landing.

"Sitrep?" Mac asked, staring at the carnage spread before him. Well, he'd found everyone.

"They cleaned house. We've identified all but Benton," Wolf said, his voice grim.

"He's on the stairs below," Mac said slowly, still staring at the massacre before him.

Wolf's grunt acknowledged the information. He didn't ask if the scientist was alive. "We need Dr. Ansell."

Mac pushed his way farther into the room. Christ, blood and bodies were everywhere. Some bodies in lab coats. Some in jeans and T-shirts. Some slumped in chairs, some strewn on the floor, and others collapsed over counters scattered with computers and machinery. He counted twenty bodies on this floor alone.

True, the plan had called for Rawls's gal pal to enter the building once the premises were secure. But that had been back when her new energy prototype had been a threat. Judging by the bloodbath before him, he'd say that possibility was no longer an issue.

Hell, the woman didn't need to see the butchery up here. Half these bodies had been her friends.

He turned back to Wolf. "You lose any men?" Wolf shook his head, and Mac exhaled in relief. At least this damn operation hadn't cost them anyone. "Any chance you grabbed one of the bastards responsible for this?"

Another shake of Wolf's head.

Fuck.

Scowling, Mac scanned the carnage again. "So why call for Dr. Ansell?"

"The *heebii3soo* was dismantling the lab. We need to know whether Dr. Benton's prototype is here."

Mac studied the tangle of equipment spread across desks and counters. Yeah, the answer to that question was imperative. It was essential to find out whether Benton and his team had produced a second Thrive generator. If they had, it might still be in the lab. Unless the asshole they'd caught cleaning the place out had already sent the prototype up the ladder to his employers.

Although Faith had drawn a sketch of her Thrive generator, several of the machines in the lab fit her depiction of it. They'd need her to identify the actual machine.

Cosky joined him and took a long, grim look around. "Faith doesn't need to see this. There's not much we can do about the blood. But we can move the bodies."

For a moment, barely more than a blink, an irritated expression flickered across Wolf's face. And then he went all stoic again. "Already being done."

As though to reinforce his statement, several of his warriors came through a large sliding door at the opposite end of the lab, grabbed a pair of limp bodies, hoisted them up, and dragged them away.

Mac shrugged. How the hell were they supposed to know what the taciturn agent had planned? He wasn't exactly Mr. Chatty, now was he?

"Wait a few minutes before calling Rawls in," Mac told Cosky. "By the time he gets here with Faith, the dead should be cleared away." He took a step farther into the lab, his attention on a bank of computer terminals pushed up against the left wall. "Looks like the computer system is still intact."

Which was a stroke of luck. They could pull hard drives and access the data back at Shadow Mountain. If Faith didn't find her Thrive generator in the building, they could check the computer logs and—

Bomb!

The word suddenly exploded in Mac's head. He winced, unsure of who'd shouted it, or if anyone had shouted it at all. The warning was just suddenly there in his head. Filling his mind. Jettisoning his heart into his throat and his pulse into his ears.

"Out. Everyone. Now."

This time he recognized Wolf's voice, although his mind was messing with him, because the bastard was standing directly across from him, and hell, his mouth hadn't moved.

"Out!" Wolf roared. And this time Mac saw his mouth open wide, expelling the order forcefully. He must have imagined that earlier idiocy.

Spinning, he bolted for the stairs behind them. He could feel the moist heat of Cosky's breath on the back of his neck. The pounding of boots filled his ears.

"Zane," he yelled into his mouthpiece as he hit the first landing. "Get out. The place is rigged."

He didn't hear his second in command's response, not surprising considering the heavy breathing and hammering feet filling the stairwell. They'd pass right by his LC, though. If Zane was still there, he'd drag him out.

He leapt over Benton's body and hit the first-floor landing at a dead run. Zane was gone—thank Christ. The adrenaline coursed through him in hot fluid waves. He jerked the stairwell door open, scrambled around the corner, and shot down the hall.

Twenty feet to the front entrance.

How much time had been left on the timer? Not much, judging by Wolf's urgency-infused warning.

Fuck—he was in front. Cosky, Wolf, and Wolf's entire team charging after him. There wasn't enough room for anyone to pass him. Not enough time for him to stop and let Cosky and Wolf's team by. Which meant everyone's fucking survival hinged on how fast Mac's out-of-shape, desk-jockey body could get out that door.

The realization seized up his lungs. Not a reaction he could afford.

Ten feet to go.

Gunfire erupted outside. An assault rifle from the sound of it. A quick succession of shots.

What the fuck is going on out there?

Nothing he could do from here. He tucked his elbows and put every ounce of strength he had into his legs and lungs.

The front door stood partially open, hanging crookedly from its gaping top hinge. Mac leaned forward, increasing his stride, milking every kernel of speed possible from his adrenaline-charged muscles, praying that it would be enough.

Three feet.

He hit the crooked front door like an anvil, slamming it against the wall and bolting through the door. The night sky spun overhead—black velvet, brilliant with stars. Spongy grass and mud tried to grab his boots, slow him down. But there was room now, room to his right and left. Room for his team to get past him—get out of harm's—

Suddenly he was lifted up and thrown forward by what felt like a giant vibrating hand slamming into his back, shoulder, and thighs. A sonic pressure penetrated his back, squeezed through flesh and bone, numbing every cell.

Boom! Boom! Boom.

The explosions ripped overhead in quick succession—each detonation less violent.

Mac hit the ground hard, his body and mind numb, that black-velvet, diamond-studded sky still spinning lazily overhead.

Chapter Twenty-One

R AWLS SQUEEZED OFF HIS FIRST SHOT, FOLLOWED BY A SECOND AND third in quick succession. Simultaneously the Tango, highlighted in bright green by his NVD, dropped his arm, targeting Rawls's position on the ground. The *crack-crack-crack* from Rawls's SCAR-L assault rifle masked the pistol's suppressed report, but Rawls knew the bastard was firing by the kickback of the Tango's hand. The acrid bite of spent gunpowder coincided with a sharp pinch in his right side. Rawls kept firing.

The luminous figure dropped to his knees, his hand with the weapon dipping toward the forest floor. Rawls fired again, relief whooshing through him as the target slowly collapsed backward.

"Faith?" He spun on his knees to check behind him.

"I-I'm . . . I'm okay."

Her shaky voice was the sweetest music to his ears. Launching himself up and across the forest floor, he kicked the pistol from the Tango's hand. The green blob didn't move. But before he had a chance to bend down and check for a pulse, an explosion sounded behind him. The pressure wave struck a heartbeat later, knocking him off his feet.

As the pressure wave rolled over and through him, he scrambled to his knees and rotated to check on Faith. She was curled up at the foot of the tree trunk, her arms wrapped around her head as chunks of brick, wood, and Formica rained down from above.

Sweet Jesus! The blast had come from the direction of the building. His chest tightened until he could barely breathe, until his exhale sounded like a whistle rather than a breath.

Cosky and Zane. Mac. Wolf. Sweet Christ—Wolf's entire team—they'd inserted into that building. Had they been in it when it blew?

His ears ringing, he dug his toes into the ground and booked toward Faith on his hands and knees. He needed a sitrep on Faith's condition first, after which he'd head toward the explosion. Assess the situation over there.

The icy, hot rush of fear swelled. *Zane. Cosky. Mac.* He forced it back down.

Faith stirred when he reached her. Since her ears would be ringing as badly as his, he abandoned language in favor of pantomime and observation. Her pulse thumped urgently against his fingers, but it was strong and steady. Her breathing was unobstructed. No sign of pain when he moved her limbs or palpated her abdomen. She'd escaped remarkably unscathed.

The relief was almost dizzying, until the memory of his teammates bled it dry and urged him to his feet.

He yanked his backpack up by its shoulder strap as he rose. The rain of debris had slowed, but an orange burn painted the sky to the north. Should he take Faith with him or hide her in the woods? Neither option gave him peace of mind, more like turbulent foreboding, but she took the decision out of his hands by rising to her feet beside him with a wobbly smile.

They pushed through the shivering foliage and emerged on the lawn circling the building. A cloud of dark green obscured his vision through the NVD, so he tore it off and handed it to Faith. It took a good ten seconds for his eyes to adjust, but even then he could see the eerie burn of the shuttered building. It glowed like a square jack-o-lantern with malevolent orange eyes.

He headed for the building at a run, the backpack bumping along behind him, ignoring the stitch in his side. Faith kept pace beside him.

Amid the flickering red-orange wash bathing the front lawn, shadows stirred, sat up, climbed to their feet.

Upon reaching the first hulking shadow sitting on the ground, he released the backpack and dropped to his knees. He didn't realize his patient was Zane until the dark head lifted and a lean hand waved him off. Relief hit hard but disappeared almost instantly. Cosky and Mac had been in that building too.

"I'm good," Zane said, his voice so loud Rawls actually heard it through the ringing in his ears. "Find Cos. Mac."

Since his LC was coherent and mobile—or as mobile as one could get while stiffly climbing to their feet—Rawls snatched up his backpack and raced farther in field. The stitch started up again, only to suddenly vanish. He found Cosky shaking his head and stumbling to his feet. The heady blast of relief lasted a few seconds before it evaporated.

Where, sweet Christ, is Mac?

In the distance, above the trees, chopper blades beat the air.

Wolf suddenly appeared before him, his rigid face streaked with dirt and blood, his braid partially free and streaming down his broad shoulders. Rage, along with other dark emotions, sizzled in the air surrounding him.

Burnished by the fiery haze of the fire, he looked like an omen of death and destruction.

"Get everyone on the bird," Wolf said tersely.

"Mac?" Rawls caught his elbow before he could turn away.

"To the right. Your buddies are with him." Wolf shook Rawls's hand loose and started to walk away.

"Gilbert and the rest of . . ." Faith's voice trailed off entreatingly.

From the expression of dawning grief on her face, she already suspected the answer.

Wolf stopped and swung back to face her with a silent shake of his head. "I'm sorry, Dr. Ansell, they'd cleaned the building before we arrived. There were no survivors." Without waiting for her response, he walked away.

"Cleaned?"

The ringing in his ears had subsided, but her question was so low he read it on her lips, rather than heard it. Sliding an arm around her waist, he leaned in to brush a kiss across her forehead.

"I'm sorry, sweetheart," he whispered against her ear.

She slumped into him for a moment, pressing her face into his neck. The warm wetness of tears trickled down his neck and then she straightened.

Scrubbing her eyes, she shook herself. "We should see to the injured."

He nodded, frowning in annoyance as that damnable stitch in his side returned.

"Zane and Cosky are over there," Faith said, pointing to the right.

Rawls followed the direction of her finger and instantly recognized Zane and Cosky's lean frames clustered around Mac's stocky one. The commander was up, and without support—both good signs.

Thank Christ.

This time the relief was a sustained, steady burn—at least until he bent down to pick up the backpack, and the low-grade pinch in his right side morphed into a sharp, stabbing pain.

What the hell?

He straightened carefully, and reached down to probe his wet side . . . *wet?* When his fingers gently pressed the soaked area, a greasy wave of agony just about knocked him on his ass. He broke out in an icy, breathless sweat.

Well, hell. This he didn't need.

Raising his hand, he shifted until he faced the fiery-orange jack-o-lantern burning across the lawn. Even through the ruddy glow glossing his hand, he could see the wet sheen of blood.

Faith studied Rawls's face through the night vision goggles. The fluorescent glow that rinsed everything from trees to skin the same shade of crisp green made it possible to pick out facial features, but not expressions. But there was something troublesome about his stillness as he stared at his hand. Something worrisome about the sudden clench of his muscles.

Grief over the deaths of her coworkers gave way to concern. She stepped closer to Rawls, angling her head to get a better look at his hand since it seemed to have transfixed him. But the goggles she wore presented his flesh in shades of luminous green.

"What's wrong?" she asked, but her words were drowned beneath the *whop-whop-whop* of the approaching helicopter.

To get his attention, she reached out to touch his arm, surprised to find his jacket damp and cold against her fingertips. His clothing shouldn't be wet. It hadn't been raining. The forest had been dry. They hadn't even pulled the water bottles out of his backpack. There was absolutely no reason for wet clothes . . . unless . . .

The snap of a twig. Rawls spinning, shoving her to the ground, and crouching in front of her. The muffled crack of a gunshot. The thunk of bullets in the tree trunk above them.

Had one of the bullets penetrated his backpack and hit a water bottle? But he'd been facing the shooter with his pack on the ground behind him. For a bullet to hit a water bottle, it would have had to go through him.

Or . . . her stomach rolled and bile climbed her throat.

Had he been shot?

No, he couldn't have been. They'd been attacked over five minutes ago. If he'd been shot, she would have known. He would have shown signs of trauma.

"Rawls." Her voice emerged sharper this time and much louder. "What's wrong?"

"Nothin'."

She barely heard his response through the helicopter overhead. He dropped his hand and turned, swaying slightly.

Bull crap. Rawls was never unsteady on his feet. Never.

Ripping off her goggles, she caught his hand. The light from the burning building highlighted his palm, illuminating its wet gloss.

He was bleeding.

"You've been shot. Haven't you?" Her voice was remarkably cool considering she was practically yelling. They both were.

"Maybe."

There was a hint of irritated disbelief in his Southern twang. As though he couldn't believe his bad luck. That, more than anything, banked her panic. He wouldn't be annoyed if the injury had been serious . . . would he?

"Where?" she asked, already leaning down to check his arm. Through the darkness and reddish-orange miasma she could clearly see a large wet patch on his bicep.

"Right side." He gingerly poked at the indicated area, only to freeze with a hiss.

His side?

She glanced down . . . okay, his side did look wet. Her eyes darted back up, settling on his arm. So did his arm. She swiped her fingers across the wet patch and angled it toward the burning building.

Blood.

He'd been shot. Twice!

"You realize your arm's bleeding too. You've been shot twice." Once again her voice emerged cool, in control.

In contrast, her heart was pounding so hard it knocked the breath from her lungs. With her medical history, the sudden, uncontrolled urgency of her heartbeat should have launched a major panic attack. But all she could think about was Rawls, and that he was losing more blood with each beat of his heart.

"You should sit down," she said, catching his left, uninjured hand and tugging.

"There's time enough to patch me up once we board the bird," he said impatiently, glancing over to the far left where the helicopter was settling on the grass. "Right now I need to check on Mac and Cosky, and Wolf's team—make sure we don't have any serious injuries."

"We do have someone with serious injuries." Faith's voice rose with each word. "You! You've been shot! Twice!"

He glanced down, his face softening. "It's—"

"If you say it's just a scratch—or just a flesh wound—I'm going to smack you," she interrupted him with a scowl.

He had the good sense to close his mouth after that warning. But not the good sense to sit down. Fine, there was more than one way to accomplish her goal.

"Mac," she yelled at the top of her lungs. When all three of Rawls's teammates looked in their direction, she beckoned them over.

"Ah for—" Rawls locked the rest of the complaint behind his teeth.

Smart call. At least he didn't try to scurry off. Instead he watched his buddies converge on them with frustrated acceptance.

"Problem?" Zane asked, scanning Faith from head to toe.

"Not with me," she said, with a flapping motion toward the silent man beside her. She could practically feel the irritation rolling off him. Too bad. "It's Rawls. He's been shot. At least twice."

Three intense pairs of male eyes shifted to her left and locked on Rawls.

"How bad?" Zane asked, this time he scanned Rawls from head to boot.

"I haven't checked yet. But it feels like a graze."

A graze? Really? She rolled her eyes at his macho posturing. Still, he'd managed to avoid describing the injury as just a scratch or just a flesh wound as she'd requested. Why in the world that warmed her belly and made her smile even in the midst of her worry—she had absolutely no idea.

"He's bleeding," she stressed. "In my book, that's bad enough."

Cosky shrugged out of his backpack, opened it up, and pulled out a flashlight, along with a plastic white box with a red cross taped across the lid. "It won't hurt to check you out. Wolf's crew is just starting to load up."

"And some of them may need my help," Rawls said, that earlier irritation sharpening his tone.

Zane shook his head. Shifting, he scanned the lawn. "Wolf's got his own medics on the wounded. And something tells me your westernized medical approach wouldn't be nearly as effective as their native one."

She'd known that Wolf had healers on his team, their inclusion was one of the reasons he'd refused to allow Kait on the mission. Both Wolf and Cosky had claimed they didn't need her services with the other healers on board.

Faith's attention didn't budge from Rawls's face, even though she was curious as to whether these other healers conducted their healings the same way Kait did. He flinched a couple of times when Zane and Cosky removed his jacket and T-shirt, but stood stoically beneath their ministrations as they poured water onto gauze pads and wiped the wounds clean.

His shoulders, chest, and abdomen rippled with sleek, lean muscles in the flickering firelight. In fact, he looked like a piece of art, something Michelangelo might have sculpted in bronze or burnished copper. His sheer beauty took her breath away and sent tingles up and down her spine.

"You're right. They barely qualify as scratches," Zane said casually as he pressed a thick pad of gauze against his side and taped it into place. "Might need a couple of stitches so you don't keep breaking the edges open."

Scratches? They didn't even qualify as scratches? He'd been shot, for God's sake. And not just once.

Could they be downplaying the danger in order not to worry her?

Rawls must have recognized her brewing panic, because he stopped easing back into his T-shirt and took hold of her chin. He nudged it up until their eyes met. She relaxed slightly at the gentle warmth in his gaze.

"Trust me, darlin'. I'm fine. This isn't my first rodeo. It won't be my last either. I know when an injury is worth worryin' over."

Leaning down, he kissed her. Not a light brush of lips either. His mouth was hard instead—strong. As though he knew she needed an indication of his health and resilience, rather than tenderness. It worked too. Her heart rate settled as she leaned into him, returning the caress, strength to strength.

His sensual reassurance reverberated through her endocrine system long after the kiss ended, and he eased back into his T-shirt and camouflage jacket. But soon her traitorous mind found something else to worry over.

"Not my first rodeo . . . I know when an injury is worth worryin' over."

Meaning he'd been hurt before . . . shot before . . . probably countless times. An accepted hazard of his career path.

A memory struck her. Harsh as a bullet, it snagged her breath. *Moonlight streaming through huge trees. Rawls stretched across a mat of pine needles, his bloody chest motionless beneath Cosky's and Kait's hands.*

He'd died that night . . . according to him, according to Jude, even according to Pachico—the ghost he'd brought back—he'd died.

This isn't my first rodeo. It won't be my last either.

And there was a chance, a good chance even, that he'd die during the next moonlight rescue, or mission, or whatever drew him out into the darkness. Only next time there might not be a Kait to save him.

This emotion brewing between them was serious—definitely for her, but she suspected for him as well. She needed to consider his career choice and its potential effect on her mental health before things went much further.

Her gaze returned to the long, lean warrior standing so solidly beside her. When their eyes tangled, he smiled, his face softening. Sensual heat, along with tender reassurance broadcasted from his gaze. That was all it took.

Her twenty-nine years and two heart transplants had taught her the value of living in the moment. Of not questioning what the future held. Of finding joy in the here and now. She couldn't foresee what fate held in store for her, so why make decisions based on possible future events? She shouldn't. She wouldn't.

There was no way she was giving up joy in the here and now to avoid possible pain in the future.

A discouraged silence and sense of anticlimax invaded the chopper on the way home. It was a familiar atmosphere, one Mac remembered well from his stint on the teams. Not every operation paid dividends. Some flipped sideways, stirring up shit they hadn't anticipated. Some brought death and regrets and memories that stole a piece of your soul. And then there were the status quo missions. Operations that cost money, energy, and time but yielded exactly nothing.

Insertions like tonight weren't the worst, nor the best—but they rode that bleak zone into disappointment and frustration.

His ears still ringing, his entire body one big aching bruise, Mac slouched against the padded walls with Zane and Cosky on either side. Rawls had hauled Dr. Ansell—or Faith, as she'd insisted he call her—off into the corner, where they'd taken to cuddling all by their lonesome, until one of Wolf's guys had invaded their privacy long enough to do a healing. At least Mac assumed it was a healing since the bastard had pressed his palms against Rawls's side and then his arm for several minutes before retreating as silently as he'd arrived.

He scowled as he glanced at Rawls and his woman. Might as well get used to calling her Faith. From the way his corpsman was cuddling her, he'd bet they'd be seeing more of her. A lot more. Just like they were seeing way too much of Kait and Beth.

What the fuck was going on with his operators? Did men have fucking biological clocks? Christ, the motherfuckers were dropping like flies.

By the time the helicopter settled onto the super-secret tarmac masked by the ring of clouds smothering McKinley's peak, the ache in his muscles had settled into his bones. Hardly surprising considering how hard he'd hit the ground back there. A long hot shower was sounding better by the minute.

He glanced out the cockpit window as the bird sank into the shaft. Dawn rinsed the mountains a delicate shade of lavender. No shit. Lavender.

But the sight of dawn breaking over the landscape reminded him of those early days, back when he'd been part of the teams. Before he'd taken the silver oak leaf and the gold bars. Before he traded his seat in the Zodiac for a desk, politics, and bullshit protocol. Back then he'd been a vampire, just like the rest of them. Riding the beach boat or the helicopter at zero dark whenever in the endless quest to keep hearth and home safe, and then crashing on his cot to sleep the day away.

As the helicopter settled, and the door slid back, Mac watched Wolf's crew shake themselves awake and disembark in that all-too-familiar post-adrenaline shamble.

Cosky and Zane held back alongside him, waiting for Wolf's team to clear the hold. As for Rawls and the good doctor, they hadn't even emerged from their cozy little corner yet. Once the last of Team Shadow Mountain was on the ground, Mac hopped down, grunting in irritation when his entire body burned in protest.

"I still got a couple fingers left in that bottle of Jack," Mac told Zane and Cos as they joined him.

The bottle had come with the room. He wasn't sure whether it had been a gift from Shadow Mountain command or forgotten by the last occupant of the room. It didn't matter. He wasn't one to look a gift horse in the mouth.

"Sure," Zane said, with a long spine-popping stretch. "I could use a day cap."

Cosky simply nodded.

"How about you?" Mac raised his voice as Rawls slowly walked past, supporting most of Faith's weight. "You up for a night cap?"

The woman looked like she'd hit a wall. White face. Red eyes. Crumpled shoulders.

"I'll pass." Rawls turned down the offer without hesitation. "I'll see you three at fifteen hundred."

He meant the afternoon what-the-fuck-went-wrong meeting.

One hundred percent of his attention fixed on the woman stumbling along beside him, Rawls steered her to one of the electrical carts parked along the side of the hangar, lifted her into the passenger seat, and took the driver's seat. Seconds later the cart was out of sight.

"Well, Rawls has finally been bitten," Zane said, staring off in the direction the cart had taken. "Never thought I'd see the day."

Mac snorted—he could have said the same about Zane and Cosky.

"Hell," Mac said. "Most likely it's a temporary thing." He held out hope anyway. "His head's been scrambled as hell lately. Besides, they've only known each other a week. Proximity and adrenaline, when combined, can have a temporary bonding effect."

Zane shot him a dry look. "Beth and I only knew each other a few days."

"And she was your fucking soul mate, which you realized the instant you saw her," Mac said, forcing derision into his voice, which was surprisingly hard to sustain. Apparently he was getting soft in his old age. "Which makes that comparison complete shit."

"I could mention how long I knew Kait," Cosky pointed out. "But I won't, because this has nothing to do with length of time. It has to do with the way he looks at her. He's never looked that way at a woman before."

"The way he looks at her?" Mac repeated with a harsh laugh. "Christ, you've been hanging around your woman too long. She's turned you into a fucking emoticon."

Zane rubbed a tired hand down his greasy, camo-painted face. "Nah, I get it. He looks at her like he looked at Baby."

Mac cocked his head, confused. "Baby? As in his ride? What the fuck does his hot rod have to do with anything?"

"Rawls was obsessed with that damn car. Every chance he got he was out there in the driveway washing or waxing her," Cosky told him with a shrewd look in his eye, as though he knew Mac was protesting a bit too vehemently. "He looks at Faith the way he used to look at that old Camaro of his—before those bastards blew it up."

An icy mask slammed down over Cosky's face as he mentioned the car. Mac couldn't blame him. The same bomb that had incinerated Rawls's "Baby" had also destroyed every possession that Cosky had owned. Leaving him homeless, carless, weaponless, and running for his life.

"You know, Commander," Zane suddenly said, amusement glittering in his green gaze. "It's not nearly as terrifying as you seem to think."

Mac took a cautious step backward, every instinct he possessed shouting that he wasn't going to like the new direction this conversation had taken. "What the fuck are you talking about, jackass?"

"Falling in love." Zane cocked his head, the gleam in those grass-green eyes brightening.

"Yeah." Another slow step back. "I'll leave that to you pussies."

Cosky snorted. "Don't think we haven't noticed how you look at her, Mac. Fuck—you look at her the same way Rawls looks at his doctor."

What the holy fuck!

A hurricane of denial flooded him. "I don't know what you jack-asses think you're seeing. But let me nip it in the bud. I am *not* in love with Amy."

Goddamn it, I'm not.

It wasn't until their uproarious laughter filled the hangar that Mac realized he'd been the one to put a name to the emotion.

Chapter Twenty-Two

ERIC ROLLED OVER, REACHING FOR THE PHONE VIBRATING AGAINST the nightstand. He groaned beneath his breath upon recognizing the number flashing across his cell's front display. A call from Coulson never boded well for the quality of the day.

"Who in the world would call you at such an ungodly hour?" Esme's groggy voice asked from the pillow beside him. She sat up, craning her neck to see the flashing number, before collapsing back onto the Vividus mattress with a tsk-tsk. "David Coulson. I should have known." She sighed, snuggling back into her pillow and closing her eyes. "Well, answer it. The sooner you tell him to go to hell, the sooner we can go back to sleep."

Sitting up and bracing his back against the Parnian headboard that fanned out across the wall behind him, he slid his finger across the green arrow to accept the call.

"Bugger you, asshole," he said sourly into the phone. "It's three a.m., for bloody sake."

A snort greeted that complaint.

"Your English is showing." There was a distinct sneer in the American's voice.

Eric bit back his retort. Like most Americans of his acquaintance, Coulson was far too proud of his heritage and country. "What do you want?"

"You know, I can actually tell you come from stiff-lipped, upper-crust, pansy-assed aristocracy this morning. Most of the time your accent is so subtle it's barely there."

"What do you want?" Eric measured the words out, ignoring the comment about his speech.

The lack of an accent had been deliberate and hard won. A universal accent meant universal acceptance. One could avoid the stereotypical stranger suspicion if one sounded like the people you were conversing with.

A pause sounded and then Coulson continued. "We've had an interesting development arise."

Eric waited. Bloody hell, the man liked to drag things out.

"Our friendly SEALs showed up at our San Jose facility."

Eric jackknifed up against the headboard. "The hell you say! How did they connect that property to us?"

"No idea. But they were there, and they weren't alone. A Shadow Mountain team was with them."

Eric stopped breathing. Literally. "They've teamed up with Shadow Mountain?"

"Apparently so." But anticipation throbbed in Coulson's voice, rather than foreboding.

What the hell did Coulson know that he didn't? Shadow Mountain was no bloody joke. The council didn't know much about their old enemies other than they hailed from a place called Shadow Mountain and for every step the council took to shove their agenda forward, those damn Indians managed a counterstep to shove the agenda back. For decades they'd been caught in this frustrating dance of one step forward and then one step back.

"What did they get?" He ran stiff fingers through his hair. They'd been rebuilding the prototype at that facility. It had been borderline operational. To lose it now, so close to the finish line . . .

Bloody hell . . .

It would set their time line back by months.

"Nothing," Coulson said, satisfaction thick in his voice. "They got absolutely nothing. I shut the facility down last night. Took the generator with me when I left. Three of my crew stayed behind to grab the research and rig the lab. Those bastards didn't have a chance to take anything before the building blew."

Eric slumped, his heart rate settling. This was news. Good news. "You have the prototype?"

"I do. It's been rerouted to our friends at Dynamic Solutions. Link's putting together a new team. One that won't have a problem with the device's . . . repurposing."

"What about those damn SEALs? I don't suppose the blast took care of that problem." But there wasn't much hope in his voice because Coulson would have led with that news.

"No such luck," Coulson said.

"What about your team at San Jose?" Eric asked slowly, although there was little doubt the scientists were dead. Coulson wouldn't have accepted anything less.

"The bastards produced the prototype, but they refused to accept the repurposing, so I gave them all pink slips," Coulson said, a hint of gloating in his voice.

As though the deaths of six of the world's top minds were something to celebrate. Eric forced back a wave of repugnance. In war, one allied oneself with men who served the greater goal—regardless of whether one liked or respected them. As a child, it was the first lesson he'd learned at his parents' table.

"So we're still on schedule?" Eric asked, relaxing. This had to be one of the few times a Shadow Mountain attack hadn't set them back by months, if not years.

"We are."

"Are you certain Mackenzie and his men were with them?" Eric asked.

How would they have even connected? Those damn Indians were secretive as hell.

"Positive. They were caught on the cameras." Coulson laughed, that earlier hint of gloating back in his voice. "They scrambled the regular camera feeds. But those new cameras Link sent us worked perfectly. Not even a twitch in the broadcast. Those bastards, all of them, were plain as day." He paused, and for the first time, a disgruntled tone entered his voice. "Too bad they didn't arrive a bit later. Like when the place went boom."

Eric rolled his eyes. Of course the bloody sod would go and blow up a perfectly good building. He was far too explosives happy in Eric's opinion.

"Well, we know who Mackenzie and his crew have hooked up with now," Eric said.

That at least was something.

And then it occurred to him what else they knew. He froze, pure exhilaration flashing through him.

"Amy Chastain and her children were picked up by a helicopter. In light of this new information, we can assume Shadow Mountain provided that chopper, along with a safe haven," Eric said, his brows knitting.

They'd undoubtedly provided the ground crew as well, which explained why his contractors had been defeated so easily. The SEALs were bad enough. But bloody hell, once you factored in those damnable Shadow Mountain warriors, the odds increased a billionfold against . . . well, anyone.

"That would be a fair assumption, considering that the SEALs were working with them last night," Coulson agreed. Judging by his satisfaction, he knew exactly where Eric was going with this.

"And since the Chastain boys were broadcasting right up until they reached Mount McKinley—"

"We finally know where their fucking lair is. We've got the bastards," Coulson finished.

Well, not exactly, Eric allowed. It could be they'd found something to block the signal up there in Alaska—as Link had suggested—and then continued on their merry way. But Eric's instincts whispered otherwise.

The signal had disappeared at the base of Mount McKinley. The activist group called themselves Shadow Mountain. Not to mention if the boys had been secreted away inside a bloody mountain, the signal would be interrupted.

All signs pointed to Mount McKinley as the base camp for those annoying, interfering bastards—as Coulson liked to call them.

Which meant they finally had a location to target.

A smile bloomed. As it turned out, Mackenzie had done them an immense favor, one worthy of a Hallmark card—if they made one for such an occasion—he'd given them the means to kill two enemies with one missile.

Rawls anchored a limp Faith against his right side as he pressed his palm to the scanner next to his quarters. Faith leaned against him without protest, apparently so tired she could barely keep her eyes open, or her body upright. He was familiar with the effects of a post-adrenaline crash, so he knew with certainty that wasn't what she was experiencing. At least not completely. Sure, some of her exhaustion could be contributed to the recent mission—but not all of it.

Most of the fatigue came from other factors: like dying, and being dragged back to life, the battery of tests she'd undergone over the past two days, followed by a night of sex rather than sleep. And then there was her grief.

He could feel the sorrow dragging at her, weighing her down. A thick blanket of oppression sucking the life from her. He'd wager the heartache was hitting her the hardest. To lose so many friends at once. Not just her mentor, but everyone she'd worked with. Sweet Jesus—that kind of loss would hit a person hard. He thought of losing Zane and Cosky, Mac, Aiden, Tram and Tag, and the rest of his buddies in ST7, and his soul went ice cold.

As soon as the lock clicked, Rawls pushed the door open, hit the switch to turn on the lights, and half carried Faith inside.

She stirred as they stepped through the doorframe. "I should go to my own room. I'm not good company at the moment."

Like hell. But Rawls kept the thought to himself.

There was no way he was letting her suffer through the night alone. Whether she wanted it or not, she needed company. A warm body to remind her there was more than death in this world. A warm body to remind her that life was still there for the living.

"Let's get you in the shower and warmed up," he said, ignoring her comment.

"Okay." She stared up at him with the saddest, most exhausted eyes he'd ever seen. But then her gaze dropped to his bicep and the beginnings of a frown knit her brow. "How's your side and abdomen? Maybe you should go see the doctor."

"The wounds are gone," Rawls assured her. "One Bird is almost as good as Kait."

In fact, he felt amazingly good. The ringing in his ears and aches and pains from hitting the ground had been vanquished along with the bullet holes. He stared down at her paint-streaked face and red-rimmed eyes as he tugged the T-shirt over her head. After returning to the chopper, he'd soaked a rag in water to wash her face. The effort had smeared rather than removed the paint, giving her the definitive raccoon look.

She didn't protest when he started undressing her; instead she stood there, docile, while he unzipped and unbuttoned.

"I had thought we'd get there in time," she said softly, anguish thickening her voice. She absently lifted one foot and then the other so he could remove her shoes. "I thought we'd have more time."

Naked, her skin looked translucent beneath the harsh white light. Fragile. She was so thin he could clearly see the rise and fall of each rib and the points of her pelvis and collarbones.

"What happened was not your fault," he said, in case she was suffering from survivors' guilt, although from experience he knew the reassurance wouldn't sink in right away—if it ever did.

He stripped his own clothes off and then urged her into the bathroom. After adjusting the taps until the water ran two steps below hot, he eased her under the spray. She flinched slightly as the water hit.

"Too hot?" he asked, keeping his voice soft and unobtrusive.

"No." The word emerged on a sigh.

Although he wasn't within the spray zone, the steam built steadily until they were surrounded by heat and humidity.

She tilted her face up and stood there, still, while the spray hit her full in the face. He didn't realize she was shaking until he picked up the bar of soap and turned toward her.

Ah hell . . .

Dropping the soap back on the shelf, he dragged Faith into his arms and held her tight. She shuddered and pressed against him, her hot, wet face nestled in the hollow of his throat.

The shake to her shoulders was his first indication she was crying. But the tears were falling silently. The hurt so vast she couldn't give voice to it. Somehow that made her pain even harder to witness.

"There you go. Let it out," he whispered, running his hands up and down her slick back.

He ignored his own aching, a very physical one, as the wet, warm woman in his arms pressed fully against him. His dick signaled its approval with a steady increase in breadth and length, at least until Rawls mentally squashed its excitement.

Sweet Mary and Joseph . . .

She didn't need lovemaking, not at the moment. She needed comforting, she needed caring for. No matter how badly certain regions of his anatomy wanted to do more . . . a lot more.

"I can't believe he's gone." The words were a mumble against his chest.

"Who?" he asked gently, stroking his palms up and down her spine.

He tried to keep his caresses soothing, although the warm, satin glide of her naked flesh beneath his hands was anything but relaxing on his end. He wrapped a choke chain around his libido and wrestled it under control.

"Gil—" she whispered, her voice breaking. "It doesn't feel real. None of this seems real."

He tightened his arms around her, still stroking her back, wishing he could absorb her pain.

Eventually the water cooled, so he pulled back to find the soap and washrag. He lathered her up and rinsed her off and started in on washing her hair. She sighed, resting against him, as he massaged her scalp. Once her hair had been washed, conditioned, and rinsed, he turned the water off and wrapped her in a towel. The towel wasn't a particularly large one, yet it swallowed her fragile frame.

Concern rose as he dried her off, his touch gentle against the frailty beneath his hands. She was too damn thin. He should have taken her to the cafeteria before taking her to his bed.

"What's wrong?" she asked, an odd, almost cautious tone in her voice.

He glanced up to find the same wariness in her eyes. "You need to eat. Don't go to sleep yet. I'll run to the cafeteria and grab us somethin'."

She caught his hand as he started to rise. "Don't bother. I wouldn't be able to eat anything anyway."

His frown deepened. "You need to try. You're too damn thin. You can't afford to miss a meal."

A flash of hurt crossed her face, and he gently shook her.

"Don't even go there. If I didn't find you insanely sexy, you might have gotten some sleep last night. I want you healthy, that's all. Healthy enough so last night can repeat into infinity."

She chuffed out something close to a laugh, but not quite. Running her hand up his arm, she slowed at his bicep and squeezed. "I believe the fact that I couldn't keep my hands to myself had a lot to do with our lack of sleep."

Rawls locked down his response. Instead of pouncing on her, like every instinct insisted, he leaned up and over, snagging the sheets and blankets and dragging them down. Lifting her, he set her on the mattress and climbed into bed beside her. Once they were settled, he dragged the bedding over them.

Tucking her against his chest, he kissed the top of her head. "If you start questionin' how sexy I find you, just remember that I'm naked, so that's not my Heckler and Koch MP7 pokin' you in the ass."

Another of those soft chuffing sounds broke from her. With a sigh deep enough to lift her chest against his arm, she relaxed.

"If we were at my place, I'd cook you somethin' special. Like French toast," he said, pressing his lips against her hair. It was the strangest thing, but she still smelled like berries, even though the shampoo and soap in his shower was scentless.

"French toast, huh." She sounded drowsy. "Is that what you make all the ladies?"

"Only you, sweetheart."

Which was true. He'd never cooked for a woman; it had always been the other way around. His girlfriends, and he'd had a fair—albeit fleeting—share, had cooked for him. But French toast was high in nutrition and calories. A perfect combination. He'd be making a lot of it in Faith's future.

Which brought up the question of what the future held for them. Or where they'd be living. He glanced toward the counter where the coffeepot sat. If he picked up a hot plate and a minifridge, he could make do for the time being.

"Gilbert just turned sixty, he was talking about retiring. And Monica had gotten engaged. Hannah had barely returned from maternity leave. My God, her poor husband. Her poor daughter. She'll never see Ally grow up . . ." She paused, and a long raw silence built and then—"They were more than my coworkers, they were my friends."

"I know, baby." He cuddled her closer.

"I didn't really have any other friends," she added in a small voice, as though she were confessing a shameful secret.

Did she realize she'd spoken in the past tense?

He cradled her closer but didn't say anything since there wasn't much he could say.

"Dr. Benton, he was my professor and then my adviser, but I think . . . I think he was the closest thing to a friend I'd had up to that point." Her voice was distant, as though she were talking to herself.

His chest tightened and ached. Did she hear the loneliness in her voice? "Didn't you have friends as a kid?"

She sighed, and the loneliness he sensed in her increased substantially. "My parents discouraged friendships. They felt my immune system was too compromised and that any old cold or flu would be my demise."

The ache in his chest increased in proportion to the ache in her voice. "They homeschooled you?"

It was a guess, but a good one. If they hadn't wanted her around kids, they wouldn't have enrolled her in school.

"At first, but once I outgrew their knowledge, they brought in tutors. I wouldn't have gotten nearly as good an education at regular school."

Maybe not, but at least she'd have had a fucking childhood.

He forced back the anger. That wasn't what she needed right now. She needed someone to hold her and listen.

"Dr. Benton was the first person in my life who didn't treat me like a walking casualty. Who didn't assess me by my transplants or tachycardia or lowered immune system. He was the first person who saw the whole me. Faith. The good, the bad, the ordinary."

"That's why you joined his research team after college?" Rawls prompted, hoping to keep her talking.

He'd bet this kind of openness, this kind of vulnerability, was new to Faith. Her guard was down, but who knew how long that would last, and he wanted to know more about her. Everything about her.

"Maybe . . . but I still loved it. There was always something new to learn or study or do. It didn't feel like work, so I stayed late most nights and got there early. Everyone did."

"What you're describin' is life on the teams." He paused, laughed softly. "My team, that is. We train together, work together, and play together. They're my teammates, but my friends too."

He could feel her thinking that through—thinking that he still had his friends, while hers were gone.

"You still have friends, Faith," he reminded her softly. "New friends. You have Kait, Beth, Zane, and Cosky. You have me."

Did she hear the promise in his voice?

She stirred restlessly against him. "It's not the same thing. I barely know them. I thought Kait was a charlatan, for God's sake."

Rawls smiled in satisfaction. *Thought* . . . past tense again.

"There's plenty of time to get to know them. We'll be hangin' out with them a lot."

She obviously noticed the way he'd linked them because her hand slipped around his hip and wrapped around his dick.

"So we're friends?" she asked, without a hint of coyness.

He tried to concentrate on the curiosity in her voice—but sweet Jesus—he could barely string two thoughts together with the way her soft, hot hand was burning around his cock.

"That we are." His voice sounded strangled.

"Then what is this?" She pumped her hand up and down his cock before giving it a light squeeze. "Friends with benefits?"

"Hell no!" He caught her hand, easing it from his dick. "*This* is a committed relationship. The kind where if another man tries to touch you, I break every bone in his body."

She must have liked that announcement because her body melted into his. "What if another woman touches you?"

He shrugged and stroked a long, slow hand up her abdomen to cup her breast. "Then you can break every bone in my body."

She snorted out a laugh. Leaning down, she kissed the arm locked around her waist. "I don't mind . . . you know . . ." She wiggled her ass against his crotch. "Doing it, if you want to."

He chuckled. *Doing it?* Look at her getting all bashful.

"Lovemakin' can wait," he said, knowing she could feel the missile pressing against her hip.

"But doesn't it hurt?" Her hand closed over the rigid length of his shaft.

She sounded more inquisitive than worried, as though her scientific curiosity was getting the better of her.

"It's not exactly pleasant," he said dryly. "But there are plenty of things that hurt a hell of a lot more."

Like losing her in the tunnels. Absently, his arm tightened around her waist, sealing her against him until he could feel every breath she took and every beat of her heart.

The fact that she didn't protest told him his instincts were right. She needed cuddling tonight. The heat could come later.

Chapter Twenty-Three

FAITH AWOKE TO A FURNACE ROASTING HER BACKSIDE FROM SHOULDERS to toes. Dazed with sleep, she tried to wiggle away, but the band of steel wrapped around her waist tightened, dragging her flush against the heater again. Vaguely the sound of breathing registered and her memory stirred.

The vise around her waist was a male arm. A heavy male arm. The furnace against her back, a long, lean male body. The bulge nudging her bottom, either a hip or a knee or . . . something else entirely . . .

Rawls.

She squirmed back a few inches and snuggled down, contentment spreading through her in a warm, fluffy wave. It felt so good to have him wrapped around her like this. So . . . right.

But then the memory of the night before crashed into her mind. The forest, the explosion. Her friends and colleagues dead. All dead. Grief rose, drowned the contentment beneath a whirlpool of loss. So much death. So much evil.

She concentrated on the furnace toasting her from behind until the hollow raw grief eased. She wasn't going to give the bastards who'd stolen her friends the satisfaction of destroying her life as well. There was proof of life behind her. Proof of good, rather than evil. She'd focus on what was important. What really mattered—like life and friendship and love.

Love?

The realization snapped her fully awake. Fully aware.

She loved him?

Well, sure she was attracted to him, but when had that physical attraction morphed into an emotional connection?

The answer came immediately. She'd fallen in love with him the night before, when he'd vetoed his teammates' invitation in order to spend the night with her.

Looking back, the emotion had been building for days—driven by his loyalty to his teammates, his kindness toward her, his determination to do the right thing no matter the personal cost, his unfailing, unflinching courage, which he seemed completely unaware of.

But she'd fallen completely for him the day before when he'd put her first—put her life and her needs before his own.

She took a shallow breath, suddenly wide-awake. He'd used his body as a shield to protect her. Not just the night before, but ten days ago as well. Back at her lab, when he'd pulled her from beneath Big Ben. After they'd been attacked, he'd pinned her against the wall, using his flesh and bone for her protection. It had been an instant, instinctive reaction, this willingness to give up his life so that she might live, even though they'd been strangers at the time. He'd done the same thing— repeatedly—the night before.

And then he'd brought her home and he'd bathed her and held her and listened to her grieving, ignoring his own needs to focus on hers. He'd put her first the night before, above everything, above everyone, even above himself.

And she'd fallen completely and irrevocably in love with him.

Stunned by the realization, she lay there, concentrating on the warm arm pinning her to the mattress, and the big body heating the entire length of her from behind. While he'd told her that they were in a committed relationship, he'd never said he loved her. But if you extrapolated his feeling based on his actions . . .

A man wouldn't cuddle a woman all night long, ignoring his raging erection—his own needs—unless he cared about the woman he was holding . . . would he? He'd talked about feeding her, for God's sake—that alone indicated he felt something for her, right? Something beyond the physical?

Suddenly desperate to see his face, she tried to turn over. His arm tightened around her again, pinning her in place. Grabbing his hand with both of hers, she dragged it up, which loosened some of the pressure from his arm. She turned over, dropping his arm as she started the roll. Instantly his arm cinched back around her waist, locking her in place. But this time she was facing the opposite direction.

The bulge that had been pressing against her bottom was poking her in the belly now, and she knew with absolute certainty that it wasn't a hip or a knee—indeed, it was something else entirely.

Not that he seemed aware of it. She studied the relaxed lines of his face and frowned slightly. His face looked much thinner than it had at the airport terminal all those months ago. Apparently she wasn't the only one who needed feeding.

With his eyes closed, he'd lost the intensity she associated with him. He appeared almost vulnerable, or maybe just tired. Impulsively, using the tips of her fingers, she smoothed the lines between his eyes and smiled as the corners of his lips tipped at her touch. A sunny, warm glow filled her chest. When she shifted her fingers to his mouth, she felt his lips curve beneath her fingers. Her gaze shot to his eyes, but they were still shut, his face still relaxed.

Her heart melted. He wasn't even awake, yet he smiled when she touched him. Tickled by this discovery, she pressed in closer, her right hand stroking his belly while she kissed the side of his neck. Her hand took a detour to the side of his abdomen to verify that One Bird had healed him to the extent that Rawls had claimed the night before.

His flesh flowed smooth and hard and completely unmarred beneath her hand. She grinned when his heart rate quickened beneath her touch. His erection, which she'd been trying to ignore, grew more demanding, prodding rather than nudging her belly. She strung kisses down the side of his neck and then around to the front, where she nuzzled the hollow of his throat.

A raspy sound, almost a purr, rumbled in her ear. A surge of giddy excitement shot through her, and her smile grew wider. Wicked.

Slowly her hand stroked its way down his abdomen to curl around his penis. His hips arched with each pump of her hand, and the rumbling turned guttural. She lifted her head long enough to scan his face. His eyes were still closed, but the lines in his forehead and bracketing his mouth had tightened even further and there was an air of expectation about him, of breathless anticipation. She was almost certain he was awake.

Bracing her palm against his right shoulder, she pushed. He gave easily beneath the pressure, rolling over to sprawl out on his back.

Perfect . . .

Still grasping his penis, she squirmed up and over him, and went back to work with her mouth and her hand. Only this time she started her downward trek at his nipples—circling one with her tongue and then the other, before suckling.

A groan broke from him, and the arm around her waist shifted, sliding down to her bare bottom. As his hand slid between her legs, it was her turn to catch her breath and freeze. The warmth in her belly tightened and heated. When his hand went still, simply lying there, a thick, burning presence tucked between her thighs, she started moving again. Squirming against him, she trailed a line of nips and wet suckling kisses down his abdomen. With each nibbling caress along his torso, her fingers tightened around his penis, sliding down and then up in a lingering caress.

The rise and fall of his chest increased, so did the thud of his heart. This time when she lifted her head long enough to glance at his face, his eyes were open and locked on her, fiery with hunger. The heat in his eyes burned into and through her, liquefying her muscles and spiking her temperature. She jumped from hot to scorching in an instant.

Avoiding those blazing, intense eyes, she returned her attention to his abdomen, lingering over the flat washboard length of his belly. Her teeth scraped, followed by the soothing swipe of her tongue and suckle of her lips. With each caress, his flesh twitched beneath her mouth. Imperceptibly, the hand between her thighs gravitated upward until it pressed with flaming insistence against her wet, throbbing core. With each swipe of her tongue or nip from her teeth, a corresponding series of tingles spread from her core, into her belly, and down her legs.

Instinctively, she opened her legs wider and rocked against his fingers, silently encouraging his exploration. But his hand just lay there absolutely still, a sizzling, erotic distraction.

Scraping her teeth down his belly to suckle at his hip, she tightened her grip around his erection and increased the up-and-down slide of her hand. A groan broke from him, much thicker and raspier than before. The sound shot off an avalanche of satisfaction throughout her. He didn't try to hide his reactions from her. Didn't pretend her touch didn't affect him, deeply. He was so completely open about the way she made him feel.

A sense of power flooded her—of confidence. It was a heady combination and one she intended to explore in length and depth . . . after she finished idolizing his body.

By the time she reached the rigid jut of flesh claimed by her fingers, he'd stopped breathing entirely. The hand melting the flesh between her thighs sat there absolutely still, as though he didn't want to distract her.

Nibbling her way across his hip and up his penis, she replaced the long, firm slide of her hand with the long, wet glide of her mouth and tongue. He tasted salty and earthy and absolutely delicious. She managed two lingering trips from the bulbous head down to the thickened trunk and the soft, warm globes before he broke. Dragging her up and over him, he nudged her legs apart until she straddled him.

The hand between her thighs stroked up, delicately parting the folds of her sex to rub repeatedly against the wet, swollen folds. Her breath clotted in her chest. Quiver after quiver shook her as his finger rubbed its way to the little knot of nerves. Her pussy tightened and swelled, moistening with urgency.

Straightening, she arched her back and clenched her legs as fever exploded through her, rippling through muscles and veins, cinching every nerve tight, feeding the urge to bear down and take him inside.

She needed him inside her, filling her, completing her.

A finger slipped into her, stroked her once, and pulled back out. She felt the bulbous head of his penis replace his finger. And then he was pushing inside her. The hot, thick length of him filling her, stretching her, binding her to him in the most primitive way possible.

She froze above him, straddling his hips, savoring the hot thickness of him stretching her. The sense of fullness. Of throbbing heat. Of coming home.

The brilliant blue eyes holding her gaze flashed as he stirred restively beneath her. His face tightened with urgency. "Come on. Darlin', you're killin' me."

She stared down at him, at the primitive hunger stamped so clearly across his face. And a dense molten pressure settled just below her belly. Tingles prickled up her spine and down her legs. Slowly she pushed herself up with her knees, rising steadily until the thick length of him almost slipped out of her, before bearing down again, taking him back inside.

He groaned, arching his hips to meet hers, his head pressed back against the pillow. Rough hands latched on to her hips, lifting her and then dragging her back down. The liquid pressure in her belly coalesced, contracting into a tight ball of raw throbbing. She moved faster, her breath trapped in her chest, her eyes blurring, the heat rising so fast and stifling she felt ready to burst into flames.

Vaguely, she was aware of an infinite litany of guttural groans echoing in her ringing ears, but she wasn't sure whether they came from her or the man arching into her.

One of his hands dropped from her hips and slid between her thighs. It found the tight bud of her sex and rolled it between his fingers. White-hot lightning speared from his fingers into the throbbing ball in the pit of her belly. She arched and bore down, screaming as the pressure exploded. Tingles swept up and out, morphed into shudders that ripped through her body from toes to scalp.

As the tingles and shudders engulfed her, liquefying muscle and bone, she was vaguely aware of movement, of rolling. And then Rawls was above her, the heavy muscles of his shoulders bunched, his face taut, neck corded as he thrust into her.

She focused on the flushed rigidity of his face, the blind urgency in his eyes, and the tingles exploded again, sweeping through her with even more force than before. As the tingles reached her head, white static took over her mind and then she was flying and crashing, his raw, breathless shout echoing in her ringing ears.

What might have been a millennium later, she returned to awareness under the unmistakable sensation of being watched.

"What?" she asked.

Since opening her eyes was too much effort and her limbs had fallen into that post-gratification lethargy and refused to move, she sighed with contentment and cuddled into the sweaty masculine body splayed out beneath her. He must have rolled them again while she was out of it. As beds went, he was hard and narrow and hot and altogether perfect.

"You're beautiful," he said, his voice raspy and strangely solemn. Fingers slid through her hair, untangling the strands before trailing down her face to cup her cheek. "The most beautiful thing I've ever seen."

A smile threatened. Since it was a stretch of the imagination to call her the most beautiful thing he'd ever seen, he must be in what was generally referred to as the postcoital glow. Why that tickled her, she had no idea.

"You find that funny?" he asked, curiosity in his voice.

"No." She opened her eyes, letting the smile spread across her lips. "I think it's sweet."

"Sweet?" He shook his head and leaned down, brushing a soft kiss across her lips. "There's nothin' sweet about it. It's pure fact, darlin'."

Sure it was . . .

But she let the statement pass unchallenged. If he wanted to see her that way, who was she to contradict him?

He brushed another, slightly firmer, kiss across her mouth before pulling back to scan her face. "You." He leaned in and brushed another kiss across her mouth. "Are." Another kiss. "Beautiful." This time he pressed the kiss into her forehead, his lips lingering. "You have no idea how beautiful you are, do you?" Pulling back to study her face, he absently stroked her cheek with the back of his knuckles.

She laughed, turning her head to kiss his fingers. "Aren't you the one who told me, and I quote, 'You're too damn thin'?"

"You are, and we're gonna do somethin' about that." He trailed his right hand down her side until he reached her midriff, where he stopped to stroke the indentations between her ribs. "But that does nothin' to distract from how beautiful you are. Hell, once you get some meat on those bones, you'll be the most gorgeous woman in the world. Every other poor female on the planet will fade into the woodwork by comparison."

She snorted and rolled her eyes, but that light, fluffy blanket of contentment filled her to overflowing.

"You don't see it, do you? How special you are." His arm slid around her waist and tightened. "That's just one of the things I love about you. Your complete lack of ego."

Shaking her head slightly, she smiled up at him. "My ego's as healthy as the next girl's. I guess I've just been more worried about

my insides than my outsides. So I've never paid much attention to—"
Abruptly the rest of his words kicked in and she froze.

Did he say what I think he said?

"Wh-wha—" The question was strangled beneath a wave of giddy anticipation. "What did you say?"

"That you don't see how special you are?" The hand on her face slipped down to her chin and lifted her head. "That you don't have an ego?"

The smile he laid on her was full of bland innocence.

"Not that, the other." She breathed shallowly, a sense of stillness rising from within her. Expectation swelled, along with the certainty that her life was about to change irrevocably.

The expression on his face shifted from innocent to grave.

"What? That I love you?" The admission emerged as solemn as a vow.

The breath left her in a rush. "I think I love you too."

He fell back to the bed, chuffing out a breath that was half laugh. "You *think*?"

"It's just that we've only known each other *ten days*. And we've really only talked during the *past few days*. And everyone knows that extreme danger and adrenaline can mess with a person's emotions. And—" Laughter burst from him. "Why are you laughing?" she asked, eyeing him with disgruntlement.

The blue eyes that locked on her face gleamed with amusement. Periodic ripples of laughter shook his torso, which in turn rippled through her body since they were pressed so closely together.

"Because none of that matters and you damn well know it." He threaded the fingers of both hands through her hair and held her gaze. "Love doesn't subscribe to a set schedule. It happens when it happens. Sometimes it's instant, sometimes it takes years. And sometimes it takes ten days and twelve hours."

Ten days and twelve hours.

The words resonated with her. He'd listed the exact length of time they'd known each other. And she knew he was right. The knowledge that she loved him sat warm and solid in her heart, even if her mind insisted on analyzing and second-guessing.

"Besides." He nuzzled the side of her neck as his hands slid up and down her back in a soothing caress. "I reckon we're not in an almighty hurry to move things along. We'll give that scientific mind of yours plenty of time to examine and adapt and climb on board."

It was the oddest thing, but the simple fact that he'd realized her brain and heart were at odds was an immense relief. If he knew her well enough to know that, maybe he did know her well enough to love her.

She studied his relaxed, certain face.

And maybe she knew him well enough for love to bloom too.

It felt right to lie there in his arms, pressed so closely against him she could feel the beat of his heart against hers, the warmth of his cooling skin.

It felt real, this emotion connecting them. It felt strong. It felt reciprocated.

Which was more than enough to hold tight to and build on.

Mac's coffee mug froze midway to his mouth. He watched in disbelief as his corpsman, at the table to his left, set two plates piled high with eggs, bacon, hash browns, and French toast on the aluminum table in front of Faith Ansell.

Who in the hell did he expect to eat that heap of calories? While Rawls might manage to wade his way through one of the plates— eventually—his woman ate like a picky bird. She'd polish off a tenth of that mound at best.

When Rawls stepped over the bench seat and sat next to Faith, settling so close to her they were practically sealed together from hip to shoulder, Mac shook his head in disgust and lifted the mug to his mouth. Another good man down for the count. This falling in love shit had become an epidemic.

"Benji," Amy said to his right as she neatly sliced her son's fried egg into pieces. "If you spent half the time working on your breakfast as you do talking, you'd be finished eating by now."

Her youngest, sitting across the table next to Cosky, turned to scowl at her. "But Mom, it's important. I'm helping him get a dog."

A dog?

Mac caught Cosky's dry expression. Yeah, Cosky wasn't the one interested in dogs.

He studiously ignored the heat blasting him from hip to shoulder thanks to the damn woman sitting so close to him. Why the hell couldn't she have chosen a different table, hell, a different room—although he suspected a different cafeteria wouldn't have lessened the effect she had on him.

Suddenly Cosky's amused voice echoed in his mind . . . haunting him.

"Don't think we haven't noticed how you look at her, Mac. Fuck—you look at her the same way Rawls looks at his doctor."

He shuddered and banished the memory of Zane and Cosky's uproarious laughter when he'd denied having feelings for the woman.

Just because they'd formed their own personal pussy-whipped club didn't mean he had any interest in joining them. His hand tightening around his mug, he avoided the woman on his right by concentrating furiously on the couple across from him.

Cosky and Kait sat directly across from him, while Marion was a bit more to the left. Empty plates were pushed to the middle of the table and half-full coffee cups sat in front of them. Their heads were tilted together as they quietly discussed something—probably wedding plans. Assuming they managed to extract themselves from this Goddamn mess and waltz into a new life together.

With a sour shake of his head, Mac glared down into the black depths of his coffee as though the bitter liquid held all the answers to their current predicament.

The failure the night before had been a blow. No, he hadn't expected much, considering the intel had come from a Goddamn ghost. But there must have been some hidden kernel of hope lodged deep in his moronic brain, because the frustration and disappointment when the insertion hadn't yielded even one fucking clue was so thick he could almost taste the bitterness on his tongue.

"You look like someone just shot your best coon hound," Rawls said, pointing his fork toward Mac.

While Rawls's head was turned away, Faith stealthily forked three slices of bacon on top of his plate.

Mac watched her fork an egg over as well and considered ratting her out on general principle. But hell, his lieutenant had to know she couldn't eat that mountain of food. And from the way he'd demolished half his plate within seconds, maybe he'd planned on using her leftovers as a second course anyway.

With a grumpy yawn, he scrubbed a hand down his face and grimaced. "We need to recover that damn prototype of Dr. Ansell's. It's too dangerous to leave in enemy hands." He paused to scowl. "And I'm getting damn tired of coming up empty-handed."

He didn't glance at Amy, but he could clearly imagine her tight, haunted expression. This moratorium on progress hadn't just bit them squarely in the ass. It had bit Amy and her kids as well. As it stood, based on the doc's latest round of tests on Brendan and Benji, Amy's kids were well and truly fucked. That shit they'd been injected with wasn't coming out anytime soon.

The combined pressure of frustration and fury pushed against his chest, threatening to smother him.

"At least we know who has it and who's behind all this, which is more than we knew a couple days ago." Cosky straightened, shooting him an undefinable look. "We've got actual names now."

Rawls shot his buddy a surprised look. Mac knew just how he felt.

"Yeah, we got names"—he reminded Cosky sourly—"from a ghost."

Cosky shrugged. "Rawls says the names are legit. Wolf says they're legit. The lab, with the missing scientists, was exactly where they said it would be. That's good enough for me."

"James Link is our best bet," Amy suddenly said from beside him. "Manheim will be harder to reach. He's got the security to go with all that money. Link's smaller potatoes. He's accessible."

He was also the current CEO of Dynamic Solutions. If anyone had a shot at helping Amy's kids, it would be that tech-savvy company. Mac could hardly blame her for fixing her sights on the opportunity with the best odds of curing her kids.

Zane straddled the aluminum bench next to Mac and took a sip of his coffee only to blanch and gag. "Son of a bitch."

What the hell? Mac watched his lieutenant commander's face turn green.

"Beth tossing her cookies again?" Cosky asked with dry amusement.

With a grimace, Zane stood back up. "I need something to settle her stomach. Coffee seems to be her biggest trigger." He paused to scowl, a world of frustration on his face.

No surprise there considering how much Zane liked coffee. Beth's pregnancy and Zane's mirroring her symptoms was really fucking with his LC.

Mac hid a smile behind the swipe of his hand.

"Get her some crackers. Saltines, or as close as you can find," Marion advised, leaning forward so she could see Zane around Cosky's massive shoulders. "She's what? Four months along?"

"Four and a half," Zane said, blowing out a hard breath. He frowned, worry lines wrinkling his forehead. "The doc said the nausea would improve by the end of the first trimester. She's six weeks past that now."

Marion sat back and swung her legs over the bench seat. Standing, she bustled over to pat Zane's arm. "I'm sure she's fine, dear. Every woman reacts differently. I was sick well into my second trimester.

Why don't Kait, Faith, and I drop by for a visit? She might enjoy some girl talk."

"You better pick up double the rations on those crackers," Rawls told Zane with a wicked grin. "Beth's not gonna be happy if you munch on hers." He glanced toward Faith, who was watching Zane with sympathetic eyes, and he slid an egg and a couple of slices of bacon back onto her plate.

If Mac wasn't mistaken, it was the same egg and bacon that Faith had offloaded earlier.

"I'm going to set up a meeting with Wolf and his COs for later today, so make yourselves available. We need to track down that damn prototype of Faith's and take it out of play," Mac said.

With luck, their very well-equipped and tapped-in hosts would have a starting place in mind. If they didn't, then James Link would have to do.

"Let's hope they haven't discovered its nifty little side benefit yet," Cosky said, grimness hard on his face.

A shadow darkening his eyes, Rawls stopped eating long enough to glance at Faith. He caught her trying to sneak the egg back onto his plate. With a couple of quick slices he quartered it and lifted the morsel to her mouth. "Eat."

She rolled her eyes and glowered, but opened her lips, accepting the offering.

"At least we have allies now," Amy said quietly when the grim silence went on too long.

She was right. Mac relaxed slightly, taking another sip from his mug. They did have allies. Powerful ones too.

But even more importantly, they knew who their enemies were.

Assuming you could trust a ghost.

Epilogue

A S YOU CAN SEE FROM THE TEST RESULTS, DR. ANSELL," FRANCIS
Kerry said, sweeping his hand above the reams of data spread across
his desk, "we have every reason to believe your heart has undergone a
complete rejuvenation." He sat back in his office chair and pushed his
glasses up with a long bony forefinger.

From the armchair in front of his desk, Faith leaned forward to
pick up an image of the echocardiogram that had been taken two hours
earlier. Since the two prior scans had shown a thorough transformation of her heart muscle, just like this new one did, she suspected
this additional imaging had been requested to rule out any sudden
deterioration. After all, it would be a mistake to go off the immune
suppressors and Cordarone if Kait's healing had worn off and her heart
had deteriorated again.

Which begged the question—did that ever happen, and if so, how
often?

Dropping the film, she picked up the printout of the EKG she'd
undergone two days before. The description confirmed a normal functioning heart—just as the reports on the transthoracic echocardiogram
and Doppler echocardiogram had shown. The video taken of the ultrasound sessions had revealed the same as well.

A perfect. Normal. Heart.

For a moment, disbelief swelled, pressed against her chest. But it faded quickly. She'd had several days to acclimate to the possibility of miracles.

"What about the treadmill test?" Faith asked, rifling through the files, films, and printouts spread across the table. "I lost my breath pretty quickly during that. Isn't that a sign of my heart not working properly?"

Okay, maybe she hadn't accepted that she'd been the recipient of a miracle quite yet. There was a sliver of doubt remaining, a piece of her just waiting for the bad news to roll in.

"It can be, of course. But shortness of breath can also be due to a general lack of conditioning," he said delicately.

Faith's eyebrows rose. Had he just called her out of shape?

"With the exception of your breathlessness, the exercise stress test indicated a normally functioning heart. There were no irregularities in the blood flow or electrical rhythm."

Which was doctor-speak for—*Hey dummy, you're out of breath because you're out of shape. Get exercising, for Pete's sake.*

"So she can go off the cyclosporine, mycophenolate, and Cordarone?" Rawls asked.

Maybe he sensed the distance buffering her, because he leaned forward and covered the hand she had resting on the table with his. She tried to relax, to concentrate on the warmth of his hand, but the tension vibrating through her refused to back down.

"For now." Dr. Kerry pushed back his office chair and stood up. "We'll continue monitoring her. And it wouldn't hurt to keep an emergency dose of Cordarone on hand just in case."

Just in case what? In case Kait's healing ultimately reversed and her heart failed again?

"So what are the long-term effects of this . . . healing?" Faith asked. "Has a healing eventually deteriorated? Is there a possibility all these miraculous findings could disappear and my old heart will return?" Faith asked.

Dr. Kerry laughed. "Admittedly Kait Winchester's abilities are remarkable. But trust me, your heart's transformation isn't the result of some short-term magical spell. If her healings reflect the same outcome as William's and One Bird's—and I see no reason why they shouldn't— your heart should remain at its current peak condition until normal aging kicks in."

Should remain . . .

While the good doctor was babbling a convincing line of optimism, she couldn't help noticing all the qualifiers he was throwing around.

"So what was my heart's spontaneous restoration a result of?" At the baffled look he sent her, Faith frowned and rephrased. "I know Kait's at the core of this . . . marvelous outcome . . . but you said it wasn't a result of a magical spell, so what, exactly, was it a result of?"

Maybe if she had a better idea of how Kait had accomplished this phenomenon, it would be easier to believe that it had occurred and that the results would be lasting.

She could sense Rawls watching her. Did he think she was being a pessimist? Or God forbid, that she didn't want to get better?

Dr. Kerry studied her face for a moment, before slowly sinking back onto his chair. "I can't speak to Kait's ability specifically since we haven't begun testing her yet. However, William and One Bird's ability draws in and then expels energy, which in turn stimulates or even supercharges the individual's immune system and their body's natural ability to heal. So the healers themselves don't do the healing, they merely draw in and then provide the fuel to expedite the body's own ability to heal, often at an accelerated rate."

Faith nodded. That made sense. The strange tension that had grabbed her the moment they stepped in Kerry's office eased. Curiosity stirred—normal curiosity, not that suspicious, moderately pessimistic interest of before.

"So how and where are they drawing this energy from? Have you pinned it down?"

"We haven't, no," Dr. Kerry said, rising to his feet again. He walked around his desk.

She jolted slightly in excitement. "You know, maybe they're drawing from the same source that powers the Thrive generator. The pool is infinite; perhaps some people have a genetic predilection to—"

With a rumbling laugh, Rawls stood and wrapped a hand beneath Faith's arm, lifting her to her feet. "I'm sure Dr. Kerry will be happy to theorize with you another time, when he doesn't have other patients to see."

Flushing, Faith offered her hand. "Of course. Thank you, Doctor. I appreciate all you've done for me."

After a brisk, up-and-down shake, Kerry dropped her hand and eased around the armchairs. "Feel free to go through the result again, if you like. Down the road a bit, we may schedule more tests, for monitoring purposes."

A sudden flush of uncertainty hit. It must have touched her face because he glanced at her and offered a reassuring smile.

"Not that I expect there to be any need for such caution." After one last heartening smile, he disappeared out the door.

He'd misread the cause behind the uncertainty. This time the worry had nothing to do with her heart and everything to do with her housing arrangements. While Wolf and his superiors had offered them hospitality for as long as they needed it, she couldn't remain here forever. It wasn't fair to drain their resources and offer nothing in exchange.

Although . . . maybe she could offer them something in return. She could talk to Wolf about joining their team of scientists. That experimental aircraft Rawls and Zane and Cosky kept talking about had to have come from somewhere.

The fact that Shadow Mountain command was more interested in destroying the Thrive generator than acquiring it for themselves had put her mind at ease. While this base was obviously of military origin, the men here had clear limits on what they were willing to do in order to advance their cause. She could work within those parameters.

"What's wrong?" Rawls asked, sliding a warm, firm arm around her shoulder. "For a woman who was just given a new lease on life, you were damn tense in there."

So he'd noticed that, had he?

"It just . . . it just seems too good to be true." She stumbled over the explanation.

She'd accepted the fact that her heart had reached the end of the average transplant's lifespan. She'd girded herself for her looming return to the donor lists, with all the uncertainty such lists carried. Both of which made it difficult to adjust to this sudden windfall of good fortune.

"Well, believe it." His arm tightened around her shoulders, drawing her closer. He leaned down to brush a kiss across the top of her head. "And darlin', I'll be right by your side to remind you that good things do happen in life, if the doubts start creepin' in again."

She murmured an acknowledgment. But he'd just touched on the other half of the worry jumbling her all up.

It wasn't just her new healthy heart . . . it was Rawls too.

She felt like she was caught in a dream. It was a great dream—true. Heck, even a wonderful dream. But a dream, all the same.

The two things she'd wanted most from life had been handed to her with absolutely no effort on her part: a healthy heart guaranteeing her a normal lifespan and a man to share that life with.

A man who would curl her toes, give her butterflies, and thoroughly cherish her. Who would put her first, accept all her quirks—who would even die for her.

Someone who would love her unconditionally and accept her unconditional love in return.

And Rawls embodied all the qualities of her faceless, nameless dream man. He'd put her needs first time and time again. For God's sake, he'd even thrown himself in front of a gun to protect her.

But in her experience, dreams rarely came true, which made it hard to believe wholeheartedly in the miracle she'd been blessed with.

She kept waiting for the catch to kick in. For her heart to revert—or Rawls to realize he didn't love her after all. That he'd been caught up in the drama and urgency of the moment.

"You know," Rawls said, swinging her around and leading her to the door. "You just sit back and enjoy the ride, and I'll believe for both of us."

The heat of his big body penetrated her from shoulder to hip, settling into her like a warm, fluffy blanket. Warming her from the inside out, it banished the cold draft of pessimism.

Maybe, just maybe, she was being foolish. While the peril and adrenaline rush of the past few days were brand-new to her, they were old hat to Rawls. His career revolved around danger and tense situations. If such things affected him, he'd have a hundred ex-wives by now.

In fact, if adrenaline-driven emotional attachments were to affect anyone, it would be her, not him. Yet if she bypassed her head and listened to her instincts, paid attention to her heart, she knew what she felt for him was real. Her love for him wasn't dependent on adrenaline and fear for survival. It was reliant on his personality and his temperament—neither of which would change.

If she could accept the fact that what she felt for him was real and permanent—why couldn't she give him the same benefit of belief?

Besides, Rawls wasn't the kind of man to declare his love unless he meant it. Unless he was sure of it. His sense of loyalty—just one more thing she loved about him—wouldn't allow him to walk away once he made a commitment.

"You're doin' it again," he said, his arm tightening and drawing her closer. He glanced down, an affectionate, knowing gleam lighting his blue eyes.

"What?"

"Overthinkin'. Analyzin'," Rawls said, amusement in his voice.

He was right—she was. He knew her even better than she knew herself. Her tense muscles relaxed. She'd never have to worry that he didn't understand what she was feeling, what she was thinking. A flush of happiness smothered the reserve.

With a soft sigh, she leaned into him, relishing the way his arm tightened even further, locking her against his side. He felt so perfect pressed up against her—his body heat toasting her. His arm a warm, sheltering anchor. Being with him felt right, it felt natural—he felt like home.

It was time to accept the fresh start life was offering her—a new heart, a new life, and the perfect man to share it with.

Sometimes dreams really did come true.

Glossary
SEAL Terms

BUD/s (Basic Underwater Demolition training): A twenty-four-week training course that encompasses physical conditioning, combat diving, and land warfare.

Bullfrog: A nickname given to a highly respected, retired SEAL.

CQB (Close Quarters Battle): A battle that takes place in a confined space, such as a residence.

Deployment: Active combat or training, deployments last generally between six and ten months.

HQ1 (Naval Special Warfare Group 1 / the West Coast Command): HQ1 has naval bases in Coronado, California; Kodiac, Alaska; Pearl Harbor, Hawaii; and Mare Island, California. Among other naval units, HQ1 houses SEAL Teams 1, 3, 5 and 7.

HQ2: (Naval Special Warfare Group 2 / the East Coast Command): HQ2 has naval bases in Dam Neck, Virginia; Little Creek, Virginia; Machrihanish, UK; Rodman NAS, PM; and Norfolk, Virginia. Among other naval units, HQ2 houses SEAL Teams 2, 4, 8, and 10, and DEVGRU (also known as SEAL Team 6).

Insertion: Heading into enemy territory, whether it's a house or a territory.

JSOC (Joint Special Operations Command): A joint command that encompasses all branches of special operations. This command ensures that the techniques and equipment used by the various branches of the military are standardized. It is also responsible for training and developing tactics/strategy for special operations missions.

LC: A rank of lieutenant commander.

NAVSPECWARCOM (Naval Special Warfare Command): The naval command for naval special operations. This command is under the umbrella of USSOC and is broken into two headquarters: HQ1 and HQ2.

PST: (Physical Screening Test): The physical test a prospective SEAL has to pass. Minimum requirements: 500-yard swim in twelve and a half minutes, rest ten minutes, 50 pushups in two minutes, rest two minutes, 50 sit-ups in two minutes, rest two minutes, 10 pull-ups in two minutes, rest ten minutes, 1.5-mile run in ten and a half minutes.

SEAL Prep School: A crash course in preparing to take the BUD/s challenge. Prospective BUD/s candidates are put through a physical training program meant to prepare them for BUD/s. This includes timed four-mile runs and thousand-meter swims. If the candidates are unable to pass the final qualifications test, they are removed from SEAL candidates lists and placed elsewhere in the navy.

SEAL Teams: Each SEAL team has 128 men, of which 21 are officers and 107 are enlisted. Each team has 10 platoons and each platoon has 2 squads. There are 16 men per platoon and 8 SEALs per squad.

SQT (SEAL Qualification Training): SQT teaches tactics, techniques, and special operations procedures.

USSOC (United States Special Operations Command): Beneath the umbrella of JSOC, the USSOC is the unified combat command and is charged with overseeing special operations command from the army, air force, navy, and the marines.

Zodiac: A rigid-hull inflatable boat, with 470-horsepower jet drives. It can reach speeds of 45-plus knots and has supreme maneuverability. (Also known as the beach boat.)

Arapaho Terms

3ooxonouubeiht: crabby

beniinookee: general or highest-ranking official

betee: heart

betee3oo hohe': *Shadow Mountain*

bexookee: mountain lion

bih'ihoox: mule

biitei: ghost

bixoo3etiit: love

ceece'esbeniiineniiit: armed forces

ceeyoubeiht: talking foolishly

ciibehbiiwoohu: don't cry

ciini'i3ecoot: grief

heebii3soo: bastard

heneeceine3: lion

hiihooko'oet: bewitched

hiihooteet: death

hiixoyooniiheiht: charm

hookecouhu hiteseiw: little sister

nebii'o'oo: sweetheart

neehebehe': younger sister

neenii3o'neihi: behave well or be quiet

netesei: my sister

noniiteceenoo'oot: temporarily crazy

noonsoo: it is chaos or a mess

noo'uusooo': storm

notonheihii: medicine man

teittooneihi: be quiet

tei'yoonehe: baby; infant

wo'ouusoo: kitten

Author's Note

Dear Reader,

I hope you enjoyed *Forged in Smoke*, the third installment in my Red-Hot SEALs series.

If you'd like to read more books set in my Red-Hot SEALs world, or sign up for my newsletter, please visit my website at www.trishmccallan.com.

Newsletter subscribers receive new-release information, new-release early-bird pricing on selected books, and free Red-Hot SEALs novellas.

For a full list of my available books, you can visit my website or my Amazon author page: http://www.amazon.com/Trish-McCallan/e/B006GHSSI2/ref=ntt_athr_dp_pel_1

If you enjoyed *Forged in Smoke*, I'd appreciate it if you'd help other readers find this book by sharing the title and book description with your friends, reading groups, book clubs, and online reading forums.

Additionally, leaving an honest review on Goodreads, Amazon, or any other retail site would be appreciated. Reviews help clue other readers in to what they might like or dislike about a book and enhance book discovery.

I love to hear from my readers and make a point of answering every email I receive. If you have any questions or comments, feel free to email me at trish@trishmccallan.com.

As always, thanks for reading!

Best wishes,
Trish McCallan

Another Red-Hot SEALs novel
by Trish McCallan

Forged in Ember
coming soon

Editor's Note: This is an early excerpt and may not reflect the finished book.

E XHAUSTION DRAGGING AT EVERY SYNAPSE IN HER BRAIN AND SINEW in her body, Amy Chastain paused in the doorway. The hall lamp burned bright and harsh behind her, casting a thin wedge of light to the right and left of her body, which illuminated her two bundles of blanket-wrapped boys.

The small apartment the Shadow Mountain housing committee had assigned her boasted two bedrooms, a bathroom, and a small living area with an attached kitchenette. The larger of the two bedrooms barely accommodated two narrow, cot-like beds, which had been pushed against the walls in an L formation. At the foot of each bed was a four-drawer dresser. At best, the small closet behind the door held a coat or two. Her room was even smaller, with a single bed and a built-in wardrobe. Combined, the entire space occupied around four hundred square feet—maybe.

But the rooms were safe. Secure. Private.

Qualities that were much more important than space these days.

Upon reaching the bed to the right, she leaned over and straightened the collection of blankets before tugging them over Benji's shoulders. It wouldn't be long before the covers were tossed aside again. Her youngest had always been a restless sleeper—thrashing around in bed as though sleep couldn't contain his enthusiasm or exuberant personality.

Straightening, she arched her achy back, kneading the tight, throbbing muscles above her hips. At least the events over the past few days—or even months—hadn't impacted her youngest. While his father's death had dimmed his sunny personality for a while, he'd treated everything else—from their kidnapping to the flight through the tunnels with the compound exploding overhead—with uncontained excitement. Not even the battery of medical tests he'd endured over the past four days had squelched his spirits for long. But then, unlike Brendan, his older brother, Benji had no idea what the test results had yielded.

Brendan knew, even though she hadn't told him—yet. Although only four years separated her two sons, her oldest was a millennium older in maturity and perception.

Turning, Amy headed toward the bed on the left and found Brendan watching her. It didn't surprise her. She suspected that he hadn't been sleeping any better than she was herself.

Unlike Benji's trashed cot, Brendan's covers were neatly folded at his chest, the blankets smooth and straight, as though he hadn't moved a fraction of an inch since he'd climbed into bed.

She settled beside him, and reached out to stroke his cheek. "Couldn't sleep?"

He studied her face before answering, as though trying to judge what she needed to hear. Such a subtle, heartbreaking response to a simple question.

"It's going to be okay, Mom," he finally said, his calm, quiet voice filling the darkness.

And yeah, he'd found it. He'd pinpointed exactly what she needed to hear, even if she didn't believe him.

His hand rose, caught hers, and held tight.

Something else she'd needed, without realizing it.

A wave of intense sorrow broke over her—raw and suffocating—it threatened to swallow her whole. Sorrow for John, for the life that had been taken that could never be returned, for all the things she wouldn't be able to share with him through the coming years. For Benji, whose losses were still to come, when he slowed down enough to realize how much had been stolen from him. But most of all, for this child lying so still and silent beside her. This boy holding her hand.

This adult in a child's body.

Brendan had lost everything. He'd lost his father and the close, exceptional relationship they'd shared. He'd lost his school and his friends and his sports teams—which he'd excelled at.

But most of all he'd lost his innocence.

Through their kidnapping and her rape, he'd learned that sex could be used as a weapon—leaving bruises and blood and invisible wounds that cut to the soul. Through his father's death, he'd learned that you could do everything right, everything possible, and still pay the ultimate price. Through this awful, high-tech biological shit those bastards had shot into his veins, he'd learned that there were people out there capable of the most invasive, horrific acts to achieve their own goals.

While Brendan's quiet, deliberate nature had always been the core of his personality, these past four and a half months had tempered his natural demeanor into something harder, darker—heartbreaking in a child.

Unlike Benji, nothing had gone over Brendan's head. Although he hadn't said anything, he'd understood what those bastards had done to her four and a half months ago while they'd been helpless and trapped beneath their care.

She shied away from the memories, entombing them deep within her, where they smoldered and swelled and pressed outward like a pus-filled abscess ready to burst forth, spewing its rot.

But there wasn't time to deal with what had happened to her, or work through the aftermath. She couldn't afford to wallow in her own personal tragedy.

"There was something in that shot, wasn't there?"

Brendan's voice dragged her from the crumbling abyss of her own thoughts.

"Something that let them track us." While he'd framed it as a question, the certainty already sat flat and hard in his voice and the dark eyes watching her.

She swallowed and tightened her hand around his, before forcing the admission through her tight, aching throat. "It appears so."

"They can't get it out of us?" His knowing gaze didn't budge from her face, and acceptance resonated in his voice.

The dark brown of his eyes didn't match hers, or John's, neither did the color of his hair. Both were throwbacks to her father. Her biological father, not the man she'd called Dad for the past thirty-odd years. She didn't remember much of the man who'd fathered her, besides a quiet voice and strong arms. But she'd seen enough pictures to know where her sons' dark hair and eyes came from. Sometimes she wondered whether Brendan's temperament had skipped a generation too . . . but then there was Benji's hypercuriosity—neither she nor John had ever been so full of life and innocence, so where had that trait come from?

"Dr. Kerry is working on it, but they aren't sure what we're dealing with yet. In the meantime, we're safe here. The signal is blocked by Shadow Mountain." She paused to instill confidence in her voice. "They can't find us here."

He didn't look surprised. She hoped he hadn't figured out the rest of it. If Dr. Kerry couldn't figure out a way to neutralize the compound that those bastards had injected into her children, Brendan and Benji would never be able to step foot outside of Shadow Mountain again. Not without the risk of being scooped up and used in this deadly conspiracy Eric Manheim and his cronies had embroiled them in.

A beat of silence followed. A moment throbbing with unasked questions.

"Commander Mackenzie thinks Clay did this to us," Brendan suddenly said, a cold front in his voice.

She flinched, denial instinctively rising—her dad and Clay, they couldn't have had anything to do with what had happened. They couldn't . . .

"Commander Mackenzie is suspicious of everyone." Which was nothing less than the truth and had nothing to do with what her son was trying to tell her. "Mackenzie doesn't even know your uncle Clay."

Mackenzie's suspicious face rose in her mind.

Brendan was right. Mac did think Clay had been behind the injection given to her sons. But if he was right, that meant Clay was behind the rest of it too. John's murder and her, Benji's, and Brendan's kidnapping—culminating in what those bastards had done to her. If Mac was right . . . Clay was responsible for every single horrific, devastating blow since March.

It couldn't be true. It couldn't. She'd known Clay practically her entire life. They'd shared a home and an idyllic childhood. He'd been John's best friend, best man at their wedding. He was Brendan and Benji's godfather. For him to be capable of such evil, without either her or John recognizing it? No . . . it couldn't be true.

Chills swept her. She shook her head. "Clay has nothing to do with any of this."

He couldn't have. He couldn't.

Brendan just stared at her. "He was there, Mom. He brought the doctor. He's the one who told us we had to have the shot."

"Because someone else convinced him you needed the shots to get back into school. He didn't realize what you were being given." She forced conviction into her voice.

"He's FBI, like Dad—and he didn't check with the school? Have the shot tested? Dad would have." Reservation and something . . . darker . . . burned in her son's grim eyes.

"That's why your dad was senior agent in charge, and your uncle Clay isn't," Amy said. "Clay misses things sometimes."

"Commander Mackenzie would have checked." There was no give in Brendan's voice.

"We've already established that Commander Mackenzie has a suspicious nature," Amy said, exhaustion crashing over her in an emotionally draining wave. Not that she'd sleep, or at least for very long, if she headed back to her bed.

"I think Commander Mackenzie is right. I think Clay knew what was in that shot. I think he gave it to us on purpose."

"Oh, Brendan . . ." Amy's voice failed.

Another wave of sorrow washed over her, only this time it was tinged with rage. Apparently they'd taken even more from her son than she'd realized—they'd stolen his trust in family too, the surety that those closest to you had your back.

"He's never liked us, Mom." Brendan tilted his head slightly and set his jaw.

That gave her pause.

Never?

Never spoke of long- rather than short-term. *Never* referenced a lengthier pattern than four and a half months.

Brendan had stopped calling her brother Uncle Clay years before. When she'd questioned him about it, he'd just said that calling him uncle was a baby thing and he was too old for that now. She'd hadn't thought much of it at the time, assuming it was something he'd heard at school or through his friends. Had it been more than that? Had he been certain even back then that Clay didn't like him?

"Clay might not always show it, sweetheart, but he loves us." The reassurance sent déjà vu crashing through her. She'd said the exact same thing to Mackenzie in the tunnels.

Suddenly she felt mired in a case of she-who-doth-protest-too-much.

"He smiled when Benji cried," Brendan said, a flat sheen glossing his brown eyes.

Startled, Amy straightened. "When was this?"

"When Clay's doctor gave us the shot. It hurt pretty bad, and Benji started crying. Clay smiled. He liked seeing Benji hurt."

She wanted to protest, tell him he was imagining things, but she couldn't. Brendan didn't imagine things, not ever. If he said Clay had smiled when Benji cried—then Clay had smiled.

Nausea rolled up her throat. "Could he have been thinking about something else?"

Brendan's dark brows knitted, but then he slowly shook his head. "I don't think so. He was looking right at Benji, and he didn't smile until Benji started crying."

Amy sat there frozen, a dark, cold shadow settling over her.

"I know you think of him as a brother, Mom." Brendan sat up and scooted back until his shoulders were braced against the headrest. "But he's never liked us. He might smile with his mouth, but his eyes are mean. He's been like that as long as I can remember."

"Your grandpa's always been hard on him . . ." She paused, shook her head. She was making excuses. But nothing excused this if Brendan was right. If Mackenzie was right. "Why didn't you ever mention this before?"

"Because it never mattered until now."

She nodded absently. "You really, truly think Clay knew what he was doing? That he injected you on purpose."

This time he didn't pause to think about it. He nodded solemnly.

If Brendan was right, then what Clay felt for them went a lot deeper than dislike. This skated right into hatred.

Maybe Brendan was picking up on something that wasn't there. Maybe the past four and a half months had hardwired his natural suspicion and he was seeing monsters in familiar faces.

Had that been what happened to Mackenzie? Had he lost his childhood innocence too early? Had that hardened him into a suspicious adult?

God help her, she didn't want Brendan turning into another Mackenzie.

She needed to get hold of Clay and feel him out—assess him for herself—without the blinders. Find out whether she'd let childhood memories blind her to the monster her brother had become.

About the Author

Photo © 2013 JK Steele

Trish McCallan was born in Oregon and raised in Washington State, where as a child she sold her first crayon-illustrated books for a nickel. This love of writing led her to study the craft at Western Washington University. She worked as a bookkeeper and a human-resource specialist before trading in her day job for a full-time writing career. Her debut novel, *Forged in Fire*, and its sequel, *Forged in Ash*, were both finalists for prestigious Romance Writers of America RITA Awards. *Forged in Smoke* is her third book, and she currently resides in eastern Washington with her three golden retrievers, a black Lab mix, and a cat.